NIGHT MARCHERS

BY WILLIAM NIKKEL

SUSPENSE PUBLISHING

OTHER BOOKS BY WILLIAM NIKKEL

Jack Ferrell Series
GLIMMER OF GOLD
CAVE DWELLER
MURRIETTA GOLD

Max Traver Series
DEVIL WIND

NIGHT MARCHERS

By
William Nikkel

PAPERBACK EDITION

* * * * *

PUBLISHED BY:
Suspense Publishing

Cover Design: Shannon Raab
Cover Photographer: iStockphoto.com/mcrisari
Cover Photographer: Shutterstock.com/doodle

PUBLISHING HISTORY:
JMS Books, LLC., Print and Digital Copy, 2012
Suspense Publishing, Print and Digital Copy, August, 2014

ISBN-13: 978-0692267455 (Suspense Publishing)
ISBN-10: 069226745X

*For my loving wife Karen
who never stopped believing in me.*

PRAISE FOR WILLIAM NIKKEL

"Part mystery, part ghost story, and all high-seas adventure, William Nikkel's "Night Marchers" is a thrilling novel that mixes modern piracy with Hawaiian history and mysticism. A debut not to be missed!"

—James Rollins, *New York Times* bestselling author of "The 6th Extinction"

"I must say that William Nikkel knows how to draw you into his story and hold you there…. In many ways Nikkel is like a latter-day Jules Verne, having written a thoroughly enjoyable adventure tale that follows a band of scientists from sunlit coral reefs to the subterranean depths of remote coastal mountains to remarkable discoveries fraught with high danger…. And above all that, this is a thriller with a message—and one as old as the cave-dwellers."

—Gary Braver, bestselling author of "Tunnel Vision"

NIGHT MARCHERS

BY WILLIAM NIKKEL

PROLOGUE

Kealakekua Bay, the Big Island of Hawaii
8 AM Sunday, February 14th, 1779

Lieutenant Mollesworth Phillips stood his ground next to Captain Cook and watched him raise his double-barreled musket and fire at a dark-skinned warrior threatening them with a rock and an iron spike.

The native staggered back a step and straightened.

Phillips knew Cook's shot struck its mark. He'd seen the pellets hit with deadly accuracy. But the birdshot he'd watched Cook load in one of the barrels of his double-barreled musket failed to penetrate the thickly woven *purau* fiber mat protecting the warrior's chest.

Laughter erupted among the throng of natives swarming the rocky beach. Behind them, towering coconut palms stood motionless in the still morning air.

Suddenly, a renewed insolence swept over the warriors.

The tribesmen moved in a solid mass toward Cook.

Phillips knew by the concern etched in Cook's expression he regretted his decision to kidnap King Kalaniopuu. A tactic to secure the return of the cutter, the vessel the natives had stolen to strip the iron used in the boat's construction.

A stone arched overhead and struck one of marines standing a few feet away from Cook.

Cook pointed his musket in the direction the stone came from and shot a native dead with a lead ball fired from the second barrel.

The warriors attacked.

Phillips pressed closer to Cook.

His gun empty, Cook raised his sword and yelled, "Fire."

Smoke and flame erupted from the barrels of the marines' muskets and several Hawaiians crumpled to the ground.

The natives swarmed the men in a savage frenzy.

Cook shouted, "Take to the boats!"

The marines threw down their empty muskets and scrambled into the water amid a hail of stones.

Cook stood his ground and faced the mounting horror.

Phillips could not let anything happen to his captain. He held his musket at the ready and said, "Into a boat with you, sir."

A rock struck the sand in front of Phillips. A second stone hit him in the head and knocked him to the ground.

Dazed by the blow, he slowly worked his legs under him in an effort to stand.

Before he could fully gain his feet, he felt the burn of a spear thrust into his back.

He slumped forward under the blow, turned, and shot the warrior in the face from a foot away.

The native fell instantly dead in a heap of flesh.

Phillips exchanged glances with Cook. And in that moment of understanding, Cook clearly knew all was lost.

A spear stuck in the ground next to Cook's feet.

He plunged his sword into a native's belly.

Phillips tried to help his captain, but could barely stand. There was nothing more he could do. Leaning heavily on his musket for support, he waded into the water.

Gripped by a feeling of helplessness, he turned and saw Cook scan the scene in front and to the left and right of him.

Cook had to feel the same wave of vulnerability.

A volley of gunshots thundered from the men in the boats.

Several natives fell.

Cook raised his hand palm out, and motioned for the men in the boats to cease fire. Then he waved them in closer.

Phillips grasped a glimmer of hope.

He turned—and in horror—watched the men row away to a position fifty yards off shore.

He and Cook had no choice but to try and join them.

He faced Cook and yelled, "Captain."

Cook had obviously understood the situation. With the palm of his left hand held against the back of his head to protect his skull from a flurry of stones, he waded toward the nearest boat, his double-barreled musket slung under his arm.

His gaze focused in the direction of his captain, Phillips saw a warrior charge into the surf and swing his club, hitting Cook.

Cook staggered falling to his knees and dropped his musket.

Another enraged warrior rushed up before Cook could recover from the blow and thrust the blade of an iron dagger into the back of his neck.

Cook tumbled forward into the knee-deep water.

The helplessness Phillips felt a minute before, consumed him. There was nothing he could do to stop what was happening. He turned to the sound of water slapping the hull of an approaching boat and was pulled aboard by two marines. He collapsed onto the gunwale and stared toward the bloody carnage on shore.

The angry throng of natives at the water's edge shouted and raised their weapons in an obvious sign of triumph. The savage brutality of the attack swept through the warriors like a plague. They dragged Cook's limp body onto the rocks and stabbed him repeatedly with an iron dagger snatched from hand to hand in unmistakable fierce eagerness to share in the killing.

The skirmish lasted ten minutes.

Captain James Cook—the man the natives had honored as the god *Orono*—and four marines lay dead on the beach.

Phillips could only stare in disbelief as he and the men retreated to their ships.

A minute later, *Resolution* and *Discovery* opened fire with their cannons.

* * * *

At four o'clock that afternoon, 2nd Lieutenant James King of the *Resolution*, and eighty armed men boarded boats and rowed toward shore under orders not to land or fire upon the natives without first being attacked. Their mission: parley with the Hawaiians for the peaceful return of Captain Cook's remains.

Lieutenant King raised a white tablecloth in a gesture of peace, and ordered the men in his boat to row in close while the other boats lay back.

From inside his boat several yards offshore, King opened his arms wide and yelled, "We are at peace with the Hawaiians."

Koa—a priest Lieutenant King knew well—walked to the water's edge and motioned them ashore.

King ordered the men to hold their position.

Concerned there would be further violence from the natives, he waved for the priest to come to them.

Koa did not hesitate. He waded into the water and swam to the cutter.

On the beach behind him, a dozen natives paraded about laughing and shouting. Others stood watching. One warrior wore a dead marine's trousers, another flaunted Cook's sword. Some turned their backs to the men in the boats and slapped their bare butts in an obvious gesture of ridicule.

Lieutenant King's men held their fire.

Koa boarded the cutter with a dagger in one hand and a piece of white cloth in the other. He saluted King and his men by touching noses and made a crying noise King interpreted to be regret over the unfortunate quarrel.

King straightened and said, "We've come for the body of the *Orono*."

In broken English, Koa told them Cook's body had been carried into the hills and that he would go and arrange for the body to be returned. Without further talk, he leaped into the water and swam ashore.

With a wave of his hand, Lieutenant King ordered the sailors back to the ship. They'd wait to see if the natives kept their promise.

* * * *

The next five days passed amid intermittent suspicion and hostility. Between ten and eleven in the morning on the sixth day—Saturday, February 20th—Chief Eeapo dressed in a red and yellow feathered cloak and helmet, stepped onto a large rock on the beach and stood holding out a large bundle respectfully wrapped in a black and white feathered cloak.

Captain Clerke onboard *Resolution* wasted no time. He boarded a pinnace with a group of armed men and rowed ashore to accept the package.

The moment Clerke was back safely aboard ship, Lieutenant King and the other officers followed him to the great cabin where they solemnly unfolded the feathered cloak. Inside—wrapped in a white cloth—were the human remains they had been waiting for.

"We have to be sure," Captain Clerke cautioned.

None of the officers hesitated. Each man bent to the grim task of examining the body parts. The skull was intact with the lower jaw missing; the scalp was separate; the hands and arms were detached; the thigh and lower leg bones were connected. The feet, vertebrae, and ribs were also missing. All the bones showed marks of fire. The flesh had been removed and salted for preservation.

"It's Cook," Clerke decided, pointing at the scar between the thumb and index finger on the severed right hand."

Everyone nodded in agreement.

* * * *

On Sunday, February 21st, Chief Eeapo and King Kalaniopuu's son boarded *Resolution* with a bundle containing Cook's lower jaw and feet. He also brought Cook's shoes, the barrels of his musket, and a few trifles.

Captain Clerke stood on deck to receive them. There were murmurs among the crew, some angry shouts. He raised his hand to quiet the men.

Lieutenant King watched the exchange. Much had been lost, already. He hoped that one day good would come from what happened here.

At four that afternoon, the colors aboard *Resolution* and *Discovery* dropped to half-mast. Captain Clerke stood on *Resolution*'s foredeck, facing King and the other sailors and performed a memorial service. Some of the crew wept.

That evening at a few minutes before six, Cook's coffin was committed to the sea amid the thunder of cannon fire at half-minute intervals and the tolling of *Resolution*'s bell.

Captain Cook's spinal column, ribs, sword, and uniform were never recovered.

CHAPTER 1

South of Necker Island, Northwestern Hawaiian Islands
Present day

The shark appeared out of the watery gloom, a grayish blur on the periphery of Jack Ferrell's vision.

He slowly lowered the waterproof digital camera from his facemask and focused his attention on the gray-brown cruise missile of cartilage, muscle, and jagged teeth moving in a wide circle around him, propelled through the water by smooth even strokes of its rapier-like tail. Shafts of sunlight shimmered on its back. He could make out faint light brown stripes along its sides.

A tiger.

With nothing to gage the predator's size, he could only guess. Cruising the coral that close to him, the monster looked to be twelve or fourteen feet long. But taking into account magnification caused by the water, he figured the shark was closer to eight feet; big enough to cause serious injury . . . even kill.

The man-eater continued to cruise the reef thirty feet away showing no sign of leaving the area.

Jack purged air from his buoyancy compensator, and let himself sink to the bottom, his back to an outcropping of coral.

He chanced a glance at Kelly, the graduate student diving next to him. They'd been dating each other for a few months and spent time in the water as a research team while pursuing their individual scientific degrees. But this was the first time during any of their dives together that they'd encountered a shark the size of this one.

And never a tiger.

He worried Kelly might panic and do something foolish.

Kelly faced the shark, her knees hovering just above the ocean floor, the tips of her fins cupping the sand. From that angle, Jack couldn't see her eyes to judge her fear, but watched her head move as she tracked the course of the sleek killing machine.

He reached to place a calming hand on her arm.

His fingertips were two inches away when she pushed off from the bottom, kicking and clawing for the surface in a frantic dash for safety aboard the eighteen-foot Zodiac floating above them.

"No," he screamed. His words were lost in a garble of bubbles from his regulator.

He grabbed for her ankle.

Missed.

He dropped his camera, lunged, and seized the blade of her flipper nearest him.

He held on long enough to stop her assent. She glared down at him, eyes wide open in terror. Then she jerked her foot free of his grasp and kicked his mask to the side as she bolted for the Zodiac.

She shot toward the surface.

Adjusting his mask on his face, Jack quickly cleared the water from it and swam after her.

Again, he made a grab for her flailing ankle. And again, he missed.

At once knew there was no way he could stop her. He whipped his head around and looked behind him.

The eight-foot-long tiger was not where it cruised the reef only a moment before Kelly panicked for the surface.

He withdrew the knife from the scabbard strapped to his calf, and knew at once the blade was a pitifully inadequate defense against a creature so big and deadly.

But it was all he had.

The sleek shape shot past him.

He spun his head that direction and saw the man-eater dart

toward Kelly who'd kicked to within five feet of the surface.

The killing machine struck with such savage speed Jack was powerless to stop the attack.

Without hesitating to think about the chance he was taking with his own life, Jack swam full speed at the shark.

The creature sank its teeth into Kelly's thigh.

Jack saw her blood in the water. At that shallow of a depth it kept its color, a red cloud in the current.

He heard Kelly's bubbled screams.

Any second the shark would begin the horrific thrashing that would rip her leg from her body.

Desperate to save her life, he grabbed hold of the tiger's dorsal fin and wrapped his legs around the man-eater's massive form. In the next instant, he plunged the serrated blade of his dive knife into an expressionless coal-black eye, jerked the blade free, and made a stab for the other eye.

The blade sliced the water next to the broad flat head.

He cocked his arm for another strike with the knife, but it wasn't necessary. The loss of an eye was enough to discourage the shark from its attack.

The creature spit out Kelly's leg, and Jack released his grip on the killer's dorsal fin. With a whip of its sickle tail, the grey-brown predator of the deep retreated over the edge of the reef and disappeared into the depths of the Pacific.

Jack turned his attention to Kelly. Pairs of arms were already in the water pulling her up and over the side and into the inflatable. He reached up with his hand and was dragged onboard a moment later.

He ripped off his mask.

"A towel quick," he said.

His eyes were focused on the blood. He'd demanded the towel from no one in particular.

Eddie, one of the NOAA vessel's deck hands—who'd come on the Zodiac to assist with the dive—quickly pressed a folded beach towel to Kelly's injured leg. Fred—another mate from the ship—peeled away her mask and un-strapped her buoyancy compensator and air tank. He grabbed another beach towel and held it poised.

Jack quickly peeled off his own dive equipment.

"Tie your towel around that one and cinch it tight," he said to Fred.

They weren't moving fast enough.

He snatched the towel from Fred's hand and leaned in to apply the pressure bandage himself. Blood soaked through the cloth.

"Fuck!" he said. "Hurry."

Fred started the engine, threw the throttle forward, and raced toward the two-hundred-foot research ship anchored in deep water a quarter mile away from their location.

"What the hell happened down there?" he shouted above the deep-throated roar of the ninety horsepower outboard motor.

"She saw that tiger and lost it," Jack yelled. "What do you think happened?"

"I can see that," Fred said. "You should have stopped her."

Jack was in no mood to listen to shit from anyone.

"Fuck you," he said.

"Cool it," Eddie hollered. "Pay attention to what you're doing."

Eddie's voice pulled Jack's angry gaze away from Fred. Jack gave the blood-soaked towel another twist.

He said, "The fucker better keep his distance."

"Guys, it was my fault," Kelly said, her voice strained and frail. "I panicked."

"Hang in there, Kel," Jack said. "We'll have you onboard in a minute."

Kelly gripped his hand.

He smiled back in an attempt to hide his concern.

"You're going to be all right," he said. "I promise."

He furrowed his brow at the ship. They weren't getting there fast enough.

CHAPTER 2

Jack held Kelly's hand and peered up at the sailors standing at the rail of the research vessel *Albatross* while the zodiac—with him and Kelly in it—was lifted aboard the ship. No one seemed to move fast enough. Even the winch hoisting the inflatable turned with agonizing slowness.

The grip Kelly had on him relaxed to nothing. He tightened his fingers around hers to keep her hand from slipping out of his grasp and focused his gaze on her.

Her eyes fluttered shut. She moaned.

Then nothing.

The Zodiac settled onto the deck. Barbara Jorgenson, the ship's doctor, took one look at Kelly and grimaced.

"Get her inside," she said.

She pointed toward the ship's infirmary and stood to the side so the two crewmembers manning the litter could carry Kelly through the open hatchway.

Jack kept hold of her hand, ducked to keep from hitting his head on the bulkhead, and stepped through the hatchway. They rushed down the companionway.

"Lay her on the exam table," Jorgenson said.

Gloved and ready, she edged past the litter bearers, an I.V. kit and a bag of saline in her hands.

Jack moved aside but kept the towel tight on the wound.

Jorgenson found a vein in Kelly's arm, inserted the intravenous catheter, started a saline drip, and injected a syringe of painkiller. She looked at Jack.

"I'm staying," Jack said. His eyes reflected his resolve.

Jorgenson held him in her gaze a beat.

She said, "So, you're a medical doctor, too?"

He knew Jorgenson, had witnessed the doctor's testiness more than once. This wasn't the first time they'd spent time together on research projects like the one they were on now. They'd even come close to sharing a night in her cabin. The sexual tension between them remained.

He locked gazes with her.

"I'm not a doctor of anything yet," he said. "But you'll need another pair of hands. I can help."

"Jack . . ." Kelly moaned.

He watched her reach across her body and grip his arm. Then he felt her grasp loosen and her fingers slide from his skin.

He hoped it was the morphine taking effect.

Jorgenson moved Kelly's arm out of the way and took hold of the tourniquet.

"Let go," she said to Jack. "Let's see what we've got."

He released his grip on the towel and swallowed. He knew the wound wasn't pretty.

"It's all yours, Doc."

Jorgenson slowly released the knotted towel, but kept the palm of her left hand pressed to the fabric forming the compress. Then she gently lifted the blood-soaked cloth and looked at the wound. A half circle of jagged teeth marks in the shredded muscle on both sides of Kelly's thigh stood out dark red in the bloody ooze.

She let herself breathe.

"The artery's intact," she said. "Probably saved her life."

Jack sucked in an audible breath through his clenched teeth.

"You okay?" Jorgenson asked. She kept her eyes focused on the wound.

"Fine, Doc. What do you need me to do?"

"Wash your hands, slip on a pair of gloves, and stay out of the way for now."

"Is she going to be all right?"

"I think so. Her injuries certainly could have been worse. From the looks of the bite, the shark must not have been all that hungry. If he had been, he'd have taken the leg."

"Jabbing him in the eye with my dive knife might have discouraged him a little."

Doctor Jorgenson looked up long enough to furrow her forehead at Jack.

She said, "You got close enough to stab him in the eye with your knife?"

He shrugged.

"I just reacted," he said. "Guess I wasn't thinking straight."

Jorgenson huffed out a breath and dabbed at the lacerations with a pad of clean gauze.

"So . . ." she said. "Do I call you hero or dumbshit?"

"There's a difference?"

She flashed a smirk his direction and said, "Not really."

He followed the doctor's gaze back to the wound on Kelly's leg, realized the chance he'd taken. The shark could have easily ripped them both to pieces.

What had I been thinking?

He winced at a jagged flap of bloody skin the doctor dabbed with antiseptic.

"I have to admit," he said, "I've pulled some pretty foolish stunts in my time. But this tops the list. Playing knight in shining armor seems to be a habit of mine."

"You like fighting dragons?"

"Not really. I just can't stand to sit back and watch a woman hurt."

She arched an eyebrow at him and said, "So you willingly risked your life for a woman?"

"Yeah," he said. "Even if it includes fighting a dragon or two."

She nodded and quickly refocused on Kelly's injury.

"Nice," she said. "I'm sure Kelly will thank you when she wakes up. But perhaps fighting the world's dragons is one habit you should work on changing."

Jorgenson picked up a suture, eyed it, and adjusted the thread.

She began to stitch.

She said, "My guess is you'll live longer."

His thoughts flashed to other times he'd risked his life for a woman's sake. His gaze found its way to Kelly's wounds. The sight of the jagged flaps of bloody flesh brought him back. The doctor had him pegged.

Damn!

He sighed and said, "Could be you're right, Doc."

"I know I'm right, but that doesn't mean you're going to change who you are."

He watched her pull two flaps of skin together with a suture.

"Should I?" he asked.

"Can't say," she said. "We can debate the issue, later. Right now, I've got a lot of work to do to save this girl's life. And then I need to make immediate arrangements to have her flown to a hospital on Oahu."

She made one more suture and cut the thread.

Then she turned her gaze on him and said, "Kelly's not out of danger yet. She could still lose her leg."

CHAPTER 3

Jack ducked through the open hatchway and stepped into daylight, embracing the heat of the afternoon and the smell of the sea. The tropical sun cooked the deck and anyone on it, but he needed to breathe.

He closed his eyes, inhaled a lungful of fresh salt air, and slowly let it out. He sucked in another, held it, exhaled. Playing nurse to Doctor Jorgenson while she sewed row after row of stitches in Kelly's leg had sucked the breath from his lungs. The scars from the shark attack would never go away. She'd wear them for life . . . a permanent reminder of that horrific encounter.

He wondered which would be worse: the physical scarring or the mental. At least she'd have her leg. He had to assure himself that would be the case . . . in spite of the doctor's grave concerns.

But what if she did lose her leg?

Jack tried to shrug off the helplessness he felt, but couldn't.

He sighed.

Some white knight I am.

The drone of an approaching aircraft drew his attention starboard. It was too soon for the Coast Guard rescue chopper to arrive. But someone was headed their way. Coming in from the south, a small yellow and white floatplane banked in a slow descent and settled onto the surface of the ocean. Not something he would have expected to see in the Northwestern Hawaiian Islands.

He wondered who it was.

A minute later, the vintage deHavilland Beaver taxied to a stop thirty yards from the ship. Jack strained his eyes to see the pilot through the sun's reflection on the Plexiglas windshield. The guy's face was concealed behind the unyielding glare.

A beat later, the door on the left side of the Beaver swung open and the pilot stepped onto the float.

Robert?

Jack's knitted brow relaxed at the sight of his friend. Then his eyes narrowed in concern. Robert would not have gone to the expense and trouble of flying all that way without good reason. That probably meant bad news.

"Robert," he yelled and waved him over.

"Permission to come aboard," Robert called out.

"Granted," Jack said.

He leaned hard on the railing anxious to find out what had brought his friend to this remote location. On the water below, the small Zodiac they had used earlier in the day was already on its way, Eddie at the wheel.

Five minutes later, the plane was tethered to the ship. Robert stepped aboard the *Albatross* and pumped Jack's hand.

"You're the last person I expected to show up out here," Jack said. "What's up? And where did you get that plane?"

He still had no idea why his friend had gone to so much effort to rendezvous with the research ship, but realized just how glad he was to see him. He could only hope the visit was a social call.

"Had it shipped over from California," Robert said. "Neat, isn't it?"

"I flew out of Vancouver whale watching in one just like that. But since when do you have a seaplane rating?"

"Six months ago. I went stateside to get my rating and came away with this beauty. Thought it might be fun to have."

"You and your toys."

Jack knew Robert hadn't flown three hundred miles to show off his new plane. Something bad had happened, he could feel it in his gut. He readied himself for the news that was coming.

"Okay," he said. "Out with it. What's so important that you flew all the way out here to talk to me when you could have called on the satellite phone?"

Robert turned his head and gazed at the broad expanse of ocean.

All at once, it dawned on Jack why his friend was there.

"I get it," he said. "You didn't come out here to talk. You came out here to fly me back with you, right?"

Robert brought his head back around and locked eyes with Jack. That was enough for Jack to know this was not good.

"It's Katie's grandfather," Robert said. "He's dying."

It was Jack's turn to gaze at the sea. He felt as though the air had been knocked out of him. Bad news is bad news. He thought he'd prepared himself. Evidently, not well enough.

He took a deep breath and blew it out.

"Damn," he said. "I really like the old guy. But there has to be more to your being here than him being on his deathbed."

Robert took a deep breath, and as he exhaled in a sigh he said, "You're right. I got a frantic call from Katie last night. Her grandfather is desperate to talk to you. He insists he has information of vital importance, and that it's imperative you be there."

"Jesus," Jack said.

Again, he turned his gaze on the ocean. What could the old man possibly have to say to him that he hadn't told him before now?

It didn't make sense.

"I don't know," he said. "What could be that important?"

"I haven't got the foggiest idea," Robert explained. "He wouldn't even tell Katie what it is."

Jack eyed the fireball overhead and turned his head from its blistering glare. His brain felt like it had begun to cook inside his skull. The reflection from the deck of the ship didn't help.

"Let's get out of this sun," he said and headed for a shaded area on the deck.

Robert followed.

"How is Katie?" Jack asked.

"You should have kept in touch," Robert said, disappointment showing in the tone of his voice. "She loves you, ya know?"

Jack's breath caught in his throat.

Katie was never out of his thoughts completely. She'd carved a niche in his heart that would forever hold their feelings for each other. But he hadn't expected to hear Robert say what he'd said so quickly and matter-of-factly.

Robert and his damned intuition. Shit!

"Yeah . . . maybe," Jack said. "But evidently not enough to come here and fetch me there herself."

"Don't be an ass, Jack. You're the one who broke it off with her."

"She wouldn't leave Vegas. My life is the ocean. And that's a far cry from the casinos on the strip."

"You talk like she's a poll dancer in a nudie club. She's a dental hygienist for Christ's sake. Hell, she avoids the strip like the plague and you know it."

"That's the problem."

Robert cocked his head in obvious confusion.

"That she avoids the strip?" he asked.

"That she's a dental hygienist in Henderson," Jack said. "She doesn't want to leave."

"She wanted to get to know her father again." Robert snorted and added, "Can you blame her?"

Jack blamed her, but then maybe not.

Struggling with the thought, he shot an uneasy glance at Robert.

Robert shook his head and said, "Should have given her time. When she was ready, she'd have come running with bells on."

"I gave her time. Three years should have been enough."

"All I can say is if you get another chance, don't screw it up."

Jack was silent a long moment. Then his eyes locked on Robert's.

"Kelly was attacked by an eight-foot tiger shark a couple of hours ago," he said. "The fucker tried to bite her leg off."

Robert sucked in a breath.

"Damn," he said. He refocused his gaze on Jack and asked, "Kelly is the girl you were telling me about?" She'll be all right, I hope?"

Jack couldn't shake the mental image he carried of her mangled leg, the blood . . . all those stitches. She'd paid the price for his clumsiness. He'd seen the terror in her eyes; knew she was about to panic.

He should've reacted quicker.

"Some nasty teeth wounds," he said. "But I convinced the ugly bugger it was in his best interest to let go of her.

"What do you mean you convinced that shark to let go of Kelly's leg?"

"I grabbed the sonofabitch by the dorsal fin and shoved my dive knife into his eye. The fucker immediately lost his appetite for young women and spit her out."

"You did what!"

For a couple of beats, Robert just stared at Jack. He recovered and shook his head with an exasperated sigh.

"I don't know what it is with you," he said. "You're always rushing in to rescue the damsel in distress. Gonna get you killed one of these days."

"Maybe," Jack admitted. "But I couldn't let him eat her."

"Jack . . ."

Jack shrugged and said, "She needed help. I did the only thing I could."

"And like I said, one of these days you're going to pull one of your stunts and it's going to kill you."

"She's a nice girl and I care a lot for her. I couldn't just watch her die."

"Guess not. Probably would have done something just as stupid had I been in your place."

They both fell silent.

"Doc's done what she can for her. But she could still lose the leg. We're waiting for a Coast Guard helicopter to fly her to Oahu." He checked the time showing on the dial of his dive watch, searched the southern horizon with his eyes, and continued saying, "Damned chopper should arrive any minute."

Robert turned his head and scanned the sky to the south.

"I'm sorry about what happened to Kelly," he said. "But you do know you still need to go see Katie's grandfather."

Jack looked at his friend, gave a slight shake of his head.

"Don't see how I can," he said. "There's Kelly to consider. I should be close by in case she needs me. And there's my research." He waved a hand at the sea around them and continued, "I need to complete my work here or it'll be another year before I finish up my doctorate."

"The *Albatross* is going to be anchored here another month," Robert assured him. "I know, because I checked with NOAA. And Kelly will heal just fine without you hanging around feeling sorry for yourself."

"Still, I don't know . . ."

"You're frustrating, you know that? Stop making excuses and pack your bag. I took the liberty of reserving you a seat on a flight out of Honolulu, tonight."

"Tonight?'

"That's right, tonight. The old man is dying. Time is of the essence. Now pack your bag. And hope it's not already too late."

Jack raised a brow and asked, "For Kelly?"

"For Kelly," Robert said. "And Katie's grandfather."

CHAPTER 4

Coleman Treadway wanted to find out what would happen now that he had talked to Charles McIntyre—the last piece of the puzzle. He intended to make sure his grandfather's World War II buddy had told him every last detail.

McIntyre swore he had.

But had he?

Treadway's experience in matters such as this told him the old man knew more than he'd admitted.

He swirled the brandy in his snifter.

Boryenko—he was confident—would have extracted every last detail out of the old man right then and there, but a retirement home full of witnesses was not a place to carry out the noisy business of breaking bones—a skill Boryenko had mastered.

Then again, perhaps he should've been done with it.

Boryenko was willing.

The old fool's fingers would have snapped like dry twigs. Boryenko would've had his fun, and *he* would have been secure in knowing he had every scrap of information his grandfather had stupidly shared with this wartime buddy.

Foolish thoughts brought on by the anxiety of waiting, he concluded. He wouldn't jeopardize his fortune by making mistakes. A day, maybe two, would tell him what he needed to know.

He'd allow himself that.

He stepped to the window and stared at the city lights. He was not a man of impulse, but he *was* a man of action. He snatched his iPhone from the desk and speed-dialed Boryenko.

"Are they still inside?" he asked when the line picked up.

"*Da.*"

The Russian's heavy accent was a reminder he had once fought against the United States in the cold war. But Treadway couldn't have cared less. Patriotism had no place in his life. His allegiance was to himself and the wealth the world offered: masterpieces of art stolen from the Nazis who'd stolen them from the Jews, Egyptian idols plundered from the tombs of Pharaohs, Incan gold smuggled through the Russian mob operating out of Cuba.

All mine. And there is much more to be had.

Treadway blinked himself back.

He asked, "Any word from our contact?"

"Only that the old man is dying. And that his son and granddaughter are waiting for a man named Jack Ferrell to arrive. He's a former boyfriend of the granddaughter and is due to arrive tomorrow morning. I was told he's been to the retirement home several times in the past, but not in the last year. The old man insisted on seeing him. One last request before he dies."

Treadway's jaw muscles tightened.

"Then we won't have long to wait," he said. "Keep me informed."

Treadway terminated the call. He had complete faith in Boryenko Ivanov. The man didn't make mistakes.

There'd be none this time.

He sipped his brandy and smiled with smug satisfaction. His decision to stick around was paying off. The old man *had* withheld information. Why else would he be so adamant about seeing Jack Ferrell?

CHAPTER 5

Jack tightened his seatbelt and straightened his back against his seat. The tires of the Boeing 767 hit hard on the runway at the Boise Municipal Airport. He jolted forward and felt the forward inertia of the plane tug on his body as the reverse thrusters sent a shudder through the cabin.

He was glad to be on the ground.

He'd spent the entire flight thinking about the last four and a half years of his life. So much had happened since his return to the University of Oregon at Corvallis: two years to complete his bachelor's degree in Marine Science, two more years of concentrated studies for his masters . . . and now the pursuit of his doctorate. No wonder he and Katie never had a chance. With such an intense academic schedule piled high on his plate, he doubted they'd have had much time to foster a relationship even if they had tried.

But they should have tried . . . dammit!

And that's what infuriated him.

They hadn't . . . or least not hard enough.

Her refusal to move from Henderson, and the months he spent on research vessels at sea in his relentless pursuit of his dream to study the world's oceans, had kept them apart. He had his world. She had hers. And now the person who brought them together in the beginning was bringing them together again: *her grandfather.*

He stepped outside the terminal and saw Katie McIntyre waiting for him at the curb. She was standing next to her white Toyota Camry.

He stopped in his tracks, felt his stomach tighten.

Damn.

He was staring. He knew it. Not good, but that had been his first impulse. He'd forgotten how pretty she was.

He sent Robert a mental "thanks" for his persistence.

There was no denying he missed her. He hadn't seen her in a year. And until he phoned the night before to tell her he was catching the redeye to see her grandfather, he hadn't spoken to her in over six months.

Way too long.

Her comments over the phone had been curt and to the point. And although he'd expected her to be a bit cool toward him, her aloofness caught him off guard. He wished she'd been happier to hear his voice and excited about spending time together. But she had sounded as though she was only happy he was coming because her grandfather was so desperate to talk to him.

That hurt.

He wanted to say something witty to take the edge off their meeting. But his heart lodged in his throat.

"Katie," he managed.

He waved and flashed his best smile.

* * * *

Katie met his broad smile with a thin one of her own and took a couple of steps in his direction. She extended her hand as he stepped close to her.

She said, "Grandpa will be glad you're here."

He dropped his duffel bag. A simple handshake wouldn't do. He stepped past her outstretched hand, slipped his arms around her waist, and pulled her tight.

"It's great to see you," he said.

"It's nice to see you too, Jack."

She kissed him on the cheek, tried to move out of his grasp.

He held on.

"Really," she said. "We should be going."

She stiffened and pressed her palms against his chest.

"Jack, please." She tried to push him away.

He held her a moment longer, then released her to arm's length and held her by her shoulders. He wasn't letting go.

She bowed her head toward the concrete walkway at her feet. It was difficult to look at him.

He said, "I take it you're not as glad to see me as I am to see you?"

She brought her eyes up and let her gaze wander over his body. He was tanned dark from his time on the water, and heavily muscled from the rigors of daily dives. Even his rumpled pants and shirt and disheveled hair looked sexy.

But she didn't want him to know that.

She raised her chin in defiance, her eyes wide open and focused on his.

"Should I be?" she asked.

He said, "Maybe I was taking too much for granted."

She held her answer. On the way to the airport, she had given considerable thought to how she'd react to seeing him after so long. She had no idea he would stir her feelings so deeply. The moment she saw him walking toward her, she wanted to leap into his arms. But she'd fought temptation. She couldn't bear the thought of him being cold to her the way he had when he told her he didn't have time for games.

That's what he had called their relationship: *a game.*

But then here he is. And he *had* put his arms around her and pulled her tight, told her how great it was to see her.

Did he miss me as much as I miss him?

She doubted it. He had even told her he was involved with someone else.

"I don't think this is the time to talk about it," she managed to say.

He sighed and let go of her shoulders.

"Of course," he said. "How is your grandfather doing?"

"Not good. He may not live through the night."

"Katie"—he reached and brushed away a tear that formed in the corner of her eye and dropped his hand when she shied away—"I'm glad you called Robert."

"And I'm glad he convinced you to come . . . for Grandpa's sake."

CHAPTER 6

Jack had no idea what to expect once they arrived at the retirement home. The limited conversation between him and Katie on the way to Ridgeview remained strained. He had even dozed a few minutes in the warmth of the morning sun. But he was wide-awake now . . . and eager to see her grandfather.

When they pulled into the parking lot, he read the slogan on the sign next to the entrance: Assisted Living for the Golden Years.

Golden years, my ass.

The residents who called this place home had come here to live out their last days, just as Katie's grandfather had.

The old guy deserved better.

They hurried inside and Jack quickened his pace down the hallway ahead of Katie. His studies and his estrangement from Katie had kept him away, but he hadn't forgotten about Charles William McIntyre and was anxious to see him. Above all else, he wanted to tell the old guy how much he meant to him.

His feelings for the man hadn't changed. It was as if Katie's grandfather was his own flesh and blood; the grandfather Ferrell he had not been permitted to get to know and who had died alone in a place like this because of a stupid disagreement between his father and grandfather.

McIntyre had to know he wasn't one of the forgotten souls.

Jack could hear the heels of Katie's shoes clacking on the tile hallway behind him when he stopped at the doorway to room eighteen. He took a breath, gripped the doorjamb, and peered inside.

Sean McIntyre sat in a chair close to the bed, his face turned in the direction of the doorway, apparently drawn there by the sound of footsteps. Jack could tell by the deep lines at the corners of his eyes he was tired, but otherwise the man appeared well. Jack was glad Katie's father was holding up. He nodded a greeting. Katie's grandfather lay on his back, spread and blanket folded to his chest, his head turned so that he faced the window and the nearby mountains crisp and beautiful in the bright morning sun.

Much the way he had when they first met.

Jack heard the clacking stop behind him. He felt the warmth of Katie's breath on the back of his neck. She'd leaned close, no doubt to see into her grandfather's room.

He smiled at the intimacy of the situation, but kept his focus on the man he'd come to see. The same Charles William McIntyre he knew and loved, only frail and vulnerable. He'd mentally prepared himself to see his old friend on the edge of his deathbed.

It had done little good.

He sniffled, and for a moment stood remembering the first time they met. The way the aged vet's eyes lit up when *he* handed him his lost ring.

That flash of reminiscence was all it took to open the dike in Jack's mind and flood his head with memories. Finding McIntyre's West Point Class Ring on that reef in Maui and him returning it had been a pivotal point in his life. It was McIntyre's war stories that intrigued him. And it was the secret behind the ring that brought him and Katie together in a quest to free her father from prison.

A quest that almost got them killed.

"Grandpa, it's Jack." He said.

He had gotten used to calling the old guy grandpa even though they weren't related. To do so warmed his heart. And it always brought a smile to McIntyre's lips.

Charles McIntyre's eyes focused on the doorway.

"Jack," he said in a weak voice.

Jack noticed the old guy's eyes clear, the dullness replaced by the sparkle he'd seen in them the first time they met.

"That's right," he said. "I came as soon as I heard."

Sean McIntyre stood up and said, "Have a seat, Jack. Dad has something he wants to tell you."

Jack stepped to the chair Sean had been sitting in, slid it close to the side of the bed, and sat down. He drew in a breath and let it out. He felt a little guilty knowing it had taken a lot of effort and urging from Robert to get him there. Now he was sorry now he had procrastinated for even a second.

"I was on a research ship in the Northwestern Hawaiian Islands when I heard you wanted to see me," he said. "I got here as quick as I could."

Charles McIntyre closed his eyes, nodded, and slowly opened them.

"I know," he said. "Sorry to take you away from your studies, but you'll want to hear what I have to say."

McIntyre exhaled a quiet sigh and closed his eyes again.

Jack breathed deeply to remain patient and quietly waited for Katie's grandfather to explain.

But this time the old guy's eyes didn't open back up.

No! You can't . . .

"Grandpa!" Jack pleaded, gently shaking McIntyre's arm.

The old man's eyes remained closed.

An overwhelming sense of loss hollowed Jack.

I can't believe I arrived too late.

CHAPTER 7

Jack exchanged worried glances with Katie. Her eyes were just as pleading as his.

He refused to believe he hadn't gotten there in time.

Her grandfather would not give up, even in death. He'd fight.

And that's what he was doing now.

Jack prayed for him to come back to them. That's when he saw old man McIntyre's chest rise and fall ever so slightly.

He looked closer to make sure it wasn't his emotions refusing to accept reality.

Again, he saw the old guy's chest expand and fall.

McIntyre was still with them.

Thank God.

Damn he loved this old guy.

He gently shook the aged vet's arm and said, "Grandpa . . . you old coot, don't do this to me. There's something I need to tell *you*. I love you as if you were my own grandfather; maybe more . . . we all love you."

He peered up at Katie and her father; saw the concern etched in their furrowed brows, tears welling in the corners of their eyes. He struggled to find the right words, but none came.

He gazed at the old guy and took a deep breath.

"Come on, Charlie," he pleaded. "You're not leaving us yet. You wouldn't . . ."

After what felt like an eternity to Jack, old man McIntyre's eyes fluttered open to the sight of three anxious faces hovering over him.

No one spoke.

Jack watched Charlie McIntyre suck in a labored breath through his mouth. Then he saw the old guy's eyes open and focus.

"Those sad faces are for me?" he said, his voice weak.

"You had us a little concerned," Jack said.

That made the corners of Charlie McIntyre's lips curl up.

"Pay attention to what I tell you," he said. "I've held a secret all these years and you're the only one I can trust to help."

Jack sighed and edged closer.

"Secret?" he said. "What secret?"

"You returned my ring, Jack. You helped Katie get her father—my son—out of prison." A flicker of pride showed on Charles McIntyre's face when the old guy's gaze shifted to Katie and Sean.

"Sure. But what are you talking about?"

McIntyre gripped Jack's wrist.

"Lost relics," he said in a tone hardened by resolve. "Stolen archeological treasures. You have to find them, Jack. And turn them over to the Hawaiian government."

"Lost relics? Stolen treasure?" Jack asked, confused. He wrinkled his brow trying to understand. "You're not making sense."

McIntyre filled his lungs. His eyes grew clear and sharp, and to Jack it seemed the old guy had drawn on an inner strength his failing body forgot he had.

McIntyre tightened his grip on Jack's wrist and pulled him close.

He said, "From the war, boy . . . *from during the war.*"

Jack stood up, walked to the window, and stared at the river. He and McIntyre had talked a lot about WW II during their visits together. The battles fought in the islands, what it was like to be a soldier in the mud and the rain . . . to watch so many buddies die. What was he talking about now?

He turned and faced the old man.

"You've got me confused," he said, there was no hiding the bewilderment in his voice. "You're talking about WW II?"

McIntyre nodded.

He said, "I told you about the battle of Saipan. You know what went on there."

"Sure."

Jack's response brought another node from McIntyre.

He continued, "I learned about the lost treasure a few hours before the Japanese banzai attack on the night of July 6th and 7th. We were all hunkered down, Jack; every last mother's son . . . waiting, wondering; not knowing if we were going to live or die. It was a time for talking about wives and girlfriends. The women you left behind and the one's that got away. A time for sharing secrets . . . those true and those made up."

Jack didn't quite know what to think.

"We talked about the battle of Saipan," he said. "Even that Lee Marvin got shot in the butt there, but you never mentioned anything about a lost treasure."

"That's because I thought it was a story dreamed up by a lonely, frightened soldier wanting to have a secret to share; something to talk about. Now I have reason to believe the story is quite true."

"But lost treasure, that's a bit farfetched, isn't it?"

"You found that ring of mine, didn't you?"

"Yeah, but . . ."

"Like I said, I thought this was a story fabricated by a soldier wanting to impress his buddies. It might still be . . . but I don't think so. As I told you, a lot of soldiers believed they were going to die on that island. Too many already had. Everyone figured they'd get it next. Sergeant Martin Treadway was one of them. That night he confided in me he'd dreamed his death. It turned out he did die in that banzai attack. But not before he told me about a cave full of relics he and two other soldiers discovered in the cliffs above Kealakekua Bay on The Big Island of Hawaii."

Jack inched closer, drawn in by the possibility there could be some truth to the story after all. He'd been to the Bishop Museum, seen the displays, but only from a distance, and with a thick pane of glass between him and the artifact's.

"The bay where Captain Cook was killed," he said.

"You know the story then?"

"A little," Jack said with a shrug. "From what I remember, Captain Cook and some of his men tried to kidnap one of the

Island's kings so they could ransom him for a boat the natives had stolen. He was stabbed to death on the beach trying to flee the warriors who had become enraged over the incident."

"Not just stabbed, Jack. The warriors snatched the fatal dagger out of each other's hands while they took turns stabbing him."

Jack narrowed his left eye slightly as he envisioned the gruesome scene. He'd tasted fear on more than one occasion, experienced the desperation that spurred a willingness to do anything to survive the moment, but couldn't imagine the horror Cook must have felt in those final seconds of his life when he knew all was lost. Did he even feel the first stab of the knife?

"If I remember right," Jack said, "Cook's crew never did recover his entire body, did they?"

"Only the long bones, hands, feet, and skull were recovered," McIntyre said. "The rest of his body parts, sword, and uniform were never returned."

"And that's what Martin Treadway claimed he had found?"

McIntyre nodded.

"That's right," he said. "Sergeant Treadway believed they'd found the final remains of Captain Cook, the dagger that killed him, and the bones of King Kalaniopuu, the old king that Cook was trying to kidnap."

"And they looted the tomb so they could sell the artifacts on the black market?"

"Precisely. According to the Sergeant, he and his two buddies packed the bones and relics into a watertight crate and smuggled them out on a small plane."

"So how did Treadway happen onto this find?"

"Treadway prided himself on being a self made archeologist. According to the story he told me, he stumbled onto his first burial site by accident. After that, he spent every minute of his off time scouring the islands for the tombs and graves belonging to ancient Hawaii's *Alii*."

"So he didn't just luck onto the discovery of the century?"

"I'm sure luck had a lot to do with it. But as I explained, that wasn't his first find. He bragged about the amount of money he'd made in the year he had been stationed on Oahu; said he had a buyer on the mainland willing to pay big dollars for artifacts, and accomplices in key military positions that enabled him to smuggle the antiquities stateside via military transport. According to Treadway, once the antiquities were delivered to the buyer, the money showed up in a special bank account. As soon as that happened, he gave his partners their share, keeping the bulk of the money for himself."

"I take it something went wrong with his operation?"

"It did, indeed. Treadway was flying a Piper Cub he'd secured at the last minute to transport the crate of artifacts to Oahu. Everything boiled down to time. He had to get the artifacts to his contact that night or risk having to sit on them until the next cargo flight out of Hickam en route to the mainland. And there was no way to know when that would happen. The problem was, he didn't make it. The engine died and the plane went down in the drink off the island of Kahoolawe."

"I'm surprised the army didn't shoot his ass down. We had shore batteries and pill boxes all along that end of Maui."

"From what he told me they threatened to. Said the plane's engine gave out on him before they had a chance to."

"Sounds like Madam Pele got her revenge."

Jack again waited while McIntyre paused to take a few breaths. His old friend was clearly drawing on every last ounce of strength to tell the story. But his smile suggested he relished the idea of Pele taking her wrath out on Sergeant Treadway.

"With everything going wrong," McIntyre said a moment later, "Treadway thought the same thing. He actually laughed about it. We both did."

Jack scoffed, "I'm not so sure it's anything to laugh about."

"Perhaps not." McIntyre took a sip of water and added, "But Treadway started out thinking it was. Said he'd refused to take stock in any of those silly superstitions he'd heard about the Goddess Pele taking her wrath out on people who did something that pissed her off. But afterwards, when he realized he'd made the find he dreamed of only to be on the verge of having the priceless relics slip through his fingers, he figured there just might be something to the superstitious mumbo jumbo he'd been hearing, after all."

"So what happened to the artifacts?"

"His plane sank, but not before he was able to wrestle the crate out of the cockpit and use it as a raft to drift to Kahoolawe."

"So that's where Treadway ended up?"

"Him and the crate. Only he drifted into a lava tube."

Jack smiled and said, "This story keeps getting better and better."

He noticed Katie and her father—as he had—moved close when Charles McIntyre started talking about the stolen artifacts. They were both quiet, clearly caught up in the story.

Perhaps as much as he was.

He said, "And Sergeant Treadway was by himself in the plane?"

"There was only room for him and the crate."

"Figures."

McIntyre swallowed. His breath rattled in his chest.

He gripped Jack's arm and said, "Bear with me, Boy. A couple hundred feet inside, Sergeant Treadway ran aground on a sandy beach that had formed there. He pulled the crate onto the lava high above the sand line to keep it safe, then swam out. At first light, a patrol boat picked him up. And that afternoon he flew out to Oahu. Two days later, he was on a troop transport headed for Saipan. He and his unit shipped out before he had a chance to return for the relics."

Jack straightened in his chair. He didn't quite know what to make of the story.

"Well?" he asked over his shoulder at Katie. "What do you think?"

She shrugged and said, "Sounds plausible, but I don't know."

Jack turned his attention back on her grandfather and said, "You mentioned that initially you didn't believe the story. Why do you believe it now? What caused you to change your mind after all these years?"

McIntyre's eyes narrowed into a hard glare.

"His grandson."

CHAPTER 8

McIntyre gasped and breathed a couple of ragged breaths. The talking clearly taking a toll. But he continued to draw on the little strength he had left. He motioned a hand at his son in an obvious gesture for him to explain.

Sean McIntyre spoke up, "I walked in about fifteen minutes after they left. Dad told me what happened. Two nights ago, he got a visit from a man named Coleman Treadway and a big brute-of-a-sonofabitch Dad wasn't introduced to. Coleman Treadway claimed his father had died recently and that he wanted to talk about a letter he found in his father's possessions.

"A relative of the long dead Sergeant Martin Treadway?"

"But I didn't realize that at first," Charles McIntyre continued. "The name Treadway didn't ring a bell for me . . . not after fifty some-odd years. It wasn't until this Coleman Treadway character told me he wanted to talk to me about a conversation I had with his grandfather about some artifacts lost during the war that I made the connection."

Jack had no problem connecting the dots.

He nodded and said, "The ones in the cave."

"Precisely," Charles McIntyre said, and explained, "It seems Martin Treadway had written his wife a letter before his death in that banzai charge. Apparently that letter found its way into his son's hands and eventually into the hands of Martin Treadway's grandson Coleman Treadway."

"That's how he knew to talk to you."

"That's right. He said his grandfather wrote in the letter that he'd told me everything. He wanted to know what I knew."

"What did you tell him?"

"The story I just told you, only I left out the part about the lava tube."

"You didn't trust the Sergeant's grandson?"

"I'm old, Jack . . . and dying. But I can still smell a rat."

"Didn't Coleman Treadway already have that information . . . from his grandfather's letter, I mean?"

"I don't think so. At least that's not the impression I got. Could be good ol' Sergeant Treadway didn't want to chance the information would fall into the wrong hands. I'm sure he planned to go back for the relics the first opportunity he had."

"So his grandson came to you hoping to fill in the blanks?"

"I'm sure of it. And for only one reason."

"He's after the relics."

"Or what was packed in with them."

Jack locked eyes with McIntyre. The old guy had been holding something back.

"What do you mean?" he asked. "Was there something else in those crates?"

"That's what the Sergeant said, but he refused to tell me what it was. He only said it would make him a very rich man."

Jack stroked his chin, imagining what would be worth so much money that it would make someone rich. Gold, jewels . . . the Hawaiian's had none of that.

He asked, "And he wouldn't tell you what it was?"

McIntyre shook his head and said, "Not even a hint. And I'm not sure his grandson knows either. But I can tell you this; Coleman Treadway intends to have the relics and whatever else is inside that crate. And from the looks of the thug with him . . . by whatever means necessary."

"And you want me to find the crate first."

"And turn everything over to the Hawaiian government."

"Why not let the State deal with Treadway? They can find the crate if it's there. You want them to have the artifacts anyway."

McIntyre reached for Jack's arm and grasped it.

Jack felt a renewed strength there. Determination.

"You, Jack," McIntyre said. "Not some undermanned government agency. By the time they get around to taking action, Coleman Treadway will be long gone, and so will the artifacts."

Jack stared at the wall, his mind three thousand miles away. *Kahoolawe again.*

It seemed the deserted island was intent on haunting his life.

"For the ducks of it," Jack said, a long quiet moment later. "Say I agree to go after this archeological treasure. Just where in hell on that ravaged, desolate, barren island do you suggest I start looking?"

"That's one of the reasons I wanted it to be you, Jack. I have confidence in your abilities."

Great, Jack thought. Now I'm not only faced with the near impossibility of finding a needle in a field of haystacks. I have to live up to a dying old man's expectations.

Fuck!

He realized he was stuck.

He said, "Even a small island like Kahoolawe can be huge when you're looking for something the size of a steamer trunk. Every treasure map starts off from a rock or a tree. The ocean's a clean slate. I'll need a beginning point."

"My feeling is you'll figure that out when you get there."

Jack got up from his seat, stroked his chin, walked to the other side of the room and back, stopping at the foot of McIntyre's bed to gaze out the window at the fresh veil of green blanketing the nearby hillsides. Only he saw the red dirt of Kahoolawe, his mind forming a mental image of every detail he could remember about the island from the year he lived on Maui.

"You said Treadway drifted into a lava tube." He held onto the image he'd formed of Kahoolawe and asked, "Did he describe the opening or anything else about it that might set that particular lava tube apart from others in the area?"

McIntyre's eyes closed.

Jack worried he was pushing too hard and considered backing off. He checked the rise and fall of McIntyre's chest to make sure he was still breathing.

The aged vet was hanging in there.

He hoped the old guy had just slid into the past, dredging up his memory of a long ago conversation. He needed to know more and would listen as long as McIntyre had the will and strength to talk. Even so, he was concerned. The conversation was clearly taxing the old man and he might not open his eyes next time.

When McIntyre's eyes opened a couple of beats later and focused on him, he could see the man's resolve to tell every detail he could remember.

Jack stepped to the side of the bed, picked up the glass of water from the bedside table, slid his hand under McIntyre's back to help support him, and held the glass to McIntyre's lips. McIntyre took a sip and pushed the glass away. Jack eased him back onto the pillow.

"Sergeant Treadway described the entrance as being fifteen or twenty feet across," McIntyre continued, his words strained. "But with the tide coming in, only three or four feet of the mouth of the tube was exposed above the surface of the rising water. And the opening was getting smaller by the minute. That's why he swam out of there without the crate. He was afraid he would be trapped inside. The problem was, the mouth of the lava tube eventually disappeared below the surface of the waves. And in the dark, he wasn't exactly sure of its location."

"Did he say anything else that might give me some idea where to look?"

"Only that he drifted there from somewhere near Molokini crater after his plane crash landed in the water."

Jack walked back to the window and faced the glass. His mind fought fatigue to piece together the information. An enigma for sure.

"And the grandson wants to find it" he said, thinking out loud. He asked, "What did this Coleman Treadway character look like, anyway?"

"Not much older than you, maybe thirty-five or forty," McIntyre explained. "And about the same size, possibly a few pounds heavier and a couple of inches taller: say six foot two or three, two fifteen or twenty. And short black hair with a white spot in back that I think is natural. Kinda odd looking."

"Some sort of birthmark?"

"That'd be my guess."

Jack scanned the mountains and the sky looking for the portal to wisdom the old guy seemed to stare into each time he gazed out the window. But no such portal existed, except in the wise old man's mind—a lifetime of experience stored like jpeg files in a computer—experience Jack didn't have.

He'd miss Charles McIntyre a lot.

"I can't make any promises," Jack said, maintaining his vigil at the window. "But I'll do my best."

"I know I can trust you to do what's right."

"The Hawaiian's call it *pono*," Jack said. "You don't have to worry."

"If the crate's there, Grandpa," Katie offered from the other side of the room. "He'll find it. I'll make sure of that."

Jack turned at the sound of Katie's voice. His conversation with her grandfather had him so preoccupied he'd practically forgotten she was there.

"And just what exactly did you mean by that comment?" he asked.

With a firm nod she said, "I'm going with you, of course."

He was about to protest, when a hacking cough from someone in a room up the hall drew his attention to the doorway. He noticed a nurse quickly turn and step away from the opening.

Only a glimpse, but it was enough.

Caught up in the discussion, he hadn't heard or observed the nurse walk up. Now he wondered how long she had been standing at the doorjamb. Had she come to the room to check on McIntyre only to be pulled away by someone else's needs?

Or had she been listening in on their conversation?

"I wonder how long she'd been standing there?" Katie asked.

He directed his attention back on her and noticed her gaze move from the doorway and settle on him. Apparently, she'd also seen the nurse hurry away from the door. No matter how much he wanted to believe the nurse's actions were purely coincidental, he couldn't . . . and doubted Katie did either.

"My guess is, long enough," he said. "What I want to know is *why was she listening?*"

CHAPTER 9

Coleman Treadway took the iPhone from Mario Fuentes and saw him nod. It was the phone call Treadway had been waiting for. He motioned for Fuentes to stay.

"You have news?" he asked the caller.

He felt no need to exchange pleasantries with the person on the other end of the line. He was paying them for information, not meaningless conversation.

"They arrived about an hour ago," the voice said.

Treadway's jaw muscles tightened. He bit back his frustration with this person.

He said, "Tell me something I don't know."

"His son and granddaughter," the caller said. "And the man I told you about: Jack Ferrell. He's the boyfriend of the granddaughter."

"And?"

"As you know, this is the young man Charles McIntyre has been waiting for. Now I think I know why. McIntyre has been talking about a lost treasure, stolen archeological artifacts, I believe it was. I couldn't quite make out everything he was saying, but he definitely wants Jack Ferrell to recover them and . . ."

Treadway was quickly growing weary of the word game.

"My dear girl," he said. "It would be a mistake to not tell me everything you know."

"Uh . . . Well . . ." she said. "From what I heard, Mr. Ferrell intends to go after the artifacts."

He wanted to reach into the phone and strangle the woman. She was holding back. He could tell by the sound of her voice.

"And!" he said. There was no mistaking his impatience.

He heard the woman swallow into the phone.

She added, "He intends to turn the artifacts over to the Hawaiian government."

Treadway sighed. This was not the news he wanted to hear.

He asked, "What are they doing now?"

"They're all inside the room," she said. "Talking."

Treadway lowered the iPhone and tapped it against his left hand. The time for waiting was over. So were the games.

He raised the cellular to his lips and said, "Call me if you hear anything else I need to know. And young lady, never play games with me. Tell me everything the first time. I don't like having to ask questions. It'd be a shame if you were to have an accident on the way home from work."

Treadway terminated the call, tossed the iPhone to Fuentes, and turned his back. He said, "There's a minor problem that needs to be taken care of before we leave town. Get Eduardo in here."

"Yes sir," Fuentes said. "But, Sir, he's . . . uh . . . next door with Felicia."

Treadway turned, his jaw tightened with rage. It was bad enough he had to endure the nurse's incompetence. There was no way he'd tolerate that same bullshit from any of his employees.

His left eye twitched.

"I don't care who Eduardo is with or what he's doing," he said. "I want him in here now!"

"Yes sir," Fuentes said without hesitation. He turned and hurried out the door of the Presidential Suite.

Treadway stepped to the bar, poured himself a snifter of brandy, and took a sip.

So Jack Ferrell thinks he's going to steal property that belongs to me.

He chuckled at the thought.

The artifacts were his, plain and simple. His grandfather discovered them. That meant they belonged to the Treadway family—*him*. He wouldn't tolerate anyone moving in to take property that was rightfully his. In the past, whenever someone tried to take something he wanted—to double cross him in the slightest way—he'd dealt with them, quickly and decisively.

He'd deal with Jack Ferrell.

The door opened behind him. He could hear the rustle of clothes and the scuff of shoes on the tile entry. He didn't need to look to know Fuentes had returned with Eduardo.

"Sir . . ." The tone of Fuentes' voice reflected the successful completion of his errand.

Treadway slowly turned and faced the two men.

Fighting to keep his calm, he shook his head at Eduardo who stood wearing a pair of faded tight-fitting Levis and nothing else. The sight of the short rail-thin Brazilian nude from the waist up infuriated him.

He swallowed back his disgust.

It didn't help.

"Drink, Eduardo?" he asked, raising the snifter of brandy in a gesture of offering.

"*Si . . . gracias.*" Eduardo smiled and stepped cautiously to the bar.

Treadway picked up the leaded crystal decanter by the neck and casually moved it toward an empty snifter. Then as quick as a cat, he grabbed Eduardo's wrist, pressed his hand flat to the bar, and smashed the heavy decanter down on the man's bony knuckles.

The decanter broke below the neck, jagged shards of crystal gouged into flesh and bone.

Eduardo screamed and backed away clutching his broken and bleeding hand to his chest.

Treadway tossed what was left of the broken decanter onto the bar.

"Fuck on your own time," he said.

He nodded at Fuentes. The man did not appear to be shaken by the incident.

"Get this worthless piece of shit out of here," he ordered. "I'll have Boryenko take care of the problem. He knows what to do."

* * * *

Boryenko Ivanov sat at attention behind the steering wheel of the black Hummer. He'd watched Katie McIntyre and Jack Ferrell walk inside the retirement home. And for the past fifty-five minutes, he'd kept his eyes focused on the entrance, waiting for them to walk out.

They had yet to leave. He'd have seen them.

All he knew about Jack Ferrell was what the mole had told them: Jack Ferrell was a boyfriend of Katie McIntyre and he'd been to the retirement home several times to visit her grandfather.

Not much information.

Now that he had seen Jack Ferrell, he was convinced there had to be more to the man than just him being the granddaughter's lover. He was here for a reason. And it wasn't only because the old man was dying.

Boryenko had ingrained Jack's face into his memory. A habit he developed while dealing with the Russian mob. It had saved his life more than once.

The iPhone sitting on the seat next to him played the ringtone he'd programmed for his boss' private number. He picked it up and said, "*Da.*"

"They're still inside?" Treadway asked.

Boryenko glanced at his watch even though he didn't need to. He answered, "For almost an hour."

Treadway said, "Jack Ferrell has become a problem. The old man told him about the artifacts. He intends to recover them and turn everything over to the Hawaiians. I won't allow that."

Boryenko smiled into the phone. He knew what Treadway wanted done.

"Do not worry about Jack Ferrell," he said. "The girl?"

"She's of no consequence to me," Treadway answered. "Neither is her father. Do with them what you like."

Again, Boryenko smiled. This time at the thought of what he would do to the young lady if he had a few hours alone with her. When he finished, she'd wish he had killed her along with the others. Perhaps he *would* treat himself and take the young lady to a place where her screams would not be heard.

"I want their deaths to look like an accident," Treadway added.

Treadway's voice brought Boryenko out of his fantasy. His boss had obviously read his thoughts. The smirk slipped from his face.

Boryenko's eyes focused on the door to the retirement home. He asked, "Do we leave soon?"

"This evening," Treadway told him. "After you take care of the problem."

The line clicked off.

Boryenko switched off his iPhone, tossed the cellular onto the passenger's seat, and slouched behind the wheel. The boring wait had paid off. He could relax now. Jack Ferrell would be dead by dinnertime.

CHAPTER 10

Jack walked the hallway in search of the nurse he'd observed snooping outside the door to McIntyre's room. He hadn't gotten a good look at her face, but he did notice her red hair and blue uniform.

When he reached the lobby, he spied her standing next to an empty chair, a cell phone pressed to her ear. Even from across the room he could tell she was the same woman—same carrot-red hair, same sky-blue scrub top.

He remembered the nurse from several of his prior visits to the retirement home. She'd been on duty the day he first met Charles William McIntyre—when he returned McIntyre's West Point class ring. She'd greeted him with a smile then, and each time thereafter.

And now she was spying on him.

Katie huffed to a stop next to him. He turned at her approach and noticed her gaze home in on the redheaded nurse. She took a step in that direction. He reached out and gripped her arm to stop her. There was a way to handle the situation. Charging up to the woman like a pissed-off bantam hen wasn't it.

Katie shot him a narrow-eyed look that told him she wasn't happy he'd stopped her.

"What's the matter?" she asked. "Let's talk to the nosy bitch."

"Relax."

Reasonably sure Katie was going to stay put, he let go of her arm and watched the redhead talk. His thinking was dull from lack of sleep. Even so, he was sharp enough to know they couldn't be absolutely sure the nurse had intentionally eavesdropped on their conversation. And what if she had, what did that mean? Surely the woman would deny any impropriety if confronted.

And the front lobby of the retirement home was no place to cause a scene.

He decided it was best to do nothing—at least for the time being. But the incident was a wake-up call that they needed to watch their backs from here on out. And that's what he planned to do.

"Let's go back to your grandfather's room," he said, half turning in that direction.

Katie furrowed her brow and said, "You're kidding?"

"Confronting the woman will accomplish nothing. Let it alone."

"Bullshit. It'll make me feel better."

"Your grandfather is more important. Come on."

He didn't give her a chance to complain further. He took her hand in his, turned her, and started down the hallway.

She twisted in his grip and narrowed her eyes into hard slits at the redhead. Jack tugged her arm, and she hurried to keep up with him.

When they walked through the doorway of Charles McIntyre's room, Jack found Sean McIntyre sitting by the bed, his face buried in his hands.

Jack's gaze shot to the old man in the bed.

Charles McIntyre's eyes were closed; his body slack.

At once Jack realized Katie's grandfather was dead.

"Grandpa!" Katie cried. She brushed past Jack and hurried to her grandfather's bedside.

Sean McIntyre pulled his hands from his face, and through red tear-filled eyes, watched his daughter cross the floor toward the bed. His arms were open and waiting when she reached his side. He pulled her into his embrace, wrapped his arms around her, and hugged her tight around the waist.

"I'm sorry," he said. "Dad passed away a minute after you left the room."

Tears erupted from her eyes. She pulled away from her father's grasp and threw her arms around her grandfather's lifeless body.

Jack took a step forward and stopped. He ached to take her in his arms and hold her. To offer the comfort she needed, to let her cry on his shoulder the way she had in the past. But would she stiffen and push him away like she had at the airport?

He didn't want a second dose.

He sighed to himself and stuffed his hands into his pockets to keep from reaching for her. She had her father to comfort her.

A moment later, she raised her head. Her tears subsided as if the faucet had been suddenly turned off. She faced her father, and then Jack.

Jack saw the resolve in her green eyes.

"I'm going with you," she said. "Grandpa asked you to find that treasure. I'm going to be there to make sure you do."

"You say that like I don't have a choice."

"And you say that like you don't want me along."

He caught himself staring at her.

Dammit, anyway.

He wanted her . . . maybe more than he deserved to.

He let go of the fantasy, but kept his hands in his pockets just to be safe. They had faced danger together once. It had almost gotten them killed. Why tempt fate a second time.

He straightened.

"And if I don't?" he asked.

She glared at him.

That was all the answer he needed.

"My gut tells me this quest will be no walk in the park," he said. "That means we'd be spending a lot of time together, some of it in very close quarters. Worst of all, it'll be dangerous. And likely as not, in the end we'll come up empty. Are you ready for that? To work closely with me, I mean?"

* * * *

Katie tossed a nervous peek at her father. He sat there watching her . . . no doubt waiting for her response.

She brought her gaze around and let it settle on her grandpa

Charley. A tear welled in the corner of her eye in spite of her efforts to hold back. She wanted the tears to flow and cleanse away the pain of his passing. But he had told her to stay strong when he was gone . . . for her father, and for Jack. They would need her strength.

She sniffled. *Oh Grandpa.*

He'd been everything to her for so long. His wisdom had guided her during the ten years her father was in prison.

Why did people have to grow old and die?

She brushed the tear away. More than once her grandfather had insisted she and Jack belonged together. Why hadn't she listened to him when he told her to go to Jack and stand by him no matter what? But then it had been Jack's decision to move on. He was the one who had grown restless.

He was the one who was unwilling to give her the time she needed.

Why did Jack have to be so difficult?

She turned and thrust her chin at Jack. To accompany Jack or stay behind, the decision was hers to make. Not his.

"I'm part of this adventure," she said. "Whether you like it or not."

Her comment brought Jack's hands out of his pockets. His gaze shot to her father, and he motioned toward Katie with a wave of his right hand.

"She's being ridiculous," he said. "Tell her she can't go."

Sean McIntyre managed a thin smile.

"Sorry," he said. This is your fight. I'd be going myself if my health was better."

That did it for Katie.

She crossed her arms firmly against her chest. She wasn't about to let Jack or anyone else keep her from fulfilling her grandfather's final wish. Her mind was made up. She met Jack's gaze with her own and held it.

"I'm going," she said. "With or without you, I'll find those artifacts."

CHAPTER 11

Charles McIntyre's death left Jack empty like an iron claw had ripped out his guts. The sense of loss that gripped him could not have been stronger if his own flesh and blood had died.

Tears welled in the corners of his eyes, but even so, he feared Katie didn't know how much her grandfather meant to him, and wondered if that made the old guy's passing hurt even more.

He stepped to the foot of the bed. He'd stayed in the room long enough. For most of the last thirty minutes, Katie had sat holding her grandfather's hand. She hadn't shed a tear the entire time, even though she had to be torn apart inside. Like him, she needed to let go of her grandfather.

Not easy, but it was time.

Even so, something held her there. It was as if she was suppressing her feelings in a kind of demonstration—to her grandfather, to them—of her strength. But it wasn't necessary. He was well aware of how strong she was. He'd witnessed that strength first hand, so had her father. There was nothing she needed to prove to anyone.

Unless she was proving it to herself.

That thought saddened him almost as much as the old guy's passing.

"I think I'll catch a cab to the hotel and check into my room," he said. "It's been a long day, and you two have business to take care of."

Katie peered over her shoulder at him, and immediately turned to her father.

Sean McIntyre nodded.

"Arrangements have been made for a couple of days," she said, her voice firm with resolve. "We just need to inform the staff and have them call the mortuary. Dad can do that while I drive you to your hotel. You're staying at the Doubletree down the road, right?"

"You'll want to stay with your grandfather until the mortuary arrives," he insisted. "I can take a cab."

"I've said good-bye." She looked at her father, then Jack. She added, "If you're ready, we can go."

Her grandfather had meant so much to her. He wondered when the dam would break. And if he'd be the person she turned to for comfort when it did.

"You're sure?" he asked.

"Go," Katie's father answered for her. "Do what you need to do. I'll take care of things here."

Jack felt a nervous flutter as he watched Katie collect her purse. His feelings toward her weren't supposed to get in the way. That hadn't been part of his agenda.

But there they were.

"Maybe we should rethink this," he said, giving himself a moment to recover from that sudden quickening of pulse, that prickling of skin.

Katie faced him and said, "There's nothing to rethink."

There is, he thought. But she couldn't possibly know what was on his mind.

He swallowed.

He hadn't anticipated having to spend a lot of time with her. To be close to her for any length of time and not have what they once shared would be difficult at best.

And that was putting it mildly.

He believed he was over her. He'd convinced himself he'd moved on . . . even to the point of seeing other women. It came as a devastating jolt to realize he wasn't over her after all . . . that he was hopelessly in love with her.

Damn those eyebrows.

He didn't like knowing something bad could happen to her if

she joined him on this quest. But he couldn't go against her wishes, either. He took a step forward and gripped her shoulders.

"Remember," he said. "I warned you."

She stepped past him and walked out of the room.

He followed.

When they stepped out of the building and into the parking lot a minute later, he couldn't shake the uneasiness that settled in his gut. Was he edgy because of the old man's death? Or was he nervous because he and Katie were going to be spending time together again after a year of being apart? Then again, perhaps he was just anxious about the treasure hunt awaiting them on the horizon?

He stopped dead in his tracks and scanned the area in front and to the sides of them.

The morning had been choked with emotion, and he couldn't deny the effect it had on him. But that wasn't what was giving him the jitters. The redhead had spied on them from the doorway of McIntyre's room and immediately made a call.

She was reporting in.

He had a feeling someone was watching them this very moment.

Did Katie even think they might be in danger?

She'd been a couple of steps ahead of him going through the door. He noticed her walking toward her Camry. She obviously hadn't seen him stop.

"Wait up," he called out and trotted after her.

She stopped walking and faced him.

He raised his hand and waved.

She asked, "What's the holdup?"

He caught up with her and said, "I didn't really know what to think when I saw Ms. Carrot-top talking on the phone. I knew something was up and had a sneaky suspicion it wasn't in our best interest. Now I'm getting a real bad feeling about that conversation. She was reporting in to someone. How about you?"

"You're the one who kept me from talking to her."

"I didn't think she'd tell us anything even if we asked. But something's going on here that's not good. I feel it."

She glanced around as though suddenly worried.

After a second she said, "Whether carrothead would have

admitted anything or not, we should have gotten in her face. What she did was wrong."

"You're probably right," he admitted. He made a visual check of the parking lot and added, "What concerns me is this creepy feeling I have . . . like someone's watching us right now."

She took another quick look around, shrugged, and said, "I don't see a thing to make me worry. You're probably just upset about Grandpa. I am too. In fact I'm not sure anything makes sense right now."

"I suppose you're right," he said.

But he couldn't dismiss his concern that easily. He made one more quick scan of the lot.

Nothing.

"Let's go," he said.

CHAPTER 12

When Katie slowed her Camry to cross the bridge spanning the Boise River, Jack noticed a black Hummer accelerate onto the roadway from a turnout at the other end. His tired mind took a moment to process what he was seeing and by the time he realized what was happening, it was too late. They were already on the bridge.

And so was the Hummer.

The monstrous SUV swerved into their lane and drove straight at them.

"Watch out!" Jack yelled. He gripped the dash to brace himself.

"Shit!" Katie said as she braked hard.

"Reverse, put it in reverse," he yelled without it dawning on him she already had, and that they were going backwards.

"I am. I am," she hollered, twisting her back and neck to see the roadway behind them.

He tightened his death grip on the dash and glanced back and forth between the windshield and the rear window. They'd die if they didn't make it off the bridge.

The gap between the Hummer and the small import narrowed.

He could see the man behind the steering wheel lean forward and glare at them through the windshield.

For a brief moment, their gazes locked.

In that same instant, the driver's lips spread into a sadistic grin.

Then he laughed.

Jack's eyes widened.

Fuck!

"Faster," he yelled. "The asshole's gaining on us."

"I'm going as fast as I can," she snapped back.

The end of the bridge loomed a hundred feet away. He knew it was going to be close.

The massive chrome bumper of the Hummer homed in on the flimsy grill of the Camry.

The vehicles thumped.

Metal crunched.

The rear end of the Camry fishtailed.

Katie shrieked and fought the steering wheel to keep her car from slamming into the guardrail.

Jesus! Jack held on.

The car straightened out and he saw they were almost off the bridge.

Fifty feet to go.

The Hummer made another run at them.

More crunching of metal. But Katie managed to keep the car going straight.

"There!" Jack said, having spied their only chance. He released his grip on the dash and jabbed his index finger in the direction he wanted her to go. "Pull off on the right, behind the railing."

She cranked the wheel and hit the brakes hard. The rear end spun around in a one-eighty, and the car skidded to a stop on the shoulder of the roadway just in time to put the guardrail between them and the speeding Hummer.

The ploy worked. The driver of the vehicle chasing them hadn't anticipated the move.

The big SUV shot past them.

Jack swung his head and focused his gaze on the maniac behind the steering wheel quick enough to catch a glimpse of him through the side window: a big man in a suit. There wasn't time for his mind to register more.

He kept his eyes focused on the Hummer as it screeched to a stop a half a block away. He shook his head in disbelief when the driver made a quick U-turn and sped toward them.

What in the fuck hell shit is going on?

The V-6 Camry would never out-power the Hummer—in a collision or a race.

"The sonofabitch is coming back," he warned.

Her head was turned. She had obviously seen the big SUV make the U-turn. She watched it speed toward them.

"Jack . . . ?" she screamed.

He slapped the dash with the palm of his hand and yelled, "Go!"

Katie mashed the gas pedal to the floorboard. A spray of gravel shot high into the air behind them as the right rear tire dug in. The car careened onto the asphalt ahead of the Hummer.

"What's this fucker trying to do?" she screeched at Jack as her car picked up speed.

"Kill us. Drive!"

They were no match for the 325 horsepowered SUV, but they at least had a chance going forward across the bridge.

He took notice of the cars on Chinden Boulevard a couple of blocks away. If they could make it that far, they might be able to lose their pursuer in traffic.

He checked behind them.

The shiny black Hummer roared up on their tail—a heat-seeking missile in the form of an SUV homing in on their exhaust pipe.

Shit!

Leaning toward the windshield, he surveyed the bridge ahead of them. Their Camry was a quarter of the way across . . . not far enough.

A thousand thoughts flooded his mind. None of them good. The driver of the Hummer meant to crush them against the guardrail or force them through it and into the river. Either way they were dead.

He studied the intersection ahead.

Cars rolled by on Chinden Boulevard . . . their only chance.

Seventy-five yards to the other side of the bridge and a couple of blocks more and they'd be there.

He twisted in his seat and eyeballed the Hummer.

The bumper was inches away.

But Katie was willing every ounce of horsepower out of her little import to keep the gap between them.

He faced the windshield.

Twenty-five yards to go and the bridge would be behind them.

More cars sped by on Chinden Boulevard. They'd have to negotiate the busy intersection.

It was going to be tricky.

"If the traffic light isn't green when you get to that intersection," he told Katie, "you'll have to run it. Just make sure you don't hit anybody when you do."

"Hit someone?"

The Camry shot off the end of the bridge, the Hummer on its rear bumper.

The two cars collided and the lighter Camry swerved.

She fought the steering wheel and brought her car under control. A steady stream of traffic blocked the intersection ahead.

"What do I do now?" she yelled.

Before he could answer, the heavy chrome bumper of the urban tank slammed into the trunk of her car.

Their heads snapped back against their seats and then forward.

She jammed her foot down hard on the brake pedal and held it there. The Camry's tires skidded in protest as the heavier more powerful Hummer pushed them toward the speeding traffic.

"Jack! He's pushing us. We'll be killed."

He whipped his head left and right.

"Go!" he yelled. "Floor it and turn left."

She did her best to jam the gas pedal into the floorboard.

The Camry shot through the intersection well ahead of the Hummer.

Car horns blared and tires screeched, but no loud thud followed . . . no sound of breaking glass or crumpled metal.

Jack craned his neck to see behind them.

The Hummer was stopped at the intersection, blocked by a string of cars. This was their chance. They would have time to put some distance between them.

He kept his eyes glued to the rear window while Katie weaved her car in and out of traffic. After a few minutes of watching and not seeing the Hummer among the cars behind them, he relaxed a little and faced forward.

He took a deep breath, blew it out with a sigh, and ran his hands through his hair.

"Fuck that was close," he said.

"Close!" she exclaimed. "My right leg won't stop shaking."

His adrenaline had him jittery, too.

"Try and hang in there," he said. "The hotel's a couple of blocks away."

"I can't believe this is happening . . . not again."

"What do you mean?"

"Being chased by a goon in a black SUV."

"At least this time we're not running across the Nevada desert in the middle of the night." He winked at her and added, "And you're wearing more than a bathrobe and a pair of flimsy slippers."

"No shit," Katie scoffed. "What in hell do you think that was all about? Damned Hummer looked like Darth Vader coming at us."

"And me without my light saber."

"Seriously."

The smile slipped from his face. He said, "The phone call the redhead made. My guess is someone doesn't want us going after that treasure."

"Already?"

"Yeah. And he's still out there."

CHAPTER 13

Coleman Treadway plunged the tip of the antique dagger into the desktop in his room at the new Plaza Towers building.

"They're still alive?" he asked. The look on Boryenko's face betrayed him.

The big man stiffened.

"They got lucky," he said. "It won't happen again."

Treadway turned, dragging the knife with him. The point of the blade etched a deep gouge into the polished surface.

"You failed me," he said.

"There will be a funeral for the old man," Boryenko assured him. "They will all be there. I can take care of them, then."

Treadway raised the dagger, tested its needle-like sharpness with the tip of his finger, and thumbed away a spot of blood.

"You have never failed me before," he said, turning his gaze on Boryenko. "This Jack Ferrell person must be lucky, indeed."

"The granddaughter was driving. Perhaps it is her luck we are dealing with."

"Perhaps."

Treadway laid the dagger on the desk.

With his back to Boryenko, he added, "But luck can be as short-lived as a leg of lamb in a pond full of piranha."

"What do you want me to do?"

"You've gotten rid of the Hummer?"

"I parked it downtown; the keys are in the ignition. It won't be there long."

"Good. Report it stolen and make preparations to leave. I want to be on my yacht first thing tomorrow morning."

"And what of the young couple?"

"They won't leave here until after the funeral. That won't happen for two or three days at the earliest. We can be onsite before the old man is dropped into a hole and covered with dirt."

"And if they show up before we recover the artifacts?"

Treadway turned and narrowed his eyes at Boryenko.

"Then you get another chance to make sure they don't interfere," he said. "Ever."

CHAPTER 14

Jack didn't want Katie to just dump him off at his hotel and leave. All morning his mind had been awash with memories of their on-again-off-again love affair. Even the deadly encounter with the Hummer was an all too vivid reminder of their first days together in Henderson when they worked hard to get her father released from prison by proving he didn't kill her mother.

Katie had said it.

They had been chased into the Nevada desert by a big black SUV driven by a goon intent on killing them. Luck had brought them through the deadly ordeal alive. And later when the shooting started, lady luck was on their side that day, too.

Now they'd narrowly survived the clash with the Hummer.

He couldn't help wondering how long their luck would hold.

He saw the sign for the Doubletree hotel and felt the tension seep from the muscles in his shoulders. No one besides Katie and her father knew he was staying there. They'd be safe, for now.

Katie slowed to steer into the parking lot.

"I don't want you to go," he said.

She shot him a look and slowed the car to a stop just outside the entrance. "Please, Jack . . ."

He scrunched sideways in the seat and faced her. For a second he considered what he was going to say. It was for the best. He hoped she didn't misunderstand.

"That was no accident," he said. "We were lucky to get off that bridge alive. The guy was there, waiting for us. And he's still on the road—probably looking for us right now. Stay here for a while—at least until after we talk to the police—then leave. That black Hummer is easy to spot so I doubt the driver will hang around in the area too long, but you never know."

She turned away. Obviously, she struggled with her feelings. Her grandfather's death was a devastating blow to her even though she knew he was dying.

He laid his hand on her arm.

Soft warm skin—she didn't pull away.

"I loved your grandfather too," he said. "He was a great guy and I'll miss him as much as you do."

She peered into his eyes. The dam broke.

He watched her tears flow. And waited while she swiped then away with the side of her free hand.

"You say you loved him . . . fine," she said and sniffled. "But you'll never miss him as much as I will. He saved me, Jack . . . from myself and from a cruel heartless world. So don't ever, ever say you miss him as much as I do."

Her words struck him like a fist to the gut.

He sucked in a breath, blew it out.

"Go ahead and be mad," he said, "at God, the world, whatever. I agree, I couldn't love your Grandpa Charlie the way you do, but that doesn't mean I won't miss him so much it makes me hurt inside."

She blinked away another tear and sniffled.

"I am mad," she said. "Damned mad. And I don't want to be with you any longer than it takes to find the artifacts and hand them over to the state of Hawaii."

Again, she turned her head, averting her gaze.

He felt the prick of the barb.

"You hurt me," she said. "You really hurt me."

He slid his fingers from her arm. She hadn't pulled away, even in her anger. That meant something.

Or did it?

"I'm sorry I wasn't more understanding," he said. "From the way you're talking, I guess it's too late for us. What you and I had in the past is over and there's no bringing it back. But we can't forget about the maniac in that black Hummer."

"Fine," she said, focusing her gaze on him. "We can sit in the restaurant and have a cup of coffee while we wait for the police to arrive, but I'm not going up to your room with you."

That hadn't been his intention, not entirely.

He mentally sighed in relief and said, "Just so you don't leave before the police have a chance to check the area for that asshole."

* * * *

Katie sat in a booth in the coffee shop drinking a cup of tea. Jack had left her sitting there while he checked into his room and phoned the police. She'd have preferred to take her chances with the man in the Hummer rather than accompany Jack to his room, no matter how good he looked to her or how much she wanted him to take her into his arms.

She hated him for the hold he had on her—hated his angular face, his tan muscled body, his tight fitting blue jeans.

Damn him. Why'd he have to drive her hormones wild?

Katie quickly picked up her cup of tea and stared into it when she spied Jack walking toward her. She didn't want him to see her looking at him.

"The police are on their way," Jack said from a few feet away.

His voice pulled her gaze from her cup. He did look good.

She asked, "What did you tell them?"

He slid in on the cushion across from her and said, "Only that a man in a black Hummer tried to run us off of the road."

"You didn't tell them about Coleman Treadway?"

Not yet. I wanted to talk to you about that."

"You don't think we should?"

"We only know that Treadway questioned your grandfather . . . nothing more."

"Jack, I know how you think. You're concerned the treasure hunt might be off if you tell them about Treadway and the antiquities."

He stared at her.

The expression on his face told her she'd guessed right.

"Wouldn't it?" he asked.

She returned his stare.

"I can't see how it would," she said after a couple of beats. "But I agree that's a risk we shouldn't take. Grandpa asked you to find those relics and turn them over to the State of Hawaii. I'm not sure why he was so insistent you to be the one to carry out his request, but that's what he wanted."

"You have a problem with that?"

"A little, maybe. But I'll do whatever is necessary to see this through to the end."

Jack planted his forearms on the tabletop and asked, "Even if it means spending time with me?"

"You heard what I said."

"I did. And no doubt, you meant every word, today . . . tomorrow. But what about a month from now—even a week? We have no idea how long it will take to find those artifacts—or if we even can. And let's not forget about Treadway."

He had a point. She couldn't ignore that.

But it didn't squelch her determination.

"Screw him," she said. "The asshole reminds me of Brian Wesley."

"You shot Brian Wesley. Remember?"

She did remember. Even now she could recall every detail of that awful night in her house four years earlier when they laid the trap for Brian Wesley—the man who beat her mother to death.

She answered, "And I might have to shoot Treadway before it's over."

That brought a questioning look from Jack, which he followed up saying, "I thought killing Wesley made you swear off guns?"

She held him firmly in her gaze.

"We'll do whatever we have to do," she said.

CHAPTER 15

Jack stood alone with his thoughts high up on the bank of the Boise River and watched Katie and her father scatter Charles William McIntyre's remains on the water. The swift current of the swollen river swept away the gray-brown ashes almost as quickly as they settled onto the surface.

Tears filled Katie's eyes. Sean McIntyre stood quietly in the somber atmosphere under the cottonwoods.

It was obvious neither of them felt a need to say anything.

A light breeze rustled the leaves above their heads, causing Jack to look up more out of response to the sudden noise than anything else. Twinkles of sunlight played down on his face from the heavens.

He closed his eyes and let the shadows dance across his eyelids. Had it been a sign from Katie's grandfather that he was at rest in a better place, at last reunited with the loved-ones who had passed on before him?

Another gust of wind rattled the leaves more violently than before, and he opened his eyes. Perhaps that wasn't what Charles McIntyre was saying after all. Perhaps the old man's spirit was telling them enough time had been spent mourning his death . . . that it was time for them to go after the artifacts.

A short distance downriver from where he was standing, a fallen log lay perched on the edge of the riverbank. He walked to it, took a seat on the rough bark, picked up a small flat stone, rubbed it between his fingers, and stared into the water.

There had been no further attempts on their lives in the four days since the incident on the bridge. He could only wonder why.

The police officer who took the report had told them they would check the area for the Hummer. For all the good it would do.

Had Treadway even been behind what happened?

Jack sighed.

Short of a signed confession, there was no way he could know for sure Treadway had ordered the attack on them. But that was only a technicality, he assured himself. As far as he was concerned, Treadway had pulled the strings just as sure as if he'd been driving the Hummer himself.

The man isn't afraid to kill to get what he wants.

Jack didn't want to underestimate Treadway, not even a little. The ambush on the bridge more than proved the man's resolve to claim the antiquities for himself at whatever cost.

If Treadway *had* backed off, there was a reason behind his actions.

The sight of Katie's reflection on the water in front of him made Jack forget all about Treadway for the moment. He turned and smiled at her the way he had when they were together. He opened his mouth to talk.

"What are you doing over here by yourself?" she asked before he could get the words out.

He was glad she had come looking for him. Even a little surprised. She wasn't just being friendly. There were some old feelings there.

"Thinking," he said. He skipped the stone across the water and added, "I can see why your grandfather loved this river. It really is peaceful down here."

He watched her scan the area as though she was seeing the tree-lined banks and the rushing water for the first time. The hint of a grin curled her lips.

She said, "Grandpa Charlie's part of the river now."

He wondered if she felt bad about pouring her grandfather's ashes into the water. There would be no granite headstone marking his grave, no place for her to read his name and talk to him. Her smile told him what he wanted to know. The river would be there until the end of time and her grandfather would be a part of it. There was little doubt in his mind she found comfort knowing that.

There was no greater monument to the man.

"That was his wish," he said.

"I know."

He could hear the sadness in her voice.

A tear had formed in the corner of her eye. She wiped it away and added, "Are you ready to go?"

"Whenever you are," he said.

He rose to his feet and noticed her father plod off in the direction of her Camry. The man's shoulders were slumped, his head drooped forward. The spring was missing from his step.

He asked, "Is your dad okay?"

"He's coping, if that's what you mean?"

Jack sighed.

"Yeah," he said. "I guess that's what I meant."

She took off walking before he could take her hand in his and walk with her. He caught up to her in three long strides.

"If you and your dad feel like eating," he said, "I'll buy lunch. It'll give us a chance to talk."

"Talk, Jack." She stopped and with an obvious edge to her voice asked, "Exactly what is it you want to talk about?"

"Going after those artifacts."

She stood staring at him, saying nothing.

He held her in his gaze. The protective wall she'd erected around her had cracked, letting him in. Now the breach had been filled. The look in her eyes told him she waited to hear more.

He searched his thoughts.

During the past couple of days, he'd given a lot of consideration to having her along on the hunt for the relics. The risks involved were real, not imagined. It would be far better for her to remain home with her father where she would be safe.

That was the sensible answer.

Even so, he knew he'd be lying to himself if he denied his desire to have her by his side when he went after the treasure. In spite of the dangers and the likelihood they'd come up empty in the end, she deserved to be there.

Most of all, he wanted her there.

"Finding that treasure for your grandfather," he said. "That's what we're going to do, isn't it . . . you and I?"

CHAPTER 16

Jack pulled a chair out from the table for Katie and held it for her while she took a seat. Her father slid onto a chair across the table from her. He sat down on the chair to the right of Katie and directly across from Sean.

For a moment, he felt like he was looking at a younger version of Katie's grandfather.

Father and son—the same.

He scanned the restaurant not quite sure what he was looking for: prying eyes, big ears hoping to listen in on other people's business . . . someone wanting to kill them. The table he'd chosen—as far back from the other patrons eating lunch as they could get and still be waited on—provided them enough privacy to talk freely.

Katie and her father ordered iced tea from their waitress. He settled in his seat and waited. Their server's red dye-job and heavy Texas accent reminded Jack of Bonnie the cowgirl waitress who'd waited on him and Katie at the quaint steakhouse in Henderson the night they'd first gotten to know each other.

Time had a way of obscuring memories, but he'd never forget sitting across the table from Katie that evening. He'd thoroughly enjoyed talking to her, loved looking at her lips as her mouth formed the words, enjoyed her laugh, and liked seeing her emerald green eyes open wide and sparkle when she was excited about something.

And then there was the way her hands moved when she talked

... and that tender side of hers. She didn't seem to blame anyone for the tragedy that had befallen her. With her grandfather's help, she had lived with her mother's murder and her father's imprisonment as a part of life's cruel game—grew from the ordeal. And through it all she'd held onto her belief her dad was innocent. She loved her father in spite of what the police said he had done; and believed that someday he would return home to her a free man.

And her father had.

Jack smiled inwardly. *Pono*. Returning that class ring he'd found had definitely been the right thing to do.

So was going after the stolen relics.

The waitress pointed her order pad at him and asked, "What can I get you, sir?"

He blinked away his thoughts.

"I'll have the same," he said.

When their waitress walked away to get their drinks, he planted his thick forearms on the tabletop and leaned close. Katie looked at him, and he gazed into her eyes for a couple of heartbeats. That wonderful evening four years ago, he had stared into her eyes wondering what it was about her that unnerved him so. Her green eyes still had a mesmerizing effect on him.

He glanced at her father to break the spell, leaned back, and looked at her. "I've booked a flight out, leaving late tonight," he said.

Katie looked at him, her eyes steady and unblinking.

"Tonight," she said. "And just when were you planning on telling me about your plans to cut me out?"

He winced at her accusation even though he wasn't surprised by her anger. There were moments when her old self had shown through, but she hadn't truly lowered her hackles since his arrival.

"That's what I was hoping to talk to you about," he said. Again, he leaned forward and planted his forearms firmly on the tabletop. He added, "The flight is for two. I reserved a ticket for you as well ... if you want it?"

"You know I do."

"Then you'll be leaving with me?"

"Dad, you'll be okay driving my car back, won't you?"

"Of course I will," he said. "But I still don't like this one bit. A bunch of relics isn't worth your life. That sonofabitch Treadway tried to kill you once; he's not going to back off as long as you threaten his operation."

She stiffened.

"I can take care of myself," she said. "You know that."

"And you could have been killed," he pointed out. "You might not be so lucky this go around."

Jack listened to the father-daughter exchange. He was entering into a quest of no small consequence. If Katie was going to be part of it, she had to understand what she was up against, and how her father felt about it.

"I know you love me," she said to her dad. "I love you too. But you're not going to change my mind."

The wrinkles relaxed from the corners of her father's eyes.

He said, "You're my daughter . . . my only daughter. If I lose you to Jack when this is all over with, that's great. He's a good man and he'll take care of you. But I lost your mother because of a slimeball exactly like Treadway. I don't even want to think what it would do to me if something like that happened to you."

Jack was a bit taken aback by Katie's father's comment: the part about *him* and Katie ending up together. Not the part about Treadway being a slimeball.

"You're right," he said to Katie's father. "This will be no cakewalk, that's for sure." He took a deep breath and added, "I suppose it's a moot point, but it's still not clear to me why you didn't turn this information over to the Bishop Museum or some state agency so they could recover the relics."

The answer to his question didn't come right away. And in that moment of silence, he thought he detected a flicker of uncertainty in Katie's father's eyes. Was it concern for his daughter's safety . . . or was it that deep down he wanted them to reunite and wished it were under more normal circumstances?

"Dad told me about his run-in with Coleman Treadway," Sean said to Jack. "But he didn't tell me about his plans for you. I had no idea he intended to dump all this on your shoulders." He paused and stared at his hands. Then went on, "Thinking back, I firmly believe he hoped the quest would bring you and Katie back together. From the way he talked these last few months, I got the impression he wanted that more than anything. I can't say I don't agree. As far as turning the information over to the museum or some state agency goes, I don't think that was an option for him."

The old guy was playing matchmaker. Jack felt his face heat up. A metaphorical cherub slinging arrows.

"I'm sure there is more to this than Grandpa Charlie playing cupid," he said. "Love's grand, but I'm going because I believe returning those artifacts to the Hawaiian people is the right thing to do."

Sean said, "I applaud you for carrying out my father's wish in spite of the dangers involved." The wrinkles returned to the corners of his eyes. Facing his daughter, he added, "But Katie, that doesn't mean your grandfather intended for you to jeopardize your life?"

"Of course he didn't," she scoffed. "Grandpa would never want that. But you said it yourself. He wanted this quest to bring me and Jack together. Well, it's doing that. Maybe not exactly the way he wanted it to, but I'm going along. And nothing you say will convince me to do otherwise."

"Honey," he said. "By rights it should be me going . . . not you, not even Jack."

"But that isn't what Grandpa wanted."

Jack felt a sudden urge to switch the focus of discussion to the treasure and off him and Katie. He watched her eyes settle on his. Having felt the sting of her newly barbed tongue more than once, he wondered if she'd had anything to do with her grandfather's request or if she'd latched onto it for leverage against her father.

He felt he needed to say something to back the man up. He'd bought Katie a plane ticket. It didn't mean she had to use it.

No matter how much he wanted her there with him.

"You know damned well your dad's right," he said. "That incident on the bridge was only the beginning. Treadway won't be content to just sit back and watch once we show up looking for that treasure. And if that's not enough, the military blew the hell out of Kahoolawe for a lot of years using the island for target practice. We could very well have tons of unexploded ordnance to watch out for. Not to mention nature's obstacles: tiger sharks, giant morays, unimaginable surge, vicious crosscurrents. A team of experts with a boatload of fancy equipment and the blessing of the government would have a hard time doing what we plan to do."

"We're not going to be on the island."

"You don't know that. Bear in mind, Kahoolawe was designated an island reserve and returned to the State of Hawaii some years back. The Kahoolawe Island Reserve Commission was established to manage it. That means they control the island. And they patrol the water around it."

"Yeah . . . so what's the problem?" Her eyes remained focused on his.

"That *is* the problem," he pressed. "The KIRC doesn't want people motoring ashore at will and wandering around the place. Except for certain days of the year, no one is allowed within two miles of the island. Even then you have to keep your boat moving and you can't get any closer than the thirty-fathom isobath that surrounds its shoreline. Daily patrols enforce compliance with the law."

"So what you're telling me is we can't even get close to the island to look for these artifacts?"

"Not without permission from the KIRC. And that's something I wouldn't count on. Given the Hawaiian's belief the bones of their *kupuna* should be left alone, I doubt they'd give us permission to search for the remains of old King Kalaniopuu, or even Captain Cook. And given the possibility there are still some unexploded bombs and ammunition lying around out there, I'm sure the KIRC frowns on people blowing themselves apart poking their heads into holes they have no business exploring in the first place."

"If that's the case, how do you plan to find the crate?"

She had him in a corner.

"Simple," he said. "We figure out a way to get onto the island without anyone knowing it. Then we're careful about where we step."

"That's your plan?" She laughed.

CHAPTER 17

That following morning, Coleman Treadway stood staring through the windscreen of *Trident's* bridge. With the grace and speed of a pod of dolphins, the twin bows of the gleaming white hundred-foot yacht sliced through the rolling swells westward through the Alenuihaha Channel a mile south of Maui, Hawaii. *Trident's* rich, sleek lines and state-of-the-art double hull were a testament to beauty and speed.

Kahoolawe in the distance. He pressed binoculars to his eyes and focused them on the island.

"Bring the boat in close along the east end. I want to get a good look at the shoreline before we anchor."

"Yes-sir," Karl Ward, the captain of the *Trident*, said. He tightened his grip on the helm, made a slight course adjustment, and added, "Sir, you know I can't take *Trident* in any closer than two miles. There're patrol boats."

Treadway's jaw muscles tightened. He pulled the binoculars away from his eyes and shot Captain Ward a hard look.

"You bear the title of captain on this boat because I allow you to," he said. "Don't let your limited authority onboard *Trident* go to your head. I'm well aware of the two-mile safe zone around the island and don't need you to remind me."

He brought the field glasses back to his eyes and added, "Stupid asshole military and their unexploded bombs. Maintain a heading northward two miles offshore and not an inch more."

"Yes-sir," Ward said.

Treadway lowered the binoculars at the same time Yvette Monet stepped onto the foredeck. His gaze locked on the former French beauty queen. Clad only in a yellow thong bottom and sunglasses, she moved with the elegance and poise of a jungle cat, her bronze skin glowing in the midmorning sun.

One of the reasons he kept her around was because he liked watching her walk. He took a moment to appreciate her long legs and firm round bottom.

Yvette took a seat on the edge of a padded chaise, glanced up at the ship's bridge, and stretched out on her stomach.

She knows she's being watched.

The hint of a smile formed on his thin lips. The same game every time she paraded around on deck; half dressed, flaunting her body. Always the French beauty queen walking the runway. There for the crew to admire, but not touch. She belonged to him. And that made the game all the better.

So much woman—his eyes narrowed—tonight he would make the wildcat purr like a kitten.

He congratulated himself on not having married. A condition he believed tiresome. The female companions he'd chosen were easily discarded when they no longer pleased him. To have a wife meant signing a written contract that would be complicated to break when the relationship grew tedious. Divorce in such a case would surely prove to be messy, and in the end extremely costly . . . in money and public exposure. His life's plan was to avoid both.

The Italian import he'd recently tired of had cost him a couple of not-so-perfect diamonds and a few thousand dollars in clothes. A paltry expenditure considering his enormous wealth. But the gesture had been a generous offering by his way of thinking. And it had more than compensated her for the bruises she'd suffered during sex games played out for her pleasure as much as his. Skilled violence, in business or in sex, was a tool no successful man could ignore.

He used it often, and it always served him well.

He faced Boryenko who stood next to him. The big man stared

straight ahead. A granite buttress—unmoving even in the ocean swells.

"We will be onsite in a few minutes," Treadway said. "I hear there are a lot of sharks in these waters."

"Many, Sir. Big ones—tigers. They feed on the turtles."

"And a tourist or two, I suspect."

"Sharks attack swimmers here every year. A month ago a man was killed, another bitten."

"You keep track of such things?"

"Only when it interests me."

Treadway couldn't resist a smile.

He said, "I want you on deck with me when we reach the island."

"*Da.*"

A few minutes later Karl Ward eased back on the throttles and pointed the bow on a northerly course along the east facing shore of Kahoolawe. Treadway stepped from the bridge, tugged on his panama hat, and walked aft to the port side of the rear deck. From there he studied the rugged shoreline through his powerful binoculars.

The day he found the letter, he knew it wasn't going to be easy to find the crate his grandfather had left hidden here so many years before. Now he saw exactly what he was up against. Certainly a challenge, but he'd faced worse.

Movement at the bottom of his field of vision broke his concentration. He scanned the water and found what had caught his eye.

A dorsal fin.

It was time his employees learned the price of insubordination. He handed the binoculars to his steward and turned to Boryenko who'd followed him on deck.

"Assemble everyone on deck and bring Eduardo to me," he said. "I want him to have a good close look at the island."

Boryenko nodded.

A half minute later, he returned and shoved Eduardo against the railing next to Treadway. The rest of the crew stood back, watching.

Treadway studied the frightened look on Eduardo's face.

"Sir," Eduardo said. His eyes widened and followed Treadway's gaze to Boryenko. His body shook, and he pressed himself tight against the railing.

Treadway's left eye twitched.

"Tie him," he said.

In the same breath, he nodded at a length of heavy nylon rope coiled on the deck near the stern. He added, "With that . . . and leave a long leash."

"No!" Eduardo's voice cracked. He made a move to run, but Boryenko's iron grip stopped him in his tracks.

Boryenko caught a nod from Treadway and hammered a fist into Eduardo's face. Blood gushed from the young man's nose and mouth. His body went slack in the Russian's arms.

The big man hefted Eduardo's weight under one arm and carried him to the fantail. He dropped him onto the deck and tied the rope tight around his chest with the knot in back. That done, he secured the other end of the line to a cleat on the transom. Then he hoisted Eduardo to his feet.

Treadway stepped to where Boryenko stood holding the skinny Brazilian propped against the transom.

Eduardo moaned and tried to raise his head.

Treadway slapped him awake, gripped his chin hard, and held on.

"So you think it is okay to fuck women on my time, huh?"

He flipped open a small folding knife and held the open blade in front of Eduardo's face just long enough for him to see the razor sharp steel reflect the sun. When the Brazilian's eyes widened with understanding, he grabbed the young man's bandaged ruined right hand and slashed his wrist.

Blood pumped from the wound.

Treadway took a step back and watched Eduardo's eyes bulge in horror.

"Throw this piece of shit overboard," Treadway said to Boryenko. "And get this mess cleaned up."

Boryenko nodded, and without a word, he lifted Eduardo from the deck and dropped him over the transom.

Eduardo clawed at the air with his hands and feet, splashed into the water, and went under. The coils of rope disappeared over the transom, then pulled tight. Eduardo's body skimmed the surface like a gigantic marlin lure.

Within minutes, the first dorsal fin appeared in *Trident's* wake.

A few seconds later, a larger fin broke surface directly behind Eduardo.

"That didn't take long," Treadway said to Boryenko with a satisfied look.

Boryenko's stoic expression didn't change.

"A ten footer," he said. "Maybe twelve or thirteen."

They watched the larger fin disappear beneath the surface.

A second later, the water erupted into red foam. The rope jerked and Eduardo let out a high-pitched scream that ended in a gurgle when his head disappeared beneath the surface.

"All stop," Treadway shouted into his hand-held radio.

Trident's engines cut to idle and the boat slowed.

Eduardo popped to the surface and flailed at the bloody water. Again, his high-pitched screams were silenced when his body was drug under.

Treadway grasped the rope and felt a couple of hard tugs, then a final fierce jerk that yanked the line from his hand. More dorsal fins moved in from the sides and behind. The water boiled red.

Treadway gave the scene a dismissive wave. He turned from the railing and scanned the crew members assembled there.

"Get back to work," he said. "And bring lunch. This business with Eduardo has made me hungry."

He walked to a padded deck chair and took a seat.

"And tell Yvette to join me," he said to Boryenko. "I want to look at something pretty while I eat."

Boryenko nodded and began pulling in the nylon rope that now hung slack in the water.

Treadway waved his steward over and motioned for the binoculars in the man's hand. He snatched them out of his servant's grasp. Playtime was over.

"Instruct Karl to head for Molokini Crater," he ordered. "We'll begin our drift from there."

CHAPTER 18

Treadway squinted against the glare from the sun and scanned the water port and starboard of *Trident*. His gaze settled on the cluster of dive boats anchored in the protective embrace of Molokini crater's compact crescent shape.

His radio crackled, followed by Karl Ward's voice saying, "We are approaching Molokini now, Sir."

Treadway raised his radio and said, "I have eyes."

The sight of a hundred vacationers face down in the water, bobbing up and down on long tube-shaped yellow Styrofoam floats—like so many giant bananas cast adrift on the ocean—made him want to laugh. He didn't believe in vacations or the absurdity of spending hours in the water staring at a bunch of fish. It was a waste of time better spent acquiring the world's riches.

Money meant power. Power meant money. He never let himself forget that. It served him well as his mantra.

He realized that from the very first day he started receiving an allowance, he had not squandered his money. He saved, bought, and traded shrewdly . . . always maximizing profit—even at that young age. In doing so, he nurtured his innate obsession with power and money and neglected any interest he had in the trivial pursuits of kids his age.

He built his financial empire on the foundation of the discipline he'd established in those early years of his life. And although he inherited a large sum of money from his parents at the age of twenty when they were killed in a private plane accident in France, it was his dogged determination and shrewd business practices that allowed him—by the age of thirty—to quadruple the family assets passed on to him.

The death of his parents had come as a shock, but what he regretted most was that they had squandered so much of their fortune on prodigious donations to museums and libraries across the United States, Canada, the UK, and Europe; a terrible waste.

And a contradiction to the very foundation of *his* beliefs.

A mistake he would not repeat.

Why give money to the world's museums when it was his belief the riches contained within those walls belonged in his prized collection of priceless antiquities from around the world or sold on the world market to further his substantial wealth.

Fortunes like his brought the opulent lifestyles afforded those with money. His parents had theirs and he had his: the chalet in Colorado, the villa in Italy, the *Trident*. All an important part of the money game; a game he'd mastered.

Most of what he had amassed came from black-market dealers and could never be shared with the world. But that mattered little to him.

Just thinking about the Aztec and Egyptian gold, flawless jewels and precious coins, sculptures and priceless masterpieces of art— all the irreplaceable riches he had stolen from the world—made him smile even now. The priceless treasure-trove concealed in the hidden chamber behind the walls of his villa in Italy served his desires and no one else's.

Even those rare antiquities purchased on the open market had been done so with the utmost privacy and discretion. He prided himself on his ability to conduct business with a subtle flair that kept his name out of the news and off the cover of magazines and supermarket tabloids.

A must for a man in his position.

From the beginning, he understood the importance of loyalty and dedication, and handpicked his employees based on that doctrine. With the exception of Eduardo—who turned out to be less than satisfactory—his discipline had served him well.

He did not make mistakes often, and it saddened him that Eduardo's sexual appetite proved to be a flaw that made him unreliable. The young man displayed innate abilities worthy of respect, but his inability to keep his pecker in his pants made it necessary to eliminate him.

A minor inconvenience, but essential to the operation.

Feeding an incompetent, untrustworthy employee to the sharks was a testament to how he handled problems . . . and a shot of adrenaline to his system. He did not dirty his hands with such matters often, but when he did, he took pleasure in the kill.

The ultimate power of one man over another.

He settled onto the cushion in his deck chair, unrolled the two-foot by three-foot nautical chart of the Alalakeiki channel between Kahoolawe and Maui, and spread the map out on the table in front of him.

From what his grandfather wrote in his letter and the information obtained from the nurse and the shriveled up old man in the retirement home, he knew the artifacts lay in a lava tube on Kahoolawe. But the only clue he had to the exact location was that his grandfather had drifted there after crash-landing in the channel near Molokini crater.

Not much to go on, but it was a start.

He pictured his grandfather's plane gliding in low over Molokini, calculated where it had crashed.

They had to be close.

"Cut the engines," he said into his hand-held radio. "We'll begin our drift from here."

The twin diesels went quiet. Voices wafted over from the crater to fill the silence. Treadway knew *Trident's* sleek lines had drawn looks from guests and crew aboard the dive boats and even some of those in the water. The yacht's magnificence always drew people's attention. The stares intruded into his privacy, but he'd learned to tolerate them.

The price of being rich.

Again, Treadway's handheld radio crackled to life. "The engines have been cut, Sir." Karl Ward's voice reflected his uneasiness. "At what point do you wish me to restart them?"

Treadway keyed his radio. "Captain Ward, do I need to remind you that you can be replaced?"

"But the two-mile limit, Sir. What . . . ?"

"We are experiencing engine problems. It cannot be helped. Drift until I signal you to start the engines."

CHAPTER 19

Jack tilted his head back and closed his eyes to let the warmth of the tropics embrace his face. He liked the mountains—had since he was a kid. The trip to Boise had given him a chance to soak in the serene ruggedness and enjoy the change in climate. But he was glad to be back on Maui. The sun and humidity agreed with him . . . maybe as much as the ocean.

"You coming with me?" Robert asked from his perch slouched against the front fender of his Toyota King Cab. "Or are you going to stand there in this heat and work on your tan?"

Jack kept his eyes closed and his face raised to the sun.

"You in a hurry?" he asked.

"Not in the least," Robert said. He pushed off the fender and stood next to his truck, waiting. "But the curb outside an airport's baggage claim area just isn't my idea of a happening place to hang out. So unless you're considering heading inside to the bar, I'd like to get going."

Jack smiled at his friend and said, "A might touchy, aren't ya? To think I actually asked you to pick us up."

"More like told me."

"You guys . . . I swear." Katie brushed past Jack and walked over to Robert's 4x4.

Robert met her as she walked up, slid a flower lei over her head, leaned down, and kissed her on both cheeks.

Katie raised the plumeria blossoms to her nose.

"How beautiful," she said, letting the lei rest against her chest. "And it smells wonderful. Thank you."

Robert beamed.

"Can't let a beautiful woman come to Maui and not get properly leied," he added. He hefted her two bags over the side of his pickup and set them in the bed.

"Speaking of pretty ladies," Katie said. "Where's Kazuko?"

"Oahu," he grinned, "working."

Jack footed it over to where Robert and Katie stood talking.

"Since when do you have a problem with a little sunshine?" he asked, dropping his tote in next to Katie's luggage.

Robert peeled off his cap, combed back his short curly hair with his fingers and said, "You think my beautiful golden locks turned white as corn silk because I'm afraid of a little sun?"

Jack took a peek at Robert's hair and asked, "Then what's the problem."

"Shit, man . . . it's hot out here." Robert stepped to the driver's door as he talked. "And it's making me thirsty."

"We can remedy that. First, how'd you make out on the boat situation?"

"Kimo set us up with one that belongs to his cousin. A forty footer with a wide beam and a flat bottom for stability. A real workboat according to him. Three hundred a day plus fuel. No way could we have done better."

"I'm sure you're right."

"Of course I am. Now, if you're through jacking your jaw, I suggest we head for Maalaea Harbor. That's where the boat is."

"I thought you were thirsty?"

"I am. While we're there, we can grab an ice-cold beer at Buzz's. I'm sure you and Katie are ready for some real food, and I could use a bite to eat, myself. And since you're the one who opened his mouth and said he could remedy my thirst problem, you're buying."

Katie slid on a pair of sunglasses and opened the rear passenger's door of Robert's Toyota King Cab and commented, "I see nothing's changed between you two in the last year and a half, has it?"

"What?" Jack and Robert asked at the same time.

95

She shook her head and said, "Get in the truck. I'll buy."

The traffic out of Kahului airport crawled with summer vacationers. Robert jockeyed his pickup for position, and Jack kept quiet.

He didn't want his chatter to distract from the driving.

"How long do we have use of this so-called workboat?" he asked Robert as soon as he settled into a lane.

"Kimo's cousin is off island for another two weeks," Robert answered. "I hope that's long enough."

"It'd better be." Jack thought about Robert's plane. "What about your deHavilland Beaver? We could use it for some aerial reconnaissance."

"Could, if it wasn't being worked on."

"Mechanical problems already?"

"Nah, routine maintenance. But it has to be done."

"Figures."

"Cheer up. I've got something really neat to show you that I think will put a smile on that ugly mug of yours."

"Ugly, huh?"

Robert flashed him a grin. Then all trace of humor disappeared from his expression when he asked, "You think that Coleman Treadway character you told me about is here yet?"

"I'll be surprised if he isn't."

"So we'd better get our asses in gear?"

"If we want to find those artifacts before he does."

Robert passed a slow moving car, found a gap in the tangle of traffic, and pressed the gas.

"Honestly," he said to Jack. "Do you think we stand a chance in hell of pulling this off?"

"God willing and the creek don't rise."

Robert scrunched his face at Jack.

"Creek don't rise?" he said. "Can't say much for your grammar, but I know you. What you're really saying is you think we're fucked from the get-go."

"We can do this," Katie spoke up from the jump seat in back. "We have to. My grandpa wanted those relics found and turned over to the state. That's what we're going to do. And there's no getting out of it."

Robert arched his brow at Jack.

"Don't look at me for an answer," Jack said. "You know how she gets once her mind is made up."

Robert rolled his eyes and added, "Heaven help anyone who gets in her way."

"Right," Jack snorted. "But we still have to find the artifacts, and that's not going to be easy."

"Nothing worthwhile ever is." Robert studied Katie in the rearview mirror. He said to Jack, "But then you should know that."

Jack knew exactly what his friend was getting at. His only chance of avoiding the subject was to play stupid.

"What?" he asked.

"Think about it," Robert said.

Katie couldn't help but hear the exchange between Jack and Robert. She asked, "Are you going to let me in on your little secret?"

Robert watched Jack shift uneasily in his seat.

"No secrets," Robert said. "Just me giving Jack, shit. He needs a kick in the ass from time to time to keep him in line."

"Not from you I don't," Jack answered.

Robert chuckled.

Jack sighed long and hard. He took another breath, let it out, and faced Robert. There had been a tone of irritability in his voice that he regretted.

"Sorry," he said to Robert. "You didn't deserve that. Going after these relics has me all fucked up. The idea of finding a lost treasure is intriguing as hell. I just can't shake the feeling something bad is going to happen out there."

Robert smiled.

"Relax," he said. "We're going to have fun. We'll get you two changed into some comfortable clothes, lathered up with suntan lotion, a tall cold drink with an umbrella in it . . . why hell, you'll feel like you're on vacation. And with Katie along, I have someone nice to look at instead of your rangy old ass."

The corners of Jack's mouth curled up, but just slightly.

"I happen to think I have a good looking butt," he said. "That's what the women tell me anyway."

His comment bought him a look from Katie.

Robert reached over and jabbed him on the shoulder. He felt like he was getting it from both sides.

"Come on, pal," Robert said. "I told you, it's going to be fun."

Jack couldn't shake the gloom shrouding him.

"I've been telling myself that," he reassured Robert. "But that bastard Treadway has already tried to stop us once. I'm sure that's not the last of it."

"I swear you're going to worry yourself to death one of these days." Robert pointed at the ocean ahead of them as he talked. "That isn't some back-water bridge in Idaho that any idiot with a car can drive to. That's our element out there. If the artifacts are on Kahoolawe, we'll find King Kalaniopuu's bones and whatever else is in that crate and drop the whole lot into the hands of the Hawaiian authorities before Treadway even figures out where to start looking for them."

Katie leaned forward and gripped the sides of Robert's seatback. "Don't say *if*," she offered with a tone of self-assurance. "Besides, how hard can it be to find a lava tube? There can't be that many along that stretch of the coastline can there?"

"Au contraire, little one," Robert said over his shoulder. "More than you think. But keep in mind, over the years the military blasted that island to hell and back. Even if the crate was there, that doesn't mean it wasn't blown to bits a long time ago."

Katie leaned back in her seat, crossed her arms against her chest, and said, "I refuse to believe that."

Jack mentally shook his head at her resolve. He flashed Robert his I-told-you-so look.

"Trust me," he said to Katie. "We're going into this expedition with the belief the artifacts are there. I wouldn't have it any other way, neither would Robert. And we'll keep searching until we run out of places to look."

She turned her head and gazed out the side window.

After a couple of beats she said, "That's all I needed to hear."

Jack turned and faced the windshield. Katie's on-again off-again bitchiness bored into his skin, grating on his nerves like a swarm of mosquitoes out for blood. And they weren't even on the water yet.

Jesus.

But then she wasn't any more touchy than himself. They both needed to improve their attitudes if they were going to get along.

"Katie," he said. "You need to lower your hackles a bit. I thought you understood how seriously I'm taking your grandfather's request."

She sniffled.

"I mi . . . miss him, Jack." Her voice shook with emotion.

Jack could tell from the quiver in her voice her eyes had filled with tears. And for good reason. He realized he had let himself forget how fresh the loss was for her—and him.

"I know," he said. "So do I."

"Did I tell you I talked to a preacher friend of mine?" Robert said when Jack and Katie fell into an uncomfortable silence.

Jack arched a brow at his friend. He had an idea what was coming.

"A preacher friend of yours," he said. "That's hard for me to believe."

Robert checked the mirror and saw Katie looking at him, teary-eyed. He winked at her reflection.

"Sure," he said, his eyes refocused on the road. "He's the pastor of a small church in Florida. The story goes like this." He took a breath and explained:

One Sunday, while counting the money in the weekly offering, this pastor friend of mine found a pink envelope containing $1,000 in fifties. The next week, it happened again: a pink envelope with a $1,000. All of it in fifties. The following Sunday, he watched while the offering was collected and saw a little old lady put the distinctive pink envelope in the plate.

Another week went by and another envelope showed up in the plate, then another, and another. Finally, overcome by curiosity, he approached the kindly old lady and asked, "Ma'am, I couldn't help but notice that you put $1,000 a week in the collection plate."

"Why yes," she replied before he could say more, "every week my son sends me money, and I give some of it to the

church."

"That's wonderful," he told her. "How much does your son send you?"

The old lady responded, "$10,000 a week."

Well, to say the least, my friend was amazed by the amount of money she was receiving. He looked her in the eye and asked, "Your son is very successful; what does he do for a living?"

"He is a veterinarian," she answered.

"That is an honorable profession," he said. "Where does your son practice?"

The old lady straightened and proudly said, "In Nevada. He has two cat houses in Las Vegas and one in Reno."

Katie managed a chuckle, brushed a tear from her cheek, and said. "Honestly, Robert . . ."

Jack rolled his eyes. Always the jokester.

"Katie's right," he said to Robert. "Nothing's changed."

Robert grinned. And then he shrugged and asked, "Would you have expected less?"

Jack snorted and said, "Not from you I don't. I just don't know where you get this stuff."

"Jimmy Durante said it. I gotta million of 'em."

Robert drove his pickup into the lot below Buzz's Wharf and parked.

"All ashore that's going ashore," he said as they climbed from the cab.

"I changed my mind," Katie said to Robert. "You're buying."

Robert laughed.

They climbed the stairs to the restaurant and lucked onto an open table overlooking the harbor. Katie took the chair next to the window. Jack sat in the chair next to her. Robert sat down in the window seat across the table from them.

Drawn by the view, the three of them turned and faced the glass. Jack knew what flashed through their thoughts: Maalaea Harbor, its array of power and sailboats, the blue expanse of white-capped ocean beyond. And ten miles away, Molokini crater—a dark hash mark on the horizon. And to the right of that, Kahoolawe island: barren and mysterious.

"There it is boys and girls," Jack said with a slightly raised brow. "As soon as we get our asses in gear, we get up-close and personal with her."

Robert pointed a finger in the direction of the harbor, raised his glass in a toast, and with a nod of his head added, "And right over there, my friends, is our boat."

CHAPTER 20

Jack couldn't help himself. Having gotten a glimpse of their boat from a distance, he found it impossible to curb his curiosity. He raised a hand to his mouth and stifled a belch. Now he wished he hadn't stuffed down his plateful of fish & chips in a rush to get down to the docks for a closer look.

He gulped one last drink of water and slid his chair away from the table. "Ready?"

"And rarin'," Katie and Robert said as though their response had been carefully choreographed. They shot each other a surprised look.

On their way through the parking lot, Jack and Katie made a stop at the restrooms so they could change out of their Idaho clothes. A couple of minutes later Jack emerged from the men's room wearing a pair of khaki shorts, a multi-colored aloha shirt consisting of mostly reds and yellows, and rubber flip-flops. Katie stepped out of the ladies room dressed in the yellow *I love Maui* short-cropped t-shirt Jack bought her at the airport gift shop, and the white shorts and New Balance jogging shoes she brought with her from Idaho.

With their luggage locked in the cab of Robert's Toyota pickup, they walked onto the dock where their boat was tied.

So what do you think?" Robert asked, jumping aboard.

Jack eyeballed the antiquated craft from bow to stern.

He peeled the ball cap from his head, scratched his scalp, and said, "I believe I've seen this boat before."

"Could be," Robert agreed. "Kimo's cousin has had it moored here forever."

Jack chuckled and said, "I meant in the movies . . . the *Orca*."

Robert grinned and shook his head.

"Nah," he said. "Jaws ate that one."

"Exactly."

Jack walked to the end of the slip and stood there, while he gave the boat a long look. His eyes focused on the name painted across the transom: *Hele Auana*.

His knowledge of the Hawaiian language was practically nonexistent, but certain phrases he'd heard stuck in his memory. *Hele Auana* was a Hawaiian term he learned from a University of Hawaii graduate student.

According to him, Hawaiians considered it bad luck to say they were going fishing. *Hele Auana*—go wandering—was one of several ways a native would announce his intention to catch fish.

Ho`oponopono—making things right—was another Hawaiian phrase he'd learned. Beautiful Ellery Seaport had taught him that gem. Actually Robert had, but Ellery was the reason behind it . . . she and her father.

Their rapacious behavior had compelled him to want to *make things right*. That's why he broke his engagement to Ellery, and exposed her father's underhanded scheme to exploit the Hawaiians in a casino venture on Kahoolawe.

Now he, Katie, and Robert were headed to that barren pile of lava to look for lost antiquities. But their scheme was not to exploit the Hawaiian people by raping their land or stealing sacred possessions. They intended to find the ancestral king's remains and return them to the Hawaiian's for repatriation. To makes things right—or simply *pono*.

So much had happened; so much was yet to happen.

He stared at the name on the boat: *Hele Auana—Go wandering*.

Hauntingly appropriate, especially given the circumstances. But was it a sign of good fortune to come or a premonition of bad.

Superstition and sea monsters had been an important part of

seamen's lives throughout the centuries. While working the family salmon boat in the ocean off the coast of his hometown of Fields Landing in Northern California, he'd often stared into the deep-blue wondering if the stories about giant serpents attacking ships were true. Now that he had spent a significant amount of time underwater, he'd seen enough strange creatures to know anything was possible.

The depths were slow to give up their secrets.

He shook off the ghostly images and concentrated on the lines of the vessel in front of him. *Hele Auana* had a wide beam and a high sloping bow that led him to believe it would provide a stable platform from which to work. And short of an attack by a giant squid, the boat would handle the afternoon trade winds and whatever rough sea the breeze kicked up.

That was all good. But hours and hours of baking in the intense tropical sun had faded the paint and cracked the fiberglass in a few places. The craft was every bit of twenty or thirty years old. That made him wonder about the engines, or worse yet, engine.

"It floats," Jack said, tugging the cap back on his head. "But does it run?"

"Hop aboard and let's find out. According to Kimo, both engines were overhauled a month ago."

Robert tossed a set of keys to Jack.

Jack snatched the keys out of the air with one hand, stepped onto the gunnel, and hopped onto the rear deck with the ease and grace of a man who'd spent a substantial number of years on the water. Robert followed close behind him and climbed the ladder to the flybridge. Katie jumped aboard next.

Once she was safely onboard, Jack left her to poke around the deck and took his place on the flybridge.

"No time like the present," he said to Robert.

Jack inserted the ignition keys and fired up the twin diesels—first one, then the other. With the starting of each engine, a gush of bubbles erupted in the water just beyond the fantail, followed by a billow of blue smoke that quickly dissipated in the wind.

Jack eased the throttles forward taking the twin diesels up to fast-idle. After a few seconds of letting them run at that speed, he eased back on the dual levers. The engines burbled smoothly.

"Sounds good to me," Robert offered with a grin. "What do you think?"

Jack arched a brow and said, "The proof will come when we're on open water."

He raised the RPMs on the diesel motors one more time, brought them back to idle, shut them down, and added, "But I have to agree. The engines do sound strong. If none of the other equipment on this tub works worth a shit, we'll at least make it to the island and back."

"This stuff looks interesting," Katie said from below.

Jack shot Robert a look and hurried down the ladder. He found Katie standing at the hatchway into the cabin, her attention focused on something inside. He edged next to her.

"Holy shit," he said.

For a few quiet seconds he stood in the hatchway with one hand gripping the doorjamb while he gazed in at the items piled on the deck. Not the latest or most revolutionary SCUBA equipment available on the market, but reliable and more than adequate for their needs.

A plethora of good times diving with Robert tugged at his memory, bringing a smile to his face.

"You did good, Robert," he said without turning to look at his friend.

He stepped inside and eyeballed the collection of masks, fins, regulators, buoyancy compensators, knives, and spearguns, all bearing the scars of heavy use. His gaze settled on two yellow hard-plastic cases—twice the size of his carryon—sitting off to the side of the other equipment. They looked new.

"What are those?" he asked.

Robert let Katie enter ahead of him. Once she was inside, he scooted past her and grasped one of two yellow plastic cases. His eyes focused on Jack.

"I told you I had something neat that would put a smile on that ugly mug of yours," Robert said. "They arrived yesterday."

"Back on ugly, are we?" Jack asked him.

"Couldn't resist."

"Right," Jack said. "Well I can't smile if I don't know what they are."

"As you know we won't be able to get closer than a few hundred yards from shore," Robert explained. "We'll need these little babies to take us in. Without them we'll use most of our air just making the swim."

Jack didn't interrupt. He watched Robert flip the latches on the case and opened the lid. Then he stepped to his friend's side and eyeballed the contents in the open case. Robert had been right. He couldn't keep from smiling.

"Jetboots," he said.

"The latest model," Robert answered.

Jack bent and probed the equipment inside the case. He'd used various types of underwater scooters a number of times over the course of his research, but never Jetboots. He'd heard about them, even seen a pair. But he had no idea how they would perform.

"Ever use these?" he asked.

"In a swimming pool, once," Robert explained. "Piece of cake. Your set's never been used."

Jack wasn't convinced.

"Best thing since canned beer, huh?" he asked.

"Maybe not the best, but close to it." With a sweep of his hand, Robert motioned at the other dive equipment and added, "You recognize this stuff, I'm sure."

"How could I forget."

Robert shrugged. "All the schooling you've crammed into that head of yours these past three years could have fogged your memory."

"It was your idea I go back to school, remember? Besides, it won't be long before I have my doctorate and I'll have time for the simpler things in life like whipping your ass at golf."

"After we find the artifacts," Katie chimed in.

Robert added, "And make sure they are repatriated."

"You got it," Jack said as he reached and picked up a scratched and faded lime-green Princeton Tec dive light. He switched it on. "Still works. And the other equipment?"

"As good as when you left it."

"That's what worries me."

CHAPTER 21

Jack glanced from Robert to Katie, breathed in deeply, and let his breath seep out.

His crew.

He shook his head.

From the beginning, he'd been quick to recognize the dangers that lay ahead on their mission. He knew all too well the unpredictable nature of the sea and the deadly creatures that lurk beneath the surface.

The good-natured joking going on between him and Robert had always been their way of reducing tension when faced with adversity. The friendly banter with his buddy had taken some of the edge off his concerns, but the dangers were still out there and he couldn't let himself forget that.

Were Robert and Katie involved in a quest best left alone?

He'd shared enough exploits with Robert to understand his way of thinking. Always the cautious one when it came to taking risks of this type—Robert had jumped at the opportunity to join in the expedition. If his friend was holding true to form that meant he wanted to be along to play big brother and watch out for their safety. And of course, there was his curiosity.

Robert liked a good adventure.

Katie—on the other hand—was not there for the adventure. Nor was she there to play big sister. She—with her pit-bull tenacity—had insisted on being part of the mission strictly out of devotion to seeing that her grandfather's wishes were carried out as promised.

Both motivations were admirable in their own right. But would he be able to live with himself if anything happened to either one of them?

He forced aside the thought of any of them dying because of a few trinkets and some two hundred year-old bones. He had more than his share of hang-ups, but a death wish wasn't one of them.

Whatever the dangers, large or small, they would approach each one with utmost caution and find that crate of artifacts. And the three of them would return with the treasure safe and sound—no injuries and no regrets.

He'd make sure of it.

"You two feel like taking a little boat ride?" He jabbed his thumb in the direction of the sky. "There's enough daylight left to run out to Kahoolawe and back. That'll give us a chance to check out this old tub's engines and get a look at what we're up against. Do that, and tonight we plan our attack."

"I'm up for it," Robert assured him, and to Katie asked, "How about you?"

"Just tell me what I can do to help," she said.

Jack surveyed the dive equipment. The items needed to be stowed so that they wouldn't be tossed around in the swells.

He pointed his finger and instructed, "Stack this dive stuff against the bulkhead and make sure those tanks are secure. We don't want 'em rolling around. I'll go topside and get the engines warmed up." He looked at Robert and said, "Cast off the bow and stern lines once we're ready to get underway."

Robert headed aft, and Jack stepped from the cabin.

A gust of wind caught his cap as he walked onto the outer deck. He snatched the bill with his hand before the gust peeled the hat away and spun it backwards on his head. The trade winds that swept across the sugarcane fields of central Maui and through Maalaea Harbor every afternoon, buffeted the boat with enough force to make the old girl stretch her starboard mooring lines tight.

Pausing with one hand on the ladder leading to the flybridge, Jack listened to the old boat creak, felt the hull bob under his feet.

He heard the clank of air tanks banging together, followed by a mild curse from Katie.

Jesus . . . and they weren't even out of the harbor yet.

From the controls on the flybridge, Jack jockeyed the twin throttles with practiced skill and maneuvered *Hele Auana* in her slip to put slack in the lines so Robert could untie them from the turn-cleats on the dock.

He looked down at Robert, who moved quickly to unlash the lines and jump aboard. It made him feel good to realize he and Robert still worked well as a team.

Robert stood on the rear deck along with Katie while Jack backed the boat out of the slip. Once they were clear of the dock, he waved up at Jack and flashed him a thumbs up.

Jack eased *Hele Auana* forward.

"Next stop Kahoolawe," Robert said to Katie.

The wind buffeted the boat, gusts blowing hard off the mountains.

Katie raised her hand to her face and brushed back the strands of long brown hair that pasted themselves in her eyes and mouth.

"This hair is going to drive me crazy if I don't get it tied back out of my face," she said. "I'm going inside and find something to use for a scarf."

Robert's gaze followed Katie into the cabin. Then he peered up at Jack standing at the controls up top, shook his head, and climbed the ladder.

"This ought to be fun," he said from the top rung, in a voice loud enough to be heard over the rush of wind and bellowing of diesel engines.

"A bit dicey for sure," Jack said. "Better hold on."

Robert hopped onto the upper deck. "Better than an *E*-ticket ride at Disneyland."

He nodded at the small duffle bag sitting at Jack's feet. "What's in the bag? You've been carrying that thing with you since I picked you up at the airport."

"A portable GPS. We're going to need it."

Jack grinned and added, "Here we go."

Pushed by the powerful diesels, *Hele Auana* plowed into a swell surging its way into the mouth of the harbor. Saltwater curled from the bow in a crashing wave of foamy froth; spray shot high into the air. The concerns Jack had about seaworthiness of the boat in rough water dissipated in the wake behind the vessel's transom.

Again, the bow plowed into a swell, and again the sea parted and rolled away.

His tight-lipped expression broadened into a grin as he throttled up, sending more foam and spray curling off the bow.

Cruising the ocean on a two-hundred-foot steel-hulled NOAA research vessel didn't give him the exhilaration manning the controls of a forty-foot fishing boat heading into open water did.

Now he knew the sea, its hardships and danger, had forged him into the person he was. And even though his younger brother Deacon had grown into a man old enough to assume the day-to-day operation of the family fishing business, he felt a tinge of longing for the life he'd had captaining his father's salmon boat.

"Is there room for three?"

Katie's voice pulled Jack from his thoughts. Over his shoulder he saw her holding onto the ladder, her head just high enough above the decking for her to see into the flybridge. He swallowed hard and twisted in his seat to gaze at her smiling from her perch on the ladder.

She'd tucked her long dark hair under a faded Dodgers ballcap, a handful of wild strands spilled out from underneath. Her designer sunglasses—he noticed—stood out in stark contrast to the dingy cap.

When a tinted lens caught the sun's rays, reflecting them in a flash of dazzling light, he remembered how her emerald green eyes sparkled with flecks of gold in the sun. And how he found it hard to turn away whenever he gazed into them.

Even looking into her eyes through dark glasses, he could feel the hold they had on him.

She never looked better.

Over the past couple of days, he had been trying to not think of Katie in a romantic way, and failing miserably. Now he caught himself fantasizing about her eyebrows. The first time they met, he'd lain awake in bed alone late that night trying to figure out what it was about her appearance that intrigued him so. Then he realized it was her carefully shaped, luxuriously thick eyebrows that drove him nuts.

And still did.

"We'll make room," Jack said as he slid over in his seat far enough to give her room to sit.

When the boat plowed through the next swell and started down into the trough on the other side, Katie scrambled up the ladder and onto the edge of Jack's seat.

In the next instant, *Hele Auana's* bow crashed into the next swell. Froth and salt spray shot high into the air.

She looked at Jack and asked, "You sure this is a good idea?"

Jack made a slight course and speed adjustment, turned his head to meet her gaze, grinned, and asked, "You did check to make sure the boat has life preservers onboard, didn't you?"

CHAPTER 22

Treadway rolled the chart into a tight tube, tucked the map under his arm to keep it from being blown away, stepped to the railing, and stood looking at Kahoolawe. The drift was taking longer than he imagined. Still, the distance between *Trident* and Kahoolawe had narrowed to where the coastline stood out vivid to the naked eye.

In the last half-hour the wind had picked up, moving them ever closer, but on a more southerly course than anticipated. And with the wind came a change in the ocean's surface. The gentle roll had quickly turned to a frothy chop that rocked the yacht.

He scanned the water astern and noticed that many if not all of the boats crowding Molokini crater were departing for safety inside Maalaea harbor.

No amount of rough water would keep him from the relics he meant to have.

Nothing would!

With his free hand, he raised the powerful binoculars hanging from a strap around his neck, held them to his eyes, and searched the rugged cliffs of Kahoolawe no more than a mile and a half away. They were well inside the restricted zone and close enough for him to get a clear look at the obstacles between him and the treasure. There were a thousand nooks and crannies large enough to conceal the treasure his grandfather had written about.

He'd search them all if that's what he had to do to find that crate.

He oriented himself by mentally triangulating his position, using landmarks on Maui, Molokini, and Kahoolawe as reference points. Taking a few seconds to close his eyes and let his imagination work as he formed a mental image of his grandfather as a young soldier holding onto the wooden box, swept along by the current. Had the crate drifted this same path?

He'd know soon enough.

He carried the rolled chart back to the table where he'd been sitting, spread the map out in front of him, and fighting the wind, gazed at the X he had penciled in an inch to the north of Molokini crater to mark the location of *Trident* at the beginning of the drift. Running his fingertip across the paper, he located his reference points and roughly calculated his present position. A few more minutes of drifting and he'd plot *Trident's* exact location using the yacht's GPS system and add another X.

He couldn't help notice the rolled parchment was beginning to look like a pirate's treasure map.

He smiled. That's exactly what it was.

The handheld radio sitting on the table, crackled to life.

"What is it?" he responded with irritation in his voice.

"There's a boat approaching about a half mile off our bow," Captain Ward said from the bridge.

Treadway had wondered how long it would take. "A patrol boat, no doubt."

"I can't tell, but that would be my guess."

"What is our current position?"

"Let me check, sir."

When Captain Ward's resonant voice came over the radio, giving the GPS coordinates, Treadway noted them on the chart.

He keyed his handheld two-way and ordered, "Continue our drift. If that is a patrol boat coming to run us off, stay on the bridge. I'll handle them. And remember, we're having engine trouble."

"Aye, sir."

Treadway set the radio on the tabletop and studied the chart. Placing a ruler with one end of its straight edge on the X marking the starting point and aligning it so that the edge crossed his present location, he penciled a dark gray line to show their direction of drift. Then he extended the line to where it intersected the south end of Kahoolawe. Directly above the line he wrote *Drift 1* and the date and time.

Without a third and fourth reference point to plot by, there was no way he could be sure the line of drift would have continued on their present course, but for now two points had to be enough.

There would be more before they were done.

Satisfied for the moment, he rolled up the chart and secured the map inside the main salon. Then he hurried forward to check on the boat headed towards them. When he arrived on the bridge, he found Captain Ward facing the windscreen, watching the vessel a quarter of a mile away and coming fast. The bow of the speeding boat plowed the rough water, sending spray high into the air.

The game had begun.

He stepped from the bridge and stood at the port railing, waiting. The hot sun beat mercilessly on his neck. The wind tugged at his clothing. He was glad he wouldn't have to stand there long.

The patrol boat slowed and then drifted alongside *Trident*, the amber caution lights mounted on the bar above its cabin, flashing. Now he could clearly make out the words painted on the hull: Department of Land and Natural Resources.

A male voice boomed over a loud speaker. "These are restricted waters. You must leave immediately or be subject to arrest."

Treadway waved to the uniformed officer who stepped from the cabin on the patrol boat and pointed at *Trident's* stern where the two massive thousand horsepower diesel motors were located.

"Engine trouble," he said. "The captain informed me we should be underway momentarily."

"Is there anything we can do to help?" the voice asked.

Treadway removed his wide-brimmed panama and mopped his brow with a silk handkerchief. He still hadn't gotten a clear look at the man talking into the microphone or the officer who stepped from the cabin. The men aboard the patrol boat had a clear view of him standing in the sunlight, while long-billed caps pulled low and wraparound sunglasses with dark lenses obscured their faces.

A definite disadvantage in a game of subterfuge.

He stuffed the handkerchief in his rear pants' pocket and

returned his hat to his head, pulling it low on his brow. It was best if the officers did not get too good a look at him.

"My captain assured me they have the situation under control," he said. "But perhaps you could . . ."

Treadway paused in mid sentence and turned in the direction of *Trident's* bridge where Captain Ward stood watching. That was the signal for the captain to start the engines. A moment later Treadway heard the twin diesels catch hold and rumble at a fast idle.

With a broad smile firmly planted on his lips, Treadway faced the patrol boat.

"It appears we won't need your help after all," he said. "We will leave the area immediately."

"Very good, sir," the voice over the speaker boomed. "We'll stand by to make sure you have no further mechanical problems."

Treadway waved off the DL&R officers and twirled his hand above his head, index finger extended into the air. The massive diesels' RPM's increased sending a swirling mass of froth and bubbles astern. *Trident* moved slowly away, the gap between the two vessels widening as the yacht picked up speed.

The patrol boat's appearance, though half expected, surprised him all the same. He had not believed they would show up so quickly to intercede.

Boryenko stepped from the bridge and stood next to Treadway at the railing. The big Russian gazed in the direction of the departing patrol boat.

"How unfortunate," he said. "Perhaps it won't be so easy getting ashore on Kahoolawe after all."

"Do not fret my Ukrainian friend," Treadway said, keeping his gaze focused on the DL&R boat. "This operation will be a piece of cake compared to those we've conducted in countries prone to shooting first and asking questions later."

"Da," Boryenko said. "I forget. This is America."

"We'll be careful none the less."

CHAPTER 23

Mario Fuentes lifted a hand to his brow and shaded his eyes. The *Hele Auana* burbled past him no more than a hundred feet away.

He still had his hand to his brow when he saw the dark haired young man at the helm glance his direction.

The corners of his lips curled into a narrow smile.

When the dark haired man looked away, Fuentes extended his right arm in front of him and pointed his index finger—thumb cocked—as though his hand was a gun. He kept his gaze firmly locked on the dark-haired man aboard *Hele Auana* and lowered his thumb onto his extended index finger. One shot, one kill. He hadn't made the slightest effort to turn or even see who might be watching.

He didn't care.

His smile grew. He fired his finger two more times . . . first at the girl who stepped onto the lower deck, then at the blonde-headed man on the flybridge.

They were lucky, for now.

He fast walked along the jetty keeping up with the boat. Fifty feet from the end of the breakwater, he stopped and watched *Hele Auana* plow into the first swell; saw the girl scramble topside. He continued on to the mouth of the harbor and watched the boat through binoculars. The ten-power magnification brought him up close to the three people seated together, cozy, as if they were on holiday.

He raised his satellite phone, keyed in a number, held it to his ear.

"They're leaving the harbor now, sir," he said when he heard Treadway's voice. "The name of the boat is *Hele Auana*. The other man I told you about—the one with blonde hair—he's with them."

"They are headed this way?"

"*Sí.*"

"Who is at the helm?"

"The girl's boyfriend, sir."

You're sure?"

"Positive. I followed them here from the airport . . . watched them get on the boat.

"Is there something you want to say?"

Fuentes took a breath. Treadway must have heard the exasperation in his voice. He had to choose his words carefully.

"This following them, it's tiring," he said. "In Columbia, I would have tossed a grenade aboard the boat and blown it and the three of them to hell. No games. No waiting. Only pieces for the fish to pick at.

His comment brought a chuckle from Treadway.

"Patience, my bloodthirsty friend," Treadway said. "You know their car?"

"*Sí*, a white Toyota pickup. It's parked in the lot."

"Very good. Make it appear as if it's an accident."

* * * *

Treadway squinted through the windscreen of *Trident* at the approaching boat. He checked his watch. The old boat had made better time than expected.

The name of the vessel continued to be obscured behind an almost constant wall of saltwater spray. Whenever the spray cleared enough for him to begin to make out the letters, the bow dipped and crashed into another wave, sending more saltwater roiling off the hull.

He raised his binoculars to his eyes. The rise and fall of *Trident* made it difficult for him to hold the approaching boat in his field of vision. He cursed under his breath. Then the curtain of water obscuring the approaching boat's name cleared as if he had willed it.

Hele Auana.

So the fly in the ointment *had* arrived.

He scoffed at the thought and pressed the powerful field glasses tight against his eyes. For a few seconds, he studied the faces of the three people on the flybridge. He adjusted the magnification from ten times to twenty times normal and focused in on the dark haired man at the helm.

Jack Ferrell.

Treadway's left eye twitched.

A full thirty seconds later, he lowered the binoculars. There was no doubt in his mind where the boat was headed. *Kahoolawe!*

He handed Boryenko the field glasses. "It appears my competition has arrived."

Boryenko peered through the glasses a moment, and lowered them. "They do not look like much of a threat in that old boat."

"Looks can deceive."

Speaking over his shoulder at Captain Ward, Treadway said, "Let the boat pass, then cut the engines and drift a few minutes. When they're about a quarter mile out, come about and maintain a course off her stern."

"Aye, sir."

Treadway saw the three people on the flybridge face in his direction when *Hele Auana* cut through the waves a hundred feet off *Trident's* port side. Jack had brought the boat in close. Which was of no consequence.

He was sure Jack's intention was to give himself and his two passengers a good look at *Trident's* superb lines.

It only made sense.

There was no way Jack or his two friends could know whose eyes watched them through the tinted glass.

Treadway's lips curled up at the corners. He nodded to himself.

If the old man *had* withheld information about the location of the treasure, he'd know soon enough.

CHAPTER 24

Jack soaked in the roar of the boat's twin diesels. Ahead of them was Kahoolawe. He kept his eyes focused on their destination as the boat droned and pounded its course toward the small uninhabited island.

Three miles out, they passed a convoy of snorkeling boats heading for the safety of Maalaea harbor. Salty spray kicked up from *Hele Auana's* bow, coated his lips. He licked it away and studied his crew.

He knew Robert never had a problem with a little rough water. Katie on the other hand was no seadog. For the moment, she seemed to be holding her lunch down. But would it stay that way? Perhaps the adrenaline fueling her determination helped take her mind off the motion of the boat.

He needed her to stay strong.

"With some luck," he said, "the waves will flatten a bit once we're father south in the channel where the trade winds aren't as strong."

Katie nodded in the direction of the passing charter boats crowded with vacationers and said, "They're the smart ones. In an hour they'll be showered and sipping Mai Tais in a bar on a beach."

"Can't fault them for that," he answered. "A Mai Tai would taste good about now . . . or better yet a margarita to go with the salt caking my lips."

Robert slid from his seat in a move toward the ladder. "No Mai

Tais or margaritas, but I've got a few beers stashed below. Fosters around?"

"Absolutely," Jack and Katie said in unison.

A couple of minutes later, Robert returned with three bottles of Fosters and passed them out. They all three clanked bottles and he settled into his seat.

He leaned toward Jack and asked, "How much do you know about Kahoolawe?"

Jack eased back on the throttles so they could hear above the engine noise, took a sip from his bottle, and ran the back of his hand over his mouth.

He said, "Only that the military used it for target practice and it's currently being held in trust for the Hawaiians."

"And you?" Robert asked, looking at Katie.

She shrugged.

"Most people know what you know. Me too . . . until I did a little research after you called and let me in on your plan to recover the artifacts."

Jack was not surprised he'd done the research. He doubted Katie was either. They were both familiar with Robert's appetite for detail.

"I'm listening," he said.

"Quite interesting reading, really," Robert began. "The ship-to-shore bombardment by the navy began in 1941—after Pearl Harbor—and ended in 1994. That's what locals remember most. But there's more history to the place than fifty years of being shot at and blown to pieces by every weapon under the sun."

"For instance?"

Robert grinned. "For instance you'd never guess Kahoolawe served as a penal colony from 1826 to 1853—actually, so did Lanai."

"The Hawaiian version of Devils Island, huh?"

"Sort of, I suppose. According to what I read, when the first missionaries arrived in Hawaii in 1820, the Protestant faith ingrained itself in the Hawaiian royal families, as well as the general population. In 1829 Queen Kaahumanu and Kuhina Nui—the prime minister of the Kingdom—proclaimed the *Edict of 1829* which banished followers of the Catholic religion to Kahoolawe as one of several identified punishments. Eventually, crimes like rebellion, prostitution, theft, and murder were added to the list. Headquarters for the penal colony on Kahoolawe was located at Kaulana Bay. In 1853, the law which established Kahoolawe as a penal colony was repealed."

"Jesus."

"Thought you'd find it interesting."

"Okay, I'm interested. What happened then?"

Robert's grin told Jack he'd said the magic words.

"In 1848," Robert continued on, "King Kamehameha III initiated land reform which became known as the *Great M'hele*. As a result, the traditional Hawaiian concept of land stewardship was replaced with the western legal concept of land ownership. The lands were subsequently divided between the King and his *Alii*"— Robert shot a look at Katie—"*Alii* means nobles. Portions of land were also set aside for government use, and processes put into place to enable private individuals to be awarded land."

"Sounds like medieval Europe," Katie pointed out.

"Prior to 1848, yeah . . . kind of."

"And Kahoolawe," Jack probed.

"Kahoolawe," Robert explained, "was considered land of the government; and in 1858 the first of many ranch leases was issued. But the number of cattle, sheep, and wild goats exploded into a major problem. As early as 1875, many parts of the island were denuded due to overgrazing. This in turn caused a substantial loss of soil from accelerated erosion. After Hawaii's annexation in 1898, the island was ceded and transferred from the Republic of Hawaii to the United States. Under the Organic Act of 1900, the territorial government was authorized to use and possess the island until the federal government acted. Kahoolawe continued under territorial management with a ranch lease until 1910."

"That explains it," Jack said. "That barren hunk of rock doesn't look like there's enough forage on it to support even one cow, let alone a whole heard of them."

Robert tried unsuccessfully to stifle a laugh.

"Another joke?" Katie asked.

"On them," Robert said. "In 1910 the Territorial Board of Agriculture proclaimed the island a Forest Reserve, which unfortunately turned out to be a complete debacle. Since the Forest Reserve designation prohibited the hunting of wild goats on the island, the proliferation of goats continued to degrade the land. Realizing forestry efforts were futile given the goat problem, the Territorial Governor withdrew Kahoolawe from its Forest Reserve designation, and in 1918, transferred the island to the Commissioner of Public Lands for management purposes."

It was Jack's turn to laugh. He could picture all those animals running around the island unchecked, eating everything green in sight. Man sure had a way of screwing up nature.

Still chuckling, he said, "So now it's one big goat ranch, I suppose."

Robert shook his head. "Not really. There was a late ranching period that ran from 1918 to 1941, but the bombing of Pearl Harbor brought that to an end. After the attack, Kahoolawe was placed under martial law and the military took control of the island. It remained in their hands until 1994 when the State of Hawaii designated the island and its surrounding waters as a reserve."

"Boom . . . ! So much for the goat problem."

"You're right about that. But it was actually an Executive Order issued by President Eisenhower in 1953 that put an end to the goat problem. The Navy was directed to eradicate, or reduce to less than 200, all cloven-hoofed animals so that the Territory of Hawaii could initiate soil and reforestation studies to render the island safe for human habitation when it was no longer needed for naval purposes."

"Jack mentioned unexploded bombs and ammunition," Katie said. "What about that?"

"A lot of removal of munitions was done," Robert said. "But there's still plenty of live ordnance to worry about on the island."

"A little checking?" Jack asked. "Jesus, you did a thesis on that island."

Robert shook his head and said, "Not really. Just some light reading on the internet."

"My ass. Remember when I told you that you should have gone back to law school, well . . . you should have."

"Let's not start that again."

"Yeah . . . well, you certainly have the mind for that kind of work."

"And I inherited enough money so I don't have to put up with the headaches that go along with being a lawyer."

Jack snorted and said, "You got me there."

"And speaking of money," Robert said, pointing to the twin-hulled yacht approaching off their port bow, "That's what I call opulence."

With the tip of his finger, Jack adjusted his dark glasses higher on the bridge of his nose and scrutinized the gold letters painted on the hull.

"*Trident*," he said. "I like the name."

Jack brought *Hele Auana* in a little closer to admire the yacht's fine lines. Then a queer feeling crept up his spine.

He narrowed his eyes at the pilothouse.

For a few heartbeats, he breathed silently, taking in deep breaths through his nose.

The tinted windows prevented him from seeing inside, but his gut told him the three of them were being carefully scrutinized.

And it wasn't mere curiosity fueling the person's interest.

CHAPTER 25

Jack kept his eyes focused on the dark glass a moment longer, then turned the wheel to starboard, widening the gap between the two vessels.

He pushed the twin throttles forward another notch.

Hele Auana crashed into a large swell and sent spray and foam into the air.

He watched the posh ship pass them and continue on a course for Maalaea Harbor. He had no idea what it was about seeing the yacht that made him jumpy, but it did.

Perhaps it was the anticipation of the treasure hunt.

The feeling of unseen eyes boring into him faded, and Jack refocused his attention on Kahoolawe, now just a few miles ahead of them. Molokini sat about a half mile off their port bow. They had to be close to where Sergeant Treadway's plane went down during the war.

"Something bothering you, Jack?" Robert asked.

Jack saw Robert and Katie looking at him. They had evidently picked up on his concern. He decided not to raise the alarm . . . not yet.

"Probably nothing," he said. "I'm thinking we should be close to where Sergeant Treadway's plane went down."

"Right," Robert said. "There's plenty of daylight left. Want to cut the engines and drift awhile to get a bearing on where he might have floated ashore?"

Jack took another quick look at Molokini and Kahoolawe. A few miles and a lot of water separated the two. They had to start somewhere.

"Sounds good to me," he said.

He throttled back and retrieved the duffle lying on the deck next to his feet. He removed a hard plastic yellow case and opened the lid. He tipped it toward Katie so she could see the device inside.

He explained, "This is where the GPS comes in."

Katie eyed the compact navigational device in Jack's hand. "I know a GPS will give our location"—confusion showed in the tone of her voice—"but how's it going to help us find the lava tube?"

Jack switched the unit on. It took a moment for the GPS to fire up. He had given considerable thought to how they were going to narrow the search area to the location with the highest probability. He had a plan—quite simple really. And surely not at all original. But even so, the odds of running into the exact lava tube were just marginally better than winning the California Lottery.

Numbers in longitude and latitude appeared on the screen. He noticed Katie lean close, obviously paying close attention to what he was doing.

Speaking to Robert, he said, "If you'd be kind enough to fetch up that chart of the channel, we'll mark our initial location, then three or four locations along our line of drift. Once we've done that, we'll connect the dots with a line extending to Kahoolawe and see where it leads. We can repeat the process from maybe a half dozen different starting points and come up with a general area to concentrate our search."

"You've got my vote." Robert rose from his seat and edged past Katie.

"Thanks," Jack said to the top of Robert's head as he disappeared from view down the ladder. "Let's just hope it works."

Jack focused his gaze on Kahoolawe looming in the distance. Steep. Rugged. Barren.

Waves pounded the rocky palisades.

He inhaled a breath and let it out. A plan—no matter how flimsy—was better than no plan at all. He wanted to remain optimistic, but couldn't ignore the many factors at work on the outcome.

Was the wind blowing the night Treadway's plane crashed? And if that was the case, which direction and how hard? Had the currents in the channel changed over the years? Were the drift coefficients for a man clinging to a crate the same as they were for a forty-foot boat? These were just a few of the nagging questions sloshing around inside his mind.

Perhaps they should pack it in and buy a lottery ticket.

He scoffed at the notion. Why waste the money? He'd only bought one lottery ticket in his life and he hadn't even come close to picking the winning numbers.

Maybe his luck would change.

Robert returned with a pencil and the nautical chart of the channel between Maui and Kahoolawe. He spread the map out on his lap.

"Ready when you are," he said when he had it held in place with his arms to keep the wind from peeling it away.

Jack read off the GPS coordinates while Robert located them on the map. When he saw Robert pencil a small X on the chart northwest of Molokini, he interlocked his fingers behind his head and slouched in the seat.

"Now we drift," he said.

Robert looked up from the map and gazed in the direction of Kahoolawe's rugged coastline. "You know the American submarine commanders used those cliffs for torpedo practice?"

Jack read into what Robert was saying. "You think one of those torpedoes could have destroyed the lava tube?"

"It's a possibility."

"One I don't even want to consider," Katie interjected. "The artifacts are there and we're going to find them."

She'd paid attention. That made Jack smile.

He'd witnessed Katie's tenacity first hand. She hadn't given up on her father . . . even when a jury of his peers said he was guilty of killing her mother. And she'd held onto her grandfather's West Point class ring.

That ring . . .

Jack mentally sighed. So much had begun and ended with him finding that ring.

Time had not erased his memory of Ellery Seaport . . . rich, drop-dead gorgeous Ellery Seaport.

Even now, when he closed his eyes he could picture her beauty and feel the heat of her lovemaking stir him. And that wasn't all. She'd caused him to realize what it was like to have an addiction. That's the only way he could describe the hold she had had on him: an addiction . . . to beauty . . . to sex.

Even so, he'd begun to see her for the rapacious creature she was. No different than the tiger sharks stalking the water off Maui. She'd devour anyone who stood in her way. She'd almost devoured him. And then he found the ring.

But why him?

With so many people swimming that reef every day, the only explanation he had come up with was that he'd been chosen to do so by a higher force. God or Goddess, it was destiny that led him to Katie.

Once again, they had come together in a common cause for a greater good: find the stolen artifacts and turn them over to the State so that they could be repatriated in a manner befitting the ancient king. Katie would settle for nothing less . . . even if it killed her.

He wasn't going to let that happen.

He reoriented himself and read off their GPS coordinates a second time. When he'd done that, he watched Robert pencil another X on the chart and connect it to the prior X with a growing line: An invisible trail across the ocean. Thousands of trails exactly like this one, left by thousands of boats over the last seventy years, crisscrossed the channel. Which trail led to the treasure?

"We're getting close," Robert cautioned, yet again.

There was no way Jack could forget about the two-mile limit. And ever-present obstacle that worked against them. One they'd have to overcome.

I'm aware of that," he said. "I don't need your constant reminders."

"Right. Keep in mind that DL&R patrol boat has cruised by twice."

"I haven't forgotten," Jack answered. Hawaii's Department of

Land and Natural Resources seemed determined not to let him forget about it.

Another of the obstacles he'd given considerable thought to.

Finding a lava tube submerged in water is hard enough when you can walk right up and look. Having to do it from two miles away was near impossible.

There was one glimmer of hope.

The open trolling periods on the first and last weekend's of each month. But they would be restricted from going any closer than the thirty-fathom isobath . . . plus their boat had to be moving the entire time.

They'd have to find a way.

By late afternoon, they'd made three drifts. Each one brought a passage of time that seemed longer than the one before. And by the start of their fourth drift, a minute felt like an hour. The trade winds had died, and the ocean had flattened to a gentle roll.

"Even with this hat on I feel like my brain is going to boil," Katie said. "The wind at least made the heat bearable."

"Yeah," Jack agreed. "And you need something stronger than sunblock fifteen. That fair skin of yours is turning a nice shade of red."

"Got some ninety at the condo," Robert offered.

Katie didn't bite. Neither did Jack.

"What we need is a sunshade," he said. He lifted the aluminum framework folded against the dash of the flybridge and shook his head in frustration. "If you ask me, Kimo's cousin needs to invest in some canvas. The patio's bare."

Robert scoffed. "What do you expect for three hundred a day?"

Jack turned his look of frustration on Robert and asked, "Is that going to be your answer every time I find something on this old tub that doesn't work?"

"Depends."

"On what?"

"If you're whining or not."

"I'm going down to get another bottle of water," Katie said, stopping the banter. "Can I interest you two nutcases in one?"

Robert ran his forearm across his brow. "Sounds good to me."

Jack raised the plastic bottle he'd been drinking out of and tilted it slightly to the side. "I've got a couple of swallows left."

"I'll bring you another," she informed him. "I don't want anyone dying of thirst our first day out."

"Thanks," he said. "And while you're down there, put on more sunblock."

Without answering, she stepped to the ladder and started down.

Jack swept the horizon with his gaze and narrowed his eyes at the dazzling white yacht sitting a half mile away. He'd thought the fancy boat had stayed on course to Maalaea Harbor. But five minutes after their wakes crossed, he noticed *Trident* come about and maintain a position a quarter mile astern of them.

Coincidence?

He took a deep breath and let it out in a silent sigh.

Not likely.

Now it looked to him like *Trident* was anchoring off the west end of Molokini in clear view of their drift.

He scratched the back of his neck. That same creepy feeling he had minutes earlier when he envisioned someone checking them out through the dark glass of the yacht's bridge, nagged him.

The scenario just didn't feel right.

They were being watched.

Then a thunderclap of realization hit him.

Treadway!

CHAPTER 26

Colman Treadway sipped his chardonnay and returned the glass to the table on the rear deck where he sat watching *Hele Auana* drift. A small gust of wind ruffled the canopy above his head.

The wind had died off considerably. He welcomed the brief breeze that cooled the sweat on his brow.

He asked, "Are you enjoying the crab, my dear?"

Yvette Monet shoveled in a mouthful of the tasty white meat and licked a dribble of drawn butter from her lips. She chewed and swallowed the delicacy as ravenously as a starving child would a piece of stale bread. Smacking her lips, she washed down the lump with a gulp of chardonnay.

"Absolutely fabulous," she said. She took one more sip of wine, swallowed, and speared another forkful. "You know how much I love crab."

He did know, and he watched her gobble down another large bite. She might have been a beauty queen, but her table manners were disgusting. He considered how lucky she was to have a great body. Without it, she'd be another ill-mannered slob taking up space in the world.

He smiled. "Perhaps you'd like something else?

She stifled a belch with her napkin. "I do wish you'd quit staring through those stupid binoculars and pay more attention to me."

Treadway chuckled and raised the binoculars to his eyes. "Eat your crab, dear."

She pursed her lips. "You've been staring at the stupid boat all afternoon long. You're not looking at another woman, are you?"

He focused in on Katie in the distance and watched her climb down the ladder from the flybridge and step into the cabin. The things he could do to her. Perhaps he'd make it a point to show her what a real man was like.

Treadway lowered the field glasses and laid them on the table next to his glass of wine. He picked up his two-way radio, keyed it, and said, "If they head in, follow them. But maintain some distance."

"Yes, Sir," Karl Ward's voice crackled back.

Treadway tossed the radio on the table. Palming the sharp knife lying next to his plate, he slowly rose to his feet.

Yvette's eyes focused on him as he moved. Aware but naive to his intention. He stepped around the table and stood behind her, slightly to the side. She tilted her head and peered up at him. He gazed down at her.

His left eye twitched.

And in the next instant, he grabbed hold of her hair, showing her the shiny blade.

Her eyes widened.

He liked that: *fear! Lust!*

The same . . .

Immense pleasure coursed through his body when her eyes widened even more as they followed the cold steel down to her bikini top.

He slid the sharp edge between her breasts.

Her breath caught in her throat with a gasp.

She looked up at him, and he pulled her head back.

Her lips parted a fraction. Her chest rose and fell, her breasts pressing against the blade with each inhalation.

He held her a couple of breaths longer, eyeing the twin mounds of soft tanned flesh. Then he sliced through the slender strap holding the skimpy top together and pressed his lips to hers.

CHAPTER 27

Jack eyed the yacht. *Trident* hadn't moved from the west end of Molokini.

Once again, a shiver of uneasiness danced up his spine. There was no doubt in his mind they were being watched.

He checked the time.

Fifteen minutes remained of the hour he'd allowed for the drift. Each one had been the same; sixty monotonous minutes of bobbing like a rubber duck cast aside in a child's bath.

A sitting duck.

They needed to wrap things up and head in. It was a little after six. The sun was well on its way down. Another few minutes wouldn't change a thing.

"I'm calling it a day," he said.

"Probably a good idea," Robert agreed.

Jack read the GPS coordinates to Robert and watched him pencil the final X on the chart.

"Do you think the guy was lying?" Robert asked, glancing up from the chart to look at Jack.

"Hell . . . I don't know what to think."

For the hundredth time, Jack visually traced each of the lines marking their prior three drifts. Having done that, he eyed the line Robert had just penciled in to connect the final X.

The result was the same.

"According to the information here, he'd have missed Kahoolawe all together." He ran his index finger along the lines of travel and off the edge of the chart. "Next stop, the Solomon Islands."

Katie leaned close. Jack could tell she was studying the map.

After a couple of beats, she said, "Maybe when his plane went down he was closer to Kahoolawe than he thought." She pointed her index finger at the southeastern corner of the island and explained, "If we shift the four drift lines west a mile or so, he could've gone ashore somewhere around this small bay, here."

"Kanapau Bay . . . ?" Jack stroked the stubble on his chin. "Maybe . . . but that doesn't match with the story told to your grandfather."

"I've been out here at night," Robert said. "So have you, Jack. Without a moon, it's dark as molasses. My guess is he wasn't sure where his plane went down."

Jack shook his head from side to side in frustration. Their calculations weren't working out. Something wasn't right. But what?

"I don't want to start second-guessing his story, now," he said. "We'll be done before we start."

Katie furrowed her brow. "No way I'm giving up."

Jack sighed. "I'm not suggesting we do. I'm thinking something else went on that night that altered his direction of drift."

Robert looked at Jack. "Are you thinking the wind might have been blowing hard that night?"

"I'm not sure what I'm thinking. The trade winds wouldn't do it, though . . . not even if they were twice as strong as they were earlier. They blow basically the same direction we've been drifting. It has to be something else."

Katie tipped the plastic bottle to her mouth and sucked down the last gulp of water. Screwing the cap back on, she tapped the empty container against her knee. She clearly shared Jack and Robert's frustration.

"It's been a long day and I'm beat," she said. "I vote for heading in for a shower and some dinner. Our minds will work better after a cold drink or two."

"I'm for that," Jack agreed. To Robert, he asked, "You?"

"Damn straight."

"Good enough. Stow the map and I'll get this tub started."

Jack cranked over the engines, let them idle a moment, and eased the boat around while Robert rolled the chart and secured it in the cabin below.

"Let's hit it," Robert said when he was back in his seat.

Jack shoved the throttles forward.

The twin props bit and churned the water, forcing the bow to rise in the water. After a few seconds, the boat leveled and he set them on direct course to Maalaea Harbor. Starboard of them, *Trident* sat at anchor.

Concern knitted his brow as he stared at the yacht. Instinct told him they had been spied on. The feeling was still there in the pit of his gut. Which, by itself, didn't worry him all that much.

But what would happen next?

CHAPTER 28

Treadway heard *Trident's* anchor being lifted. He slid off the king sized bed in his master suite and smirked at Yvette Monet's nude body. Her right breast mounded above her arm she had draped across her chest. A pool of sweat filled her bellybutton. The narrow strip of pubic hair glistened with moisture. The scent of their sexual exertion hung heavy in the air.

A lioness in her lair.

He licked the blood from his lip where she had bitten him.

"Come back to bed, *mon amour.*" Her other breast fell free when she snaked her arm out to him.

"Enough for now," he said. He turned his back to her and stepped toward the private bathroom adjoining his suite. "Go to sleep or get dressed. I have business topside."

"But my itch is begging for more."

"Then scratch it."

A few minutes later Treadway stood in the center of the suite, showered and dressed in shorts. Yvette sat on the side of the bed, looking at him. She was still nude.

She fell back on the rumpled sheets. "These things you are chasing, they mean more to you than I do?"

He slid on his shirt and began buttoning it. Now he wished he had cut her throat and fed her to the sharks along with the worthless piece of shit Eduardo. She was becoming tiresome and demanding.

Two traits he detested in a woman. He'd replace her as soon as he returned to France.

Maybe sooner.

The thought made him pause. If he picked himself out a tight-bodied Hawaiian girl it would make his possessing the artifacts of her ancestral king all the sweeter.

"I can have my choice of a hundred women just like you," he said. "The artifacts are irreplaceable, a value far beyond that of female flesh."

She pursed her lips. "You are so mean to me, *mon amour*. But I love you anyway."

He scoffed at her. "You speak of love as if you know what it means. Your mouth is better suited for other things my dear."

Out of the corner of his eye, he saw her move. He quickly fastened the last button on his shirt, stepped out of the suite, and pulled the door closed behind him. Just as the latch clicked, a hollow thud of something heavy hitting the wall reverberated into the passageway.

His left eye twitched.

He stood gripping the knob. His heart raced. She'd pay for that childish display. He took a deep breath, let it out, and hurried topside.

When Treadway entered the bridge, he noticed the captain had resumed a course a quarter of a mile astern of *Hele Auana*. He snatched the binoculars from Carl Ward's hand, raised them to his eyes, and focused on the heads of the three people sitting on the flybridge of the departing boat.

His left eye twitched.

Staring through the powerful lenses, he asked, "They left when they finished their fourth drift?"

"Yes, Sir."

"What do you make of it?"

"They did exactly what we were trying to do when that DL&R patrol boat interfered. From here it appeared each of their drifts could have put them ashore somewhere in the area of that bay on the southeast corner of the island."

Treadway turned and scanned Kahoolawe with the field glasses.

"That's where we'll concentrate our search. Just as soon as we see what our friends are up to."

Captain Ward cleared his throat.

Treadway lowered the field glasses. "You have something to add?'

"Sir, there's another possibility to consider. Without plotting their coordinates on this chart"— Captain Ward held up a curled map—"I can't be sure, but it's also likely they would have missed the island entirely if the boat had kept going."

Treadway glared at Karl Ward. "Are you saying my grandfather would have drifted right past Kahoolawe if his plane went down where he said it did?"

"It's a possibility, Sir."

"Nonsense. Give me that chart."

Treadway grabbed the map of the Alalakiki channel out of Captain Ward's hand and unrolled it. "My grandfather drifted ashore near Kanapou Bay." He smoothed the chart flat with the palm of his hand. "I'm sure of it. We were drifting that direction when the patrol boat interfered, and that's the direction *Hele Auana* headed each time they made a drift."

"Yes, Sir. But we weren't able to finish our drift, and without their coordinates, we can't be sure where they would have ended up."

"We don't need their coordinates. My grandfather wouldn't have lied about this. In his letter, he said he floated ashore on Kahoolawe. That's what he did."

Treadway jabbed his index finger at the paper. "And Kanapau Bay is where I'm going to start looking."

CHAPTER 29

By the time Jack steered *Hele Auana* into Maalaea Harbor, the sun was a bright orange ball disappearing behind the shadowed outline of Lanai. The air was humid and dead calm, not even the slightest breath of wind. And in the dying light, the sea behind them stood out a blue gray slate. Farther out, where the ocean joined with the heavens, Kahoolawe loomed dark, barren, and mysterious. Above them, wisps of clouds glowed red like a fire in the evening sky.

I'm ready for a shower, a bite to eat, and a good night's sleep," Katie said with a yawn.

Jack pulled back on the twin throttles, letting the boat idle toward its slip, and took a quick look over his shoulder to see if *Trident* followed them in. The yacht appeared to be drifting a half-mile out. He brought his head around, caught a glance from Robert, and resumed his vigil forward.

"Speaking of a night's sleep," he said. "I forgot to ask where we'd be staying. Were you able to get Katie and me rooms nearby?"

"No need," Robert said. "You're both staying at the condo in Kihei. Since Kazuko is off island at our house on Oahu, Katie can have the bedroom." He grinned at Jack. "We can flip for the rollaway, loser gets the sofa."

Jack removed his sunglasses, let them hang from the strap around his neck, and rubbed his gravely eyes. Earlier in the day, he had been charged by the adrenaline that went along with getting their quest off to a running start. Now—like Katie—all he could think about was sleeping for at least eight hours straight.

He exhaled a drawn-out sigh and said, "You pick. As tired as I am, the floor would feel good."

Ten minutes later, they had *Hele Auana* tied in her berth. Katie wandered up the ramp to the public restroom. Robert and Jack milled about the boat, giving her a final once-over and making sure the lines securing her to the dock, were tight.

Robert stooped and tugged on the starboard stern line where it was tied to the cleat on the dock. When he straightened, he asked, "Is it still sitting out there?"

"About a half-mile. You noticed *Trident* follow us in, too, huh?"

"That fancy Yacht's been dogging us all afternoon. I thought about mentioning it earlier, but then I noticed you quietly keeping an eye on it so I figured you didn't want Katie to know."

"Thanks, buddy. No need getting her all worked up over something we're not sure of."

"You do think Treadway is on that boat?"

"If I had to guess, yes. So do you. Otherwise it doesn't make sense, them spying on us all afternoon."

"Could be he's sitting out there waiting for the opportunity to screw with us."

"What bothers me most is he knows our boat." Jack scanned the harbor. Someone had to have tipped Treadway off. And they might still be out there, now . . . waiting. He asked, "Do you think we should chance leaving the dive gear onboard?"

Robert's shoulders sagged. "I lugged all that junk down here so we wouldn't have to haul it back and forth. But now . . . Shit. Guess we'd better take it with us . . . the gear that's worth something, anyway. We can leave the tanks. They're heavy and awkward to haul around. Besides, I don't think they'd bother with them."

"Sounds like a plan to me. While we're at it, let's not forget the chart we plotted our drifts on. I want to look it over tonight." Jack fought a yawn. "If I can stay awake, that is."

"Stay here," Robert said. "I'll grab the stuff we need from inside and hand it over to you."

Robert returned with the two yellow plastic cases containing the jetboots. He stood them up on the deck, and one at a time, hefted them over the gunwale and into Jack's waiting hands.

"You know," Robert said, "if that *is* Treadway on that boat, he's a rich sonofabitch. He could have all kinds of fancy gadgets at his disposal."

"I'd say you're right," Jack scoffed. "Even to charter a yacht that size, he'd have to be loaded. Grave robbing must be a lucrative business."

"Antiquities, Jack. The man deals in lost relics. He's an antiquities dealer."

"A fancy name for grave robbing."

"Removing a golden idol from a tomb somewhere isn't exactly like pulling a wedding ring off the finger of a rotting corpse."

Jack arched a brow at Robert. "Isn't it?"

"In many cases, yes. Depends."

"I suppose it does."

"Unfortunately, there are people in the world who would dig the gold from their mother's teeth if they thought someone would pay a bundle to add the fillings to their display case." Robert faced the open ocean in the direction of *Trident*. "I don't know Treadway, but already I don't like him."

"I have a feeling you think we ought to leave the relics where they are."

"It's a thought. But I also know you have a promise to fulfill. And I couldn't sleep knowing Treadway stole those artifacts away from the Hawaiian people and we did nothing to keep that from happening."

Robert disappeared into the cabin and a minute later walked out carrying two buoyancy compensators, a couple of regulators, and two dive lights.

Jack reached and took the equipment from Robert's hands. "I'm the one who made the promise to Katie's grandfather. You're not bound by anything."

"I'm bound by my promise to you. I said I would help and that's what I intend to do."

"But I'm saying you don't have to."

Robert gave a dismissive snort. "Know this, Jack. Those relics, if they exist, should be repatriated. I wouldn't be here if I didn't believe that was your intention." He jabbed a thumb over his shoulder in the direction of the yacht. "Like I said, I'm sure not going to sit back and let King Kalaniopuu's bones or any of the other artifacts end up in that asshole's private collection."

Jack smiled. "Treadway might have all kinds of fancy gadgets, but I've got you. I'd say I'm one up on him."

"Don't forget Katie."

Jack chuckled. "You're right. The guy's positively fucked."

"Am I interrupting something?"

Robert and Jack looked at Katie walking toward them.

"Some guy talk is all," Jack said. "We decided to take the bulk of the dive equipment with us. Don't want to chance someone sneaking aboard tonight and stealing it."

Katie glanced from Jack, to Robert, and back to Jack. "You're worried about Treadway, aren't you?"

"So are you," Jack said. "I know you haven't forgotten about that Hummer. Neither have I. We have to watch our backs."

Robert dug into his pants pocket and withdrew the keys to his pickup. He held them out to Katie. "If you'd be kind enough to fetch my pickup and park it up top"—with his extended hand, he motioned in the direction of the parking spot that had been vacated at the top of the ramp leading to the dock—"Jack and I'll haul this stuff up there."

By the time Katie drove up in Robert's Toyota, they had the dive equipment piled at the top of the ramp. Two minutes later, it was loaded in the bed. Katie climbed into the rear jump seat, and Jack handed her the chart and the duffle bag that contained his GPS unit.

"That's it," he said climbing into the front passenger's seat. "Let's hit the road."

"Next stop Kihei," Robert said.

The road out of the lot was a short straight shot to Honoapilani Highway. Robert accelerated into traffic and settled back in his seat. He took notice of Katie's reflection in the rearview mirror and saw her rubbing her eyes.

"You'll be in a hot shower in ten minutes," he said over his shoulder.

She smiled at the side of his face and lowered her gaze to the windshield.

Robert focused on the roadway ahead, but not before he noticed Katie's eyes widen in the mirror. He saw the Honda dart in front of them at the same time he heard Katie yell, "Look out!"

Robert swerved.

The three of them held their breath.

The right front tire of his pickup left the pavement and furrowed the soft shoulder, sending up a spray of rocks and dirt.

Their bumpers missed by inches.

Robert fought the steering wheel to keep control.

The truck straightened.

Katie released her grip on the back of Robert's seat. "Whew. That was close."

"Too close," Robert sighed. "They ought to outlaw those fucking zipper cars. They're a God damned menace to the highways."

Jack let his body sink into the seat. "You won't get an argument out of me."

"Me either," Katie said.

Robert searched out her reflection in the mirror. "Maybe we should all have a shot of Don Julio before we take our showers."

"I'll go for—" Jack heard a thunk against his door, felt something bite his leg.

"Damn . . ." He clutched his calf.

Suddenly there was a loud ka-clunk of metal breaking.

Then the front end dipped low on the passenger's side and skidded on the pavement.

Sparks shot into the air.

The 4-Runner jerked to the right.

"What the f—" Robert swallowed his words.

In that same instant, Jack leaned back and reached for the handhold mounted above his door, grabbed it, and held on.

Through the passenger's window, he saw the front tire on his side of the truck wobble off toward the cane.

"You just lost a tire," Jack said, his voice laced with disbelief.

Jesus. He tightened his fingers around the handhold.

With the tire and wheel gone, the hub buried itself in the dirt shoulder.

The front bumper dug in.

A wall of dirt and gravel erupted in front of the grill and pelted the hood. A golf-ball sized stone hit the windshield and cracked it.

Katie screamed.

Robert gripped the steering wheel. His knuckles white under the strain.

"Dammit," he said. "Hold on."

The airbags exploded into Robert and Jack's faces.

The pickup truck plowed a path to the cane, hit a snarl of roots, bounced, tipped, and slowly settled onto the passenger's side and stopped. The deflated airbags hung limp from the center of the steering column and glove box. A dust cloud passed over the wreckage and dissipated among the stalks of cane. The catalytic converter crackled as it cooled.

Dead silence swept the interior of the cab.

"Fuck," Jack gasped, blinking his eyes open.

The windshield had cracked, but somehow remained intact. Outside, cars pulled to a stop on the side of the road. People got out and stood gawking; several others sprinted toward the wrecked truck.

Katie groaned, fumbled with the latch to her seatbelt, released it, and fell against the passenger's side of the cab. She managed to work her legs and feet under her, squatted and put a hand on Jack's shoulder. "You guys all right up there?"

"Son of a bitch," Jack gasped.

He released his seatbelt and wiggled to a kneeling position with his back to the broken windshield. "Robert, you okay up there?"

Robert hung limp from his seatbelt and shoulder harness. He didn't answer.

Katie cried out, "Robert!"

CHAPTER 30

Robert moaned, blinked, and looked around. "Shit . . ."

"You can say that again," Jack said as he pushed Robert off him.

"You all right, Jack?" Katie's voice cracked. "Robert, talk to me. You okay?"

"Let's get out of this thing before it catches fire," Robert said, rolling down the driver's door window.

"Sounds like your mind's tracking." Katie took a deep breath and let it out. "You had me scared."

Robert squirreled through the open window, kneeled on the outside of the door, and reached in to Katie. "Hand me the chart and GPS, and I'll help you out."

He set the chart and duffle aside and steadied Katie as she pulled her body free of the cab.

Jack waited until Robert and Katie were safely on the ground before he hoisted himself out and joined them.

He stretched and worked his jaw where the air bag punched him.

"Shit," he said. "Feels like Tyson got me with a right cross."

"Me too," Robert said. "Anything broken?"

Jack rubbed his right arm where it had banged the door when the truck rolled onto its side, then bent and probed the red crease on his right calf. Not a cut, more of a burn. It had stung like hell when it happened. But what caused it? They were still on the road.

The tire hadn't come off yet.

"Only your truck," he said.

Sirens blared in the distance.

He saw Katie looking in the direction of the sirens. Robert stared at his pickup and shook his head. They both appeared bruised, but otherwise unhurt. He limped over and joined them.

"Cavalry's coming," he said.

Katie glanced at him, then at Robert. Concern showed in her eyes.

"You sure you guys are okay?" she asked.

"Just marvelous," Jack answered. He noticed her hands shaking. Clearly, she was on the edge. "How are you doing?"

"I feel like I've been kicked around in a barrel by a rodeo bull but yeah, I'm all right." She brushed tears from the corners of her eyes. "Just a little shaky . . . and sore."

"Robert?" Jack asked. He still worried about Katie. "Anything broken?"

"Like you said, my truck."

Jack patted him on the shoulder. "So you're all right, then? You were out cold, ya know?"

"I'm fine," he grumbled.

"Good. You talk to the police. I'll collect what's left of our stuff."

Jack turned and scanned the cane for the spilled SCUBA gear and his and Katie's luggage. Even though the sun had dropped below the horizon, there was still enough light for him to see by. Katie joined him when he started walking toward the cane. He liked that. And it brought back memories of when they had been chased into the desert by Brian Wesley's goon—that's what she had called the man, a goon . . . and it fit: big, ugly, and dangerous.

She proved her salt that night. She hadn't given up. Just like she wasn't giving up now. Back then that tenacity had saved her and probably him.

"I've never seen that happen before, a wheel coming off a vehicle like that," she said, still shaky.

"It happens," Jack acknowledged. He fought temptation to put his arm around her. "Not very often, but it does happen."

He leaned over and examined the tire and wheel. The tire

was flat and the sidewall mangled. The lug holes in the rim were wallowed out and a couple ragged where the nuts pulled through.

He'd seen damage like that before, on a boat trailer his family owned when he was a teenager. The wheel had come loose from the hub because in his rush to change the flat tire and run off to play baseball with his friends, he had forgotten to tighten all the lug nuts.

If one of Treadway's henchmen removed all but two of the lug nuts securing the wheel to the hub, it would account for the damage to the rim. No doubt, the person unscrewed the nuts figuring the remaining lugs would break under pressure once he, Robert, and Katie were on the road.

He inserted his index finger into one of the wallowed out holes and felt its ragged edge. He nodded to himself.

Someone had tampered with that wheel, but he'd never be able to prove it.

That explained the wheel coming off. Not the tire loosing air the way it had. From the look of the tread, the heavy-duty radial was almost new and shouldn't have been punctured when the wheel came loose from the hub. At least that's the way it'd gone with the family's boat trailer.

He studied the wound on his leg. Unless . . .

The rim had chewed the sidewall in places, normal in a blowout. But areas were still intact. That's where he found the pencil-sized hole.

A bullet!

CHAPTER 31

Jack left the tire lying there. If he was right in his thinking, the stakes had just been raised. Even so, he was in no hurry to share this bit of information. Not until he was sure.

He hurried to help Katie gather their stuff. Since Robert's pickup truck had slowed considerably and settled gently onto its side like an old hound dog going down for a rest, the luggage and dive gear had been scattered only a few yards away. The hard part—he and Katie quickly discovered—was fighting their way through the dense growth of cane to gather the scattered equipment from the field.

By the time the police officer finished talking to Robert, the luggage and dive gear sat in a neat pile a few feet away from the wrecked Toyota. Traffic still slowed on the highway as drivers craned their necks to satisfy curious eyes, but many of the bystanders who had stopped to help, were climbing back into their cars to leave.

"Looks like the dive gear came out of it all right," Jack said to Robert when he walked up. "Sorry about your pickup."

"No worries. It's insured."

"Yeah, but I know how much you like that old truck."

"She's been good to me, all right . . . might even have some miles left in her. But it's still just a pile of metal. We're what's important."

Robert pulled his droid from the holder on his belt. "I'll make some calls. We'll be back on the road in no time. And Katie, don't worry. You'll get that hot shower. It's just gonna take a tad longer than I promised."

Jack saw him dig a card out of his wallet and noticed the AAA logo at the top. He watched him tap a number into the phone and quietly listened while Robert talked to someone about sending a tow truck to the location. Robert read off some numbers and returned it to his wallet. That call took no more than a minute or two.

Robert pressed the button that broke the connection, and said, "Tow will be here in fifteen minutes."

"Thank God for triple A. You know that wheel didn't –"

"Hold on a sec," Robert said. "I've got another call to make."

He scrolled to a preset site, pressed a button—presumably auto dial—and raised the phone to his ear. While he waited, he said, "We'll need something to drive while my truck's being fixed."

Jack sighed inwardly. The wheel had not come off by accident. Someone had loosened the lug nuts. They might even have shot at them. He wanted his friend to know what was happening before they went any further. In case Robert wanted to back out.

"It's me," Robert said a couple of seconds later. With the phone pressed to his ear, he wandered over to the front of his pickup. He squatted and moved his head as if he was inspecting the undercarriage.

Jack got the odd sensation Robert had walked away so that he could talk in private. His friend examined the busted hub with his fingertips, but his eyes were not focused on the damage or the pickup truck. His gaze swept the area and the car loads of people gawking at them from the roadway as though he looked for something, or someone.

"What's up," Jack asked when Robert switched off his phone.

"A friend's going to loan us his old truck," he said, walking back to where Jack and Katie stood by the pile of luggage and dive gear. "He should be here in a few minutes." He looked at Katie, smiled, and added, "Then you'll get that shower I promised."

"And it'll feel good," she said. She nervously scanned the area and let her gaze settle back on Robert. "That was no accident. Jack can explain. My guess is Treadway got here ahead of us."

Jack arched a brow at Katie. He hadn't mentioned Treadway or that in all likelihood he had been behind the accident. She had come up with that on her own . . . which shouldn't have surprised him.

He wondered now if it had been a mistake not to tell her about the yacht.

"Someone loosened the lug nuts on that wheel," Robert said before Jack could. "I figured that out from the start. And I believe we're all in agreement Treadway's pulling the strings." He looked at Jack, then Katie. "You saw that yacht out there, the big fancy one? It's been dogging us all day. Jack and I believe—"

"Treadway," she finished for him. She looked at Jack. "And you thought it best not to tell me."

Jack shrugged. He was screwed.

"I didn't want to alarm you until I knew for sure," he said. "Now I realize I should have told you the moment I suspected something. It was a mistake on my part and it won't happen again. My feelings for you just got in the way."

She glared at him and warned, "It had better not happen again. I'm in this to the end. Remember that!"

He'd seen that scathing glance one too many times over the past few days. He'd let her have her way. It was time for that to change.

"When are you going to get that burr out from under your saddle?" he asked. "What happened between us happens to a lot of people who have deep feelings for one another. You had your life and I had mine. I . . ." He started to reach for her and straightened. It would only hurt worse to have her pull away from his touch. "I love you, Katie. I always will. And for that, I'll make no apology."

She turned and faced the ocean, said nothing.

"Well at least you know how I feel," he said. He held the back of her head in his gaze a couple of beats longer. She stood with her arms crossed, looking everywhere but at him.

He faced Robert and asked, "Did you tell the police your suspicions about this so-called accident?"

Robert's attention shifted Katie to Jack.

He huffed.

"I didn't see the use," he said.

Jack shook his head and cautioned, "Lug nuts don't loosen themselves."

"Sure they don't. But what could I say?" Robert motioned

toward his overturned pickup with a sweep of his hand. "Shit happens. You know it, the police know it. How would I prove this was anything more than negligence on my part?"

Jack could see Robert's reasoning. If he insisted someone tampered with the lug nuts on that wheel, he'd have to provide the police with a motive. The only motive they had was Treadway wanting to keep them from finding the treasure. That would mean telling the authorities everything. Once they did that, their treasure hunt would be over. Treadway might not win, but neither would they. With no evidence to prove a crime had been committed, Treadway would sail off to play his deadly game somewhere else, and they would be left sitting on the beach staring at Kahoolawe in the distance wondering if Charlie McIntyre's story was true.

He locked gazes with Robert and asked, "So you're good to keep going?"

"Those relics are out there," Robert said in a matter-of-fact tone. "Let's get busy and find them before that asshole on that fancy boat does."

* * * *

Jack, Robert, and Katie stood back from Robert's pickup and watched the driver of the tow truck winch the Toyota upright.

All three of them walked over to take a closer look at the damage. Jack stepped to the passenger's door and found what he had suspected. A pencil sized hole, similar to the one in the tire.

Definitely a bullet.

He turned and peered into the cane field. Someone must have been hiding in the cane with a scoped high-powered rifle waiting for them to drive by. The loosened lug nuts weren't enough. The shooter wanted to blow the tire to add stress to the wheel. Insurance that it would break away from the hub. The shot that hit him must have been a miss.

There was no doubt in his mind. Treadway wanted them dead, or at least hurt bad enough to have to abandon the search.

And he wanted the wreck to look like an accident.

The horn from a car stopped on the side of the road, sounded.

He turned and saw Katie and Robert look that direction. He followed their gazes to where a gray, raised, half-ton Dodge Ram pickup and a blue van sat parked on the dirt shoulder.

Robert smiled. "Our ride is here." He took off walking toward the Dodge pickup.

Jack filed away his thoughts about the shooting and followed his friend. "Wait up. Isn't that Kimo?"

Robert turned, kept walking. "We're using his cousin's boat, why not his uncle's truck?"

Why not, indeed? Jack hadn't seen Kimo in two years. His first thought was that his friend hadn't aged a bit; that he even looked a few years younger. It brought a smile to his lips to know the captain's job Robert had gotten Kimo aboard one of the Whale Foundation's boats, had worked out well for him. The man deserved a break.

Jack waved at Kimo, then shot a look at the person inside the van. The guy sat turned in the driver's seat, looking at them out the open passenger's door window.

One of Kimo's relatives, Jack thought. The man, obviously Hawaiian, had thin white hair hanging past his shoulders, narrow deep-set eyes, and dark skin from years in the sun. He had to be at least seventy.

Jack watched the man's head move as he took the next few steps. He smiled at the old guy and turned his gaze on Kimo, who stood in front the truck reaching for Robert's hand. He took another step, paused, and checked out the driver of the van.

The old Hawaiian still watched them.

He thought it ridiculous, but Jack got the feeling he was the person the old guy was looking at. Too much drama for one day. He needed a shower and a stiff drink.

And for people to stop trying to kill them.

But he doubted that would happen. Treadway meant to have those relics at whatever cost.

Jack shivered at the thought.

What would the man try next?

CHAPTER 32

Jack blinked his eyes trying to bring the dimly lit living room into view. The voices he'd heard had come as part of his dream. Then a sharp rebuke from Robert brought him awake. He focused on the front door.

Ajar.

More voices. People talking in hushed tones.

Robert's voice.

He glanced at his dive watch: 4:10.

He slid his legs off the side of the rollaway bed and sat up on the edge of the thin, narrow mattress. He rubbed the sleep from his eyes with his fingers and then gazed down at himself. He had on the khaki shorts and t-shirt he'd put on after taking a shower. That made him realize he'd fallen asleep in his clothes.

He didn't even remember lying down.

Fully awake now, his first thought was that Treadway had tried to finish the job the deadly stunt with the pickup had failed to accomplish. He grabbed Robert's practice putter from where it leaned against the wall. This was the second time a *Ping* putter had been his choice of weapon.

Holding the club down at his side, he crept toward the open front door. Listening. Wondering.

He still couldn't see Robert, but he could hear him talking. What he was saying didn't make sense: something about having the situation under control.

What was that all about?

And who was he talking to?

Jack stayed out of sight off to the side of the doorway, gripped the doorjamb to steady himself, poked his head around, and peeked outside.

What the hell . . . ?

In the glow of the walkway lights, he could see Robert—naked from the waist up, wearing board shorts and a pair of flimsy rubber sandals—standing fifteen feet away at the end of the cobblestone path leading to the condo. The white-haired old Hawaiian who'd watched them from the blue van stood a couple of steps away. They appeared to be engaged in a serious conversation. Robert was doing the talking, but he'd lowered his voice.

Jack strained to hear, but Robert stopped talking before he could make out more than a word or two. There was no response from the Hawaiian. Whatever Robert had said to the old man, was brief and conclusive. He saw Robert place a reassuring hand on the old guy's shoulder.

He caught himself holding his breath. He breathed.

The concern he had for his friend's safety turned into confusion. Given what he'd just seen and heard, he didn't know what to think. He propped the putter against the wall, stepped into the open, and saw Robert and the old man stare in his direction. They seemed surprised by his appearance in the doorway.

Of course they did, they had no reason to expect me to be there.

He stepped onto the walkway and began walking toward them. Whatever was going on, he intended to be part of it. But after traveling only a few feet, he saw the old man nod at Robert, turn, and disappear into the night.

"What was that all about?" he asked Robert from a stride away.

Robert stepped past Jack and continued walking toward his condo.

Taken aback, Jack turned and stared.

"We can talk inside," Robert said over his shoulder. "I don't want to disturb my neighbors any more than I already have."

Jack followed him inside, and shut the door.

"Okay," he said. "Talk. Who is that white-haired old man, anyway?"

Robert turned and shook his head.

"That white-haired old man," he said, "is Kimo's uncle Keoni. What are you so worked up about?"

"Him showing up here at four in the morning . . . the two of you standing outside in the dark talking, that's what. Call me paranoid, but how in the fuck would you feel if the roles were reversed? You're supposed to be my friend, for Christ's sake. I was worried. You should have roused my ass out of bed and let me know what was going on."

Robert's expression softened. "Okay, Jack. You want to know what's going on, I'll tell you. Keoni stopped by to make sure we were all right."

"At 4 AM?"

"They know about Treadway, I told them."

"Who's the *they*, you're referring to?"

"Kimo and his uncle. Couldn't ask to use their stuff without letting them know what's going on, could I?"

"No? I thought we were paying them three hundred a day . . . plus fuel?"

"They're doing us a favor."

"And the treasure, I suppose you told them about the artifacts and what we're doing here?"

Robert stood looking at Jack.

After several beats, he said, "Only as much as they need to know."

CHAPTER 33

Jack held Robert's gaze. Nothing in his friend's eyes betrayed his thoughts. But there was a hint of something . . . a side to Robert he hadn't seen before.

He considered the effect Kimo and his uncle knowing about the treasure would have on the quest. *Nothing* . . . providing they didn't interfere. Kimo could even be of help. They needed someone to drive the boat while he and Robert were underwater looking for the entrance to the lava tube.

"Okay," he said, "so they know. I guess there's no harm in that." Jack checked the time on his watch. "It'll be light in another hour or so. If you'll point me toward the coffee maker and fixings, I'll whip us up a cup and we can take another look at that chart. Then we'll need to wake Katie and load up and go. I want to be on the water by the time the sun's up."

"Good idea. Coffee maker is on the counter, coffee and filters are in the cupboard above. But I don't know what good it'll do us to spend more time staring at that chart. Nothing's changed."

"Won't hurt. And we can orient ourselves while we plan our day."

"Nothing like a good adventure to get the blood moving. I'm going to make a pit stop and slip on a t-shirt. I like my java strong."

Jack had the coffee brewing by the time Robert walked into the kitchen. They took a seat at the table to wait for the coffee maker to finish dripping.

Robert stroked back his wet hair and stifled a yawn. "It's warm outside for this early in the morning."

"Humid too . . . and you can smell the ocean. Could be we're in for a blow from the south. That might mean rain."

Jack unrolled the chart onto the tabletop in front of him and pressed it flat with his forearms. Speaking across the sheet of paper at Robert, he asked, "What's the scoop on Kimo's uncle? Something about him gives me the willies."

"Scares you, does he?" Robert winked. "That's because he's a *Kahuna*. Keoni lives in the *Honokohua* Valley—a mystical place for several generations of Hawaiians. It's located on the northern end of the island. Quite beautiful, really. There's a waterfall at the end of the valley that'll take your breath away. He's lived there all his life. So did his father, his grandfather, and his grandfather's grandfather."

"No wonder he makes me uncomfortable. You say he's on our side?"

"He loaned us his truck, didn't he?"

"He did at that."

Robert scooted closer to the table. "So tell me, how's that woman friend of yours doing?"

Jack furrowed his brow. "Katie?"

"No. The young lady from the ship, the one bit by the tiger shark."

"I called the hospital from my hotel room in Boise and talked to Kelly on the phone. She sounded positive. The nurses were pumping her full of antibiotics and watching for infection, which I understood is standard procedure for a shark bite. According to her, the doc says she's going to be fine. Problem is, he doesn't want her to do any diving for a while. She's pissed about that because it's going to put a kink in her studies."

"So that shark didn't talk her into considering a career change?"

"Apparently not."

"Well, at least she has the leg."

"And a nasty scar to remind her to keep her wits about her when a man-eater cruises by."

"And where does Katie fit in the picture?"

Jack glanced in the direction of the bedroom. He thought he had put his feelings for her behind him when he started dating other women. Now he knew he hadn't. He loved her. And always would . . . even if they were not able to sort out the differences between them. Which appeared to be the case.

But was it?

He didn't know what to think. She had cried herself to sleep. He'd heard her sobs from the living room. Robert had to have heard her as well.

Was she crying because their quest to fulfill her grandfather's dying wish was well under way, or was it something else?

"What can I say?" he said. "I love her. We just can't seem to get on the same page. Every time I think things are going to work out between us, it gets all fucked up. I guess we just want different things out of life."

"So what you're saying is, it's up to her?"

"She knows how I feel."

"Did I tell you the one about the colonoscopy?"

"What the hell, man? It's too early for one of your jokes."

"It's never too early for one of my gems . . . or late, for that matter."

"I'm going to hear it anyway so get it over with."

Robert chuckled and said:

All the organs of the body were having a meeting, trying to decide who was in charge.

"I should be in charge," said the brain, "Because I run all the body's systems, so without me nothing would happen."

"I should be in charge," said the blood, "because I circulate oxygen all over so without me you'd all waste away."

"I should be in charge," said the stomach, "because I process food and give all of you energy."

"I should be in charge," said the legs, "because I carry the body wherever it needs to go."

"I should be in charge," said the eyes, "Because I allow the body to see where it goes."

"I should be in charge," said the rectum, "Because I'm

responsible for waste removal."

All the other body parts laughed at the rectum and insulted him, so in a huff, he shut down tight.

Within a few days, the brain had a terrible headache, the stomach was bloated, the legs got wobbly, the eyes got watery, and the blood was toxic. They all decided that the rectum should be the boss.

"And...?" Jack asked. He didn't need to be reminded of Robert's habit of using witticisms to get a point across. He was making one here.

"Simple." Robert said, looking Jack in the face. "The ass hole is usually in charge!"

Jack would have laughed if Robert's joke hadn't struck a nerve. What he said made a lot of sense.

He mentally shook his head.

His thoughts cleared, and he realized he had tried to take charge of his and Katie's relationship based on his needs more than hers. That made him the asshole. Perhaps they should try again. And this time do it on equal terms.

"Point taken," Jack said. "Now let's look at this map."

The drift lines stood out clear on the paper.

"Nothing's changed," Robert insisted. "Unless the plane landed in the drink a lot closer to Kahoolawe than Sergeant Treadway described to Katie's grandfather, he'd have drifted past the island and on out into the Pacific."

"I can read the map. But ..."

"But you don't want to accept what the facts show."

"Not if they are wrong."

"Wrong?"

Jack pointed at the cliffs along Kahoolawe's central coast and said, "Yesterday I'd have sworn our drifts would have put us ashore here. The scenario fits more with Katie's grandfather's recount of Sergeant Treadway floating into a lava tube. But our drift lines, told us different. Still . . . I don't know. Something's not right."

"Facts don't lie."

"If the facts are correct."

"They are in this case. Those X's prove it."

Jack stroked the stubble on his chin. "Then we will have to assume he went down"—he tapped the chart with his index finger—"somewhere out in this area. That means we need to concentrate our search along the coast near *Kanapau* Bay on the southeast end of the island."

"I told you that yesterday," Katie said from behind him.

Jack and Robert turned at the sound of her voice.

"You're up," Jack said.

"Who could sleep with all that talking going on?"

She poured herself a cup of coffee, stepped to the table, and peered down at the chart. "Have you figured out how we're going to do this yet?"

Jack used his index finger to trace his planned course. "We'll cruise the coast along southeast end of the island, making sure to stay outside the two-mile limit, and check it out through binoculars. We don't want that DL&R boat getting nosy. Anything that looks promising, we'll mark on the chart."

She leaned closer.

After a beat, she asked, "But how are you going to check anything out with the boat two miles offshore?"

"That's what Robert's fancy jet boots are for. But we'll be considerably closer when we use them. The first Open Water Trolling weekend for May starts this Saturday. That gives us one more day to scope it out from a distance. Then we move in closer."

Robert slid his chair back and stood up. "This'll be fun. I just hope it doesn't turn into a wild goose chase."

Jack didn't respond. He rose to his feet, eyeballing the chart. The X's stood out clear and decisive. Had they continued their drift, they would have missed Kahoolawe altogether. Yet Treadway's grandfather drifted ashore contrary to their data.

Why?

They had to be missing something.

But what . . . ?

CHAPTER 34

Jack pointed *Hele Auana* on a course toward Kahoolawe. He'd been surprised to find no one had tampered with the boat. The SCUBA tanks were sitting where they had been stacked; the two-way radio and depth finder hadn't been ripped loose or smashed. The engines ran smoothly. It would have felt like a holiday on the water had it not been for the edgy feeling from the close encounter with death the day before.

He looked to the east, then behind him at the harbor. He brought his gaze forward and smiled. They were getting a good early start. The eastern horizon showed the first blush of dawn, but the sun had yet to rise above the cane fields. Maalaea Harbor clanked, banged, and thunked to life as it did every morning at first light: a beehive of activity in preparation for the race for Molokini crater. Behind them, crews aboard the snorkel-tour boats loaded supplies and readied the decks for passengers that wouldn't arrive for another hour. Other boats idled in line waiting to have their fuel tanks filled with diesel.

But for now, only a couple of fishing boats left the harbor ahead of them. The sea spread out strangely calm; barely enough rolling swell to remind them they were on the open ocean and not pleasure-boating on a small lake.

He shoved the twin throttle levers forward and took the boat up to cruising speed. Saltwater curled off the bow and fell in a frothy spray that hissed and dissipated.

"Isn't she something?" Jack said, nodding at Katie who sat Indian style on the foredeck, staring into the water.

"She is at that. But what's she doing down there?" Robert asked. "I figured she'd want to be up here with us."

"I think she's looking for porpoises. I told her they sometimes like to ride the pressure-wave kicked up by the bow."

"A somber start for a treasure hunt."

"She misses her grandfather."

"Rightfully so, but are you sure that's all it is?"

"You suggesting she's thinking about me?"

"I think she wishes life could have turned out different."

"Don't we all, to a degree?"

"Sure, but we move on with our lives. She seems to be stuck. You two—"

"Get off it, already," Jack interrupted. "It just wasn't meant to be."

"You might be right. And I was getting to that if you hadn't cut me off. As I see it, Katie spent half her young life trying to prove her father's innocence. That gave her a goal to strive for. Once she secured her dad's release from prison—thanks to you—she didn't know what to do with herself. It was more like she had existed for a purpose. I have a feeling that's why the two of you couldn't pull it together. She didn't know how to live a normal life. Now she has another goal to give her purpose: this quest to fulfill her grandfather's dying wish. That's why she's here, now—alive with vitality; ready to take on the world. When we're done—however it turns out—my guess is she'll be even more lost."

"Unless I save her?"

"I wasn't necessarily going to say that, but yeah, now that you brought it up."

"I'm just not sure I'm the right person for her."

"No?"

Jack narrowed his eyes at Robert. "No!"

Robert huffed.

"Since we're on the subject," he said, "there's something I wanted to ask you."

"Shit . . ." Jack shook his head. Robert was on a roll.

"Out on the boat yesterday afternoon," Robert began, "last night, and this morning with Katie listening, I haven't had a chance to bring this up, but now that she's busy porpoise watching and we're on the verge of diving together, I've got to know. That business with the tiger shark, what was that all about, really?"

Jesus . . . Jack couldn't believe what he was hearing. Exactly as he figured, Robert wasn't going to let up on him.

"I didn't know what else to do," he explained. "The knife was all I had."

"I think there's more to it." Robert held him in his gaze. "You like playing White Knight to the rescue."

Jack had hoped his admission would put an end to their conversation. It obviously hadn't. And Robert was right.

He felt his face heat with embarrassment. Beneath the knowledge his reaction to the shark attack on Kelly had been impetuous and downright crazy, there was the knight-in-shining-armor pride of knowing he had saved the damsel in distress.

Just as he had Katie back in Boise.

"It's natural enough for a guy to want to do that," Robert said when Jack didn't answer. "A lot of men want to prove things to themselves, to others. It makes them feel manlier when they do things they think are impressive. What you did to that shark, Jack . . . was downright impressive. You saved that girl's life. The problem is, you seem to be making a habit of putting your life on the line for other people—primarily women. I don't think you took those risks to prove you're a man . . . to them, or yourself. But something's driving you."

"And that concerns you?"

"This white-knight syndrome could get you seriously hurt or dead."

"It's my life."

"Yeah . . ." Robert gazed at the broad expanse of sea. "But I don't want you doing anything stupid on my account. I couldn't live with myself if you got hurt because of me."

"You getting old and scared or what?" Jack said. "You're not even in the water yet and already you're worried about me pulling my knife on some tiger shark that's trying to eat your rangy ass?"

"Joke it up, Jack." There was no hint of amusement in Robert's voice. "You and I both know you take chances . . . unnecessary ones. That concerns me. And it's not only sharks I'm worried about. Treadway played his cards twice. It's only luck you're not seriously hurt or dead; me and Katie along with you. That asshole won't back off if he sees us nosing around. We have to stay focused and watch our asses."

"Don't you think I know that?"

"Sure you do. I just want to make sure you're head is on right. It's not just your white-knight syndrome that worries me. I've seen the look in your eyes. Katie being here with you has you all fucked up. And Kelly, someone you care a lot about . . . feeling guilty about her lying in the hospital hurt while you're spending time with the woman you love . . . shit, it's gotta screw up your brain."

"I won't deny having Katie here is a distraction. She makes my blood boil, does every time I'm near her. Even now looking at her down there on the deck, I'd like to take her inside the cabin and make up for lost time. But I know that's not going to happen. So relax, my thinking is as clear as ever."

"You're thinking? That's precisely what has me concerned."

Jack slapped Robert on the back. "You worry too much. Hell, chill a bit. You said it yourself, this is going to be fun."

"Yeah . . . just do me a favor. Don't throw your saddle on any sharks out there."

Jack laughed. "Trust me, once was plenty."

"Good enough," Robert said. He nodded at Kahoolawe. "Now let's get this done. You still owe me a round of golf."

"And you owe me a beer."

Jack shoved the throttles levers forward to give them another five knots.

Not that getting there a few minutes sooner would change much.

From a couple of miles away, he could make out the white hull of the yacht glaring in the morning sun.

"You see what I see?" he asked, leaning toward Robert.

"Can't miss him," Robert answered.

Katie climbed onto the flybridge and stood holding onto the

narrow windscreen. In the next instant, *Hele Auana* plowed through an unexpected swell rolling in from the south. The bow of the sturdy boat rose and fell. Katie staggered a step and regained her balance.

She asked, "How much longer?"

"At this speed, four or five minutes," Jack said. He throttled back a few knots. "But we have a problem."

"What problem?" Katie held on with both hands to keep from being flung forward by the sudden slowing of the boat. When she regained her balance, she let go with one hand and motioned them forward. "Crank this thing up and stop wasting time."

Jack and Robert pointed at the yacht at the same time.

"Treadway," Jack said. "He beat us there."

She shaded her eyes with her hand and squinted in the direction of the fancy boat.

"I guess my mind was on something else," she said after a moment. "How'd he know where to look?"

"The sonofabitch watched us yesterday. I'd say he drew the same conclusion we did."

"That's not fair."

Robert laughed and said, "I don't think Treadway knows the meaning of fair."

"The bastard." Katie practically spat the words out.

"The question is"—Jack squinted at the yacht—"how do we proceed from here?"

"I say we proceed as if he wasn't there," Robert answered. "We might be looking at the same section of coastline, but that's all he'll know."

Jack picked up the binoculars sitting on the dash in front of him, raised them to his eyes, and focused in on the boat, half expecting to see Treadway on deck staring back at them. No one was in sight. That concerned him. It seemed odd Treadway would let them cruise into the area without showing at least some interest in their arrival. Surely, he knew by now his plan to get them out of the way, failed.

He lowered the binoculars and looked at Katie waiting to hear her answer.

She knitted her brows. "The bastard wants us out of the way real bad. He might try something."

Jack thought about that. He hadn't told them about the shooting. Now seemed like a good a time.

"Before we go any farther," he said, "I need to tell you both there's a possibility we were shot at yesterday?"

Robert stiffened. "What do you mean shot at? When? Where?"

"Not at us, exactly," Jack told them. "At your pickup."

"My pickup?"

"That's how the tire blew. I wouldn't even have known had it not been for this." He pointed to the red crease on his calf. "The first shot missed the tire and went through the passenger door."

"So they weren't shooting at us," Robert said.

"That's how it looked to me."

"And I agree," Robert said. "If they had been, we'd be dead. Treadway wanted it to look like an accident. He might try something else, but I don't think he'll start blasting away at us with a rifle. Not out here with the other boats around. And for sure not with that patrol boat keeping an eye on things."

"Accident or no accident, I don't like the thought of guns being involved," Katie said. "But I'm not ready to back off. Not now."

Her voice was shaky. Jack figured it was more out of anger than fear.

Robert looked squarely at Jack. "I guess it's your decision."

Jack shrugged. "I say let's let him know we're here."

CHAPTER 35

Jack kept the engines' RPM's up and maneuvered *Hele Auana* alongside the slow moving *Trident*. He raised a middle finger at the bridge of the yacht even though he couldn't see Treadway through the tinted glass. There was little doubt in his mind the bastard was on the bridge watching them.

He grinned and kept his finger raised high in the air as they sped past. His childish display of crudeness wouldn't get Robert a new pickup truck, but it did release some of the anger.

Hele Auana's wake slammed into the side of *Trident's* hull. Spray shot into the air, but the wave had little effect on the movement of the much bigger boat. A blast of the yacht's air horn reverberated across the water. Treadway had gotten the message. Jack breathed a silent sigh of relief that the obnoxious sound had not been the sharp crack of a rifle shot.

"I'd say that went well," Robert said.

"I thought you'd like that." Jack raised his hand for a high five.

"Crude, but effective." Robert slapped his palm against Jack's.

Katie took her turn, slapping Jack's palm, then Robert's.

Robert nodded in the direction of Kahoolawe and said, "What do you say we get down to business?"

"Fine by me." Jack checked on *Trident*, started to turn away, then paused and gave the yacht another look. A circuit breaker in his memory banks, tripped. The lines of the boat seemed different in a small way.

Something was missing from the deck . . .

The Zodiac!

All at once, it dawned on Jack what Treadway's scheme was. He'd put a search team ashore during the night.

Jack swept his gaze across the water to the rugged shoreline. The sun was fully up now, and Kahoolawe's coast stood out bright in the morning light. He squinted hard but couldn't see anyone moving about along the water's edge. It didn't matter; he knew they were there. The missing Zodiac was proof enough. No other explanation made sense. Treadway's men had gone ashore in the inflatable under the cover of darkness and were there now, hunkered low in the shadows, waiting for nightfall to return.

Not a bad plan.

It would be a simple task for Treadway's men to conceal the small boat from view during daylight, and later—when it was dark—emerge from hiding to search the rocky shoreline from underwater using dive lights or from the Zodiac with the aid of night-vision goggles.

Treadway had already shown his contempt for the laws of society and an ardent willingness to kill to get what he wants. From the start, Jack accepted the reality it would be necessary for them to break the law at some point during their quest—just being on Kahoolawe without permission was a crime, as was the looting of Hawaiian artifacts. But they planned to turn the artifacts over to State officials, so that didn't really count.

Or did it?

He could only wonder how far he would have to go to fulfill his promise.

He shot a casual glance at Robert, at Katie. He knew what Katie was made of—had seen it firsthand—and he had known his friend long enough to have a good idea what he was capable of.

They'd carry the quest through to the end no matter what it took, short of one of them dying.

So he hoped.

They needed to draw on every ounce of willpower and determination if they were going to stand a chance of succeeding.

Three Jack Russell terriers against a pack of wolves.

The question he had to ask himself was would they know to quit if the time came.

Before one of them died.

He eased off on the throttles and brought the boat around two hundred yards off *Trident's* starboard bow. There, he moved the throttle levers to idle. Letting the boat drift, he raised the binoculars to his eyes anxious to spot Treadway's search team ashore. He wanted to know what the three of them were up against.

The best money can buy, he was sure.

Robert picked up the binoculars he had stashed on his side of the flybridge and joined in the search. "You seem like you're looking for something," he said with his eyes pressed to the lenses. "Other than the lava tube, that is."

"I am." Jack lowered the field glasses, but kept his gaze focused on the island. "Did you notice anything different about Treadway's yacht?"

"I think I was distracted by you flipping him that bird."

Katie and Robert twisted at the waist and peered in the direction of *Trident*.

"What are you talking about?" she asked. "How can a boat change over night?"

"The boat itself didn't change," Jack said. "Just the way it was outfitted."

Robert scoped in on the yacht.

"I don't . . . Wait!" he said. "The Zodiac, it's gone."

"You got it," Jack answered. He raised his ten-power Bushnell's to his eyes and resumed his vigil of the rugged shoreline. "I'm thinking Treadway put a search party ashore sometime during the night."

Robert brought his glasses around and focused in on the lava outcroppings above the tide line. "And they're on Kahoolawe right now, hiding out in those rocks."

"I'd bet on it."

CHAPTER 36

Jack lowered the binoculars and rubbed the blurriness from his eyes. Treadway's men were there. But where?

"If they went ashore, then that's what we should do," Katie said.

"Possibly." Jack locked gazes with her. "But what'll happen if our paths cross with those men's?"

"We make sure that doesn't happen." Katie's voice reflected her resolve in the matter.

"It's inevitable," he said. "And when it does, there'll be a fight. I'm not sure I'm ready for that."

"You confuse me, Jack," she said. "I thought you'd be anxious to mix it up with Treadway."

"I'd love to get my hands on Treadway's neck. But we wouldn't be going at it toe to toe with Treadway. It'd be his men. And we don't have any idea how many there are, or if they're armed."

"You can bet they're armed," Robert interjected. "They've already shot at us once."

"Fine," Katie groused. "So we let them steal the treasure right from under our noses. Some promise."

Jack clamped his jaw shut to keep from losing control of the anger that surged inside him. Robert was no coward. Neither was he, far from it. She knew that. She also knew the dangers involved. Yet she appeared eager to send them up against a group of armed men.

What was going on with her?

"We'll do what's necessary," he said. "But we'll ease into the situation so as to not hang ourselves out to dry. Know this, Katie, I haven't forgotten the promise I made to your grandfather, and won't. So don't bring it up again."

She fell silent, tears formed in her eyes.

He immediately regretted letting his anger show in the tone of his voice. Treadway changed the rules of the game. The stress had to be getting to her.

"I'm sorry for getting upset," he said. "I know you didn't mean anything by what you said."

She wiped her eyes. "I did mean it, Jack. I wanted you to get hurt. Not Robert, you. I don't know why, but I did. Everything that's happened . . . I'm all messed up inside. You . . . me . . ."

She buried her face in her hands.

"Then we have to get you un-messed," Robert said.

Katie took her hands away from her face and glanced nervously at Robert, then Jack. She sniffled.

Her tear-filled eyes seemed to plea for forgiveness.

Jack laid his hand on her arm in reassurance. The warmth of her skin made him pause. He collected himself.

"We're all on edge after that incident yesterday," he said. "Finding Treadway here ahead of us this morning didn't make matters any easier. But we can pull this off no matter how many men he has ashore. Besides, who says they're even looking in the right place." He nodded in the direction of *Trident*. "The asshole doesn't know any more than we do—maybe less. Otherwise he'd have the artifacts and be gone from here."

She swiped away the tears and offered a shaky smile.

"Then let's get busy and find them," she said. "I can't wait to send this guy packing."

"Thatta girl," Robert said. "Blast his scurvy-riddled innards. Hoist the main sail. Prepare for battle."

Jack chuckled. "Now we're playing pirate, are we?"

"Aye, mate. 'Tis you Captain Jack Ferrell that brings the brigand out in me." Robert winked at Katie. "Let's do 'em the dirty."

That made her grin. Jack had to smile.

"Let's start our drifts and see what we can see," he said.

The morning started out warm, and got much warmer. And with the rising of the sun, the humidity climbed off the charts.

Hele Auana floated on a flat gray sea. Time slowed to a crawl.

Trident cruised back and forth in the same area. More than once the two boats passed within a hundred feet of each other. But Treadway didn't make a move to stop them.

Jack couldn't understand why the man hadn't shown himself. Treadway's arrogance would surely force him outside, if for no other reason than making an appearance to let them know he was watching.

Jack blew off the thought. Whatever scheme had been hatched was happening on shore.

And that bothered him.

He jerked his head sideways at *Trident*. "That smug bastard figures he has us beat."

Robert lowered his binoculars and rested them in his lap. "On thing's for sure, we're not getting anyplace doing this."

"You didn't think it was going to be easy, did you?"

"Easy, no . . . but I wasn't expecting impossible. I can't see shit from this far out."

"Neither can Treadway. At least we're even in that respect."

Robert raised his field glasses to his eyes. A few heartbeats later, he sang, "Fare thee well and a due to you fair Spanish maidens. Fare thee well and a due to you ladies of Spain . . ."

"So now you're on to Jaws?"

Robert pointed and said, "That looks like a big God damn dorsal fin to me."

Jack didn't need his binoculars to see the shark. A fifteen-foot tiger—the biggest he'd seen—swam up to the boat and made a lazy circle around them. "Jesus that's a big sucker."

"If we had a harpoon gun we could put a few barrels on him . . . if we had barrels, that is."

"Easy, Quint." Jack stood and peered over the side at the monster. He felt Katie brush against him when she moved to his side to check out the man-eater. Robert stood behind them looking over their shoulders.

Robert chuckled and said, "He looks hungry."

"He does at that." Jack pointed toward *Trident* and hollered down to the shark, "You've got the wrong boat. If you're looking for lunch, it's over there."

As if the shark understood what Jack had said, the tiger bumped the hull with its broad head, kicked its crescent tail, and swam off in the direction of the yacht.

"Your schooling teach you that?" Robert asked, laughing.

Jack turned. "Teach me what?"

"Talking to sharks." Robert nodded at the water. "Seems that big tiger understood what you said. Maybe you should have talked that shark out of biting Kelly instead of stabbing him in the eye."

"Who said it was a *him*?" Jack nodded in the direction of the fin slicing through the surface of the ocean fifty feet away. "I just hope that brute over there isn't around when we go into the water. One close encounter was enough for me."

"Close encounter? Stabbing a shark in the eye?" Katie pivoted and rested her weight against the side of the flybridge. "What are you two jabbering about?"

Robert glanced from Katie to Jack and said, "You didn't tell her?"

Jack sighed. He'd planned on telling Katie, but then he decided there was no reason to. That is, till now.

"A tiger shark bit a diver on my research team," he explained. "I was the only one who could help her so I stabbed the sonofabitch in the eye to make him let go. It's no big deal."

"You stabbed a shark in the eye to save someone's life and it's no big deal. You could have been killed."

"Robert's already lectured me on that point. I'd just as soon let the subject drop."

"Not until you tell me who Kelly is."

"What does it matter? If you'd been in the water when that shark attacked, I would have done the same thing. End of story."

"Fine," she looked away. "Just don't go taking any unnecessary chances."

"Chances?" he scoffed. "Shit . . . a while ago you were eager to have me mix it up with Treadway's men. Now you're worried about me getting bit by a shark." He shook his head. "I don't know

173

about you."

She pushed off the rail and glared at him. "Not wanting you hurt because of some stupid stunt you might pull and not wanting you to let Treadway's men steal the treasure from under our noses are two different things. Christ, Jack. Give it a break."

"Both of you need to cool your jets." Robert pointed his index finger to starboard. "We have a visitor."

CHAPTER 37

Jack swallowed his response to Katie's comment. She was driving him nuts. He shifted his attention in the direction of the water where Robert pointed.

He straightened.

Katie turned and stared, her hands gripping the starboard edge of the flybridge.

Robert rose to his feet and edged between Katie and Jack.

Trident slowed, throttled down to an idle, and drifted to a stop twenty-five feet off their starboard bulwark.

Robert draped his arms around his two friends' shoulders and pulled them in close to him. "What I wouldn't give for a deck lined with cannon. We could give him a broadside."

Jack stifled a chuckle. Back in the day, Treadway would have been the person flying the skull and crossbones.

"I'm with you on that," he said. "We'll hear what he has to say."

They watched and waited. A minute later, they saw Treadway make his appearance on deck. Treadway had on khaki shorts and a blue and yellow flowered aloha shirt. A Panama hat sat at a slight angle on his head. His right hand gripped a short fat glass filled with a red liquid, a celery stalk protruded from the drink.

"Smug bastard, isn't he?" Katie muttered.

"Good morning Mr. Ferrell," Treadway called out. "That is your name: Mr. Jack Ferrell?" His voice was neither harsh nor threatening. He spoke in a tone just loud enough to be heard above the engine noise.

"We can cease with the pleasantries, Mr. Treadway," Jack called back. He had no desire to talk with this man in a manner befitting friends or respected enemies. The man was neither. He had shown himself to be a thief and a killer. "What is it you want?"

"Want?" Treadway gripped *Trident's* railing with his free hand. "I want what is mine. Nothing more."

"Yours," Jack scoffed. "You only have the gall to call those artifacts yours. Your grave-robbing grandfather stole those relics and lost them. Now you're after them. You're nothing more than a glorified grave robber."

"Strong words for so early in the day, Mr. Ferrell. Especially from someone trying to steal them, himself."

Jack didn't answer.

After a moment, Treadway sighed. "I see we are at an impasse."

Jack grinned, and held it a second longer.

"A shame," he said. "You can always pack it in and sail off to wherever it is you came from."

Treadway raised his drink in salute. "Not possible. You see I mean to have those artifacts. And I will . . . it's only a matter of time."

"By that, I take it the team of men you put ashore last night aren't having any luck?"

"What makes you think I have men ashore? That's against the law, you know?"

Jack couldn't resist another smile.

He pointed at *Trident* and said, "The Zodiac, it's gone."

"Ah, yes . . . quite astute of you Mr. Ferrell."

"So tell me, Mr. Treadway, if we find the artifacts first, what then?"

"Treasure hunting is a dangerous business. Accidents happen: deadly ones."

Katie wedged her foot onto the top edge of the flybridge and started over.

Jack caught her movement out of the corner of his eye and placed a hand on her shoulder. He was sure she had it in mind to dive in after Treadway.

"Calm that Irish temper of yours," he said, "and listen."

She narrowed her eyes at Jack and said, "He needs his face slapped."

Jack acknowledged with a sight nod of agreement and told her, "Let the man have his say."

She settled her feet flat on the deck and crossed her arms tight against her chest.

Robert leaned close to her ear and whispered, "Relax and enjoy the show. Jack's having fun."

"Speaking of accidents," Jack called out to Treadway, "you owe Robert a new truck."

Treadway straightened. His calm exterior slipped.

"I owe your friend nothing," he said. "There are a lot of crazy drivers on the island. He should have been more careful."

"There are crazy boaters too, Mr. Treadway," Jack told him. "Remember that." With a sweep of his hand, he gestured toward *Trident*. "I'd hate to see something happen to that fancy yacht."

Jack noticed the corners of Treadway's lips curl slightly and slip back into a thin hard line. The man was obviously finding it difficult to control his temper.

"I'll make you a deal, Treadway said, "Let me pay you for your gas and lunch . . . dinner, too. Then go home and forget about your foolish promise to that crazy old man."

Foolish promise . . . crazy old man . . . my ass.

Jack's jaw muscles tightened, hardening his angular features. It took every ounce of willpower he had to maintain his calm.

Suddenly his concern shifted.

Dammit . . . *Katie?*

Treadway had surely struck a nerve with her too. Given half a chance, she would leap over the railing to get at the bastard.

He checked. Ready.

He breathed a silent sight of relief. Robert held her by the shoulders. But her red face told him his fear had been right on. She would have been over the side and in the water if Robert hadn't been there to stop her.

"Keep your money," Jack said to Treadway. He crossed his arms tight against his chest to hide his balled fists. "We'll take our chances."

Treadway's gaze hardened. His left eye twitched. "We'll see, then."

Jack did not wait for Treadway's next move. Speaking to Katie and Robert, he said, "Let's get away from this prick before I ram his ass."

"It's a good thing I'm not driving this boat," Katie grumbled. "I'd do it."

"Yeah, and then we'd be in the water swimming with that big-ass shark." Jack gripped the wheel and reached for the controls. "Hold on."

Robert scurried to his seat. Katie gripped the edge of the flybridge and held tight. Jack shoved the throttles forward, sending the *Hele Auana* in a large arc to the north.

When he eased off on the throttles, they were a quarter of a mile away from *Trident*. He let the boat drift. Speeding through the water helped dispel some of his anger, but he still felt like hitting something. He wished he was on the driving range with Robert. Then he could whack the shit out of a bucket of golf balls.

"That fucker!" he said, hammering the dash with his fist.

"It was all I could do to stand there and listen to that shit," Katie added. "Can you believe that guy?"

"One thing's for sure," Robert said. "I'm scratching Treadway off my Christmas list."

Robert's joking helped calm Jack's anger. He filled his lungs and breathed out.

"Might as well," he said. "I'm pretty certain he's not going to get you that new truck."

"Enough jokes." Katie slumped against the side of the flybridge and faced Jack and Robert. "What do we do now?"

CHAPTER 38

Jack shaded his eyes with his hand and tilted his face at the blazing sun. Sweat beaded his brow and soaked the pits and chest of his T-shirt. He lowered his gaze and fiddled with the bare framework of what had once been a folding canvas sunshade. The frame appeared to be in working order.

"We drift some more," he said. "And let's see if we can tie a tarp or some beach towels to this. I don't want to fry like we did yesterday."

"I know just the thing," Robert said and took off down the ladder and into the cabin. He reappeared with a red, white, and black moth-eaten blanket that looked like it had been picked up at a roadside trading post in Mexico, and a spool of 250 lb monofilament fishing line.

"Perfect." Jack stripped his sweaty shirt off over his head, wiped the perspiration from the mat of dark hair on his chest and pits, tossed the tee onto the dash, and began unfolding the blanket. He shook his head at the colorful pattern.

"Anyone sees this," he said with a chuckle, "they're going to think they've happened onto a boatload of Cuban refugees."

Robert slid off his shirt, flexed the kinks from his muscled back, mopped his tanned pecs, and tossed it on the dash next to Jack's tee. Helping Jack with the shelter, he said, "At least the sun won't be beating down on our heads."

"It's still plenty hot," Katie was quick to point out. "I hope Kazuko is okay with me borrowing one of her swimsuits." She unbuttoned the thin white cotton blouse covering the orange bikini top that barely held her breasts in and tossed it onto the deck next to her feet.

Jack stood holding the blanket and watched her unsnap her shorts, peel them over her hips, and let them fall to her ankles.

Jesus . . .

She stepped out of her shorts, scooped up her clothes, dangled them over the edge of the flybridge, and let them drop onto the lower deck. "I'm going down for a bottle of cold water. Can I get you guys one?"

Jack hadn't been able to take his eyes off her.

Damn.

The shorts and thin blouse she'd been wearing had been more than enough to stir his hormones. Seeing her standing there with hardly anything on—large breasted, firm bodied—made his head swim with desire, remembering how much pleasure they had given each other.

He felt himself becoming aroused and tried to focus his thoughts on the cold bottle of water she'd offered.

It didn't work.

He noticed her watching him stare at her. It felt as though a fist plunged into his gut. He wondered if she wanted him as much as he wanted her.

"This is stupid," he muttered just above his breath. He couldn't look at the woman and not want her.

Double damn!

He averted his eyes and to keep from reaching for her. Busying himself with the blanket, he noticed Robert ogling Katie. A bit of jealousy pricked his heart. But there was no way he could hold anything against his friend for looking.

She was beautiful.

"Some water sounds good," he said.

"Me too," Robert said. His gaze shifted about. He was obviously trying hard not to gawk at her. "And don't worry about borrowing Kazuko's suit. She has a drawer full. I'm just glad you found one that fit."

She tugged at the edges of the bikini top. "The bottoms are fine. It's the top I'm having a little trouble with."

Jack dropped the blanket.

She smiled and scurried down the ladder.

"Pardon me for staring," Robert said to Jack once she was out of sight. "But I couldn't help myself when she peeled off those clothes."

Even though Katie had just left the flybridge, Jack watched the ladder, hoping to see her climb back up. When she didn't show, he turned to his friend and told him, "Don't give it a second thought. A sight like that would make a blind man blush."

"She's a nice looking lady, no denying it."

His thoughts obviously on something else, Robert gazed in the direction of the yacht in the distance.

"Treadway really pushed your buttons back there when he called Katie's grandfather a crazy old man," he said. "You tried hard not to show it, but he did . . . sure as shittin'. I saw your knuckles turn white when you balled your fists."

Treadway had pushed his buttons, Jack thought. More than he cared to admit.

"Truth is," he said, "Treadway had all three of us going. Katie would've been over the side after him if you hadn't stopped her."

"I suppose. But this isn't about her."

"No?"

"Jack, you told me what happened in Henderson, but we never did really *talk* about it. I think that shooting screwed you up more than you think." He looked at Jack in a way that made it clear it was important for him to hear what Jack had to say.

"Scarred maybe, but killing that man didn't fuck me up. It just let me know I can do what needs to be done when it's necessary."

Robert stood looking at Jack a moment, then nodded. "Good enough. Let's get this canopy rigged."

By the time Katie returned topside, Jack and Robert had the metal frame up and the blanket tied in place. It was cooler under the makeshift sunshade, but the air was still hot and muggy without a breeze.

"I can't believe how still the air is," Katie said when she handed the guys their water.

"It makes for smooth sailing," Jack said, taking his bottle of water from her. "But I have a feeling we're in for a blow."

The hint of a rising breeze ruffled the wool blanket above their heads. The surface of the ocean rippled. He unscrewed the cap, gulped down half of the water, and lowered the container from his mouth. On the southern horizon, a bank of cumulus clouds billowed high in the sky.

A gust of wind from the south swept the bridge. He snatched their T-shirts just in time to keep them from going into the water.

"I knew we were in for some wind," he said. "If this keeps up, it's going to get messy out here."

"Can we stay out?" Katie asked. She spread her feet apart to keep her balance.

"It'll bounce us around some, but yes . . . for now anyway."

"First Treadway," Robert groaned. "Now the wind decides to come up and blow us off the water. What's going to happen next?"

Jack grabbed up his binoculars and said, "Let's not think about that now."

"Hard not to."

For over an hour, they drifted and scanned the coastline with binoculars. The south wind continued to build with the rising heat of midday. Jack found himself having to reposition the boat more often to stay beyond the two-mile limit.

At this rate, one or two more drifts would be it.

He had just shut down the engines when a gust of wind buffeted the boat with enough force to make him reach for a handhold. He focused his attention on the direction the boat drifted.

All at once the thought that had been bouncing around in his head since early that morning, jelled.

"Let's pack up and head in," he said.

"You're not giving up?" Katie gasped. "What about Treadway? We need to find that lava tube before his men do."

He flashed her and Robert his best toothy grin and chuckled.

"Don't worry about Treadway," he said. "He's looking in the wrong place."

CHAPTER 39

The wind howled a mournful tune in the rigging by the time Jack put the final cinch on *Hele Auana's* mooring lines. He stood and watched the whitecaps crest and break beyond the entrance to the harbor. No place for a small boat to be.

"We got off the water just in time," he said. "No one's searching for anything out there right now. I'll bank on that. Even Treadway on that big boat of his is being bounced around pretty good."

"Wouldn't bother me a bit if the boat sunk," Katie grumbled as she stepped toward the ramp leading to the parking lot.

Jack watched her walk. She wore the shorts and blouse, but he could still see the orange bikini top through the thin cotton material. He was glad no one could read his thoughts. There had to be a law against what was running through his mind.

"She just needs something to eat," Robert offered. "Buy her a hot fudge sundae with extra hot fudge. The chocolate will mellow her out."

Jack frowned at Robert.

His friend . . .

Jack asked, "Where do you come up with this stuff?"

Robert grinned and said, "I pay attention."

"Right."

Jack focused on Katie. Buying her a hot fudge sundae was the last thing on his mind. He left Robert standing there on the dock and jogged after her.

"Wait a minute," he called out to the back of her head.

She kept walking.

"Katie, please," he said. "You're not being fair."

He caught up with her at the top of the ramp. "Hey, I said wait a minute. Am I that hard to be around when we're not out there looking for those damned artifacts?"

She spun on him.

"I don't have anything against you," she said. "It's Treadway; I hate the man."

"Fine." Jack calmed a bit. "You hate Treadway. So do I. Robert probably does too. But why do I get the feeling you're always walking away from me?"

"Is that how you see it? How can someone as smart as you be so stupid?"

"So I'm stupid, now?"

Her eyes narrowed.

* * * *

Katie needed to breathe.

At least she hadn't lost her temper and slapped him like she wanted to. She took a gulp of air, startled at the amount of anger she'd been holding inside. And what a surprise it was to realize she wasn't just angry at Jack. That she was angry with herself as well.

She'd let their breakup fester inside her, refusing to acknowledge it was no one's fault the relationship had fallen apart. They had simply taken different paths: his, the ocean he loved; hers, the desert town she'd grown up in and a father who needed her to help put his life back together.

And still Jack occupied her thoughts, constantly.

At the moment, she felt as though she was made of glass so delicate it would shatter into a thousand pieces with the slightest touch of his hand.

Jack was beautiful. No amount of anger denied it. His eyes—as blue as the ocean that meant so much to him—could see right through to her heart. His angular chin with its dark stubble, his soft full lips, addled her brain with a sexual punch that made her want to kiss him. He was trim, fit, and bronzed dark from many hours in the sun. His shoulders seemed broader than she remembered, his arms muscled and hard as granite, his stomach flat and rippled under his tight-fitting T-shirt. The hard work of ocean research agreed with him.

She allowed herself the pleasure of admiring his body.

Her thoughts trailed off. "I can't do this," she said. "Not now."

He stood there looking at her, and she felt the heat from his deep blue eyes, seduce her.

I'm a grown woman, for God's sake. I can resist a man's charm. Even if the man is Jack Ferrell.

She closed her eyes and fought off a wave of emotion. He had a way of sneaking past her defenses every time he came near her.

Damn him. I can resist, can't I?

* * * *

Jack gripped Katie's shoulders to stop her from turning and leaving. He's seen the spark of passion in her green eyes. The fire still burned.

"You're not walking away," he said. "Not this time. We have to settle this once and for all. I can't ignore our feelings for each other. And I don't think you can either.

"Time makes it easier, Jack. What we had is gone."

"Is it?" He pulled her against him, put his arms around her, and held her tight.

"What do you feel?" he asked. "Dammit, what do you feel?" He pressed his lips to hers.

She gave in to his kiss for a few beats of her pounding heart—warm and dreamy—then pushed him away.

"This isn't the answer" she managed.

"No?"

She gazed at the ground.

"You still haven't answered my question." Jack's jaw was set, his words firm with resolve. "What do you feel?"

"Hurt!" She finally said. She looked at him through tear filled eyes. "And need. I do feel, Jack. And you drive me crazy with want every time you touch me. Is that the answer you were searching for?"

He leaned close and kissed her, slower this time, and gentle.

He pulled away from her lips, but held her close, his face inches from hers. "Now that we've got that out of the way"—his voice soft and tender—"maybe we can be civil to one another."

Katie wedged her hands between them and rested her palms flat against his chest as if to keep her balance. A gust of wind swirled her dark hair. Working a hand free, she brushed strands from her face and gazed into his sea-blue eyes.

"I love you," she said.

"What?" Distracted by her closeness and the emotions whirling around in his mind, he wasn't sure he heard her correct.

She leaned into him and kissed *his* lips this time.

Soft. Tender. Sweet.

Even as she pulled away.

"I said I love you." The tone of her voice was dreamy.

The words were familiar. They had said them to each other a hundred times. But this time they sounded different. They were laced with a sincerity he hadn't noticed before.

He fought off a shiver. "I never want to lose you, Katie."

She gazed into his eyes. "Are you saying you love me?"

He smiled, engulfed by inner warmth that coursed through his body.

"With all my heart."

With those words humming inside his head, he let his fingers slide down her arms to her hands. He held on and turned his head to search for Robert. His friend stood on the dock, watching, smiling.

"If you're ready, we can go," Jack said to Robert loud enough to be heard over the din of creaking bow and stern lines and clatter of rigging. "We have preparations to make.

Robert jabbed a thumb in the direction of their boat and asked, "What about the dive equipment?"

Hele Auana lurched in the wind. Jack watched her stretch her portside mooring lines tight. He scanned the dock. People there were climbing into cars and driving off in the direction of the highway.

"Leave it," he said. "No one is going to be poking around here in this weather."

CHAPTER 40

Jack led the way up the stairs to Buzz's Warf for a late lunch. In spite of the gale that chased them off the ocean, their mood stayed light. The tension that had hung like a dark shroud of gloom around Jack and Katie's necks since their reunion, all but disappeared, replaced by a different tension. A sexual desire bordering on animal lust that would have to be satisfied . . . and soon.

Even so, he ached to get back on the water. He'd explained his revelation to Robert and Katie on the boat ride in. The south wind was the key. Robert was the kind of guy who made sure he had the answers before questions were asked. To know he had gotten one over on Robert made him feel good.

"I can't believe I didn't Google the weather on the night Sergeant Treadway's plane went down in the channel." Robert shook his head. "It's not like me to overlook an important detail."

"Don't feel bad, buddy." Jack gave Robert a friendly clap on the shoulder. "I totally forgot about the Kona winds. The smell of salt and seaweed wafting in off the ocean early this morning should have been clue enough."

"Yeah . . . well I don't miss details like that. I'll check the internet, but you're sure about this, aren't you?"

Seeing their boat drift toward Kahoolawe, propelled by current and a strong south wind told the story. A Kona wind had been blowing hard that night back in 1944. Jack *was* sure of it. And that meant Treadway's grandfather drifted ashore somewhere along the island's central coastline.

He smiled. Just as he'd first thought.

He extended a calloused hand to Robert in an offer to shake and said, "A bottle of Don Julio say's I'm right."

Robert ignored Jack's proposed bet, saying, "I don't need to take that wager to pay up. I've got a bottle at the condo. We'll drink on your idea instead."

"Then shake on a successful mission."

The two friends shook hands.

Over the next hour, they ate burgers, talked, and laughed at Robert's jokes.

Their plates were carried away, and the double hot fudge sundae Jack ordered Katie when she left the table to use the restroom, arrived. Robert stifled a chuckle when he saw her eyes light up at the sight of all that chocolate.

Jack winked at Robert and said, "You were right."

Katie eagerly sucked a dollop of hot fudge from her spoon, savored the rich taste with an audible "Mmm," and swallowed.

"Right about what?" she asked, the edge of her question softened by what could only be interpreted as utter contentment.

Jack smiled at her and said, "Eat your hot fudge."

"Seriously." She dug her spoon in for another bite.

"Chocolate," Robert said. "A girl's best friend."

She chuckled. "You guys are terrible."

They laughed in agreement.

"I've been thinking," Robert said, his voice turning serious. "It'd be a good idea to invite Kimo along when we head back out. If we have to make a dive tomorrow—and I'm sure that'll be the case—we'll need someone to run the boat." He met Katie's gaze. "No offense, my dear. He's a boat captain and knows these waters."

She jabbed her spoon into her ice cream and pursed her lips as if she was pouting.

"Darn," she said. "I was looking forward to sailing off and leaving you two bums behind to swim home."

Jack's heart warmed. It was nice to hear her laugh and join in the joking around.

"Swim?" He said. "No way . . . not with that big-ass tiger swimming around out there. He'd have us for dinner for sure."

Katie grinned and added, "Don't think I hadn't counted on that."

"You'd do that to me." Robert gripped his chest over his heart, looking hurt. "I thought we were going to run off together."

Katie dismissed him with a flick of her hand. "That was only a ploy to see how far you would go."

"That cinches it," Robert said, straightening in his chair as though he was taken aback by her comment. "I'm getting Kimo to drive the boat."

"Good idea," Jack said.

Robert snatched up the check in spite of Jack's objections, and scurried off to pay the bill while Katie finished her sundae.

She scooped in the last bite, and they met Robert at the door.

Twenty minutes later, he braked to a stop at the curb fronting his condo and handed Jack the key to the door.

Jack eyed the key suspiciously.

Robert winked and said, "Have fun, kids. I'm going to talk to Kimo."

"Don't you want me to come along," Jack asked.

"Nonsense, I've got it covered. Enjoy yourselves."

Jack didn't argue. He had an idea what Robert was up to. He and Katie slid out on the passenger side and watched Robert drive away.

"That was nice of him," Jack said.

"What's that?"

"Him giving us time alone."

Jack took Katie's hand in his, gently gripped it, and led her to the door.

On the stoop leading inside, he paused and gazed down at her. She stood looking up at him through her wonderful green eyes.

"I do love you," he said.

CHAPTER 41

Jack lowered his lips onto Katie's in a tender kiss to expose the desire surging inside her. Her soft full lips parted to let his tongue inside as her fingers searched out his shoulders, his neck. She pulled him tight against her. A soft moan rose from her throat.

Breathless, they let their lips separate.

He fumbled with the lock. His hands shook so much he could hardly work the key. He was sure that if he didn't get the door open in the next second or two, he'd have to take her right there on the stoop or explode.

The door opened and they stumbled inside. Jack kicked it shut behind them and raced Katie to the bedroom.

His mouth crushed down on hers as they fell onto the bed together. His mind whirled with need.

"Katie." Jesus, he could hardly breathe. "This is crazy. We're crazy."

"I know," she said. "Kiss me again. Hurry."

Their tongues probed and entwined, feeding a hunger long denied. Their bodies pressed together, hands searching out familiar curves. Everything about what they were doing hurt and satisfied at the same time.

"I want you," she murmured into his ear. "God, how I want you."

Her words struck him as though he'd been hit with a hammer. He pulled away and gazed at her in the afternoon light.

He gasped, "You do?"

She tugged at his shoulder in obvious desperation to pull his chest tight against her breasts.

He'd been ready to dive into her the way he did the sea. Eager to peel her out of her clothes . . . that orange bikini. To touch her warm silky skin and have what he had let get away. But the need to explain kept him from giving in to the desire that threatened to rip his pounding heart from his chest.

"I thought you didn't," he whispered. "It hurt to let you go, but I—"

She put a finger to his lips, took a deep breath, and let it out. "I never stopped wanting you, Jack. Even when I thought I was mad at you."

He reached out and buried his fingers in her hair. Nothing more needed to be said.

The way a rising tide consumes land, he let himself be devoured by the hot-edged hunger that had driven them there.

His lips brushed her neck and found her ear. Soft moans of pleasure escaped her lips.

At the same time, he felt her fingers explore his body . . . a touch so familiar, so unbelievably sensuous it made his skin tingle.

"I want to see you," he said.

Mindful not to give in to his urge to rip her clothing off, he carefully unbuttoned her blouse.

Clearly seduced by the tenderness of his touch, she sat up and let the cotton fabric slip from her shoulders and fall to the bed. In the next moment, she undid the orange bikini top and tossed it aside.

The paleness of her breasts beneath stood out in stark contrast to the pink-brown of her two-day tan, a feast for his eyes, his touch.

"All of you," he said, dizzy with desire.

Katie undid the snap, and he pulled off her shorts.

His breath caught in his throat. *My God!*

"Now, Jack." She peeled his T-shirt off over his head, tugged at his board-shorts. "Make love to me, now!"

With those words swimming in his head, he lowered her to the bed. He ran his lips over her breasts, teased her erect nipples with his tongue. His fingertips traced the curve of her side, her hip.

They found her pubic hair and danced through the dense triangle of soft curls.

He knew how to touch her . . . how to pleasure her.

She began to moan.

His own breath caught in his throat. She was so moist with need. *My God . . .*

He felt her hips shudder under his touch as pulses of pleasure sent her soaring.

Her fingers teased the mat of dark hair on his chest. Then her hands moved lower.

She guided him into her, and immediately he engulfed himself in her silky sweetness.

Slow at first, they began to make love . . . then she took him full into her and cried out as her body tightened and shuddered in release.

He fought to control his own need to let go and took her to the precipice and over the edge again. Then he exploded into her, his moan of ecstasy merging with hers.

Her nails clawed at the skin on his back, her body bucked and jerked under him as wave after wave of sensation overtook her. Tears welled; a sob escaped her throat and ended with her crying out his name.

CHAPTER 42

Jack woke to the sound of the wind howling outside and the murmur of voices in the kitchen. Katie hadn't stirred next to him.

He lifted his watch from the bedside table and checked the time: a quarter after five.

Katie rolled onto her side and hugged the pillow.

She settled. He watched the corners of her lips curl into a smile . . . a gentle sigh of contentment.

One less demon haunting her.

He eased off the mattress, pulled on his board shorts, and stepped barefooted from the bedroom to see what the discussion was about. When he padded into the kitchen, he saw Robert and Kimo sitting at the table. They were engaged in conversation. An open can of diet Pepsi sat in front of each of them.

"It's really blowing out there," Jack said.

He saw them both turn and face him.

"Good, you're up," Robert said. "Kimo was just telling me he thinks we should go back out tonight—if the wind stops blowing, that is—and make more drifts. The open-water trolling weekend goes into effect a minute after midnight. He figures that if we can get on the water before then, we can get a head start on it if we run without lights. Treadway won't expect that. And with any luck we can be in and out of there before he figures out what's going on."

"There's also a minus tide tonight," Kimo added. "But it won't

194

be at its lowest until two. By then we can swing in nice and close and search the shoreline with my million candlepower spotlight. If that lava tube is there, we'll see it."

Jack liked their plan. He smiled and nodded in agreement.

To Kimo, he said, "So you took Robert up on his offer to run the boat?"

It was Kimo's turn to smile. "No way would I pass up the opportunity to put the screws to that rich *haole* asshole."

"I take it you're all right with what I'm doing, then?"

"You wouldn't be using my cousin's boat or my uncle's truck if I wasn't."

"I figured that. I just wanted to be sure."

"No problem, as long as you keep your promise."

"You know about that?"

"Robert explained everything."

Jack detected suspicion in Kimo's voice; saw it in the way the man looked at him. He had a gnawing feeling the old Hawaiian agreed to join the expedition for reasons other than simply driving the boat.

For a moment, Jack considered the ramifications of having Kimo along.

None.

He had no intention of going back on his promise.

"It's a plan then," Jack said. "We'll wait for this blow to slack off enough to flatten the water a little, then head out. We need the wind to be blowing enough to affect our drift, but I prefer not to be tossed around like a cork in a child's tub. The *Hele Auana* is a fine big boat, but it's not that big."

"Rubber duck," Robert corrected with a smile.

"What?"

"Rubber duck, Jack. Not cork."

Jack rolled his eyes. "Whatever."

Kimo pushed away from the table and stood. "Call me on my cell if you decide to go out tonight. I'll meet you at the boat."

"Count on it," Jack said.

He and Robert followed Kimo outside. In the heat of the late afternoon sun, they stood on the walkway in front of the condo and waved to their friend as he drove out of the parking lot. A gust of wind off the ocean—not quite as strong as those of the past hour—rustled the fronds of a nearby palm. The tempest showed signs that it might be letting up.

Robert gazed at the ocean.

After a breath, he said, "You and Katie worked things out, I see—at least for now."

Jack flashed a faint smile. "Seems so."

"No regrets?" Robert eyeballed Jack, clearly interested in what his response would be."

"Only that I let her get away in the first place." Jack shook his head from side to side and added, "I'll tell you what, something had to give. I don't think I could have survived another day the way things were going."

"So I gathered," Robert said. "Just keep in mind that conversation we had. You two belong together. There's no doubt about that. The question is: will she be willing to get on with life once this quest is over? I hate to say it, there's a chance she won't. I don't want to see you beating yourself up over her decision if she doesn't."

"Not going to happen."

"Her not changing or you not beating yourself up over it?"

"Take your pick."

Robert looked at Jack as though evaluating what to say. "Right . . ." he said, and started up the walkway. "What do you say we go inside and you wake up that girl of yours so we can hear what she has to say about our plan?"

Katie emerged from the bedroom just as they walked through the front door. She had on a white terrycloth robe pulled tight around her.

"Did I hear talking?" She fought back a yawn.

"Kimo was here," Jack said from the front door as he walked over to her.

She reached up and caressed his cheek with her fingertips. He touched her hand. Soft smooth skin. Warm. Her eyes, green as emeralds, wide open and focused on his. Pupils large and dark as pools of oil in the dim light.

He struggled to control his breathing.

196

"Kimo thinks we should head back out tonight," he said. "If the wind slacks off."

She smiled sheepishly. "And use darkness to get the jump on Treadway?"

"You were listening?"

"No. It's just that I was thinking the same thing."

"Why on earth didn't you say something?" Robert asked before Jack did.

"I'm not really sure . . . it's dangerous out there at night. I figured it was a stupid idea."

"Well it's not a stupid idea," Jack said. "And I think we're all in agreement on that."

"So we're going?"

"If the wind dies down enough . . . and it looks like it's going to."

"How do we get around the two mile limit?"

"You're forgetting the first open-trolling weekend for the month begins at 12:01 tonight," Robert said. "In the dark we should be able to move in nice and close to the shoreline."

"Plus there's a minus low tide at two in the morning," Jack added. "That means the opening to the lave tube will be exposed."

"Great." She glanced anxiously back and forth between Jack and Robert. "But it'll be dark. How will we see it?"

In a reassuring voice Jack said, "Kimo has some monster spotlight he's bringing along. If the lava tube's there, we'll see it."

"Be a good idea to ice down some bottles of water and cans of Pepsi. And I'll whip up a pile of sandwiches to take with us." She was wide awake now and all smiles. "It's going to be a long exciting night."

CHAPTER 43

From atop the flybridge, Jack watched Kimo stride down the dock with a SCUBA tank hanging from each hand and a massive spotlight strapped on his back. At sunset, the wind slacked off just enough to make it safe for them to be on the water. Overhead, patches of dark clouds billowed and floated by.

Jack could tell the clouds retained their moisture. So far the lull held, but he kept a nervous eye on the sky and water in the quickly fading sunlight.

"Robert," he hollered down to his friend who stood on the rear deck, fussing with the switch on one of their dive lights. The beam flashed on and off. "Kimo's here and he's lugging a couple of extra tanks and that big-assed light of his. You wanna give him a hand before he busts a gut."

Robert moved to the starboard railing and took the tanks from Kimo, who hefted them across one at a time. That done, Kimo lifted a nylon strap over his head and handed over the gigantic spotlight he'd told them about.

"Shit this thing weighs a ton," Robert said, adding a second hand to keep from dropping it.

"It'll burn a hole in your retinas if you look into the lens when the light's on," Kimo warned. He held out a small nylon bag he'd unclipped from a belt loop on his cutoffs. "You and Jack might need this."

"What ya got there?" Jack asked from his perch.

A sly grin creased the old Hawaiian's face.

"An underwater GPS," Kimo said, nodding in the direction of a vessel bobbing in a slip across the harbor. "I borrowed it from Seaport."

Jack had noticed contempt flash in Kimo's eyes. The man obviously held on to the belief Seaport owed him for lost wages.

Perfectly understandable as far as Jack was concerned.

He focused his gaze on the fancy forty-one foot sport-fisher backed into its slip, outriggers raised. The cabin stood out dark and lonely. He didn't need to see the name *Ellery Queen* painted across the stern to know the boat. Even from a hundred yards away in the growing darkness, he recognized the lines of the Hatteras. He'd captained Thomas Seaport's expensive toy for a short time while engaged to his daughter Ellery. But not until after Seaport ordered him to fire Kimo.

He still felt the sting of having to prove his loyalty to the rapacious bastard. That's what the firing had been about, and no one could convince him otherwise. Not that anyone besides Robert tried. And now that he was thinking about it, he believed it fitting Kimo took the initiative to borrow Seaport's GPS.

The payback was well deserved.

"Good thinking," Jack said. "Now let's get this show on the road."

Fifteen minutes later, they left the protection of the harbor. Behind them the lights of Maalaea showed bright. Above them the slice of moon had already climbed high in the sky. Its cool white light shimmered off the surface of the water lighting their way. But even so, Jack had to keep their speed down to be safe.

So much can happen on the ocean, especially at night.

From his vantage point on the flybridge, he scanned the sea. A lone figure at the helm—the way he preferred it. Below him on the rear deck, Robert and Kimo leaned against the transom, talking. Katie had retired to the cabin.

All's well.

He relaxed and breathed in the ocean air—with only his thoughts for company.

So much could be resolved on a night like this.

In the glow of the moon, he could just make out the dark shape that was Kahoolawe in the distance. Beyond, the horizon melted together in blackness. He had spent many a long lonely hour on the bridge of his father's salmon boat, staring at the black waves of a rolling sea, a carpet of stars overhead for a ceiling. It was easy for him to understand how early seamen could think they would fall off the edge of the world if they sailed too far from land.

A half an hour out, Robert and Kimo climbed the ladder and joined him on the bridge.

He made eye contact with Kimo and gesturing at the wheel with his free hand, asked, "Feel like taking the helm for a while?"

"Sure," Kimo said. "Get some rest if you want to."

"I just want to check on Katie."

"She's in the cabin," Robert said, sagging into the portside seat.

Jack turned the wheel over to Kimo and went below. It was easy to fall back into the rhythm of being with Katie as a lover. They fit together nicely when their conflicting worlds didn't get in the way.

He found her sitting at the galley table, her chin resting on her fists. A gas lantern burned on the tabletop in front of her.

"Asleep?" he asked.

She raised her head. "Just thinking."

He wanted to believe she was thinking about him, them together as a couple . . . the lovemaking they'd shared only a few hours earlier. But deep down, he knew something else plagued her thoughts.

"Thinking about us?" He smiled. He held onto the hope that was the case after all.

Her expression remained stoic.

He wondered if she had heard him.

"Conception," she said. "Death. Why a person's life turns out the way it does."

"The meaning of life?" Jack scoffed. "People have pondered that question since the dawn of time."

"Not people, Jack." Her voice had a slight edge to it. "I was thinking about myself—how things turned out for me, not everyone else in the world."

"So you *are* talking about us?"

A faint smile creased her lips. "I guess I am."

"We just need to move forward, Katie. There's no changing what happened to either of us. The future is new and fresh. We can make it what we want."

"Can we? Or are our lives written ahead of time by a higher force?"

"Can't answer that. But I do know I want to think I have control over what's yet to come. And I plan to make the years I have left the best they can possibly be."

"You sound awfully sure of yourself."

"I am. Now, turn off that lantern and come outside with me. It's cooler on deck and the night sky is fantastic."

"I'm still worried you—"

He raised his index finger to her lips. "You worry too much." In the same breath, he pulled his finger away and said:

One day the madam of a brothel opened her door to see a rather dignified, well-dressed good-looking man in his late 40's or early 50's standing on the stoop.

"May I help you?" she asked.

"I want to see Valerie," the man replied.

"Sir," said the madam. "Valerie is one of our most expensive ladies. Perhaps you would prefer someone else?"

"No. I must see Valerie," the man replied.

Just then, Valerie appeared and announced to the man that she charged $1,000 a visit.

Without hesitation, the man pulled out ten one-hundred dollar bills, gave them to Valerie, and they went upstairs.

After an hour, the man calmly left.

The next night, the same man appeared again, demanding to see Valerie.

Valerie explained that no one had ever come back two nights in a row—too expensive—and there were no discounts. The price was still $1,000.

Again the man pulled out the money, gave it to Valerie, and they went upstairs.

After an hour, he left.

The following night the man was there again. Everyone

was positively astounded that he had come for the third consecutive night.

But again he paid and again he and Valerie went upstairs.

After their session, Valerie questioned the man. "No one has ever been with me three nights in a row. Where are you from?"

The man replied, "South Carolina"

"Really" she said. "I have family in South Carolina"

"I know," the man said. "Your father died, and I am your sister's attorney. She asked me to give you your $3,000 inheritance and that's what I did."

The moral of the story, three things in life are certain: Death, taxes, and being screwed by a lawyer.

Katie opened her mouth, a word forming on her lips and hanging there. She sighed, and after a moment said, "Leave the joke telling to Robert. They don't sound near as funny coming from you."

"It was that bad?"

"I guess there are worse things."

He gazed at the bulkhead, and right through it . . . all the way to the water off the south end of Kahoolawe where they had last seen Treadway. He was out there still . . . somewhere.

"Yeah," he said in an almost whisper. "And he's on that yacht."

CHAPTER 44

The rain hit hard. A squall swept in on *Hele Auana* like a runaway freight train. The downpour only lasted five minutes. But in that brief period, enough rain fell to drench the deck and everything topside.

Jack and Katie scurried into the protection of the cabin to stay dry. Amid their laughter, they could hear Robert and Kimo thumping and bumping on the deck above them. They couldn't help laughing even harder knowing their two friends had to be getting soaked.

When Jack was reasonably sure the clouds weren't going to open up on him, he started for the door, turned and said, "I'm going to check topside."

When he looked at Katie, she covered her mouth with the palm of her hand to keep from laughing. A snorting sound came out instead. He started to laugh, making a kind of snorting sound himself. That made him want to laugh all the more. He clenched his jaw tight behind his smile to get control.

They had lost all semblance of composure. It felt good to let go . . .

At the top of the ladder, Jack paused and held on. Robert and Kimo sat huddled under the dripping blanket sunshade staring at him.

He asked, "A little wet up here?"

"It depends on what degree of wet you're referring to," Robert groaned.

"Go down and dry off. I'll take it from here."

"You're on."

Jack edged past Robert and Kimo and took a seat behind the wheel, giving them room to climb down. Once they were below, Katie climbed up and joined him.

They looked at each other trying hard not to laugh. It wasn't quite working. They giggled like schoolchildren.

He hooked a finger in the direction of the rear deck and asked, "Did you see those two drowned rats scurry down the ladder?"

"Yeah. They were positively soaked."

"To the bone." He swallowed one last chuckle.

He had barely collected himself when a drop of water streaked his cheek.

"Shit," he said. "I've been slimed."

That did it for Katie. She started laughing all over again.

"That's not funny," he said as he began folding down their makeshift sunshade that Robert and Kimo had raised to block the rain. "I don't *even* want this damned blanket dripping on me. No telling what those stains are."

Katie managed to stop laughing and helped him fold the top down. The cloud that drenched the boat and his two friends moved on, opening up a dazzling display of stars. Lower on the horizon behind a dense bank of clouds in the distance, the moon was hidden, keeping the sky dark, and the tiny pinpoints of twinkling light, vivid in the clean air.

He slouched in his seat, laced his hands behind his head, and stared at the heavens, letting his knees steer the boat.

"I do love a clear night sky," he said to her after a quiet minute. "Especially on the ocean."

"Reminds me of the desert," she said. "Stars as far as you can see."

The wind whipped a wisp of her hair into her mouth. When she reached to tuck the wild strands behind her ear, she lowered her gaze. In the distance, lights from a lone boat glowed bright in the night.

She pointed. "Is that Treadway's yacht?'

"Probably. With a search team ashore, I doubt he's strayed too far." He grabbed the set of binoculars hanging from the hook next to him. "Too dark to be sure, but yeah, it's him."

"That means he'll be able to see us."

"Not when we switch off our running lights."

"Is it going to be safe?"

"We'll be drifting when we do. Plus we'll have four sets of eyes keeping a watch on the water around us. As long as the moon shows itself again, we should be fine. It's when we turn on that big-ass spotlight of Kimo's and start flashing that beacon around that we'll stand out. I just hope it takes Treadway a while to realize he's been had."

"And if it doesn't?"

"I don't think he's a man of words."

"You'll be careful?" She placed a clammy hand on his arm.

"We'll all need to be careful." He rose to his feet and peered into the darkness at the landmarks he could barely make out. "I think we're about where we need to be. I'm going to begin a drift."

"Robert," Jack hollered down, his hands cupped to his mouth to keep his words from being swept away by a gust from the south. "Hand me up the chart and the GPS. It's time to find out if I'm right about this Kona wind."

CHAPTER 45

Jack shut down the engines and switched off the red, green, and white running lights. Without the reassuring rumble of the twin diesels for comfort, a lonely silence settled in. He fought off a shudder of helplessness. They were a dark spot on a black ocean. The only noise was the slap of the waves against the hull.

"Now we drift," Jack said in a voice just loud enough to be heard. "Eyes on the water."

Robert's head appeared above the top of the ladder. He held the GPS unit in his right hand with a finger hooked around the rung in front of him. He groped for the top rung with his left.

Jack reached to help his friend up.

The wind that had slacked off minutes before gusted.

Hele Auana lurched.

"Shit!" Robert cried out. His left hand flailed as his head dropped from view below the flybridge.

Before Jack could grab his friend's hand, a loud thump sounded from below.

He scrambled to the ladder and looked down. Robert lay sprawled on the deck. But he was moving.

Jack let himself breathe.

"You okay?" he asked.

"Busted my ass," Robert groaned, rubbing his butt. "But yeah, I'm fine."

Jack watched Kimo reach with his left hand to help Robert to his feet. It appeared as though Kimo was holding his right arm tight against his body to immobilize it. "You sure you guys are all right."

Robert rubbed his butt. "I said I was fine." He held up the GPS he'd been holding. "Your GPS isn't, unfortunately. I think I landed on it."

"Never mind the GPS." Jack strained to see Kimo in the darkness and asked, "Kimo, you okay?"

"Not sure," Kimo said. He bent and straightened his right arm at the elbow a few of times. "When Robert fell back, he landed on my shoulder and damned near tore my arm out of its socket."

Jack left the boat to drift and hurried down the ladder. He didn't bother with the last few rungs and dropped to his feet.

Katie watched from above.

Jack wouldn't let himself believe the worst. Not tonight. Everyone had to remain healthy and in one piece if they were going to have any chance at all of succeeding.

"How's it?" he asked Kimo. "Nothing broken?"

"Arm's okay." Kimo raised his right arm a few inches and slowly rolled the shoulder joint while massaging it with his left hand. "Shoulder hurts like hell, but I don't think it's dislocated. I should be fine to drive the boat. But I don't think I'll be doing much heavy lifting."

Jack gave Kimo's injured shoulder a good long look.

Fuck!

He took the cracked GPS from Robert and fingered away a piece of plastic housing. He gave the unit a shake, heard the insides rattle.

"Dammit," he said. "I don't like the way this night's starting out."

Robert shrugged. "We still have the GPS Kimo brought along."

Jack tried switching on the broken navigational device. Nothing happened. No surprise there.

He handed the unit back to Robert and said, "One's better than nothing. But we won't be able to set up a rendezvous point like I hoped. We needed two GPS units to do that: one for us in the water so we'd know where to be waiting and one for Kimo on the boat so he'd know where to pick us up."

"What were you planning on doing before Kimo showed up

with that second GPS?" Robert asked. "You had to have had some plan in mind."

It was Jack's turn to shrug. "Truth is, I hadn't really thought about it."

"There's another way," Kimo said. "I'll just have to steer in close to shore while it's dark and drop you two off to do your exploring. You can flash a light or something when you want me to come back in and pick you up."

Jack took a few breaths to consider the situation. He didn't like the odds of ripping out *Hele Auana's* bottom on some unseen coral outcropping in shallow water, but he liked the option of making a long swim at night with fifteen-foot tiger sharks cruising the area even less.

Realizing they had little choice, he nodded imperceptibly and said, "We won't need those fancy rocket boots if we do that. Sorry, Robert. But it's best if we don't have to mess with them unnecessarily."

"Damn," Robert said. "I was really looking forward to the ride."

Jack patted Robert on the shoulder. "We'll take them to the beach when this is over with and play. Right now, they're just something else to worry about. And we don't need them banging into any unexploded ordnance."

"Wouldn't that be a blast?"

"Literally," Jack said. He turned to Kimo and asked, "Can you climb the ladder? I'd like to have four sets of eyes on the water from up there. It makes me nervous to be drifting out here without any lights on."

"Don't worry," Kimo said. "I can make it." He turned his face to the sky and added, "At least we have *Hinaikamalama's* light shinning down on us."

Jack hadn't discounted the moon. But would it be enough?

He watched a fresh bank of clouds move in front of the bright crescent.

They were thrust into darkness.

He said, "You mean, did."

CHAPTER 46

On the flybridge, Jack switched on the borrowed GPS and read off their coordinates. Robert—with Kimo keeping watch—fought the chart to keep the wind from blowing it out of his hands.

Jack noticed the map wasn't cooperating.

"Don't bother trying to plot 'em," he said. "We can always do that later if we need to. Just write them down. "

The south wind continued to blow, though not quite as hard as the gust that sent Robert flying. Overhead, the clouds remained dense and impenetrable to the moon's light—a menacing reminder of the squall that drenched them earlier.

Caught in the grip of the wind and the current, *Hele Auana* moved ever closer to Kahoolawe.

Kimo held Jack's high-powered binoculars pressed to his eyes. "Night Marchers," he announced, pointing to the south.

"Night Marchers?" Jack took the binoculars from Kimo and raised them for a look-see. "What are you talking about? Where?"

"There." He pointed again.

Jack saw them, the light from three electric torches bounced along the shoreline way to the south of them.

Treadway's search team.

"Not Night Marchers," he said. "Treadway's men."

"What are Night Marchers," Katie asked, straining to see what Jack and Kimo were looking at.

"Spirits . . ." Kimo breathed with a hint of wariness. "*Ka huakai o ka po: Marchers of the night.* All Hawaiians believe in the power of spirits to return to the area they knew on earth in the form in which they appeared while alive."

"These *Ka hua ka ka* . . ." she attempted.

"*Ka huakai o ka po,*" Kimo corrected.

"These Marchers of the Night," she went on. "Are they your run-of-the-mill zombie type dead people, or is there something special about the way they died . . . like being murdered or something?"

"There are many types, but the spirits are usually chiefs or gods who march on paths they marched on in life. Thunder, lightening, and a sudden downpour of rain occur when Night Marchers march."

Katie gasped. "We had that downpour just a while ago."

Jack chuckled. "Superstitious, are you?"

"I just want to be prepared." She turned her attention back on Kimo. "What happens if you run into one of these Night Marchers?"

"You don't want to interfere with the *Ka huakai o ka po,*" Kimo warned.

"They can hurt you?" Katie asked, clearly caught up in the legend.

"Usually, a spirit marches ahead of the procession, calling out *kapu*—a warning for the living to flee. Unless one of the person's *aumakua*—family spirit—is among the marchers, a spearsman will kill anyone who lingers."

"What if you can't run?"

"Then you must take off all your clothes and lie down face up, breathing as little as possible."

Kimo's answer piqued Jack's interest and made him smile. He'd heard the legend; and he knew what a person was supposed to do when confronted by Night Marchers: prostrate yourself before the chief is what he'd been told.

He decided he liked Kimo's version better. "I can see it now. A pathway full of naked people."

You're serious?" Katie asked Kimo. "You really have to take off all your clothes?"

"It is the best way. They will pass you by thinking it is a shame for you to lie there uncovered."

"And if you don't take off your clothes?" Robert asked.

Jack wanted to laugh. Robert had been the one who told *him* the legend . . . and retold it . . . and retold it—usually when they were hanging out on the beach at night, drinking beer and shots of tequila. Obviously, Robert was playing along with Kimo's taking-your-clothes-off version as well.

"Then you must lie perfectly still and close your eyes," Kimo said, the tone of his voice remained serious. "And hope they think you are dead."

"Does it work?" Robert questioned, appearing concerned he might have to take his clothes off in front of someone.

"Sometimes." Kimo made a violent stabbing motion and said, "But more likely the guard in front will kill you."

"Glad I'm not bashful," Robert glanced down at himself. "My clothes are coming off for sure."

"Mine too," Katie said. "I certainly don't want to be skewered by some native spirit."

"You do that"—Jack winked at Katie—"and I'll join you. We'll really give those spooks something to look at."

"We make jokes," Kimo said. "But remember this: the *Marchers of the night* are real."

CHAPTER 47

After a half hour more of listening to waves slap the hull, Jack called out a third set of bearings to Robert and mentally plotted them. On their present course, they'd make landfall a full two miles north of where Treadway's team of henchmen searched.

He smiled; confident he had solved the mystery.

He'd know for sure soon enough. He just hoped they didn't tear the bottom out of the boat in the process.

A distinct possibility.

He heard waves breaking on the shoreline before he saw the jagged lava. The others obviously did too. They stared expectantly into the darkness. The cliffs stood out a dim shadow barely visible against the night sky, the rocks at the water's edge were coal-black basalt appendages of doom for boats straying too close to the coast. He cranked over the engines and breathed a sigh of relief when diesels rumbled to life.

"The tide is not all the way out yet," he said, and waved a finger at Robert. "But it might be enough. If your butt's up to it, turn on that big assed spotlight you hauled up here and let's have a look-see."

"My butt's fine," Robert grumbled, reaching for Kimo's light.

"I'll have to take your word on that."

"Smartass." Robert balanced the million candlepower spotlight on the dash and switched it on. A bright cone pierced the blackness. The base of the cliff lit up a hundred yards away. He swept the rocky shoreline with the beam looking for any sign of an opening to a lava tube.

All eyes were on the circle of light probing the nooks and crannies along the tide line. Only Jack divided his attention between the rocks on shore and the water around the boat. He still had the receding tide and coral outcroppings to worry about.

A mishap here would doom the expedition.

The search was slow going. For over an hour, he motored *Hele Auana* south along the cliff. He was following his instincts, now, as though an unseen conscious from above guided his way. And maybe that's what it was.

They were close; he could feel it.

Several times he throttled back so they could focus the beam on a promising shadow or cleft in the rock.

But each time they came up empty.

"Tide's almost out," Robert said. "And there is only so much coastline along here for us to search. You'd think we would have spotted the opening by now. It's my guess the military blasted it to bits."

"I've considered that possibility," Jack said. "Ever since you told us Navy sub commanders used these cliffs for target practice."

"No one said this was going to be easy," Katie chimed in.

Jack chuckled mockingly. "No shit."

"Speaking of shit," Robert said. "Did you know it has been scientifically proven that if we drink one liter of tap water each day, at the end of the year we'll have absorbed more than one kilo of Escherichia coli—*E coli*—the bacteria found in feces. In other words, we're consuming one kilo of poop each year. But we don't run that risk drinking beer, wine, rum, whiskey, tequila, Vodka or liquor of any kind, because alcohol has to go through a purification process of boiling or filtering or fermenting, or any combination thereof."

"Your point?" Jack asked. He had an idea what was coming.

Robert grinned and said, "Water equals poop. Liquor equals health. So it's better to drink liquor and talk stupid than to drink water and be full of shit."

"Is he always like this when you two get together?" Kimo asked, looking at Jack.

"Mostly. But then you know how he is."

"Do I? That's not how he is around me. He must save those gems for you."

Jack saw Robert smile.

"What can I say, Jack?" Robert threw his free hand up in front of him in a helpless gesture. "You bring out the best in me."

"Just keep shining that light," Jack told him. "That lava tube's here, and we're going to find it."

As if Madam Pele had stepped in to lend assistance, the clouds parted and the wind slacked off to almost nothing. The partial moon lit up the water around them. The swell rolled ashore but with less force.

Wondering if the worst of the weather was past them, Jack scanned the sky above the horizon to the south. He saw only blackness. Then his hope shattered when he saw a sliver of lightening streak the sky over the Big Island sixty some-odd miles away—too far to hear the rumble of thunder. But it was there.

Is this the lull before the storm?

He didn't want to think that was the case.

His eyes dropped below the horizon. The lights on *Trident* stood out as bright dots on a slow-moving shadow. It appeared Treadway had the boat's generators running at full capacity. With the south wind reduced to that of a light breeze, the deathly quiet of night returned. Even the slightest sound carried effortlessly across the water. In the stillness, between the crashing of waves, he thought he caught the faint sound of music onboard the yacht a mile and a half away.

Jack felt his face tighten.

Smug bastard, indeed.

He watched the yacht a few seconds.

You might not be worried about being seen. But I am.

He stared anxiously at the round circle of bright light sweeping the shoreline. All he could do was hope the storm held off, and that Treadway didn't notice the unmistakable beam from the powerful spotlight and decide to come looking.

Another half-hour passed. Jack considered and re-considered

all the cards stacked against them . . . against him and Katie. Then, out of the corner of his eye, he saw Kimo straighten.

"There," Kimo called out.

The Hawaiian's voice startled Jack. He turned to see Kimo pointing toward shore. Robert held the light steady. Everyone's eyes focused on the spot.

Jack centered his attention in that direction. There was only one thought on his mind now.

They had found the lava tube.

An oblique shadow maybe two feet high at the tallest point and eight to ten feet wide showed above the wave line below a protruding shelf of lava at the base of the sloping cliff. The beam of light seemed to disappear into the darkness inside.

A lava tube.

But that wasn't all.

Concentrating on what lay before them, he narrowed his eyes until his brows knitted together. A couple of beats of his pounding heart later, his forehead relaxed a bit. But his gaze remained firmly locked.

Not on the cave itself. But on the object wedged in the opening.

A torpedo!

CHAPTER 48

Coleman Treadway sipped Napoleon brandy from a crystal snifter and savored the soothing sound of Mozart's Symphony #28 in C Major. Yvette played devilish eye games with him from where she lay sprawled on the sofa on the other side of the luxurious salon. Her flirtations intensified with the melody.

For a split second, he considered dragging her to his cabin for amusement. His French pet would be more than willing to help him recapture some of the elation he'd experienced earlier in the day when Boryenko informed him his men had located a lava tube and were investigating.

But he wasn't in the mood.

The artifacts weren't there. The team had to keep looking.

He let his eyes close. He simply wouldn't allow himself to dwell on simple setbacks. Besides, he was a dozen steps ahead of Jack Ferrell. The search team would find the artifacts and secure them aboard *Trident* before Jack and his friends even figured out where to look.

The buzz of the intercom stirred him from his revelry. He pressed the button below the speaker.

"This had better be important?" His irritation showed through in his voice.

"Hate to trouble you, Sir. But could you come topside?" The heavily accented voice of First Mate Hayden Fiske, the brash young

Aussie recruit standing night watch on the bridge, boomed from the speaker. "I think there is something you need to see."

Treadway fought off the wave of annoyance. What could there be of interest for him to see at night.

"What is it?" he asked, impatient.

"A spotlight, Sir."

Treadway knitted his brow in thought. He hoped he was wrong. "Pray you're not mistaken."

He didn't wait for a response.

He burst through the doorway leading to the bridge ready to feed another member of his crew to the sharks. He wouldn't stand for any more incompetence.

"What do you mean, spotlight?" he asked with an edge to his voice sharp enough to cut frozen meat. "Where?"

"There, sir, about a mile and a half off our starboard bow." Fiske pointed a shaky finger. "Isn't that a spotlight?"

He held his breath.

Treadway stepped toward the broad windscreen and faced the tinted glass. The red-orange illumination from the instrument panel lit up his scowl in an unearthly glow. To the north, he saw a bright white beam pierce the night and light up Kahoolawe's rocky shoreline.

He grabbed the binoculars out of the first mate's hand and held them to his eyes.

"Jack Ferrell," he muttered a moment later. Perhaps he would keep Fiske around a little longer. He'd proved useful.

Treadway didn't like mistakes, least of all his own.

The south wind had changed the line of drift.

Admitting he had become overconfident and narrow minded in his search was not something he was going to do . . . to himself or anyone else.

He'd simply miscalculated.

His grip tightened on the field glasses as he lowered them from his eyes and fought off an urge to hurl them at the glass. His mind filled with the image of Jack Ferrell holding up his middle finger in defiance.

So he thinks he's outwitted me.

Treadway swallowed back his rage. Jack Ferrell had managed to anger him yet again. Twice in one day. That type of unmitigated insolence was not acceptable under any circumstances.

Jack and his friends would have to pay the price.

Death!

The game, Treadway reassured himself, was far from over. He would not accept failure, ever.

He gave himself a quiet moment to think and plan.

His mind calmed as it always did. And having considered his options, he decided to give Jack and his crew of misfits some time and space to work. He'd let Jack think he'd outwitted him, and wait to see what they turned up. If they found the prize, he would simply move in and take it.

He laughed to himself.

Regardless, they would die.

CHAPTER 49

Jack kept an eye on *Trident's* lights. The yacht showed no indication of a major course change. He had expected Treadway to be steaming their direction and couldn't believe the asshole hadn't seen the powerful spotlight.

Nothing Treadway had done over the past week led Jack to believe the man was anything but shrewd and careful. It was possible the asshole was asleep in his fancy stateroom, or that the light had not aroused his lookout's suspicion.

But Jack wouldn't let himself believe that . . . not even for a second. The man's treachery would not allow their spotlight to go unnoticed.

Treadway had to be up to something.

He just hoped he was wrong about Treadway steaming toward them to intervene. They needed time to investigate the lava tube—time to navigate a minefield of ordnance—time to find a way past that unexploded torpedo.

In daylight, the task would be hard enough to pull off safely. At night, it was going to be damned near impossible.

"What do you think, Kimo?" Jack peered over the side at the dark water and then at the shoreline. "Can you get us in close enough so we don't have to swim too far?"

"If you stand on the bow with the light shining in the water and guide me, yeah. Otherwise I wouldn't chance it."

Jack turned and faced Robert. "You ready to get wet?"

Robert grinned and said, "You mean wetter . . . sure."

"It's a plan, then." Jack saw Katie knit her luxuriously thick eyebrows at him. It was obvious she was concerned about him and Robert diving in that inky blackness.

"Relax," he said to her. He stepped close, reached, and gently cupped her chin with his right hand. "We'll have dive lights to guide us in." He pulled his hand away, but not before he let his fingertips glide lightly along her cheek. "It'll be a kaleidoscope of color for us once we switch them on."

"I want us to find those relics," she said. "But I don't want you injured. Promise me you'll be safe."

Jack flashed his best grin.

"Piece of cake," he told her.

He expected a comment back.

She just looked at him in the moonlight as if the wanting in her eyes alone would keep him safe.

For a full ten count, he couldn't tear his gaze away from her beautiful emerald green eyes . . . and those wonderful thick brows that drove him crazy. Finally, he made himself forget about all one hundred and twenty-five pounds of sensuality he was leaving behind . . . what he had to lose if something went terribly wrong.

He couldn't afford the distraction.

He faced Robert and said, "Time's a wastin'."

"We'd better wear wetsuits and weight-up heavy," Robert suggested.

"Is the water that cold?" Katie asked.

"No," Jack answered. "But we don't know what we'll be rubbing up against in the darkness so it's best to have a little protection."

Robert winked at her and added, "It's positively creepy down there if something you can't see brushes your bare skin."

Jack noticed Katie hug herself and rub her arms. He couldn't help smiling at her uneasiness. She had broken out in gooseflesh, no doubt imagining the ocean's nasties they'd be encountering under water.

"Don't let Robert scare you," he said. "It's an aquarium down there."

Her silence betrayed her uncertainty.

Ten minutes later, suited up in a blue and black Body Glove eighth-inch neoprene nylon-two Farmer-John style wetsuit, Jack stepped to the bow rail, kneeled, and clicked on Kimo's spotlight.

The powerful beam stabbed the water, lighting up the seabed thirty feet below.

He waved a hand, and Kimo edged the boat forward.

The bottom rose surprisingly quick.

Two hundred feet from shore in about fifteen feet of water, he threw up a hand in a signal for Kimo to stop. In the heavy surge, he didn't want to chance getting any closer. Jagged ridges of black lava and coral-encrusted rock jutted up from the bottom ready to gut the boat.

He lugged the heavy spotlight aft and hopped to the rear deck. Katie was there to meet him. Robert—suited up and ready to go—arms crossed in front of him—leaned against the starboard gunwale.

They were waiting on him.

He handed Katie the spotlight—which she took with both hands—and to Robert, said, "Let's get this show on the road."

Robert nodded at Jack's dive equipment on the deck and said, "Waiting on you."

In the moonlight, Jack saw a tank, regulator, and buoyancy compensator rigged and ready.

"Now why didn't I know that?" he said.

He helped Robert with his tank and got a thumbs-up.

That done, he made a quick visual check of the dive gear sitting on the deck to satisfy himself the equipment was hooked up correctly. It was. He pressed the purge valve in the center of his Scuba Pro regulator. An expected spurt of air hissed back at him.

"Let's do it," he said. And with Robert's help, he slid his arms into the buoyancy compensator and buckled it on.

Two minutes later, they stood at the port side gunwale. Armed with a Princeton Tec underwater light and a four-inch dive knife strapped to his right calf, Jack slid on a pair of dive fins, grabbed his mask, spit into it, rubbed the saliva around with his finger, and rinsed it in the ocean.

Ready, he flashed Robert a thumbs-up and said, "Don't go scaring anything down there."

"You're the shark killer," Robert replied with a chuckle. He slid on his mask, inserted his regulator into his mouth, and rolled over the side.

"Fucker," Jack said too late to be heard. He positioned his mask over his face, put his mouthpiece in, and tumbled backwards into the water.

The sea below the surface was absolute darkness—an enveloping blackness with no up or down, just total nothingness. Jack switched on his dive light and saw Robert do the same. Their flashlight beams swept across each other.

Jack adjusted his mask, tilted his head back, pressed his fingertips to the top of the faceplate, and exhaled through his nose to purge the water that'd seeped in. Pinpoints of light danced on the surface—starlight reflected by the water.

He circled his thumb and middle finger at Robert and saw his friend answer with the same okay sign.

No further communication between them was necessary.

They purged air from their buoyancy compensators and sank slowly to the bottom. The cool seawater that leached through Jack's wetsuit and collected on his skin quickly warmed to body temperature making him feel safe and secure. Almost dreamy. Had it not been for the coral surroundings, he could have been submerged in the oversized bathtub in his condo in Oregon.

Jack spread his legs and settled onto his knees when his flippers touched bottom. A strong surge made it exceptionally difficult for him to hold his position. Robert settled onto the sand next to him, and they began swimming on a heading provided by the compass strapped to his wrist.

The water to the side and behind them remained an inky void. Ahead—in the beams of their handheld lights—the coral lit up in a brilliance of color that Jack always found a little startling at first sight. In the daylight, the coral would be a drab greenish brown with only an occasional display of muted red. The light from their flashlights brought out the natural colors. He saw reds, yellows, whites, and oranges. Raccoon Butterfly fish, Moorish Idols, and

Sergeant fish darted in and out of the light beams—their bright black and yellow striping showing up in stark contrast—as did the colors of the Yellowfin Goatfish with their bright yellow lateral stripe.

Jack was surprised at how relaxed he felt. Even when a four-foot moray eel swam out of a crevice to investigate the light, his mind did not register concern. He felt warm and cozy, totally at home in the sea. So much so he forgot why he was there. All those brightly colored sea creatures swirling around him.

He removed his regulator from his mouth feeling as though he no longer needed it.

He could breathe with the fish.

CHAPTER 50

Jack felt a vague sensation of having a regulator jammed into his mouth. There was a spasm in his chest, a retching sound.

His own.

He breathed in, gagged, and threw up in the mouthpiece. He blew out and sucked in a sour-tasting breath, then another and another and another. The fog began to seep away from his consciousness.

A voice called out in the distance. No, it was next to him . . . a familiar voice calling his name. His mask was ripped off. He felt the night air on his face and heard the voice again: Robert yelling.

He saw a translucent white beam waving back and forth in the darkness. It came from something in Robert's hand: his underwater light.

Jack rolled his head to the side. The hull of a boat . . . he could see the hull of a boat next to him.

After what seemed a year later, he felt hands grip his arms, his body being lifted, his butt thump against something hard.

"Jack . . . Jack . . . you with me?" Robert repeatedly slapped Jack's cheek. "Open your eyes . . . there we go . . . that's good. Look at us, Jack . . . let us know you're all right."

As the remaining layer of fog lifted from his consciousness, Jack felt scratchiness in his throat and tasted sour, acidy vomit. His brain felt like it would split open inside his skull. He heard Katie plead: "What the hell happened? Is he all right? Tell me he is okay."

Then her face appeared above his, staring down at him. Her hands stroked his hair back. Her voice: "Jack, talk to me. Are you okay?"

Jack managed to keep his eyes open and whispered, "Yes."

"That was close," Robert said. "Too damned close."

Jack forced himself up on one elbow, coughed several times, and studied the three nervous faces watching him.

"What happened?" he croaked. "I was fine, then I wasn't."

Robert held Jack's regulator under his nose and pressed the purge valve. Air from the tank shot up his nostrils. "Carbon monoxide." He scrunched up his face. "By rights you should be dead."

"I'm not sure I'm not," Jack said, his voice sounding more like his own. The scratchiness in his throat seemed to be easing.

Katie pulled his head onto her lap and continued to stroke back his hair.

She asked Robert, "How could something like that happen?"

Kimo spoke up. "Jack's tank is one of the two you left aboard. Robert, you have one of mine. Someone had to have tampered with your tanks."

Robert retrieved the other tank they'd left onboard that first night and opened the valve. He leaned close to the rush of air and took a whiff. He turned his head to the side.

"Carbon monoxide," he said. "Just like the other one."

"Fuck! I can't believe I didn't notice the air was bad." Jack rose to a sitting position. He was getting over the effects of the CO2 poisoning and getting mad. "Jesus, I'm an experienced diver for God's sake."

"Don't beat yourself up, Jack." Robert set the bad tank next to the one he'd removed from Jack's back. "It's not pure carbon monoxide. They only spiked the air in the tank with enough to do the job."

"Whoever did this definitely knew what he was doing," Kimo said. "My guess is Treadway has a compressor onboard that fancy boat of his. Probably funneled exhaust fumes into the intake. It's a good thing Robert took one of the tanks I brought onboard or you two would be floating belly up out there."

Jack struggled to his feet and leaned against the transom. All eyes were on him and he knew his friends were anxiously awaiting his next words. He could tell by the way they looked at him—even Katie—that no one wanted to be the one to say give up and go home.

The decision was his to make.

CHAPTER 51

Treadway lowered the powerful binoculars from his eyes for the tenth time in as many minutes. He cursed the darkness.

It infuriated him to not be able to see what Jack Ferrell was up to. He'd switched off the boats running lights but movement of the beam from the spotlight showed their boat neared shore. They were taking a closer look . . . but at what?

Had they found the lava tube . . . the artifacts?

The questions ate at him like a cancer. Not even Yvette's tight ass could keep him below decks.

She'd tried . . . always ready, always wanting. He'd thought a few rounds of sordid sex-play with her would help pass the hours while Jack did the work. But he had quickly tired of her games.

There was only one game on his mind and that was securing those relics.

Enough of waiting.

He picked up a satellite phone, punched in a number, and held it to his ear. "Boryenko," he said several seconds later, "Looks like Jack has found something on the coast north of you. Leave Fuentes and Diederich there to continue the search, you take the Zodiac and see what it is Jack has found."

"Maybe the surprise we left for them will save us some trouble," Boryenko answered, reassuringly.

"Perhaps . . . but I don't want to take the chance they discovered their tanks had been tampered with."

"Sir, I assure you I only put in enough CO2 to do the job. It would have taken a few minutes—"

Treadway raised his hand in a quieting gesture as though the Russian could see him and said, "I'm not doubting your skills, my trusted friend. You certainly know your job, well. But we can't be too careful."

"I think I would like it better if they are still alive when I get there."

"Have I not allowed you your indiscretions?"

"I do what you expect of me. But there are some things I need to do for myself."

"You're still upset about Idaho?"

"They got lucky."

"Not this time. I've grown weary of their meddling. If they are alive when you get there, do what you like with Jack and his blonde-haired friend. But remember this, the woman's mine. I have plans for her."

Treadway heard Boryenko laugh the way he did each time his twisted pleasures were about to be satisfied. He smiled to himself. The big man's undivided loyalty would not go unrewarded. Perhaps he'd let Boryenko have a turn with the meddlesome woman before he disposed of her. The Russian's sexual appetite—not unlike his own—required a special type of partner: young women who would not—or could not—complain to the authorities.

Katie McIntyre would not live long enough to complain to anyone.

First Mate Hayden Fiske clearly had not wanted to interrupt. He stood, waiting.

Treadway switched off the satellite phone and said, "Get Captain Ward up here. We're changing course."

Treadway stepped to the windscreen and stared into the dark. He didn't like feeling as though a rug was being pulled from under his feet. He'd planned on giving Jack and his team of do-gooders time to complete the work. But then he'd seen their boat move close to shore. That meant they had found something. He couldn't chance the treasure would—by an underestimation of cunning on his part or simple accident—slip between his fingers.

His quest for the world's valuable antiquities had taught him that even the best plan was not foolproof. And that improvisation was the key to true success. He pictured Katie: brash, young, willing to scratch his eyes out if given the chance. Now he had another plan for getting his hands on the treasure.

One he liked even more than just swooping in at the last minute like a common pirate to take it from Jack.

CHAPTER 52

Jack inhaled several deep breaths. The fresh ocean air leeched the poison from his system. But not all at once. He knew the process would take time, time they didn't have. Treadway would not sit back and wait. And neither would they.

He wasn't about to let that rich asshole win.

"We've got two good tanks," he said. "That's more than enough air for Robert and me to swim in, have a look around, and swim out."

No one spoke for a moment. And in that couple of beats of his heart, he believed he saw a spark of relief in the eyes of his friends.

"Are you sure, Jack?" Katie stepped close to him and placed the palm of her hand on his cheek. "You don't have to do this."

Jack took her hand in his and kissed it.

"Don't I?" he said. "I made your grandfather a promise, remember?" He faced the night sky envisioning heaven high above them and added, "The old guy's up there now, waiting to see if I'm a man of my word."

"He's up there," she said. "But I also know he'd understand if you decided it's too dangerous to continue. He wouldn't want you to kill yourself over a box full of artifacts. It's just not worth it."

The yacht's lights blazed in the distance. He'd made his promise. He'd keep it.

"And let Treadway win," he said, "no way."

"The man's a persistent bastard," Robert offered. "No telling what he'll do next."

"Bastard is right," Jack agreed. "But he's not going to get his grubby hands on those artifacts. I won't let that happen."

Robert nodded and sighed. "There's other ways to resolve this, Jack."

Jack straightened, bolstered by resolve.

"Not for me," he said.

"At least give your body a chance to purge the poison from your system," Kimo suggested. "Better yet, let me go."

Jack could feel the lingering effects of the CO_2 poisoning. He ignored the pounding inside his head.

"The promise I made wasn't just to Grandpa Charlie," he said. "I made a pledge to myself. No one is doing this for me."

Three sets of eyes stared at him, but no one said a word.

Jack figured his friend's could tell by the resolve in his voice it was useless to debate the issue further.

"I'll change out your tank," Robert said, a few uncomfortable seconds later. "You stay there and breathe in as much fresh air as you can."

Twenty minutes later, Jack hoisted his tank and buoyancy compensator atop the gunwale and slipped it on. He buckled the strap tight and slid on a pair of leather gloves—an added piece of protection from the sharp edges below. He intended to minimize the chance he was taking. Katie hovered close, but didn't say anything to try and change his mind.

He was glad for that. He pressed his clammy wetsuit against her breasts in a hug tight enough to carry them both through the dive. And when he released her, he kissed her in a way to remind her they were more than friends.

"It'll be a piece of cake," he said, holding her by the shoulders.

She offered a shaky smile.

"You said that last time," she pointed out.

He purged a burst of air through his regulator and grinned.

"Air's better this time around," he assured her. "In there and out . . . ten minutes . . . fifteen, tops."

He pulled her close for a reassuring hug. Over her shoulder, he noticed *Trident* make a course change. The brightly lit side windows of the salon slipped from view and he stared at the red, green, and white running lights. The yacht was heading straight for them.

They'd have to work fast.

He and Robert rolled off the gunwale together, their dive lights switched on. This time there was no shock at the sudden display of color, no staring at fish. They swam off in a direct line for the lava tube.

Jack heard the underwater drone of *Hele Auana* motoring off. A lonely sound, like a sad farewell between parting friends . . . or lovers.

But that was not the case.

Kimo and Katie would cruise back and forth a safe legal distance from shore, he reassured himself. And bring the boat back in close when he and Robert flashed their lights signaling they were ready to be picked up. Their hope was that in the darkness, Treadway wouldn't know exactly where to look for the lava tube, giving him and Robert time to enter the cave, find the relics, and swim out.

That was the plan they had all agreed on. Now they just had to make it work.

Running the risk of using up a large portion of their precious oxygen supply, Jack set a vicious pace toward their objective.

Don't hold your breath to conserve air. Just breathe normal, he kept reminding himself.

He hoped Robert did the same.

In spite of the bass-drum chorus thumping inside his head, Jack's vision remained clear, the fog had disappeared. But the unrelenting headache made it difficult for him to concentrate. He was sure the remaining effects of the CO_2 would wear off soon.

Several times during their first minutes of the dive, he exchanged anxious glances with Robert. He knew his friend worried about him being back under water so soon and wanted to assure him he was okay. Each time he caught Robert looking his direction he circled his thumb and middle finger and motioned ahead.

In there and out . . . ten minutes . . . fifteen, tops. That's what I told Katie.

Jack used the reminder to keep them forging ahead. They

couldn't waste even a second.

To the sides—at the fringes of their light beams—coral-encrusted lava jutted up in a menacing wall of jagged edges. A couple of feet beneath them, the seabed was course sand with an occasional outcropping of lava for them to negotiate around.

Taking it all in, Jack realized they were swimming in a sort of trough leading to the lava tube—a gouge in the island where molten rock had once flowed like a river.

The current from the waning tide tugged and pulled at them in this underwater conduit. One moment they could barely make headway using hands and flippers. The next, they rocketed forward, uncontrollably.

Near shore, the surge worsened.

A section of reef jutted out in front of Jack, but he couldn't stop.

He was at the mercy of the surge catapulting him forward.

Unaware that the carbon monoxide in his system slowed his reflexes, he extended a gloved hand too late and slammed into a wall of coral and rock.

He groaned into his regulator and pushed off, only to be sucked backwards.

Again, he was at the mercy of the surge.

He grabbed hold of a basket-ball-sized chunk of lava protruding from the sand and held on. He searched out the source of Robert's light beam and noticed he'd done the same.

And he was pointing.

Jack aimed his Princeton Tec dive light in that direction and strained to see through the swirling silt.

At the farthest reach of his vision, a jumbled mound of coral and algae-encrusted lava that stood out in contrast to the surrounding area, littered the sandy bottom. Above the rock fall, a wedge of darkness swallowed his light beam. And directly above that, the bottom of a long, massive, algae-covered cylindrical tube hung at an angle just below the turbulence on the surface.

The torpedo!

They had reached the opening to the lava tube.

Jack sucked in a breath and held it in spite of everything he'd learned about diving. He swore to himself he had just seen the torpedo rock back and forth in the surf.

Only an inch or two, but it had moved!

Fuck!

Had the mass of fallen rock and the unexploded torpedo not been there to block the entrance to the lava tube, they would have had an unobstructed opening extending a good eight feet under water.

An easy swim in.

Instead, they faced an unstable barrier of high explosives.

CHAPTER 53

Jack sloshed back and forth in the tidal surge like a drunken sailor on shore leave. By holding onto fissures in the rock outcropping with the fingers of both hands and digging the tips of his fins into the sand, he maintained his position.

They didn't have time to spare.

But plunging forward without a plan could lead to certain death.

He checked his air gauge: 1600 pounds. He'd started the dive with a slight overfill of 2300 pounds per square inch.

Robert had to have a couple of hundred pounds less than that. He'd used at least that much on the first dive.

What he feared had happened. Fighting the current and vicious surge was eating up their air supply at an alarming rate.

He checked his watch. They'd been down fifteen minutes already.

Surely, Katie didn't actually expect them to be in and out that soon.

The minutes were counting down and they still had to get inside the cave to see if the artifacts were even there. And in the meantime, Treadway wouldn't be content to cruise around up top and watch.

The parasite would do anything to stop them.

But what . . . ?

Jack knew it wouldn't be good.

His heart raced.

They had to get inside and find those artifacts.

In the swirling silt, it was hard for him to tell the size of the opening at its tallest point, but he believed he could squeeze inside if he wasn't wearing his air tank. But he still needed the lead weights in his buoyancy compensator to hold him down or he'd float to the surface like a cork and be smashed against the rocks by the waves.

What he wouldn't give for an old-fashioned weight belt.

He knew he was breathing way too fast. And at that rate, he'd quickly bleed his tank dry. If that happened, he would have to surface and risk death in the waves pounding the cliff.

He had to relax or he'd never make it in and out of the lava tube alive.

He noticed Robert was waiting for him to lead the way inside. He almost wished the roles were reversed and Robert was the person calling the shots.

Enough seconds had been lost thinking about what he was going to do. It was time to finish what they had come there for.

Damned torpedo.

He couldn't ignore it. The way the instrument of death sloshed back and forth in the tide, it could go off at any moment without any help from him.

He raised his palm in a signal to wait, felt a slack in the surge, swam over, and grabbed hold of Robert's outstretched hand just in time to keep from being swept into the wall of jagged rock.

Without wasting even one more second trying to use hand signals to explain his intention, he unbuckled Robert's tank, pulled it from the BC, and handed it to him. Then he turned his back, hoping his friend had caught onto the plan.

There was no mistake. Robert pulled the tank free, handed it to him, and motioned ahead.

Jack gave the okay sign and waited. His timing had to be right.

The surge slacked as a wave crashed and rumbled ashore.

Now or never.

Jack kicked hard toward the opening, shined his light inside, and squirreled through the gap between the jagged rock and the torpedo, dragging his tank behind him.

Dropping to the floor of the lava tube behind the barrier of stone, Jack discovered the surge wasn't as bad as it had been on the other side. But above him, the sea funneled through the opening with the force of a fire hose.

He'd been lucky.

He couldn't help worrying about Robert.

In the next instant, he felt the tide slack off.

Now, Robert. You can do it.

Robert's tank came through first, followed by his light, then his body.

Jack watched his friend sink to the silt five feet away just as another rush of water streamed through the narrow opening.

Jack made a move toward Robert and stopped.

Something was wrong.

Robert's light beam bounced around.

He was struggling . . . but with what?

Jack pointed his underwater torch at Robert's left hand. A large moray eel had clamped down on his fingers. The eels' writhing, curling body was tying itself into a knot around his wrist.

Robert groped, trying to grab the creature behind its head. But the eel had already begun pulling his hand through the knot using his coiled body as an anchor. Had it not been for the heavy leather glove, he'd have lost his fingers.

Jack gripped his tank by the valve to drag it with him and kicked off to help.

When he reached his friend, Robert was pounding the eel with his right fist. But the eel seemed unaffected by the blows. Its jaws continued to work.

A fraction of an inch at a time, the back-slanted teeth drew Robert's fingers deeper into its mouth.

CHAPTER 54

Jack drew the dive knife from the scabbard strapped to his calf. His only thought was to stab the eel the way he had the tiger shark.

He raised the blade, and started forward.

A fraction of a second later, he saw a flap of leather tear away and wisps of blood rise from a crescent hole.

The moray unknotted itself, lashed once at Robert's arm, and slithered over the rock pile. Jack followed the creature with his light beam until it disappeared from view on the other side.

He turned the circle of light on Robert who'd focused his own light on the injury to his hand. Robert flashed him an OK with his thumb and middle finger and reached for Jack's tank to return it to the mount on his BC. Jack had to trust that his friend was all right.

With their air tanks in place on their backs, they swam another forty feet before the sandy bottom began to rise sharply. Sixty feet in, their heads broke the surface.

Jack rolled onto his butt in three feet of water, pulled off his fins, and stood up. For a few beats of his thumping heart, he just stood there staring through his faceplate. Then he spit out his regulator and slid his mask onto his forehead.

He heard Robert rising out of the water a few feet to his left and noticed he had his mask perched on his forehead and his regulator out.

"Fucking unbelievable," Jack said, flashing his light beam around the cavern.

Robert's beam crossed and re-crossed Jack's.

"You got that right," Robert agreed. "I find it hard to believe no one's been in here since Treadway's grandfather."

"Access to the island is restricted—specifically, no diving. You know that." Jack jabbed a thumb over his shoulder in the direction of the opening. "And let's not forget about the torpedo. Five hundred pounds of live explosive is a deterrent for anyone in their right mind."

"Didn't stop us."

"I said anyone in their right mind." Jack grinned. "We're stupid."

"You think so?" Robert swept the ceiling and walls with his light. "Get a load of this place."

The beam from Jack's Princeton Tec pierced the blackness in front of him. The tunnel continued on, looking like a half-flattened radiator hose that was being pressed down on by a giant hand from above. The lava tube was about fifteen feet wide and perhaps ten or twelve feet tall. The darker, coarser basalt was coated with a smooth, thin, metallic-like coating that made the rock appear as though the stone floor, walls, and ceiling had been glazed over to give them a silvery luster.

"Looks like we're inside a glazed doughnut," he said.

"You're right about the 'glaze' part," Robert explained. "Actually, it's a coating of magnetite crystals. The luster comes from the tiny facets of magnetite on the surface."

"Looks like something out of Jules Verne's *Journey to the Center of the Earth*."

Robert chuckled. "Where are the giant mushrooms?"

Jack shot him a look and said, "That's where they found the dinosaurs. We don't need any prehistoric monsters getting in our way."

"They found the lost city of Atlantis, didn't they?"

"No lost city here," Jack said. "Just a crate full of precious artifacts if we're lucky."

Twenty feet in front of them, coarse sand and crushed coral had washed in over the millennia to form a beach on the sloping stone. The beach ended six or seven feet above the surface of the water, marking the high-tide line.

Jack sloshed ashore and deposited his dive gear on the sand. Robert did the same. Had it not been for the lava grotto, Jack would have sworn they were on a secluded beach in Kihei.

He pointed his beam into the tunnel. "I hope these batteries have a good charge."

Robert added his beam to Jack's. "Just pray there're no dinosaurs."

They took cautious steps forward to where the beach ended, then stopped to probe the tunnel with the narrow cones of light. The lava tube continued on with a gradual slope upward before the tunnel disappeared from view around a turn to the right thirty feet in. The inside of the wall there slumped and flattened out about four feet above the floor to form a rock shelf.

Both of their lights settled on the top edge of this shelf and held fast.

"Holy shit," Jack said. He took a couple of steps closer. "There it is. Do you know what this means?"

Robert nodded, his mouth agape.

He swallowed. "We got here first."

CHAPTER 55

From two hundred yards away with his naked eye, Treadway could not only see *Hele Auana's* running lights, which had just switched on, he could make out her shadowed silhouette against the moonlight shimmering on the waves. The boat had moved offshore into legal waters.

He raised the binoculars, again cursing the night.

The moon made it easy for him to spot the boat, but the bright crescent moved in and out of openings in the clouds blowing past overhead. There wasn't enough light to illuminate the deck and whoever was onboard.

With the aid of the powerful lenses, he studied the boat. There were two people on the flybridge. Looking at their dark profiles, he couldn't tell for sure which two. But judging from the long hair and curve of breast, one of them was the woman.

Katie.

Seeing Katie was no surprise. He hadn't figured her to be a SCUBA diver. That was Jack Ferrell's specialty. Since it appeared there were only two people onboard, he had to assume Katie and Jack's blonde-headed friend had dropped Jack near shore. It would make sense Jack's friend had stayed aboard to drive the boat.

He clenched his jaw. He was sorry now he had made the decision to have Fuentes join the search team. If he had left him at the harbor to keep an eye on the boat, he would know for sure who was aboard.

He swept the shoreline with the field glasses. If Jack was on shore, it was because they had found the lava tube.

The smart ass might even already have my artifacts.

Again, he brought his gaze to bear on *Hele Auana*. The boat had moved from its position of a minute ago, but just barely. Another sign Jack was ashore, searching. No doubt, Katie and his friend were idling back and forth waiting for a signal to steer in close and pick him up.

He wasn't about to let that happen.

"You know what to do," he said over his shoulder to Captain Ward. "Take us in close on our port side, but stay to their stern. I want to lure Katie down off the flybridge. And make sure Fiske and Dolon are ready. I don't want any foul-ups."

"Yes, Sir . . . I've already done that, Sir. They'll slip over the starboard side the moment we stop."

Treadway stepped from the bridge as the two boats came together. There was ten feet of water between them, just enough distance to keep the waves from smashing the hulls into each other.

"You've been busy, Ms. McIntyre," Treadway didn't attempt to hide the irritation in his voice. "I truly did not expect to see you out here in the middle of the night with the weather the way it is. All sorts of bad things happen in the dark."

Katie gripped the edge of the flybridge. "You can go fuck yourself."

"Such talk for a lady. You surprise me."

"I'm sure you've heard it before. A man like you brings out the best in people."

Yvette—wearing a white sheer robe parted in front, exposing her red lace bikini underwear and bare breasts—stepped from the bridge and stood next to Treadway. He caressed her shoulder while holding her in his gaze. "Fortunately, not everyone shares your opinion of me, or your naive ethics."

"Then she's as vile a person as you are."

"Ah yes . . ." Treadway smiled, clearly amused by her comment. He turned and motioned toward Kimo with his hand. "I see you've added a new member to your crew. That must mean Jack and that blonde-headed friend of his are ashore looking for my treasure."

"Fuck off, Treadway," Katie said. "This isn't your treasure."

"Quite the contrary. My grandfather found it, so by rights it belongs to me."

"Those relics belong to the dead, not the living."

"Such a noble thought for a filthy mouthed whelp of a woman. Your poor grandfather did a lousy job of raising you."

"What do you know about my life?"

"A person with money can find out many things."

"Then you know my grandfather was a wonderful man. He did everything for me."

"I know you had a whore mother and murderous father."

Obviously, Treadway had pushed Katie's buttons to the breaking point. She flew down the ladder and dashed across the rear deck to the transom where she was closer to Treadway.

She seized the railing in a death grip that turned her knuckles white and glared at the multi-millionaire.

"You're a pig, Treadway." She practically spit the words out as she said them. "A filthy, vile pig." Her body shook.

Kimo strode next to her and placed a calming hand on her shoulder. In a clear sign of defiance, he raised his chin at Treadway and said, "It's time you leave."

Treadway grinned. His plan was working perfectly. Both of them had taken the bait.

"Stand there beside her if it makes you feel better," he offered. "But this is between me and the young woman."

Katie silently glared at Treadway. The edge of a rain-filled cloud moved in front of the moon. She could still see him in the dim cool light, but not his nasty grin. He'd turned into a faceless silhouette.

"I'm only calling a spade a spade," Treadway said. He had to keep her attention focused on him.

"Kimo's right," she said. "You have no business here. Leave!"

"Ah, but I do."

Treadway's pulse quickened when he saw his two men slip aboard the rocking boat unnoticed. When Fiske's long muscled arms wrapped tight around her breasts from behind in a massive bear hug, he grinned with satisfaction. Time was up for her and the Hawaiian.

"Easy there, Sheila." Fiske's voice was unmistakably Australian. "Don't want you to hurt yourself."

"Let go of me." Katie kicked backwards at her attackers shins. He gripped harder. She gasped.

Kimo turned to help and was clubbed down by her assailant's partner.

She shrieked a strained feeble sound as Kimo fell. The old Hawaiian lay limp and unmoving on the deck. Her anger turned to fear as she fought to take a breath against the Aussie's vise-like grip.

"Get this ape off me," she groaned. You have no right to be doing this."

Treadway laughed. "Surely you have a few minutes to spend with an old friend."

The cloud that plunged them into darkness, moved on and the moon eased into view. The boat lit up around Kimo's body sprawled on the deck next to Katie. An oily wetness glistened in the hair on the back of his head.

She spun on Treadway and glared in the direction of his self-righteous smirk. She visibly swallowed as if fighting an urge to throw up.

"I have nothing for you," she said. "Time or otherwise."

"But Jack does." Treadway waved a hand. "Fiske. Dolon. Bring her."

Katie screamed and felt a hand clamp over her mouth. The next moment she was flung over the side.

Hauled onboard the yacht by her two attackers who had jumped into swells after her, she coughed and gagged salt water.

She stood soaked to the bone on the aft deck of the yacht. A puddle forming at their feet, Fiske—with a smug smile—and Dolon—his tattooed arms crossed in front of him—flanked her on both sides.

She planted her fists on her hips, raised her chin, and glared at Treadway and Yvette standing in front of her.

"You'll pay for this," she said. "I promise you; you'll pay."

"Wrong." Treadway motioned for her to be brought inside. "*You* will."

Fiske's hand clamped so quickly, so painfully around her arm, he left her with no choice but to comply.

"Put her in Yvette's cabin," Treadway said as Katie was ushered past him.

Katie's gaze fixed on Yvette, clearly catching a look from her. Unmistakably feral. The evil that showed in the woman's eyes and the curvature of her mouth betrayed her wickedness.

The golden tan seeped from Katie's face as she was dragged into the dimly lit salon. Treadway watched with satisfaction from the doorway, well dressed, straight backed, and square shouldered. A jackal, but looking very much the part of being a prim and proper gentleman.

"You can't do this," Katie screamed, as she was drug into a companionway and down steps leading into the bowels of the yacht.

CHAPTER 56

Jack worked the sharp edge of his heavy-bladed dive knife into the slit between the lid and the box and pushed down on the black plastic handle. He moved the blade a few inches down the widening gap and repeated the process.

He and Robert had lifted the wooden crate—about the size of a steamer trunk—to the floor of the lava tube and were kneeling beside it, surprised by how well the wood had withstood the ravages of time and moisture. Their guess was the wood had been preserved with a coating of creosote or similar type of waterproofing.

"How are we going to get this crate past that torpedo?" Robert asked, the tone of his voice anxious with anticipation. He held both lights steady as Jack worked at the final corner.

"We'll figure out something." Jack shoved down on the handle of the knife. "First, let's see what we have."

A final nail squeaked loose.

"Got it!" Jack said. He slid the lid aside.

Robert leaned in close with their lights.

"I'll take that," boomed a voice, clearly Russian.

Jack jerked back reflexively at the unexpected sound of a voice behind them. Robert did too. Apparently, he hadn't heard the man slip from the water, either. The constant sloshing of the tide flowing in and out of the lava tube made it impossible to hear someone rising out of the surge, especially from thirty feet away.

And a visitor was the last thing either of them expected.

Jack turned to look behind him at the same time Robert did. A huge hairy-knuckled fist hammered the side of Robert's jaw.

Robert went down on the stone floor and stayed there. The dive lights spilled from his hands, illuminating the cavern.

Jack recoiled from the attack and raised his knife in self defense. A foot crashed into his wrist.

The knife flew from his hand and skittered across the rock.

He stumbled and fell.

Without a second's hesitation, he crabbed backward and managed to get to his feet.

"Who the hell are you?" he asked. The words spewed from his mouth without a thought as to what he was saying.

"I am glad now," the Russian said, "I missed you and the girl on that bridge."

Jack's jaw tightened.

"The Hummer," he said, thinking out loud. "You rotten sonofabitch, you tried to kill us."

The big man smiled. "And now I get to finish the job."

Stooped low, feet wide apart, arms raised in front of him, he came at Jack in a sort of half-circle as though he were a grizzly bear expecting to squeeze the life from Jack's body.

Throaty growls and mutterings in Russian escaped his lips as he moved in for the kill.

Jack sidestepped his attacker, shoulders down, braced.

His heartbeat raced.

He spied his knife where it had skidded to a stop on the floor of the tunnel, five feet away from where he was standing. He took a step in that direction.

The big man moved in front of him.

Jack swallowed.

With little choice, he raised his fists defensively, and stared into the Russian's dark eyes—wild, primordial. King Kong, that was what he called the big man who had chased Katie and him into the desert—the man he'd shot and killed. The name fit here, too. So did Sasquatch.

But this time he was armed with a four-inch knife.

And he'd already lost that.

The Russian made a grab for his wrist.

He pulled away and swung his fist down hard on Big Foot's forearm. His knuckles connected with a solid slab of muscle.

The Russian grinned.

Jack readied himself, his hand throbbing from the blow.

It felt like he'd struck an oak limb.

Clearly unaffected by his attempt to inflict injury, Boryenko sidestepped in an obvious move to come in from behind.

Jack turned with the big man in a deadly dance.

Low, guttural sounds continued to emanate from the Russians throat as he waved Jack toward him with his fingers.

Jack knew he was being taunted into a fight. He had no intention of taking on the hairy giant by himself unless he had to. He chanced a glance at Robert. He hadn't moved from the spot where he'd gone down.

"You never did tell me your name," Jack asked, trying to buy himself some time. Robert could come to any moment. Maybe together they'd have a chance against the Russian Big Foot.

"Does it matter?"

"Guess not."

The big man smiled. "Boryenko."

Robert moaned, causing Jack to turn his head and look.

Boryenko lunged.

Jack caught the movement out of the corner of his eye and rolled sideways. Somehow, he managed to come up on his feet.

Boryenko crashed into the crate spilling it on its side. In spite of his size—moved incredibly fast. He was on his feet in a second and coming straight at Jack, knuckles bared.

Jack took a step to his left, but not fast enough.

A fist as hard as a block of granite, struck him a glancing blow on the side of his head. An explosion of lights burst inside his skull.

Boryenko grabbed him around the chest, pinning his arms to his sides. He could feel the life being squeezed out of him.

His vision blurred.

He lifted his feet and heaved with his arms in an effort to loosen Boryenko's hold on him so that his body would slide free.

The vise tightened around his chest.

He felt himself blacking out. His thought at that moment was that he was going to die in a lonely hole in the ground, with a pile of two-hundred year-old relics and a dead friend for company.

His life shouldn't end this way.

He moved closer to the edge of darkness. A nightmare, this was all just a nightmare. He'd have an opportunity to hold Katie in his arms again.

Then the vise lost its hold on him and his butt hit hard on the stone floor. The rock walls and ceiling came into focus, but his mind still wasn't tracking all that well. But it tracked enough for him to know he had to move, had to get away from Big Foot.

He rolled and rose to his feet on wobbly legs. His mind cleared and the scene in front of him began to register.

Robert stood stooped at the waist, feet spread, legs bent, chin against his chest, his left hand gripping his knee for support, and a cantaloupe-sized stone weighting down his right hand. Boryenko stood a couple of yards away moving his head from side to side like a prizefighter shaking off a punch from his opponent.

"Robert," Jack muttered. He took a step toward his friend.

A roar like nothing Jack had heard before pierced the air.

Big Foot.

He turned and saw Boryenko standing ten feet away with blood streaking down his cheek. Even in the dim light from the two underwater electric torches cast aside on the stone floor, he could see the fire in the man's eyes. But that wasn't what worried him. The big Russian gripped the dive knife in his right hand.

And it was pointed at them.

CHAPTER 57

Katie stood in the middle of Yvette's cabin. Fiske had her arms pined to her sides. His long, strong fingers dug painfully into her biceps. Yvette and Treadway stood with their backs to the door, their eyes fixed on her. She tried to pull free.

"You can let go of her now," Treadway said to Fiske, stepping to the side far enough to expose the doorway. "And wait outside."

Katie jerked out of the man's grasp and rubbed the red finger marks on her arms where he'd gripped her.

She raised her chin at Treadway. "What have you done with Kimo?"

Treadway didn't answer. When the door closed solidly behind him, he faced her and said, "I'm afraid there has been a tragic boating accident. Your Hawaiian friend and that scow you called a boat rests on the bottom of the ocean with the fishes."

Katie felt a tear well in the corner of her eye. "You kill a kind old man and talk as though it was nothing."

"That old man *is* nothing."

"He has a family, kids . . . people who love him."

"That is of no concern to me. And I advise you to not waste any more time worrying about him. It's *you* that you should be worried about."

She wiped the tear from her eye and stiffened. She had to be strong.

"So what happens now?" she asked. "You hold me prisoner here?"

"Something like that."

His eyes narrowed into a steely glare. He added, "Forget about whatever it is you're considering. You and your friend Jack Ferrell have caused me enough problems. If you think that for even one second I would hesitate striking a woman, think again."

He'd obviously noticed her glancing around the room. Her back remained straight. Her eyes focused on his. "I'm sure you're the kind of man who takes pleasure in hitting women."

His mouth tightened into a narrow hard smile.

She sucked in a breath, held it.

He stepped close, clamped a strong hand around her left wrist, and leaned to within a few of inches of her face. "If I wasn't a civilized man, I'd break you . . . one bone at a time."

She stepped back and struggled against his grip. Her Irish temper spiked. She raised her right hand, poised palm open, ready to slap his face. "Get your fucking hand off me, you pig."

Her words met the back of Treadway's hand as it slammed into her cheek.

Stars exploded in front of her eyes. Her knees weakened.

She found strength and straightened.

Fighting back a flood of tears, she slowly brought her face back around and glared at him.

Treadway met her stare and held it firmly in his own. Silent seconds passed. There was no mistaking the resolve that settled in his steel-gray eyes.

She braced herself.

"Young lady," he said—his tone matter-of-fact. "There are many people in this world who believe torture and corporal punishment have no place in modern society. I for one do not agree." His tight smile returned. "I am a firm believer pain and swift, decisive punishment is important for maintaining discipline and control."

"That includes children, I suppose."

Appearing to ignore her comment, he stepped to a teakwood cabinet secured to the bulkhead and poured two snifters of brandy from a crystal decanter sitting on a tray on top. He held one out to Katie.

"Have a sip of this my dear," he said. "It will warm you in your wet clothes."

She couldn't believe Treadway. What kind of man talks about how much he likes to inflict pain, hits a woman, and then casually offers her a drink?

A psychopathic monster.

She couldn't help worrying about what he would do next. Even so, she wasn't about to bow down to him.

"Keep it," she said. "I don't drink."

He shrugged. "Have it your way." He handed the snifter to Yvette. "Fetch her a towel. She's quite wet."

Katie managed to remain defiant and strong, but felt herself coming apart inside. Perhaps she should have taken the brandy.

She clasped her hands in front of her to keep them from shaking. "I don't need a damned towel. What I need is for you to stop playing this game and tell me what it is you have planned for me."

"Ah, yes . . . you are most astute. This has turned into a game— one I have no intention of losing. As to your question about what am I going to do to you . . . ?"

She saw his gaze shift to her breasts.

She followed it there and noticed her erect nipples and large dark areolas showing beneath her wet t-shirt.

Modesty was the least of her worries but she wouldn't give him the satisfaction. She crossed her arms against her chest to cover herself.

He chuckled. "Relax my dear. It's not me you need to worry about. My French pet Yvette will be the one who'll see that you don't get lonely."

"So am I supposed to believe rape is not part of your agenda?"

"Rape. Another one of the ugly words you're so fond of." He took a sip of brandy from the remaining snifter and said, "You do like annoying me Ms. McIntyre. I won't deny I take women when and where I want them. But I assure you, they come to me willingly."

"Now I guess I'm supposed to show my gratitude for your wholesome hospitality by being a good little captive?"

"Show me gratitude . . . ?" He threw his head back and laughed.

"You'll be begging me for mercy before Yvette is done with you."

She felt as though she had been suddenly hollowed. She'd noticed the sparkle in Yvette's dark eyes, had thought it odd and dismissed it. Now she knew the gleam had been anticipation.

Katie swallowed. She couldn't have been more scared than she was right now.

Still, she had to remain strong . . . resist until Jack got there.

But could she?

She dug deep for that last ounce of strength and clenched her jaws tight.

This was not going to happen.

She took in a breath, raised her chin, and said, "Jack will not sit back and let you or your sick bitch do this to me."

From the smirk that formed on Treadway's face, she could tell he wasn't impressed by her threat.

"Ah, yes," he said, "your precious, Jack Ferrell." He leaned close. "You remember that bridge in Boise?"

"Yes," Katie said almost involuntarily. She hadn't wanted to answer. She didn't like the direction his question was headed.

"My man Boryenko was driving the Hummer that day. He takes special pleasure in eliminating problems for me. And it angers him when an opportunity to do what he likes most slips through his fingers. Like having the two of you get away from him that day on the bridge."

Katie took a deep breath, steeled herself. "Where is this headed?"

He smiled. "My big Russian friend is taking care of Jack and his blonde-headed friend as we speak. And I assure you, Ms. McIntyre . . . this time he will not fail. Jack Ferrell and his friend—"

"Robert," she said, cutting Treadway off. "His name is Robert Foster."

"As you wish. But knowing his name changes nothing, young lady. Jack Ferrell and Robert Foster are dead men."

CHAPTER 58

Katie felt her already weak knees going, but stiffened them before they totally collapsed under her. She couldn't believe Jack was dead—wouldn't believe Jack was dead. Nor was Robert or Kimo. They had to be alive. She couldn't be left there on her own with this crazy man.

Again, she drew on strength she didn't know she had.

"Your friend will find Jack a handful," she said, defiantly. "Robert, too."

"I assure you, Boryenko does not lose."

Her mind whirled with possibilities. None of them acknowledged Jack being dead. Treadway had known where to find their boat, but he didn't know the location of the lava tube. Boryenko wouldn't either.

Stalling, she pointed at the brandy. She needed a stiff shot of booze.

"I believe I will have that drink." She took a step toward Treadway's glass sitting on the cabinet. She eyed the heavy crystal decanter. A fine weapon if she could get her hands on it.

He raised his hand in a gesture that stopped her.

She stood her ground.

He handed her the snifter and said, "I hope you're not entertaining any thoughts of using that glass as a weapon. It's pitifully inadequate. You'd only succeed in annoying me. And you've seen what I do when I'm annoyed."

She put aside the idea of going for the decanter. He was right. Hitting him with the snifter would only piss him off. Her face still hurt where he had hit her. She didn't want to give him an excuse to inflict any further pain on her.

He enjoyed it too much.

But she had to do something.

Her only hope—she realized—was to keep the man off balance as much as possible and pray Jack got there soon.

"Make no mistake," she said. "Jack is very much alive and well. He and Robert will be coming for me." She fixed him in her gaze, portraying confidence. "But then you know that. So, since you are so intent on my company, I assume you intend to trade me for the relics."

"Hold onto your silly thoughts if it makes you feel better."

"I intend to, Mr. Treadway. Jack's coming . . . they both are."

"Let's suppose for a moment you're right. I don't trade. I take what I want. And when I do, I'll decide what I'm going to do with you and him. This game has gone far beyond acquiring a few antiquities. It's personal."

"My grandfather's dying wish was that Jack find those antiquities and return them to the Hawaiian's for repatriation. That's what we intended to do. What I want is your word you will let us go if we give them to you."

"You're assuming you have them."

"Let's pretend we do."

"Pretend nothing. You forgot about Boryenko. My man will not let that happen."

"*Mon amour*, I am sad," Yvette whined in interruption. She took a step toward Katie, reached out and fondled her chestnut hair. "You said you were going to give me this American bitch. What of your promise?"

Katie had noticed Yvette staring at her.

"*Allez-vous faire enculer, salope*," she said, slapping Yvette's hand away.

Treadway waved Yvette off. "Calm yourself a moment."

With an amused smile, Yvette stepped to the foot of her

bed and stretched out on it with the poise of a jaguar. Her robe parted revealing twin, firm mounds of flesh and bare skin to her bellybutton. She sipped her brandy, but her gaze never left Katie.

Treadway arched his brow at Katie. "You speak French. I would not have expected that from a dental hygienist."

"Enough to tell that French trollop to go get fucked. I have a few choice words for you too if you care to hear them."

"I'm not impressed by your bad language."

"And you sicken me. To you, I'm nothing. To me, you're a rich asshole unworthy of the oxygen you breathe. If I had my way, you'd be put down like the rabid dog you are."

He took a quick step toward her, stopped, grabbed her wet t-shirt, ripped it from her shoulders, and let the tattered shirt fall to her waist, exposing her breasts in humiliation. Then he slapped her hard on the side of the face before she could protest.

"Insolence angers me," he said. He grabbed her jaw and made her look at him. "It would be best if you remember that."

He glanced over his shoulder at the bed. "Yvette . . ."

CHAPTER 59

Jack stared at the heavy stainless steel blade of the dive knife and imagined it plunging deep into his stomach. The sharp serrated edge would slice through his organs severing bowel and artery. He would not go out like a stuck pig; curled up on the floor, holding his guts in with his hands, and praying for a miracle.

And what about Robert?

He checked.

Robert was still on his feet, but barely. He stood hunched over with his left hand on his knee for support. His right arm hung limp at his side. He still gripped the rock, but it was obvious he barely had the strength to hold onto it.

They were screwed.

Jack scanned the stone floor at his feet. Robert had used a rock. Perhaps . . . ?

His gaze fell on the wooden crate. A gleam of metal in the spilled relics winked at him.

A sword.

Out of the corner of his eye, he saw the Russian come at them with the knife held low and threatening.

Jack dove for the relic. His fingers tightened around the hilt.

He turned and saw Boryenko sidestepping Robert. Somehow, Robert had managed to straighten, but the hand holding the rock still hung down at his side.

Boryenko would kill him for sure.

Jack had no choice.

Boryenko made his move toward Robert.

Light flashed off the polished stainless steel blade of the dive knife.

At the same time, Jack plunged the antiquated Samurai sword into Boryenko's chest just under the sternum.

The Russian's eyes widened.

Jack let go of the handle and scooted backward on his butt. Watching. Waiting.

For a moment, Boryenko stood there staring at him. His mouth opened and closed. But no words came out . . . only a gagging groan and a trickle of blood.

Jack locked eyes with the Russian, amazed he was still standing.

Then the knife slipped from Boryenko's fingers and he toppled to the side like a felled redwood.

Jack heard the man's skull crack against the stone floor. Blood pooled under the body and ran down the stone slope to the sand.

Breathing hard, Jack scrambled over to Robert who sat on his heels probing a slice in his wetsuit, to the side and just below his right breast.

"Are you all right?" Jack asked, his hand outstretched in a silent plea. His friend had been stabbed. He wanted to do something to help.

"Screwed up my wetsuit." Robert turned and showed Jack. "But he missed me."

Jack sat back and sighed. "Fuck!"

"You can say that again." Robert sat down next to Jack. He rubbed his jaw, working it back and forth, and added, "That asshole almost took off my head. Like being hit with a sledge hammer."

Jack breathed in, held it, and massaged his ribs. He was sure one or two were cracked. "Goddamned animal. Fucking Big Foot, if you ask me."

"And you killed him. Damn . . . I can't believe it. You really killed that crazy sonofabitch."

Jack furrowed his brow at Robert and said, "You tried."

"I only hit him with that rock to keep him from stabbing you."

"And I killed him to keep him from killing us. He would have, you know. He'd have killed us both."

Robert didn't comment. He quietly fingered the slice in his wetsuit and stared at the slack body of the dead Russian.

Jack let him have his moment. Clearly, Robert realized how close he came to dying.

A few heartbeats later, Robert inhaled a deep breath, huffed, and said, "Well, one thing's for sure. He was no match for that samurai sword."

"You asked me once what it was like to kill someone." Jack gave Robert a long look and said, "Now you know."

"I only hit him with that rock," Robert pointed out. Then he said, "But you're right. I *was* trying to kill him. And it wasn't a difficult decision to make when I saw him crushing the life out of you."

"And it's easier the second time. I'm not sure that's good. But it *is* easier."

Robert nodded almost imperceptibly. Jack knew they would be talking about this incident for a long time to come.

For a few beats, they sat and breathed.

Jack could feel his nerves calm.

All at once, Robert straightened and gave him a sideways look.

"That samurai sword," Robert said, "it came from the crate?"

Jack hadn't thought about it. He had just been glad the weapon was there for him to grab. Thinking about it now, the Japanese sword did seem out of place in a crate of Hawaiian antiquities.

What was the story behind that?

He shrugged at the thought and commented, "Probably a war souvenir Treadway's grandfather was sending home. It would have been worth big bucks."

"And the other stuff?"

They both turned their heads and gazed curiously at the crate spilled behind them. The precious antiquities had been packed in leaves from ti plants. From what they could see, most of the contents lay scattered on the stone floor.

They scooted closer and eyeballed the artifacts: a red and yellow-feathered cape and helmet, carved wooden idols with mother-of-pearl eyes, war clubs embedded with shark's teeth, wooden daggers, short-handled spears, bone fishhooks of all sizes, a koawood paddle, and two multicolored *tapa*-cloth bundles secured with cords made of plant fiber. A large bone from a leg protruded from the open end of one, a charred rib from the other. And there was a rusted sword of the type worn by Captain Cook. The antiquities Treadway's grandfather spoke of.

Jack exchanged gazes with Robert. For a several seconds neither of them said anything.

Finally, Jack said, "It's all there, just like Katie's grandfather said."

"Sure looks like it," Robert said. "Now, how do you propose we get all that stuff out of here? Sure can't float it out."

"We'll come back for it with a waterproof bag. Make a couple of trips if we have to."

Robert worked himself to his feet, nodded at Boryenko's body, and asked, "And Big Foot?"

"Leave him for the crabs." Jack couldn't have cared less about Boryenko's body or the antique sword protruding from his hairy belly. Then a shockwave of realization pierced the quagmire of molasses that had been his brain since his CO_2 poisoning.

Katie!

Jack jumped to his feet. "We need to get back to the boat."

CHAPTER 60

Jack ignored the pain of his damaged ribs and quickly slid the heavy steel air tank from its mount on his buoyancy compensator. They knew from their swim in they wouldn't be able to make it through the narrow opening with tanks on their backs.

He steadied it on the sand in front of him and lifted the air gauge close to his face to read the pressure. "My gauge says a thousand pounds. Yours?"

Robert didn't answer.

Jack checked on his friend. Robert had his tank sitting on the sand in front of him. But his eyes were locked on the dead Russian.

Jack too had found it hard not to look at Boryenko's body. Obviously, being part of having just killed a man affected Robert more than either of them realized. But now was not the time to ponder the morality of taking a human life.

They needed to get back to the boat.

"Hey, Robert," he called out. "Your air pressure, how many pounds do you have?"

"Sure, yea . . ." he mumbled. Finally, he blinked and tore his gaze away from the bloody body lying less than ten feet away and eyed the air gauge attached to his tank. "Seven hundred. It's going to be close if we're wrong."

"Not likely that's the case. I can't imagine Big Foot dog-paddling it here from Treadway's fancy yacht." Jack looked toward the opening of the lava tube. The sea surged in and out foamy under the torpedo. In the beam of his dive light, the bristling bubbles glowed bright white against the darkness surrounding them.

"My bet is he beached *Trident's* Zodiac nearby and swam in." He swept his light beam to a set of mask, fins, and snorkel scattered on the sand a few feet away. "He didn't have a tank."

"Probably on that small stretch of beach fifty yards south of here that we saw from the boat," Robert suggested. "The other possibility is that he anchored the inflatable in front of the lava tube just beyond the waves."

"Let's just hope the boat's still there." Jack rose to his feet and strapped on his buoyancy compensator, slid on his mask and fins, looped the wrist cord of his Princeton Tec dive light over his hand, and grabbed his tank by the valve. "Ready?"

Robert already had a grip on his tank with his left hand. He flashed a thumbs-up signal with his right and backed into the water.

When they were knee deep, they gave each other a final thumbs-up, inserted their regulators into their mouths, and slid into the submersed grotto.

With the tide still on its way out, the water sloshing over the rock pile at the mouth of the lava tube was only inches deep now. The torpedo hung precariously from where it had lodged in the mouth of the tube. The night sky showed dark and foreboding on the other side of the narrow opening.

Jack paused, remembering the moray that had bitten Robert. The incident had been quickly forgotten in all the excitement. Now it loomed as a reminder of impending danger. The creature's home was in a hole in the reef on the other side—maybe just a few feet away.

Forcing aside all thoughts of the eel, He kicked his fins hard and scooted over the slimy rocks, dragging this air tank with him.

Halfway through, a jagged lip of lava snagged a strap at the bottom of his buoyancy compensator. He twisted to free himself and felt his back hit against the torpedo. In spite of its considerable weight, the huge steel tube rocked an inch.

Fuck! Jack froze.

More than half a century of wave action had worked to free

the torpedo from where it had lodged in the lip of the lava tube. Now it teetered as though carefully balanced. He could only hope the torpedo stayed put a little longer. There was no way to know if the ordnance would explode. Time and salt may have corroded the detonator or maybe it had been a dud to begin with. When the tube full of TNT finally fell, he didn't want to be there to find out.

He closed his eyes and gently worked his body back and forth to free his buoyancy compensator.

He felt the nylon strap come loose.

Relief flooded over him. But his back still rested against the torpedo. Surly his body wasn't keeping the massive piece of ordnance from falling.

He stopped breathing and relaxed away from the metal tube. It held.

He didn't linger even a second to consider his good fortune. He wiggled through and sunk into deeper surge on the other side.

The thought that he could be blown to bits replaced the concern he had about being bit by the eel. He brought his head above the surface and let his feet hang in the water below him. He kicked and felt the tip of his fins brush sand and rock, but it was too deep for him to stand. He treaded water with one hand and pointed his flashlight beam at the dark opening, while struggling to maintain his position in the current.

Robert squirreled through the gap and slid into the sea. His head broke the surface next to Jack. He spit his regulator into his hand. "What-in-the-hell was the holdup back there?"

Jack pulled his regulator from his mouth. "Got hung up. See if you can spot the Zodiac."

Their light beams swept the surface of the water. The moon had dropped low on the horizon behind Kahoolawe. Rain clouds had moved in adding to the darkness.

The beam from Jack's Princeton Tec found the sixteen-foot Zodiac twenty feet away. The tiny craft bobbed and jerked in the churning surf. Robert's light beam settled on it a second later. They both kicked in that direction, without a word to each other.

Hampered by towing their heavy air tanks through the powerful surge, it took them a full two minutes to swim the thirty feet. It felt like a lifetime. Jack pulled himself into the Zodiac with a shove from Robert and promptly helped Robert aboard.

Breathing a sigh of relief that the key had been left in the ignition, Jack fired up the outboard while Robert unhooked the anchor line clipped with a "D" ring to a grommet on the bow.

Jack shoved the throttle lever forward, engaging the 35 hp outboard. The inflatable struggled against the surge, then the propeller bit the turbulence and the boat shot forward.

Two hundred yards away, the lights from *Trident* glowed bright. The red, green, and white running lights of *Hele Auana* should have been clearly visible nearby. Jack didn't like what he was seeing . . . or wasn't seeing.

"Do you see the boat?"

"Not ours."

Fuck!

"Switch off your light," Jack yelled to Robert who kneeled in the bow illuminating the water ahead of them. We don't want Treadway or someone standing watch aboard the yacht to see us."

They sped forward in the Zodiac. The inflatable bounced and slapped the water as it rode up and over the rough swells. Salty spray shot into the air. The trough between the building mountains of water was a dark valley with no visible lights, not even those on Maui across the channel.

As the boat climbed the crest of each swell and dropped into the trough beyond, they frantically searched the wave tops for any sign of their boat.

The bottom fell out of Jack's stomach. *Hele Auana* had disappeared . . . and along with it, Katie and Kimo.

With that single thought plaguing him, he ignored his concern about the fancy yacht and circled the area where their boat should have been. With darkness working against them now, he peered into the night, scanning the waves.

Hele Auana just wasn't there.

The Zodiac peaked and dropped into yet another dark trough.

Robert saw something in the water and yelled, "Lookout."

His warning came a second too late. The inflatable skidded off the partially submerged bow of a boat.

Jack throttled back. Luckily, the smooth fiberglass hull of the sunken boat hadn't punctured any of the inflatable's air chambers.

"What the hell . . . ?" He scanned the water to see what they'd hit.

All he could see was an ocean of ink.

"Turn on the light," he yelled, and quickly brought the Zodiac around.

When Robert lit up the wreckage, Jack's jaw muscles tightened at the sight of the name staring at him from under three inches of water.

Hele Auana.

Anger filled the hollowness in Jack's chest as Robert swept the beam from his dive light over the surrounding water. Jack grabbed his Princeton Tec and added its beam to the search.

Where are the bodies? There should be bodies if Katie and Kimo were aboard when the boat sank.

He held onto that sliver of hope, refusing to believe they were dead.

While Robert continued to probe the darkness for their two friends, Jack gazed into the night. He needed to think. He should never have left them alone on the boat. His last words to Katie haunted him.

A piece of cake. In there and out . . . ten minutes . . . fifteen, tops.

He was responsible for what happened here. His recklessness might even have killed her and Kimo.

Unless.

He glared at the yacht a hundred yards away. *Treadway!*

The bastard.

He remembered the look on Treadway's face the day before. Obsessed. Ruthless.

And the monster had taken Katie and Kimo.

CHAPTER 61

Katie stood dazed by the vicious slap from Treadway. Powerless to stop him, she felt his surprisingly strong hands grasp her wrists and shove her against the bulkhead and pin her arms above her head. The stars spinning in front of her eyes cleared as realization of what was happening set in.

She tried to kick and wiggle free from his hold on her, but the powerful muscles concealed beneath Treadway's loose-fitting shirt held her firm against the expensive wood paneling.

Across the room, Yvette slid off the king-sized bed with a feline litheness that punctuated her jaguar presence. With her sheer robe hanging open, she stepped between Katie and the door. She raised her hands in front of her, arms outstretched. "Giver her to me, *mon amour.*"

Treadway smiled and threw Katie to the floor.

The move came with such surprise Katie didn't quite get her hands under her in time to block her fall. Her right wrist, knee and elbow hit the teak deck first, then her left wrist, elbow and knee, and at about the same time, her right cheek slammed into the hard wooden floor. She rolled onto her back and for a moment, just stared at the ceiling spinning above her.

Treadway laughed and said, "Enjoy yourself, my pet. I'll make sure no one disturbs you."

In the mist fogging Katie's mind, she heard the French woman utter a prolonged cry that resembled a mew of a spoiled housecat. In the way a feral call on a cold moonless night brings chills to a person's skin, the woman's predatory wail brought Katie out of her stupor.

She forced aside the haze, propped herself up on her hands, and rolled to a sitting position. She flexed against the soreness in her right wrist testing the injured joints usefulness; and that of her right elbow and right knee. She fingered an abrasion under her right eye and cringed at the touch.

What had she done wrong to bring this kind of wrath down on her?

As Treadway stepped past her, he paused, reached down, and tweaked the nipples of her exposed breasts. "Nice," he said; and again he laughed. Then he continued toward the door.

His final act of humiliation was more than she could endure. Tears welled in the corners of her eyes, and she stared unbelieving at the sick sadistic man as he stepped into the companionway and closed the door behind him.

Her gaze was fixed on the passageway when Yvette stepped between her and the door. She interpreted the French woman's move to be an attempt to emphasize there was no escape.

Yet!

She locked her gaze on Frenchie's eyes and kept it there.

Yvette slid out of her robe and let it fall to the floor.

Katie swallowed.

"Games?" Yvette asked in her heavy French accent. "You like games, *ma petite chatte*?"

My little pussy, Katie translated to herself. *I don't think so.*

She didn't answer the woman's vulgar taunting.

Yvette's lips narrowed into a cruel smile, and she began a slow circle like a great cat does a wounded antelope: cautious, determined . . . deadly.

"You will never want love from a man once you've had a sweet taste of Yvette," she purred, claws bared.

Katie wiped away her tears and dug deep within her resolve for the strength to stand firm. Treadway had come close to reducing her to a blubbering mess. Now Yvette was taking a turn with her.

She wasn't about to let that happen.

She'd die first. Or not!

With a renewed will to survive, she rose to a crouch.

She'd live, for Jack.

Hands in front of her open and ready, she turned with Cat Woman as the creature moved with effortless grace in the dance of predator and prey.

CHAPTER 62

Jack goosed the throttle and pointed the Zodiac at the yacht and Treadway. In front of him, with both hands gripping the nylon rope threaded through brass grommets around the bow, Robert stared ahead in obvious indifference to the salt spray hitting his face as the inflatable skipped and bounced its way toward *Trident*. No words passed between them, only grim determination.

He'd seen Robert's face pinch and harden when they couldn't find Katie and Kimo in the water. There was no mistaking that look; it was the same as the one etched on *his* face.

Pure hatred.

He hoped the couple of minutes of light they had chanced to search the wreckage of the sunken *Hele Auana* had not attracted attention from the yacht.

They didn't need a reception party.

He no longer worried about the roar of the outboard. The squall that threatened from the south moved in and fell in great sheets rain. Lightning cracked the sky, thunder boomed.

Fifty feet from the yacht, he throttled back and coasted in.

The rubber pontoon of the inflatable bumped against the portside hull of *Trident*. Jack did not wait for Robert. He grabbed the polished gunwale of the sleek double-hulled yacht and climbed up and over the side.

The classical music filtering out of the salon and the steady splattering of raindrops pelting the deck drowned out all sound of his feet hitting the expensive teak planking. The light that filtered through the curtains on the rear windows of the salon cast a dim glow on the first few feet of deck. Beyond that, there was only darkness.

He crouched on his heels and scanned the deck for movement. Nothing.

Against the hull directly to his left, was a life-ring. Attached to that was a coil of rope. Quietly lifting the life-ring from its mount, he unclipped the nylon rope and tossed the line over the side to Robert.

He returned to his crouch . . . looking, listening.

Again, nothing.

Suddenly, twenty feet away under the cover of a stripped canopy near the stern, the cherry at the end of a burning cigarette glowed bright red-orange.

Fuck!

He crouched lower.

Only one cigarette?

Slip out for a quick smoke and then back to your post . . . that's how it usually worked with smokers.

He crept to within ten feet of the single figure who stood on the far side of a wooden table, his back turned.

Jack's body shook. He'd only have one chance.

When he saw the fiery cherry flare up and glow bright red-orange a second time, he knew the lookout's hand was raised to his mouth and that he was distracted by the enjoyment of inhaling a satisfying drag.

Jack dismissed all thought of sore ribs or further damage to his battered body and dove across the tabletop at the guy.

His right foot hooked the edge of the table, dragging it over with him. But the momentum of his leap carried him forward.

His shoulder slammed into Smoker's lower spine, snapping his head back before sending him headfirst into the transom. The lit cigarette flew and landed with a hiss in a puddle of rainwater.

The table and two of the four chairs around it hit the deck at the same time Jack did. But the collision with the smoker's body had broken his fall.

He rolled and lifted the limp crewmember by the front of his shirt ready to hammer a fist into his face. It wasn't necessary. Smoker's head hung at and odd angle, his neck obviously broken.

Grabbing hold of a heavily tattooed arm, he started to heave Smoker over the side. Then realized it wasn't necessary. The man wasn't getting up. Besides, the table and chairs falling over had made enough noise without adding a loud splash to the mix.

He let the body drop to the deck.

Pumped by the adrenalin surging into his veins, every one of his senses was heightened.

He heard a faint scuff on the teak behind him.

His nerves already stretched tight, he jerked around, ready.

The tension in his mainspring relaxed when he saw Robert crouched under the canopy. Eyes on him.

Jack breathed heavily through his nose to loosen the spring another notch and whispered, "Let's check inside and see what we're up against."

Without waiting for his friend to answer, he started toward the door of the salon.

Robert reached out with a gloved right hand and gripped Jack's shoulder, stopping him.

"Already did." he said, keeping his voice low. "While you played linebacker with this asshole here, I took a peek in through a gap in the curtains. Treadway's kicked back in an overstuffed chair in the salon. There's light coming from a companionway leading below deck, but I couldn't get a good enough look to know if anyone's down there."

"Treadway's girlfriend?"

"Not in the salon."

"Katie has got to be here. She didn't go down with the boat. Neither did Kimo. We'd have seen their bodies. So we'll have to assume they are below deck with Treadway's French piece and at least one other person standing guard: most likely a man."

"I'll buy that. And . . . ?"

"There'll be another person standing watch on the bridge. My guess, the captain."

"We should have brought your sword."

Jack hadn't thought about Boryenko since leaving the lava tube. Once again, he breathed a silent sigh of relief knowing they wouldn't have to face the Russian a second time. But he and Robert still had the pretty French woman and at least two more male crewmembers left to deal with.

And Treadway.

Muffled and barely audible above the noise from the music and the storm, a woman's scream reverberated from below deck.

Jack faced Robert and got a curt nod confirming what he'd heard.

"Katie," they whispered at the same time.

In the fraction of a second it took for realization to settle in, Jack understood the true meaning of hatred.

Treadway would die for what he had done to her.

And *he* would kill him.

CHAPTER 63

Katie tensed her body ready for Yvette's next move. Their eyes remained locked on each other. And for the moment, Cat Woman appeared content with her feline game of predator and prey: the cat toying with the mouse . . . primordial, but also strangely seductive . . . a sort of foreplay stalling the inevitable.

But the dance would not go on forever. That much Katie knew . . . and feared.

She thought back to the scuffles she had in high school. It seemed some student always had a nasty comment to make about her father being locked up in prison for murdering her mother. That would push her over the edge, regardless of how big and tough the girl was—sometimes even guys.

Most of the time she'd be the one who ended up bruised and scratched. But even when she came out on top, she didn't consider herself a skilled fighter. She had been a survivor, though. And it was her will to survive that had made the difference when she killed Brian Wesley.

That same will to survive would make the difference, here.

"Treadway is going to rot in prison . . . you know that, don't you? Why let yourself go down with him?" Katie doubted her words would sway the evil facing her, but she had to try.

"*Ma petite chatte*, I have no intention of sharing a filthy prison cell with *Monsieur* Treadway. But that is of no consequence to you."

Yvette's move was quick and practiced.

Katie did not see the kick coming until it was too late to react. Yvette's foot struck her on the chin hard enough to make her head swim just shy of total unconsciousness. The room tilted and her vision blurred. For what seemed like an hour she floated above the floor, her ears ringing, then her knees buckled and she started down.

Yvette pounced on her in an instant. She scooped her into shockingly strong arms before she hit the floor and deposited her on the bed.

Katie had a vague awareness of what was happening to her: body heat, soft skin, firm lithe muscle pressing against her, a scent of perfume, a scant touch of lace, hot breath against her cheek.

"Go ahead and resist," Yvette murmured into Katie's ear. "It will make the love all that much better."

"Get off me, you bitch." The words boomed inside Katie's head. But she didn't know if the words had crossed her lips or if they had been lost somewhere in the haze between her brain and mouth.

She tried to push Yvette away, couldn't. Her arms wouldn't move. It was as though her efforts to protest were lost in a bad dream and that none of what was happening to her was real.

But it was happening.

Yvette shook her head from side to side. "You call me such bad names, *ma petite*. But I fear you misjudge me. Embrace your desires and you will see how wrong you are. A few hours in bed with me and you'll beg for my touch and no one else's."

The dreaminess that threatened to envelope Katie passed. She felt the weight of Yvette straddling her. Strong thighs and knees squeezed her in a human vise, pinning her arms to her sides.

"I said, get off me." Katie squirmed and heaved upward with her hips.

"Good . . . now we play," Yvette said with a smile. She groped and squeezed Katie's bare breasts; her thumbs teased both nipples hard.

Get off me, bitch!" Katie tried to pull her arms free. She was helpless in the grasp of the woman's strong legs.

"You tease me," Yvette murmured. "They are firm and full like two melons ripe for the squeezing. And mine to embrace. She leaned close and ran her tongue over Katie's breasts.

Katie tried to shrink into the mattress, pull away from the French woman's touch . . . will her nipples not to respond. There was nowhere for her to go.

Oh, Jack . . .

She sunk into the murky depths of humiliation and terror.

Yvette gripped Katie's hair, pinning her head down on the bed, pulling the skin tight at her temples. Savage. Primal.

Katie tried to turn her head, couldn't.

Yvette leaned toward Katie's naked breasts and traced both areolas with the moist tip of her sharp tongue.

Katie's nipples hardened in response.

"You like what I do," Yvette said, her face inches from Katie's. "I bite too."

Katie cringed. Instead of searching for words she knew could never express her disgust, she scowled at cat woman and spit into the woman's face.

Yvette leaned her head back and closed her eyelids, seductively. A smile formed as spittle streaked the side of her nose and settled on her upper lip.

She brushed away the saliva with a slow swipe of her hand. Her smile still there, she pinched Katie's nipples between thumb and forefinger and pulled back on them as if she were reining in a horse.

Katie screamed.

"Yes . . . scream. I like the screams."

Digging the nails of one hand into Katie's breast, Yvette reached behind her with the other and worked her fingers under the front of Katie's shorts that were still wet from her plunge in the ocean. She probed deeper until her middle finger slid between warm moist folds.

Katie squirmed, kicked, and bucked against Yvette's probing finger. But she didn't scream. She would not give Yvette that satisfaction.

"Come, *ma petite chatte.*" Yvette plunged her middle finger.

Katie wanted to scream.

No!

"Do not shy from me." Yvette breathed the words. "Let me hear your cries of pleasure."

Katie bit back her words. Pain and terror were no longer the controlling forces. She had moved well beyond that. She knew she would not leave the room alive. Treadway had planned it that way from the beginning. He couldn't afford to let her live, not now. She'd die at the hands of Yvette's perverted pleasures, or be hit over the head and tossed overboard somewhere far at sea.

Kill or be killed.

She thought about Brian Wesley, and she thought about Coleman Treadway—two men, different but the same. Once again, she had been left with no choice.

Still . . .

Yvette's hips began a rhythmic movement, and Katie felt the woman's hold on her arms, loosen a fraction with each thrust. But would it be enough?

She searched for a weapon she could get her hands on if she managed to free them from the French woman's iron grip.

. . . Any weapon.

She mentally blocked out what was happening to her and focused on the bulkhead above the headboard.

A three-foot long golden trident spear rested in a grove in the hands of a bronze King Neptune staring down at her.

CHAPTER 64

Jack stood facing the window in the hatchway leading into the salon. Eight feet away on the other side, the man he'd come there for, lounged in an overstuffed chair at an angle to the doorway. He got the impression Coleman Treadway was not concerned about who might walk in behind him.

Treadway's back and left side faced the door. A crystal snifter of amber liquor in his left hand sparkled in the light from a lamp on a table against the bulkhead to his right. The snow-white patch in his short-cropped coal-black hair stared at them like a lone eyeball from the dark. A symphony Jack didn't recognize played over unseen speakers, loud enough to be heard, but not so loud the music drowned out the scream they heard a minute ago.

For a few beats of his heart, he couldn't tear his eyes away from the man so intent on seeing them dead. This was the monster who held Katie and Kimo prisoner, who valued antiquities over life. Surely, he was a creature as vile as any on earth . . . or in hell.

Did Treadway have the music turned low so he could listen to Katie's cries?

Jack shuddered to think that was the case.

He looked for the devil's horns but saw none.

For a solid ten-count, he studied Treadway's apparent smugness through the window, watching, wondering. The man's complacency was puzzling.

Then he remembered Smoker. Perhaps he hadn't been sneaking a puff. Perhaps Smoker had been on watch and Treadway was secure in the belief his thug would alert him to anyone sneaking aboard.

Jack cracked a smile. Smoker should have heeded the Surgeon General's warning: cigarettes are hazardous to your health.

"He hasn't moved," Robert whispered, pressing his head in next to Jack's.

"Confident bastard, isn't he?"

"We can fix that. Let's get the sonofabitch."

Jack gripped his friend's arm. He was just as ready to charge Treadway as Robert was, but wanted a moment to consider the situation.

He calculated the distance they would have to travel: eight feet, maybe one or two feet more, between them and Treadway. Not too far to get the drop on a man sitting down, unaware.

But a mile if the man is armed and ready.

He didn't believe that was the case. Why would Treadway be sitting there armed, or even suspect Boryenko would fail to kill them? Still, he didn't trust Treadway to be anything but unpredictable.

With all that could go wrong with his plan, Jack hoped his conclusion Smoker had been on the rear deck standing watch would keep Treadway from jumping up at the sound of the door opening.

They would need that extra second or two of surprise, especially if Robert was going to have any chance at all of making it below deck to surprise whoever was down there standing guard over Katie and Kimo.

"I'll go in first and take care of Treadway," Jack said, quietly. "That fucker's mine."

"And me?" Robert asked.

"You come in right behind me and head straight for that companionway on the far side of the room and jump whoever is down below standing guard. Don't look back or stop no matter what you hear."

"But what if Treadway—"

"Save Katie and Kimo. I can take care of Treadway."

A couple of heartbeats of silence passed, Robert nodded and

held up a wooden leg from one of the broken deck chairs. "Okay, but take this. I picked it up over there on the deck."

"Keep it. No telling what you'll run into."

Robert tapped the makeshift club against his palm as if testing it and said, "Give the asshole a shot for me."

Jack reached for his friend's shoulder and gave it a reassuring squeeze. He smiled when Robert gripped his hand in return.

"On Three," he said, and counted: "one . . . two . . . three!"

Jack pulled open the door and rushed through the hatchway at Treadway, Robert right behind him.

Treadway rose from the chair, turned, and lowered his shoulder against the attack just as Jack crashed into him. The same move used on Smoker. Only the antiquities dealer met him head-on, braced, and ready.

A small flat chrome semi-automatic flew from Treadway's right hand.

Jack reached for the gun too late and missed it.

He lowered his shoulder and drove with his legs.

The deck pitched and bobbed under his feet. The quick down and out he had hoped for, had just as quickly become a no-holds-barred wrestling match neither of them could allow themselves to lose.

They continued to struggle, locked in a sort of drunken dance— arms around each other groping for advantage.

Jack was getting nowhere, but neither was Treadway.

The antiquities dealer turned out to be a much stronger adversary than Jack had figured. Under his Tommy Bahama shirt and khaki slacks, he was powerfully built and more than able to hold his own.

They hit the deck and rolled.

Out of the corner of his eye, Jack noticed Robert dash into the companionway and disappear below deck. It was up to him, now. All that mattered was that he gets Katie and Kimo out alive and well.

Jack felt Treadway's grip slip. It was the opening he'd been waiting for.

He twisted free of Treadway's grasp and bounded to his feet, fists raised.

Treadway did not try to stand. Instead, he rolled and scrambled on his hands and feet to where the gun lay on the deck a few feet away. He groped the floor searching out the pistol.

Jack grabbed a lamp from the table and threw it at Treadway's head.

Treadway turned and put his hands in front of his face to block the blow.

The lamp fell short.

Jack leaped and his hand slid across the polished teak planking to where the gun had fallen.

It wasn't there.

The teak splintered next to Jack's cheek at the same time he heard the sharp crack of a gunshot from the little automatic.

He knew the next bullet would punch a hole through his heart.

CHAPTER 65

Katie could not be sure what she heard. But it sounded like a sack of flour hitting the deck in the companionway on the other side of the door.

A scuff of feet and another thud.

Not as loud this time. But loud enough for her to hear it from the bed.

She had no idea what was going on, but something had happened outside the cabin. Yvette had obviously heard the thump and bump too, because she stopped her vulgar probing and peered in that direction.

Katie seized the moment.

There was no hesitation in her movement. Catching Yvette unaware in that second of distraction, she bucked Frenchie off with an exaggerated hip thrust and pulled her arms free from the vise of female flesh, muscle, and sinew.

Yvette landed on her side and rolled—arms reaching and grabbing—off the end of the bed before she could fully regain her balance.

That was all the time Katie needed.

Nothing more to think about, nothing to rehearse . . . rolling her plan over and over in her mind during the last few minutes, she'd practiced her escape a hundred times.

She made her move.

Pivoting on her knees, she jerked the trident spear from King Neptune's hands, and turned it on Yvette.

Cat woman was already coming at her, claws bared.

Katie plunged the spear forward with all her strength.

There was an instant of resistance; then the flesh parted when the longer center prong pierced the French woman's abdomen just above the bellybutton, followed by the shorter prong on each side. The barbs buried deep in Yvette's guts.

Katie pushed hard on the spear one more time.

Yvette shrieked and fell back, taking the golden trident with her.

Her hands wrapped around the shaft as if by reflex and tried to pull it out as she stared wide-eyed at the blood flowing from the three symmetrical punctures.

The barbs held.

Katie watched Yvette writhe and squirm with pain. Revolting. Horrible. But she felt no remorse for the creature as her venomous blood seeped from her body into a crimson pool beneath her.

Without thinking twice about leaving Yvette to die a slow agonizing death, Katie started toward the doorway.

She felt Yvette's bloody hand clamp onto her ankle.

"Screw you, *ma petite chatte*," Katie practically spit Yvette's words at her.

In the next instant, she kicked the woman's hand away and reached for the door handle.

Her fingers were an inch away when the hatchway flew open.

She jerked back in time to keep them from being broken.

Remembering the brash Aussie who had been left to guard the door, she lunged with her nails raised and ready to gouge the man's eyes out.

A strong hand clamped onto her wrist and held tight.

Her final shred of hope drained away. The fawn caught in the lion's claws.

A form came into focus as the fear and anger clouding her vision, cleared.

It can't be.

Tears flooded and rolled down her cheeks. Through glazed eyes, she stared at Robert unable to move or speak. Her mind had to be playing games with her.

Robert and Jack were dead.

"Aren't you going to say hi to an old friend?" Robert gave her back her arm.

His eyes were automatically drawn to her bare breasts. They took in the ripped T-shirt, her unbuttoned shorts, and locked on the bruises on her face.

He asked, "Are you hurt bad?"

She didn't stop to think about her exposed breasts or her bruised face. She threw her arms around Robert and hugged him.

He allowed her the moment even though there was no time to waste. That's when he saw Yvette's bloody half-nude body sprawled on the floor, the golden trident spear protruding from her firm flat stomach. Her blank lifeless eyes stared at them.

He cringed as though the realization of the sick, perverted game that had gone on here sickened him.

"We have to go," he said.

Katie had no problem comprehending the urgency.

She started to leave, but his strong hands stopped her before she could take a step. Confused, she watched him retrieve a red silk blouse from where it had been folded over the back of a chair.

"Put this on," he said. "Jack will be all kinds of mad at me for letting you parade around like that."

She gripped the front of Robert's shirt in disbelief.

"Jack's alive?" she gasped. Where?"

"He's taking care of Treadway. Where's Kimo?"

She took the blouse from his hand, unable to look at him.

Nothing more needed to be said.

"Let's go," Robert said.

"Right behind you."

She hastily tied the tails of the blouse in front of her instead of taking the time to work the buttons and followed after him not sure what they were rushing into.

When she stepped through the doorway, she saw the Aussie's feet, then his body face down on the deck—out cold . . . or dead. A broken chair leg lay next to him.

Robert saw her looking. "Caught the perverted bastard with

his ear to the door."

"He—"

The pop from a small caliber gun reverberated down the narrow companionway.

They both turned.

"Jack!" Katie muttered. She hustled past Robert and started toward the stairs leading topside.

Robert caught her by the arm and raised a palm.

At once, she realized her mistake. She forced aside her concern for Jack and followed Robert as he crept up the stairs a step at a time.

Her concern heightening, she pressed against him.

They cautiously raised their heads enough to see what was happening on the upper deck.

Jack lay on the floor, propped up on one elbow. Treadway stood over him a few feet away, right arm extended at a forty-five degree angle to his body.

The stubby barrel of a small chrome pistol pointed down at blue eyes glaring with hatred.

CHAPTER 66

Jack lay on the polished teak deck peering into the pea-sized bore of the small chrome semi-automatic. His breath caught in his throat.

Treadway's finger squeezed the trigger.

Nothing.

He squeezed it again, and then again.

Nothing.

Jack exhaled a sigh. The deadly little handgun should have gone off, but it failed to fire.

Treadway continued to squeeze the trigger.

Jack stared past the bore and saw the empty casing from the first shot jammed upright in the ejection port: *a stove pipe.*

He drove his foot into the side of Treadway's knee and heard the joint pop.

Treadway went down hard on his hands and one good knee. The handgun skittered out of his reach a few feet away.

Jack lunged for the gun and got his fingers around the grip.

Without a second's hesitation, he pulled back the slide with his other hand and shook out the spent cartridge.

The empty casing clattered to the floor.

He released the slide, jacking a live round into the chamber, and turned the gun on Treadway. The semi-automatic might jam again, but not before he got at least one clean shot.

At this range that's all he'd need.

"Okay asshole, my turn." Jack rose to his feet and stood keeping the semi-automatic pointed at Treadway.

"It's jammed. If it wasn't, you'd be dead."

Jack hand didn't waver.

He grinned and said, "Guess hell will have to wait."

Treadway worked his good leg under him and stood up, his eyes searching. "I'm telling you, that thing will do you no good."

Jack held his smile. "You want to bet on that?"

Treadway studied the bore of the gun. His left eye twitched. "I only bet on sure things. So what's your play?"

Robert and Katie chose that moment to scurry up the stairs and enter the salon.

The noise made Jack look.

In that same instant he felt his gun-hand being slapped aside.

Out of reflex, he squeezed the trigger.

Crack! The bullet splintered the teak, just missing his foot.

He swung the gun around and pointed it at Treadway who limped toward the open door leading aft. His injured leg apparently not as bad as Jack had thought.

Jack fired a second shot.

The window next to the hatchway shattered.

He fired again.

Treadway cried out, gripped his shoulder, and disappeared into the darkness.

Jack followed him to the door, spread his feet to steady himself against the rise and fall of the deck, and stood just outside the hatchway, scanning the rain and the darkness. Robert and Katie joined him a second later and stood facing the night.

Treadway was nowhere in sight.

"Where'd he go?" Robert asked.

"I don't know," Jack said.

Their heads jerked around at a thump that sounded like the lid to a storage locker closing. A second later, they heard a large splash on the starboard side.

"Sharks can have the fucker"—Jack looked at the tiny chrome semi-automatic in his hand—"and his toy gun." He threw the pistol overboard, pushed aside all thought of Treadway, and reached for

Katie.

She rushed into his outstretched arms, and he pulled her close, kissing her long and passionately.

His mind reeled from her touch. The moment he had seen her step into the salon, he had wanted to take her in his arms and never let go. And in that instant, he was consumed by the relief that flooded over him: knowing she was alive and well.

Mere words could not describe his love for her. There was only one language that could truly express his feelings. Now that Treadway was over the side and no longer a threat, he could focus his attention on her.

And that mean embracing her tight against him and planting his most passionate kiss on her wonderfully soft lips.

He reluctantly pulled away not wanting the kiss to end. As their lips parted, he noticed the bruising on her face.

His jaw muscles clenched.

The bastard. The sick sadistic bastard.

"Are you okay?" he asked, his voice sick with concern.

"I'm sure I look worse than . . ." She glanced at the floor obviously embarrassed by her appearance.

"You're beautiful," Jack said. He leaned in, gently kissed the bruise under her eye, and slowly pulled away. "I can't believe—" He gritted his teeth. "What kind of rotten bastard would beat a woman?"

She flinched at his touch and smiled past the pain.

"A dead one," she said.

He wrapped her in his arms and held her close, his eyes probing the night.

"If the asshole isn't," he said after a moment. "He soon will be. No way can he survive out there with a bullet in his shoulder and a busted knee."

He slid his arms from around Katie, realizing for the first time Kimo wasn't standing there with them. "Where's Kimo? We need to get going."

Robert answered for Katie. "He didn't make it."

"What do you mean he didn't make it?" Jack anxiously scanned their faces for the answer.

"Dead!" Katie blurted. "The man with the tattooed arms clubbed Kimo down when they grabbed me. He was still onboard our boat when they sank it. Treadway told me he was dead."

Sadness gutted Jack. There had been too much killing. No one should have died over a box of relics.

But that was how Treadway did business.

A renewed anger surged inside him.

He sucked in a deep breath through clenched teeth and shot a gaze at the starboard gunwale. *Treadway.* "That fucker!"

"You'll get no trouble out of me." The voice that boomed was deep and not one they had heard before. It came from within the salon.

The lookout from the bridge.

Struck between the eyes by his stupidity, Jack couldn't believe he had failed to remember there were still crewmembers aboard to be careful of. He silently cursed himself for throwing the gun overboard.

Clenching his fists tight, he brushed past Katie and Robert and stepped into the cabin.

The man inside raised his hands in front of him, palms out. "Whoa. You don't have to worry about me."

Jack lowered his fists, but stood his ground, ready to react. He noticed the man's distinctive cap. "You're the captain?"

"Carl Ward." He extended his hand.

Jack didn't take it. His gaze remained fixed on the captain's eyes.

Captain Ward bowed, curtly. "I understand completely. Believe me when I say you can forget about this fancy boat and me."

"Who else is aboard?"

"A cook and a maid. They're hiding below."

"And they agree?"

"They feel the way I do." Captain Ward removed his hat and offered it to Jack. "If I had a sword, I'd surrender it to you. Trust me. I've tendered my resignation from Mr. Treadway . . . or will as soon as I cruise his boat the hell on out of here and back to the mainland. I assure you; I've had my fill of Treadway's condescending bullying. Now that he's gone, I can return to being the person I was."

"What about the bodies?" Robert asked, assuming a defensive

position next to Jack. "There's one on the rear deck and two below."

"I assure you, they won't be there when I reach land."

"And the blood?"

"Where I'm going, no one will care about a little blood."

Jack nodded at the man's cap. "Keep the hat. I've got one of my own."

He didn't know why he was concerned for Captain Ward. The man had certainly played his part in all that had happened to them over the last couple of days. But there was a definite sincerity in his opinion of Treadway.

"You can manage this tub by yourself?" Jack asked, putting his trust in the captain.

"This fancy boat practically runs itself." Captain Ward's expression softened. "I'm truly sorry for the pain Treadway caused you."

Jack was touched by the captain's remorse. "You know we'll have to go to the police with this. The authorities will be looking for you."

"The ocean is a big place. I'll give you a minute to get in the Zodiac before I weigh anchor." Without another word, he turned and calmly walked up the steps leading to the bridge.

They watched the door click shut behind him. "You heard the man," Jack said. "We've got one minute."

The three of them scrambled over the portside and into the Zodiac. Jack started the engine and Robert cast off the line.

"Where are we going?" Katie asked, brushing matted strands of wet hair from her face.

A sudden crack of lightening streaked the sky, causing Jack to flinch. A boom of thunder that reverberated off the rubber pontoons followed an instant later. The storm was right on top of them. He was sure that was no accident of nature. *Madam Pele* was watching and listening.

And she was pissed.

"Kahoolawe," he yelled to be heard above the roar of the motor. "There's a rocky beach not far from the lava tube. I'll put us ashore there."

The Zodiac bounced up and over the waves in an amusement park thrill-ride that soaked them in a constant sheet of rain and salt spray. Dressed in cotton shorts and the flimsy silk blouse, Katie took the brunt of the discomfort. Jack and Robert fared better in their Body Glove wetsuits.

In the distance, *Trident* sped away at full speed. White water cascaded off her twin bows. Captain Ward was obviously making good his intentions to leave the area as quickly as possible.

Without warning, Jack eased off on the throttle and let the inflatable bob in the swells.

"The beach is over there," Robert said. He rose onto his knees and pointed.

"I know where the beach is. I'm going after the artifacts."

"The artifacts?" Robert yelled in disbelief.

"The bones were wrapped in *tapa* cloth, remember?" Jack explained. "The least I can do is recover King *Kalaniopuu's* remains—Cook's, too."

Katie laid her hand on Jack's. "You don't have to do this. Kimo's dead. We almost were. Let it go."

Jack patted her knuckles. "We've come too far to quit, now."

She curled her fingers around his hand and held it firm. "Can't you see it just doesn't matter anymore?"

"Does to me." He raised her hand to his mouth and kissed it. "The tide's coming in. If I don't go now I could lose the only opportunity I have to see this through. I've got just enough air in my tank to make it in and out if I don't dawdle. Robert will take you ashore. I'll meet you there."

"Katie's right," Robert urged Jack. "The odds are against you making it."

Jack pulled on his buoyancy compensator and buckled the straps.

He didn't worry about odds. Never had. Finding Katie's grandfather's West Point class ring in a hole in the reef after it had been lost there ten years, the shooting in Henderson, Nevada, going back to college to pursue a life dream, even finding the lava tube with the artifacts had defied odds.

And now that he thought about it, everything he'd done over the last four years had been a long shot of one type or another—especially stabbing that eight-foot tiger shark in the eye.

A neat trick, but it never should have worked.

"Put a hundred-dollar bill on the 'Don't Come' line if you like," he said. "I'm going for it."

He slipped on his mask and fins, grabbed his tank by the valve, picked up his Princeton Tec dive light, and rolled over the side and into the water.

CHAPTER 67

Jack hugged his tank as though it were a child's bobsled and rode the incoming tide through the channel in the reef all the way to the mouth of the lava tube. He didn't let himself think about the schools of brightly colored fish, running out of air, angry moray eels, or even what it would feel like to see Boryenko's lifeless body. Grabbing the *tapa*-cloth bundles of bones and getting the hell out of the basalt tomb alive was his only thought.

Until he felt the current slam him against the torpedo.

He'd seen the narrow opening looming ahead of him in a cloud of silt as the tide pushed him toward it, timed his entry . . . or so he thought. His head and one arm made it through, but his back smacked solidly into the twenty-one inch diameter metal tube.

It moved.

He felt the torpedo press down on him.

A flicker of claustrophobia shot a shockwave of panic to the nerve endings in his brain. Another couple of inches and he would be pinned against the coral encrusted rubble to die a slow agonizing death by drowning.

And if the torpedo fell . . . he'd be cut in half.

He wiggled through, dragging his tank with him.

His body slid free.

An almost overwhelming sense of relief flooded over him.

He faced the opening.

What were the odds of the torpedo picking that moment to slip from its resting place after so many years of being wedged solidly in the opening?

One in a million, one in two million . . . it just didn't matter.

Whether the movement had been caused by the impact of his body or the mounting surge from the storm and the rising tide, the torpedo had chosen that moment to rock loose and drop a few inches, narrowing the opening as if a gate were being closed behind him.

He couldn't help asking himself the one question he'd hoped to avoid.

Would the torpedo hold its present position long enough for him to get in and out of the lava tube with the artifacts?

All of a sudden, he found himself believing very much in odds.

He turned and kicked hard in the direction of the coarse sandy beach eighty feet into the tunnel. Promise or no promise, he felt very stupid being there.

All he could think about was grabbing the bones and getting out alive.

And the sooner the better.

Finally, the bottom rose under him until he could reach out and touch it. He rolled onto his butt, un-strapped his fins, peeled off his mask, and stood up facing the dark throat of the tunnel.

Despite an almost overwhelming desire to rush ahead, he slowed his feet and walked onto the sand. Something didn't feel right.

Taking one cautious step and then another, he swept the stone floor with the circle of light from his Princeton Tec.

He froze.

Boryenko's body was gone. Only a pool of blood marked the spot where he had lain.

Jack steeled himself against the possibilities and frantically swept his light beam through the dark interior.

Nothing . . . not even the crate of artifacts remained.

His mind could not comprehend the impossible. Boryenko was dead. No doubt about that. Incidents that defy explanation occur every day, but the big man could not have gotten up and swam away. Neither could the crate or the artifacts that had spilled from it.

But they had.

A chill like a million exploding micro-bubbles of cold air surged up his spine.

He shivered.

Gods and Goddesses . . . unearthly apparitions in the night . . . were these the forces at work here?

Leaving his tank wedged in the sand with his mask and fins piled beside it, he crept forward and brushed a finger through Boryenko's blood if for no other reason than to reassure himself the Russian had died there with a Japanese sword stuck through his guts. The blood was still tacky from the humidity inside the cave, and when he held his finger in front of the bright spot of his Princeton Tec, it shone deep red.

The pool of blood proved the man had bled to death. But what happened to his body?

And what about the scattered ti leaves? And the wooden crate or the treasure-trove of relics that had been strewn about, what happened to them?

Searching for answers, Jack probed deeper into the tunnel, around a turn beyond where the crate had lain with its contents spilled. He squatted and directed his light at a wet spot on the floor.

He dabbed it with the tip of his index finger.

A single drop of blood.

He anxiously swept his light beam over the glazed walls and ceiling in the tunnel ahead. He pointed the beam behind him. He could have sworn he heard a noise that didn't fit . . . or was it just a feeling, something his senses had picked up on?

Apparently nothing.

Again, he focused on the single drop of blood.

That noise again.

He felt a nervous flutter.

The blast reverberated through the tunnel. A maelstrom of Rock, coral, and water peppered the walls, floor, and ceiling.

In a brief moment of awareness, he believed Madam Pele had unleashed her mighty fury on him. The rock under his feet shook. His last thought: the dormant volcano was erupting.

CHAPTER 68

Robert beached the Zodiac, hopped into the ankle-deep surge, and helped Katie out. Together they pulled the inflatable above the tide line. Then they both turned and stared in the direction of the lava tube.

Katie crossed her arms tight around herself and paced. She and Robert had hovered in the inflatable near the spot where Jack slipped below the surface of the water, waiting for the glow from his dive light to appear in the inky blackness. They'd seen his bubbles . . . watched the narrow beam move off in the direction of the lava tube. She had wanted to stay in the area in case he needed help. But Robert insisted Jack would expect them to be on the beach waiting for him.

Jack.

She raised her hand to her cheek and held it against her skin, savoring his last kiss. There was nothing to do now but stare at the surf and watch for him to appear.

But how long would it take?

She silently prayed he was okay.

"He should be on his way out by now," Robert said with a tone of concern. He took a few steps closer to the jagged basalt outcroppings between them and the mouth of the lava tube.

Katie joined him. "Shouldn't we see his light?"

"Probably. Once he's—"

The explosion shattered the night. A ball of fire lit up the beach a fraction of a second before they were knocked to the sand.

They felt the heat of the blast, even from a hundred yards away. Bits of lava rained down on them.

To avoid the hailstorm of stones, they both faced the sand and covered their heads with their hands.

A golf-ball-sized rock struck Robert on his thigh. He tucked his knees to his chest and cringed.

Katie yelped, struck by one of the falling stones.

They both kept their heads covered.

Finally the onslaught stopped.

Ears ringing, Katie forced herself up on one elbow and looked toward the lava tube, trying to comprehend what happened. She'd felt the ground shake, heard the explosion, saw the fireball. Was the volcano erupting?

Then her eyes widened in horror.

She screamed.

"Jack!"

She struggled to gain her feet and staggered into the water. She inhaled breath after breath as she waded in up to her knees in the surf, but it was as though the oxygen had been sucked from the air.

Robert waded in after her and grabbed hold of her arm. "You can't do any good out there."

"But he might be unconscious," she gasped. "He'll drown."

"We'd have seen his light if he's out there."

Her legs threatened to give out on her. She stiffened. "Then we need to keep looking."

"Katie . . ." He squeezed her arm.

She spun her head to the side, wrenched her arm free of his grasp, and narrowed her eyes at him over her shoulder.

For a long uncomfortable moment, she glared at him.

Neither of them spoke. The only sound was that of the breaking waves.

Then tears flooded Katie's eyes and her breathing slowed. "Jack has to be out there, Robert. He just has to be."

Robert blinked back his own tears, and for a moment, he stared. "Jack's not there," he said. "And if he did make it out, the concussion . . ."

She held her gaze on him, silently pleading. She had to believe Jack had somehow survived. He had to have.

"There's still a chance," she said.

He took her hand in his and led her toward the beach.

"There's always a chance," he reassured her, but his tone lacked conviction.

She pulled back, resisting. "The Zodiac . . . we can take the Zodiac."

"We will," he said. "We'll do everything we can."

Still sobbing, she let him lead her ashore, but kept turning to peer over her shoulder at the water. She couldn't shake the feeling she was abandoning Jack.

"What happened?" she asked, clearly confused. "Was it the volcano?"

"There was a torpedo wedged in the opening. It might have—"

"A torpedo?" She stopped walking and spun on Robert.

He turned and met her gaze. "I thought you knew." His voice reflected his sincerity. "We had to squeeze past it to get inside."

"What . . . ? Where . . . ?" She could hardly speak.

"A present from the Navy, I'm sure. But I can't imagine what set the thing off. If that's what happened. Damned thing's been there for years."

"If it was wedged in the entrance, there's a chance he—." She squeezed his hand. "How far inside the lava tube was the crate of relics?"

"Not far enough." His eyes narrowed. "Unless . . ."

CHAPTER 69

Dazed and deafened, Jack blinked himself conscious. Or was he? Because the place was pitch black.

Had he taken one too many risks?

Had his luck run out?

He fingered a moist gash over his right eye and cringed. Sticky. *Blood!*

Pain and blood meant he was alive. He'd survived the explosion.

His head began to clear as he struggled to piece together what happened.

The torpedo.

There was no other explanation.

But how had he lived through the blast?

He had a vague recollection of being hurled onto the basalt shelf that once held the lost crate, and then being slammed headfirst onto the stone floor. The turn in the lava tube must have saved him from the deadly barrage of shrapnel and the worst of the concussion from the bone-crushing explosion.

Crawling around on his hands and knees, he groped for the dive light he'd been holding at the time of the explosion.

His hand touched the plastic housing; his finger found the switch. He flipped it on.

Nothing.

He shook the dive light, broken.

There was another possibility.

He was blind.

Never in his life had he known such utter blackness. Nor had he envisioned dying while wandering the darkness and solitude of a lava tube inside a volcano.

But he couldn't let himself think that . . . not yet.

His mind tilted and he feared he was going to pass out.

Then he saw it: a dim glow forming deeper in the tunnel, perhaps a hundred feet away.

He managed to rise to his feet using the rock shelf for a handhold. Was he seeing things or was this the light at the end of the tunnel that people who have died and come back, talk about?

He took a shaky step, and another.

The golden light danced on the crystalline glaze coating the walls and ceiling of the lava tube.

Torchlight.

And whoever it was . . . whatever it was . . . they were moving toward him.

He waited . . . and watched.

The light grew brighter.

He made himself breathe. Forced his hands to stop shaking.

Then a lone figure stepped into view and stopped twenty feet in front of him.

Through the mist fogging his vision and the glare of the torch, he saw a bare-chested dark-skinned native dressed in a *tapa* loincloth. A boar's tooth necklace hung around his neck. A leafy *lei* adorned the crown of his head. And around his ankle, he wore a bracelet of teeth, shell, and carved bone.

The Marchers of the Night . . . A Night Marcher.

For what seemed like an eternity, the native stood motionless in the yellow glow of the flickering torch. The ghostly appearance of the ancient warrior unnerved Jack. Was this an apparition sent to help . . . or a messenger of death?

That's what it was, Jack decided, an apparition dredged from his mind. A figment of his imagination that would disappear in a puff of smoke the moment he stepped toward it.

There was nothing for him to lose.

Except his life.

He cautiously stepped in that direction fully expecting the figure to disappear, but the native pivoted and walked deeper into the tunnel.

Jack still did not know if what he was seeing was real. No one lived or traveled in this subterranean world of stone.

Or did they?

"Hey," he called out and waited for an answer.

His voice echoed far into the tunnel. But his words faded away without a response. The warrior did not turn, did not acknowledge his presence in any way. He just kept walking.

"Where are you leading me?" Jack tried, again.

Nothing . . . not even a glance over the shoulder.

Standing amid the rubble in the middle of the tube now, he took a quick look behind him in the dim glow from the torch and saw a wall of broken and shattered stone even the ocean couldn't penetrate.

The explosion had sealed him in a rock tomb.

He hesitated a moment longer, then stepped in the direction of the fading light.

There was only one way out. Follow the warrior.

Suddenly hopeful, he strained to see as he started walking.

Ahead, the interior of the lava tube came into view as foreign as any faraway planet. The native carrying the torch appeared to move effortlessly over the stone floor.

Jack wished he could walk as easily.

Again, he stumbled and righted himself. He was having a tough time negotiating the uneven terrain.

A dozen paces ahead—in the dim glow of the torch—the tunnel was a patchwork of shadow that shifted and changed shape with each step, making it impossible for him to keep up.

His foot caught. He fell hard on one knee.

The separation between them widened, and he felt the walls close in on him with the fading light.

He found his footing and pressed onward.

But where would he end up?

He increased his pace, but couldn't help wondering if he was being led to safety . . . or into the heart of the volcano and a fiery death in a cauldron of molten lava?

His mind reeled with questions.

How far had he walked? How long had he been in the lava tube?

His dive watch was no help. The crystal had shattered on the stone floor when he fell. Without the watch, he had no sense of time. He figured he'd been walking about five minutes, maybe fifteen . . . and hour for all he knew.

Did time really matter in a world without light?

Around another sweeping curve to the right, the tunnel floor leveled out before disappearing in shadow around yet another turn.

A winding string of spaghetti.

Jack remembered he had made a slight right turn before spying the spot of blood on the stone floor—the curve in the tunnel that had shielded him from the concussion of the blast and the maelstrom of flying rock and shrapnel. He'd just made another curve to the right and the slope had leveled off.

Picturing the lay of the shoreline as he had seen it from their boat, he concluded the lave tube meandered north along the rocky coast.

But how far before the tunnel veered into the bowels of Kahoolawe?

Glancing up at the stone ceiling, he envisioned a star-filled night sky . . . the moon. If he was correct in his reckoning, only a few feet of rock separated him from the world he knew . . . and Katie, the woman he loved.

So close, but it might as well have been a mile.

Even an inch of solid rock was an impenetrable distance for a man caught alone without iron tools.

CHAPTER 70

Jack stumbled on amid the fading light.

The passage remained smooth with glaze . . . no stalagmites, no stalactites to bar his way. An open road for him to travel, but he still didn't have an answer to the question of where he was being led.

Once again, he considered odds. What odds would a Vegas casino give against him making it out of the lava tube alive? Could he even find a casino that would cover such a long shot? He figured they would be lined up to take his money.

He thought about calling out to the native, again. Ask him where they were going; see if he would answer this time. But why waste his breath. The native was leading him someplace.

He just prayed it was a way out.

Another fifty feet in, he stopped. Ahead in the tunnel—at the farthest fringes of the torchlight—he saw a mountain of basalt chunks that rose to within a foot of the domed ceiling.

Evidently, the ghost warrior had been heading for this exact spot because he floated up the mountain of stones as effortlessly as he'd traveled the lave tube and disappeared through the roof of the cave.

Immediately Jack regretted the loss of the torch. Without its golden light for company, he stood alone in the darkness.

A chill pricked the hairs on his neck and raised goose bumps on his arms.

There was nowhere for him to go.

For a long minute, he struggled with the loneliness that descended upon him in the darkness. The warrior apparition had given him hope. But without the night marcher there to guide him, all expectation of making it out of the rock hell alive, was lost.

He and Robert had joked about the lava tube when they first saw its glazed walls sparkle in their flashlight beams.

Something out of Jules Verne's *Journey to the Center of the Earth*.

Now that analogy proved to be closer to fact than not. He'd wander the lava tube until he died of starvation. Water wouldn't be a problem, he could hear it dripping. But in the center of the earth, food was nonexistent. Giant mushrooms didn't grow there; neither did monstrous flesh-eating dinosaurs. There was no lost civilization, or sunken cities with loaves of stale bread and thousand-year-old eggs, no long dead explorers of the inner world with sacks of gunpowder lying next to their bleached bones to blast a way out.

Only death.

Incredibly, his eyes began to grow accustomed to the dark. He could just make out the walls and ceiling of the tunnel, and when he looked down, the stone floor, his feet, his hands held out in front of him.

Immediately he knew this would not have been possible in the absolute darkness of the lava tube . . . not without some light.

And there was a breeze . . . a gentle wisp of air that wouldn't be there if he was sealed in.

Could it be . . . ?

He looked at the spot where the native apparition disappeared. The darkness there was not the same as it was inside the lava tube.

A night sky.

He was looking at an opening in the rock ceiling . . . a skylight out.

Was it wishful thinking?

Or was he just dreaming?

He swallowed hard, his mouth suddenly dry.

Neither . . .

The way out had been revealed to him and he wouldn't spend a minute more than necessary to make his escape. Still, he restrained his excitement and moved cautiously over the dark uneven floor.

He didn't want to stumble and break a leg when he was this close to freeing himself from his rock prison.

Now he wished he'd been able to lay down a hundred dollar bill on his making it out of the tunnel alive. Vegas odds makers would have shit their pants. And he'd have been able to retire in style.

When he neared the rock pile, he noticed the floor had become slick. He reached down and felt slime on the glaze at his feet. Ahead of him, rainwater that had fallen through the opening, pooled in recesses in the lava. The downpour outside had stopped, but it had left the stone slick with a goo that had formed over years of exposure to salt air and moisture.

He took his time now, choosing his footing carefully ... thankful he was wearing neoprene booties.

Finally, he reached the mountain of stones. A stray drop of rainwater struck him on the forehead and dripped down. Looking up, he realized the stairway out had been created when the basalt ceiling collapsed into a heap of jagged stone slabs leaving a hole where rock had once been.

He began climbing one boulder at a time.

Out of the corner of his eye, he saw the reason the ceiling had collapsed. An unexploded bomb had pierced the tunnel. It lay wedged in the boulders at the bottom of the pile.

A small rock jiggled loose beneath his foot, bounced, and struck the tailfin of the bomb.

He froze and clenched his eyes shut.

Nothing ...

No high-pitched whirring of a firing mechanism arming itself. No ticking.

He sighed and opened his eyes.

Taking his time, he moved his foot around to reposition the loose stone he was standing on so that it wouldn't fall.

The rock slipped.

He wedged the chunk of lava back in place before it got away from him.

Another hit on the bomb and he might not be so lucky.

Easy now. Don't fuck up.

Doing his best to calm his racing heart, he continued to climb.

A minute later, he poked his head through the opening.

CHAPTER 71

Jack scrambled out of his would-be basalt tomb. And for a moment he stood with his head tilted back, drawing in a deep breath. The night air was thick with salty humidity and the pungent aroma of decaying seaweed. He'd never smelled anything sweeter.

Then he remembered.

The warrior . . . ?

He scanned the darkness. There was no sign of the native with the torch anywhere. The night marcher had faded into the night as quickly as he had appeared.

He looked at the sky. Stars twinkled overhead. Was Madam Pele appeased? Had she caused the torpedo to fall when it did? Was that her revenge? He closed his eyes and thanked the Goddess of Fire for saving his life.

"Jack." Robert's voice boomed from the darkness. At the same instant, the beam of his dive light appeared from around a protrusion of black lava.

Jack dropped his gaze, surprised by his friend's sudden appearance.

Robert hurried forward, stopped in front of him, and gripped his shoulder. "My God, buddy. I can't believe it's you."

"In the flesh." Jack lips spread into a broad grin. He couldn't stop smiling.

"Jack! Jack!" Katie's voice shook as she picked her way over the rocks to get to him. "It's really you."

"You can't get rid of me that easily."

She threw her arms around his neck and kissed him. Tears flowed. "Get rid of you. My God, Jack, we thought you were blown to pieces when that torpedo exploded. How'd you ever get out of there?"

Again, Jack visually checked the area for the apparition. It seemed that's what he was.

"A native with a torch led me to that hole over there," he said. "It's a kind of skylight into the lava tube. A pile of rock leads right up to it like a flight of stairs."

"A native?" Katie questioned, clearly skeptic.

"Like a fire dancer at a luau . . . torch and everything. But he seems to have disappeared."

"So that's the light I saw." Robert jabbed a thumb over his shoulder. "We were way over there trying to figure out how to get into the lava tube to find you when I saw what I thought was the glow of your dive light." He swept his bright beam across the shadows. "This is strange. He should still be here."

"*A Night Marcher* . . ." Katie whispered the words as if she was thinking aloud.

Jack caught a glance from Robert. He'd heard her, too. Clearly mystified by the prospect, his arms hung limp at his sides, the beam from the dive light he was holding pointed at the ground.

All three of them gazed into the darkness without uttering a word.

Jack was as mystified as his two friends were. Even though he had wondered if the warrior in the lava tube was a ghostly apparition conjured up by his imagination, he had believed the man was real. Now he didn't know what to think.

Had the native been a spirit . . . a legendary Marcher of the Night?

The salt air that welcomed him to the surface was replaced with an eerie chill that crept up his spine. He knew Katie and Robert had to feel it too.

A force not their own was at work here.

"What's that?" Katie asked.

"What?" Jack saw her raise her index finger to her mouth the way she did when she was concentrating. She had her ear cocked to the wind. He mentally blocked out the sound of the ocean and listened.

Chanting!

He looked to the north, squinted. He could barely make it out, but he was certain about what he was seeing. A hundred yards away, just beyond a jumble of protruding lava, a golden glow . . . faint but visible.

"Over there," he said, pointing. "Let's go, but be careful of that hole."

With the aid of Robert's light, the three of them negotiated the football field of rocky coastline without incident. Finally, they reached the outcropping between them and the ghostly glow.

Robert and Katie started around the rock mass.

"Wait," Jack cautioned in a soft tone, extending an arm to stop them.

He wasn't sure he was all that anxious to see what awaited them on the other side. The golden glow danced and flickered against the backdrop of rock, an indication the light was from a bonfire on the beach. But who were these people?

The island was uninhabited.

"Let's take a peek first," Jack whispered

Robert chuckled quietly. "Scared, are you?"

"Let's just say I want to be sure of what we're walking into."

"I'm with you, Jack." Katie gripped the front of her blouse firmly together at the buttons. "I've already had my clothes off once tonight, and I'm not anxious to have to take them off and play dead in the path of a bunch of Night Marchers."

"I noticed you'd changed." Jack looked her up and down as though he were checking out the blouse for the first time. "Red silk looks good on you."

"When we're out of here, I'm burning this one. The former owner left her stink on it."

"Speaking of that French bombshell, what happened to her, anyway?" Jack had not thought about her till now. He hadn't seen any reason to since she no longer posed a problem.

"You mean French bitch." There was venom in Katie's tone. "The woman came down with a fatal stomach ache."

"Skewered her in the gut with a trident spear is what she did," Robert said. "Quite appropriate, I might add."

A sad hollowness descended on Jack's chest. There was obviously no love lost for Treadway's girlfriend as far as he was concerned. But he knew the pain Katie had to feel having killed the woman. Killing people in self defense was getting easier for him, but there was still a certain amount of regret even for killing someone like Treadway or the Russian equivalent of Big Foot.

"I won't ask the sordid details," he said. "When you feel like talking about it, I'll listen."

Katie sighed. "Right now I just want to be away from this place."

"Well"—Jack said—"let's take a gander at who's on the other side of this rock and see if we can get a ride off this island."

He faced Robert for an indication he agreed.

Robert shrugged.

Good enough.

Like children peeking over a backyard fence, they raised their heads above the rock barrier and stared at the figures in the firelight fifty feet away.

A familiarity about the white-haired man who stood as the center of attention of the group, pricked at Jack's awareness. But the clothing confused him.

The old Hawaiian wore a multi-colored *tapa*-cloth *kihei* slung over his left shoulder and tied at the waist on the right. And a bright red sash. A lei of feathers—most of them red, a few yellow—crowned his head.

The clothing clearly had special meaning. The man was a shaman, a priest.

It took Jack a few seconds longer to recognize the *Kahuna*, then it dawned on him who he was: the old man he had seen sitting in the van the day of the accident, and again outside Robert's apartment.

Keoni!

Kimo's uncle.

Keoni started to chant and Jack realized the *kahuna* was held in high regard by the other men standing around the fire.

On the other side of the blazing pit, three young men stood straight-backed and perfectly still with their muscled arms folded in front of them: majestic warriors of the past. And in every way—except for the facial features—carbon copies of the native in the tunnel. A long torch was stuck into the ground next to each one of them, adding to the golden glow from the fiery pit.

A fifth person—older by appearance—stood across the pit from the three warriors, but Jack could only see his back. It wasn't until the man showed his profile that he recognized Kimo.

Alive!

Jack was positive he wasn't mistaken. Kimo had shed his street clothes and stood naked except for a loincloth, but it was him.

Clearly, the native Hawaiians were engaged in a magical ceremony of religious importance. And he was part of the ceremony.

Jack raised his head higher above his rock hiding place and saw the wooden crate that had held artifacts. Every relic that'd been packed in it was gone. Not even the leafy packing remained.

He sighed. The anticipation that had been there a moment ago, dissipated. Then he spied the *tapa*-cloth bundles at the feet of the *kahuna*.

Abruptly, the chanting stopped.

CHAPTER 72

Jack gripped the rock. There was no denying a spiritual power was at work here. And he felt that power draw him to the circle of men. But what did it mean? Did his inner spirit seek the comfort of the fire? Or was it the gaze of the *kahuna* who stood staring at them that drew him in?

His instinctive reaction was to duck down out of sight and hope the spell would be broken. But then what good would that do? It was useless to pretend they hadn't been seen.

He shot a nervous glance at Katie and Robert. His trusted friend was already standing, clearly in view of the men around the fire.

Robert gestured a hand that direction and said, "Let's go, Jack."

Jack had a sinking feeling it would cause them more problems to intrude on such a sacred ceremony. Still, they needed help. And Robert seemed confident in his decision to join the group of Hawaiians by the fire.

Jack huffed.

Not more trouble?

He pushed off from the rock and stood well exposed to the group. To Robert he said, "I hope you know what you're doing."

Cautious of what they were getting into, he took his time climbing down from the jagged outcropping. He held Katie by the hand, determined not to leave her side. Robert strode into the ceremony as though he belonged there.

Jack didn't march into the ring of resolute faces the way Robert did. He purposely held back waiting to see what was going to happen. He relaxed when he saw his friend exchange grins with Kimo, clap him on the back, and shake hands.

Nothing could have made Jack happier. He'd been struggling with Kimo's death, and given the opportunity he'd like to do more than just shake the man's hand.

He took a couple of steps that direction. Then stopped dead in his tracks, stunned by what he saw.

Katie shot Jack a hard look over her shoulder. "What'd you stop for?"

Jack raised his hand in a gesture for her to wait. He could hardly believe his eyes. Robert had walked up and touched foreheads with Keoni in the honored tradition of the Polynesian islands: The custom of breathing in each other's breath . . . or life as it is believed.

This greeting clearly had significance beyond that of a simple handshake.

Robert turned and waved Jack and Katie over, saying, "Keoni has been waiting to greet you."

Jack knew Robert had become good friends with Kimo, but he had no idea their relationship had evolved this far. It seemed as though Robert was one of the family. A blonde-haired addition to the tribe.

That part was great. What disturbed Jack was that Robert—his trusted and dear friend—had apparently chosen to not tell him everything.

They have words about that, he was sure.

"Our turn," he said to Katie.

Katie didn't need any more urging. She hustled ahead of Jack, right past Robert and Keoni, up to Kimo, and hugged him. Tears streaked her cheeks.

"I'm so glad you're alive," she said. "Damn that asshole for lying to me."

Kimo embraced Katie and told her, "I hated leaving you with Treadway. But I had no choice. When I came to, the boat was sinking. They must have chopped holes in her hull or something. Anyway, all I could do was swim ashore and find my uncle and his nephews."

"Your head?" She eyeballed his scalp. "They clubbed you."

"I have a thick skull," he said. "I'll live."

"Would someone mind telling me what's going on?" Jack stepped forward and shook Kimo's hand. "I'm sure-as-hell glad you're alive. It felt like I'd been gutted when they told me you were dead. But this"—he nodded at the group—"is no home coming party."

"It is . . . sort of." Keoni stepped to where Jack stood and extended his hand.

Jack gripped it, and in the way Robert had, leaned close and touched foreheads. The Kahuna deserved the respect. And he really was glad to find him and his family there, even if something sneaky was going on.

"Then—" He looked past Keoni at Robert.

"You're correct in your assumption," Keoni said. He reached out with his arm, and with a sweeping motion added, "This gathering . . . this ceremony . . . was planned from the beginning. Robert informed us of your promise to the young lady's grandfather to recover the remains of our ancestor. He understood the importance of seeing the bones returned to my people, but it was his wish you be given the opportunity to fulfill your promise. He knows you value your word. So we gave him our word that we would not interfere as long as the artifacts were given to us once you found them."

"You planned all this?" Jack turned and scanned the scene, taking it all in. From Robert's smug expression, he knew more than he let on.

Robert shrugged.

"The ceremony, yes," Keoni continued. "But we did not know the exact location of the lava tube were the artifacts were hidden, until you located it. We would not have interfered if it had not become necessary."

Jack couldn't hold back a broad grin that creased his face.

"I'm glad you did," he said.

Out of the corner of his eye, he saw Robert smile as if his minor betrayal had been vindicated by Keoni's actions. It had. The end result was turning out the same. King Kalaniopuu's bones and those of Captain Cook would be repatriated along with the other stolen artifacts, which was Katie's grandfather wish.

They'd have a beer over all this later—Jack vowed to himself—maybe even a shot of tequila or two . . . the good stuff: Don Julio *anejo*. He'd make Robert buy. There was no way he would allow such a minor infraction of their trust in each other to interfere with their longtime friendship.

He faced the three young men. "Which one of you do I owe my life to?"

CHAPTER 73

Jack watched and waited for the young men to step forward and take credit. None of them moved.

"My nephew Iokepa found the opening into the lava tube," Keoni offered with pride. "It was he who ventured inside to find you."

Jack reached out, eager to shake hands with the young man. But Iokepa stood firm, his arms tightly crossed in front of him—a proud island warrior in modern times.

"Thank you for coming after me," Jack said, withdrawing his hand. "I owe you."

Iokepa did not respond. His expression remained stoic. Jack did not take this or his refusal to shake hands as an insult, only a show of his warrior pride.

Just as Jack was about to turn away, he saw the young man wink and smile.

He cracked a smile and nodded in acknowledgement.

Warrior pride, indeed.

Facing Kimo, he said, "We're indebted to you already. But we seem to be in a bit of a fix here. I don't suppose we can intrude on you to give us a ride back to Maui? I prefer not to put my trust in that little Zodiac if I don't have to." He looked toward the sea and added, "You have a big enough boat, I hope?"

"Of course," Keoni said. "My nephew is waiting offshore in it now. It's only a matter of signaling him in. But before we do that, we have the ceremony to complete."

The *kahuna* resumed his position facing the artifacts. Raising his hands in front of him, he faced the heavens and began to chant.

Jack did not understand the words, but felt their power.

Keoni let his incantation trail off. Then he reached down, picked up the Samurai sword, and held it out to Jack.

"There is a Hawaiian legend that speaks of the Wonderful Iron Knife," Keoni began. "Seven hundred years before King Kalaniopuu's death, a white chief with an iron knife was shipwrecked on the coast of Maui near the village of Wailuku. Three men and two women survived. Legend says they were Japanese. The captain carried a long sword which became revered throughout the islands . . . tribal wars were fought over it. Over the centuries, the sword was carefully preserved and treasured by the *alii* who possessed it. For when the Wonderful Iron Knife was matched against wooden daggers and clubs, it was an enormously effective weapon. I believe this is that great knife. You used it in battle to protect the bones of our ancestor King. You are a warrior. The sword is yours, now."

Jack accepted the fabled Samurai sword. "I am honored to receive your gift."

Keoni bent and picked up a jade box big enough to hold a pair of shoes. The lid was bound shut with a thick plant-fiber cord. He held it out to Jack just as he had the sword.

"These belonged to the Japanese survivors who brought them to trade. All this time, they have remained with the sword. They are of great value and yours to do with as you see fit."

Jack accepted the gift as he had the Wonderful Iron Knife. Only this time he did so with reservation. He remembered seeing the jade box in the spilled relics. He had no idea what was in it, but knew Keoni would not embellish its value. The prize was too great.

"I'm not sure I deserve your generosity." Struck by humility, Jack offered the box back to Keoni.

"You won the sword in battle. The box is part of the prize. It is yours."

The formality of the ceremony made Jack uncomfortable. Nothing was discussed. The *kahuna's* words were final.

He searched the expressions on the faces of other men. Kimo and his nephews made no attempt to question the kahuna's wishes—neither did Robert or Katie—but what was the price of this loyalty?

To the victor go the spoils?

Jack did not want to be singled out as a great warrior more worthy than any of the other men standing there. Killing Boryenko and shooting Treadway had been simple acts of self defense, not uncommon valor.

He had to find a way to make them understand without insulting the *kahuna's* wisdom and generosity.

"I—"

Keoni raised his hand. Jack understood the meaning. The *kahuna* was silencing him.

"These are yours." He handed Jack a *kapa* cloth bundle bound tight with a fiber cord matching the cordage tied around the koawood box. "The final remains of your ancestor Captain Cook have been returned. The promise made so long ago by my people has been fulfilled. And here is his sword."

Jack stared incredulously at the bundle and the rusty saber Keoni placed on top of it. First the samurai sword, then the jade box with its treasure, now this. He found it difficult to shoulder the weight of so much history.

Surely he was not worthy of such a great honor. "With all due respect—"

"Jack Ferrell!" His name boomed from the surf, cutting him off.

It was a voice Jack didn't expect to ever hear again. Bile rose in his throat. The man just wouldn't die.

He turned and saw Treadway standing knee deep in the frothy surf thirty feet away, a speargun leveled in his hands. The three thick rubber bands were pulled tight and locked into their notches on the spear.

The weapon was ready to fire . . . and it was pointed right at Jack's belly.

In a millisecond of awareness, Jack realized Treadway must have grabbed the speargun from the storage locker before going overboard.

And then what?

Jack couldn't see how Treadway had survived the swim ashore . . . not with a bullet in the shoulder and an injured knee.

But he had.

Jack sidestepped in front of Keoni, reached, and pulled Katie back out of the line of fire.

"You've lost Treadway," Jack said. "Give it up."

"I never lose," Treadway answered.

Jack felt the sting of the venom in the man's threat. He stepped away, separating himself from the group. The fight was between him and Treadway. He didn't even want to think anyone else would get hurt by this madman.

"But you have," he said. He kept moving, a step at a time. He didn't want to give Treadway a stationary target to shot at. "In case you haven't noticed, your captain beat feet out of here with your boat."

"He will die for that . . . as you will." Treadway raised the speargun chest high, the sharp point of the barbed spear focused on Jack's chest as he moved.

Treadway's left eye twitched.

Jack tensed.

Treadway's finger tightened on the trigger.

At that moment, a dorsal fin broke the surface of the water behind him. He fired at the same instant his legs were jerked from under him. The four-foot-long stainless steel spear went wide and stuck in the sand three feet to the left of Jack.

Jack stood his ground and watched the surf boil red. No one else on the beach moved to help. They felt the way he did.

Sharks have to eat, too.

Treadway's screams echoed into the night. Then they were lost when the shark sunk its teeth into his thigh and pulled him under.

The creature broke the surface, and Jack saw it was an eight-foot tiger. He could have sworn the shark had one scared eye.

He continued to watch as another dorsal fin . . . and another, appeared in the bloody surf as sharks swarmed in a feeding frenzy to tear off their own piece of Treadway—the scavengers of the sea moving in to take out the garbage.

Jack's only regret was that the megalomaniac hadn't suffered more.

But he *had* suffered.

For a long moment, no one spoke. The only sound was the crashing of the waves, washing the beach clean.

Then Keoni began to chant.

The rhythmic canticle calmed the boiling water as the last pieces of Treadway were gulped down.

This time Jack not only felt the power of the elder's words, he understood their meaning. The *kahuna* thanked *Kamohoalii*, the shark god of Kahoolawe, for taking revenge on Treadway.

EPILOGUE

Santa Barbara, California
Six months later

Jack stood on the dock with his back to a sixty-foot power catamaran. How wonderfully happy he was just to be alive.

The overcast that blanketed Santa Barbara's coast with a veil of gray during the summer had been replaced by a warm bright October sky. In his hands, he held a bottle of Don Julio *anejo* 100 percent blue *agave* tequila and four shot glasses.

He'd decided it was his turn to buy.

A hundred feet away, Robert, Kazuko, and Katie walked his direction. They each held a small carryon. No sight looked better to him.

"I was beginning to worry you weren't going to make it," Jack said when the trio of friends got a little closer.

"How could we not?" Robert answered. He strode ahead of the two women and embraced Jack with a handshake and a friendly slap on the back. "First class tickets and a solemn promise for a fun-filled week away from home would bring anybody running."

Kazuko caught up and punched Robert on the shoulder. "Ladies first." She leaned in and kissed Jack on the cheek. "The clod. I swear I can't take the man anywhere anymore."

Katie stood back until Kazuko finished teasing Robert. Then she brushed past him and Kazuko and slid her arms around Jack's neck.

"Careful." Jack winked. "People are watching."

"Who cares." Mussing his tight-cropped hair with her fingers, she pulled his body tight against hers and kissed him long and passionately.

"Okay, okay." Robert said when Katie finally slid her arms from around Jack's neck. "Give someone else a chance."

Katie saw Kazuko elbow Robert. She smiled. "A chance, huh? At me, or him?"

Robert knitted his brow at her. "Very funny."

"You're the man with the jokes."

"Yeah, right. What I meant was I wanted to ask him what all the mystery is about." Robert shifted his gaze to Jack. "So what gives, buddy? Your note asked us to meet you here today, but it didn't say why, only to pack light and for warm weather." He held up his bag. "Well, here we are."

"And I brought the tequila," Jack said. He held up the bottle of Don Julio. "Come aboard and I'll explain."

"Come aboard?" Confusion showed in the tone of Robert's voice.

Katie and Kazuko faced each other, clearly puzzled.

"My boat." Jack made a sweeping gesture with his hand. "That's why I asked you to meet me here—to pick up my new boat. Or new old boat as it were.

Robert noticed the name painted on the side of the hull—large scrawling green letters with gold shadowing: *Pono*.

He smiled. "*Make things right.* The name fits. I take it you sold that jade box and all those nice pearls?"

"All but one." He dug into his pocket and pulled out a jeweler's box the size of a two-inch ice cube. He handed it to Katie.

She held the small velvet-covered case in front of her and glanced nervously from Jack to Robert to Kazuko and back to Jack.

He waved the bottle of Don Julio at the gift and said, "Well?"

She shrugged. "What can I say?"

"You don't have to say anything." He flashed her his best encouraging smile. "Just open it."

Katie held her breath and lifted the lid. She gasped. "My God, it's positively beautiful."

She held the ring out for Kazuko and Robert to admire: two golden dolphins circling a single 8 mm greenish-yellow pearl. "I can't believe you did this."

Jack could hardly contain himself. This was exactly the response he hoped for. His idea for the ring couldn't have turned out better.

"A romantic," Robert said. "That's what you are, Jack . . . a hopeless romantic."

Jack winked. "You think?"

"I know."

"Well you just might be right." Jack grinned. "Come aboard and let's pull the cork on this bottle. We have some catching up to do. And as far as what I have planned, how does a week sailing down the Baja coast to Cabo San Lucas sound—a kind of maiden voyage to christen *Pono*? Plenty of sun, salt air, fishing, great food, barbeques on the beach, and lots of Don Julio tequila, what do you say . . . sound like fun?"

"Let's get that bottle open," Robert urged.

There was plenty of room for the four of them in *Pono's* spacious salon. They took seats at the galley table and Jack poured each of them a shot of tequila.

He raised his glass. "To good friends and good times.

"Here, here . . ." was the resounding answer by all.

Robert noticed the samurai sword sitting on a koawood stand mounted prominently on the forward bulkhead in front of the helm. "Nice sword."

"And sharp," Jack flashed him a devilish grin. "I believe you have one of your own?"

"Mine's rusty."

"You decided to keep it?"

"Let sleeping dogs lie, that's what I say. Besides, Cook's sword makes for a great conversation piece. It's just too bad I can't tell the real story behind it."

"All that'd do is land us behind bars. And for what . . . ridding the world of that asshole Treadway?"

Katie scoffed. "We didn't kill him, the sharks did."

Jack grinned. "You have a point. So what do we chalk that other scum we took care of up to?"

Robert raised his glass. "Practice."

That made Jack laugh.

"I still think you could have found a way to return Captain Cook's bones to England's historical society," Kazuko said.

Jack shook his head. "They belonged in Kealakekua Bay with the rest of him. Besides' we would have had to explain where we got them."

Robert draped an arm around Kazuko's shoulders and pulled her close. "Honey, you have to remember, none of this happened."

He nodded at the samurai sword, again. "What's the final story on that?"

"Well"—Jack turned and eyed the fabled antiquity—"as you know, there's no way of determining if that is, in fact, the *Wonderful Iron Knife* Keoni spoke of. But the head of the Archeology Department at the University gladly conferred with his colleagues in the field. They marveled at the pristine condition of the sword, but all agreed it was quite old."

"Did the date match?" Katie leaned forward in her chair, clearly interested. "Keoni said seven hundred years before King Kalaniopuu's death. That would make it what . . . the twelfth century. If the dates are close, it'd give some credence to the myth."

"Unfortunately, the professor wasn't able to tell me exactly how old it is, not without further examination by experts in Japan. Which I wouldn't agree to because none of that matters to me. As far as I'm concerned, it'll always be the *Wonderful Iron Knife* spoken of in Hawaiian legend."

Robert stared into his shot glass. "You still think the pearls were what Treadway was really after?"

"I'm sure he was after the whole lot, but those pearls certainly sweetened the pot. That must have been the part of the loot his grandfather mentioned only as being worth a bundle."

"What surprised me was the color," Katie said. "I thought pearls were either white or black. All of the ones we recovered were a greenish-yellow."

"That's because they're native pearls," Kazuko offered. "The pearls you're familiar with are cultured."

"She's right," Jack continued. "This whole pearl thing was an eye opener for me. I won't even tell you how many fast-talking jewelers tried their best to get their greedy hands on them before I found one willing to point me in the right direction. The bottom line is one thousand three hundred and eighty-four Akoya high quality pearls 7mm or more, plus the gold inlayed jade box they were in, one million fifty thousand . . . minus one pearl for Katie's ring."

Katie clutched the ring to her chest. "And I love it."

Jack wanted to laugh. He chuckled. "I certainly hope so."

He pulled two envelopes from his shirt pocket and slid one each across the table to Katie and Robert. "Now, the final piece of business before we get down to some serious celebrating."

"Two hundred and sixty-two thousand five hundred each," he said. "I've already sent Kimo his share. I hope no one minds, I took the liberty of hanging onto the sword. You can say it has special meaning for me."

"Keep it, Jack." Robert raised his glass in a salute. "You definitely earned it. Although I'm sure it has more than one notch in the handle."

"Speaking of notches, Boryenko's body never did show up, did it?"

"Not a trace. Keoni said not to worry. My guess is there are some fat tiger sharks swimming around out there."

"I know of an eight footer that has probably grown a couple of feet off of Treadway, alone."

"If the taste didn't kill the poor shark," Katie said. Her voice trailed off as her gaze dropped to her drink glass.

Jack reached across the table and gently gripped her hand. The bruises on her face had healed months ago, but obviously the injury ran deeper. He had feared it would. But he couldn't really blame her. His stomach still knotted up when he thought about Treadway, and the Russian who had almost killed him and Robert.

That's what the trip was for. Hopefully a long week in the sun stretching and toning her muscles, working on the tan she had started, and laughing a lot would purge that hurt—help them all forget.

"The world is definitely better off without some people in it," he said.

Robert nodded agreement. "Cliché or not, there's never been a truer statement. The world is definitely better off without that slimeball Treadway and his henchman stinking it up."

Kazuko nudged Robert with her shoulder. "Tell them about the two guys DL&R picked up at Kanapau Bay."

Robert faced Jack and Katie and chuckled. "Seems Treadway left a couple of his men on Kahoolawe. After a week of hiding out, they waved down a DL&R patrol boat, dehydrated and half starved. Seems they were quite happy to surrender themselves to the authorities. Course they didn't say anything about what they were doing on the island."

That unexpected tidbit of information made Jack laugh as well.

"Part of the group Treadway sent ashore in the Zodiac, huh," he said. "Warms my heart to know they had to sit there and watch that fancy yacht cruise past them and on out to sea without stopping or even slowing down."

"I don't think picking up passengers was on the captain's agenda," Katie offered.

Jack chuckled. "Not the way he sailed that tub the hell out of there in a hurry." He tipped his glass and stared into his tequila. "I wonder what happened to *Trident*? Scrub Treadway's smell off of it, and she'd be a fine boat to have."

Robert arched a brow in Jack's direction and grinned. "If you're truly interested in buying *Trident*, you'll probably find that ostentatious monstrosity tied up at some drug dealer's dock in South America."

"That's all right," Jack said. "My cut was enough of a down payment to buy *Pono* here. She's plenty of boat for me."

They turned their heads as they marveled at the interior of the plush salon.

"And a right fine vessel it is, too." Robert held up his glass. "To *Pono* and well kept secrets between friends."

"To Night Marchers." Jack raised his glass to Robert's.

"And to Grandpa." Katie added her glass to the toast, along with Kazuko.

Jack clinked his glass against the others held high above the table. "To Charles McIntyre. May he rest in peace."

ABOUT THE AUTHOR

William Nikkel is the author of four *Jack Ferrell* novels and a steampunk, zombie western featuring his latest hero Max Traver. A former homicide detective and S.W.A.T. team member for the Kern County Sheriff's Department in Bakersfield, California, William is an amateur scuba enthusiast, gold prospector, and artist who can be found just about anywhere. He and his wife Karen divide their time between California and Maui, Hawaii.

www.ingramcontent.com/pod-product-compliance
Lightning Source LLC
Chambersburg PA
CBHW051236260626
47162CB00002B/457